unfinished
business

unfinished
business

LEE GOOD

Red Ladies Press

First published: 2023

Cover design includes adapted images from Pixabay.com. Credits: 1274056 Pexels; 3990680 Alexa; 4092609 Gerd Altmann. Cover design and all other images by the author.

A CIP catalogue record for this title is available from the British Library.

ISBN: 978-0-9957363-9-9

Red Ladies Press (an imprint of White Ladies Press)

For further information and enquiries, email the publisher at: info@whiteladiespress.co.uk

ONE

'Aren't you ready yet, Em?' asked the girl, popping her head into the bedroom where her friend was dressing.

'Five minutes, okay?'

The girl began to pull the door closed, then paused, and pushed it open again, just wide enough to expose her face, an impish grin written across it. 'Starting to feel excited?'

Her friend looked round at her. 'Talk about a silly question. If you were getting married tomorrow, wouldn't *you* feel excited?' she replied cheerfully.

'More nervous, I think. Anyway, I *am* excited. I've been looking forward to it nearly as much as you, I think,' she said, swinging idly on the door. 'It'll be strange to think of you being married, though,' she mused.

'Mm. Well, my maid of honour,' the girl answered, placing her hairbrush on the dresser and looking up to address her friend's reflection in its mirror, 'we'll still be here tomorrow if you don't leave me to finish. Go on. I'll be down shortly.'

2

7:45 p.m.

She stood in the doorway to the living room. 'Well, what do you think?' she asked with a flourish, twirling around and coming to a stop before them again.

Her mother's face beamed with delight and love. 'Beautiful,

Emily. You look wonderful.'

She was dressed in a cream-coloured blouse, and navy-blue knee-length pleated skirt. Her golden-brown hair fell to her shoulders; her piercing ice-blue eyes sparkled with life. And her smile, set in beautifully even white teeth, could crumble even the stoniest of dispositions. She was just twenty-two years old.

Her father returned her smile. Sitting in his armchair in front of the bay window, he was a man shrunken and gaunt from illness, a stroke; a shadow of the proud man he had been only a few years before. But the sight of his daughter made his eyes brighten noticeably. He forced himself to sit upright. His eyes travelled to his wife's. The smile between them was natural and easy. Their only daughter was getting married. They had less than a day in which to enjoy her as she was. Tomorrow, she would be a married woman, and slowly and inevitably, their share in her life would diminish. But that was only natural. They were very proud of her.

'About time,' commented Julie, the girl who had popped into her bedroom earlier. She rose from the settee, where Emily's other friend, Olivia, still sat, where they had been watching *Sale of the Century* with Emily's father.

'Well,' said Emily, glancing at her wristwatch, 'About time we were going.'

Olivia, a small, pert blonde, stood up, straightening her clothes, reluctant to leave the warmth of the fire. 'I was just beginning to thaw out,' she complained.

'C'mon. It's not that cold out.'

'Have you looked out there lately?' she said. 'It's trying to sleet out there.'

'Don't exaggerate. Let's get going,' said Emily, stamping her feet one-two on the carpet-grip in the doorway, the heels of her shoes clacking on the hallway linoleum.

The two girls followed her into the hallway amidst

exchanges of parting.

'Go and get in the car,' she said, opening the front door and waving them past. 'I'll be with you in a moment.'

Her friends stepped out, and she made her way back to the doorway to the living room, where her mother was standing. She smiled at her, and stepped into the room, in view of her father.

'Dad, Mum,' she said, turning from one to the other. 'Just to say thanks for everything. I love you both very much.'

'We love you too, dear,' replied her mother, stepping over to give her a peck on her cheek.

'Your mother and I are very proud of you,' said her father. 'Have a smashing evening.'

She smiled. 'I will.' She stepped into the hall, but held back momentarily to look at each of them in turn again. It seemed that she might say something, but only smiled again.

Her father would most often conjure up this particular image of his daughter as she was at this moment: glowing in her youth and vitality, but in her expression a little sadness or regret. As if she knew.

Then, suddenly, the spell was broken, the moment lost, passed on. She altered her stance, shifting her weight to turn. 'See you later,' she said, before stepping into the hall.

'Enjoy yourselves,' her mother called after her. 'Don't make it too late.'

Then, with the slamming of the front door, she was gone.

3

She glanced back. Stepping out of the warmth and brightness of the interior into the cold night air caused her to pause. It wasn't simply the physical discomfort – Olivia had been right, it *was* almost sleeting. A light freezing rain, twinkling in the light that spilled through the living room curtains, coated her hair and clothes in tiny short-lived beads. No, there was something more, something deeper, an unconscious recognition of unease that should have no place in her life right now, but which refused to be ignored. She shuddered, trying to shrug the feeling off.

She turned towards the car. Olivia, sitting in the passenger seat of Julie's Ford Consul, was beckoning for her to hurry.

Pushing aside further thought, she hastened to the car, which now gurgled to life.

She climbed into the left rear seat, and very soon they were pulling out of the cul-de-sac onto the main road, bound for Eldonbridge.

4

9:15 p.m. The Clubhouse, Eldonbridge

Olivia came over and perched on the end of the polished wooden bench in the restaurant section. The disco floor was before them, half-full. A DJ stood in his pulpit beyond the lights and commotion.

She leaned forward. 'The next one's for you, Ames,' she said.

'Huh ... ? She looked up, frowning at her friend, not quite sure she had heard her correctly over the music. Then the sound fell away, the compere's voice breaking through a burst of static as he interrupted the song.

'I have here a request for a young lady from across the hills in Haltham, here tonight with some friends to celebrate her last night of freedom. Yes, Emily – Emily Reynolds – congratulations and best wishes for your marriage to John tomorrow.'

In his best syrupy voice, he said, 'This one's for you!' His words echoed those of her friend moments before. The track began:

> *I'm gettin' married in the mornin' ...*
> *Ding ... dong ... the bells are gonna chime ...*

She dropped her face in embarrassment as she sensed others in the place find her with their eyes. Her friends reacted to the song, singing along. Some in the crowd applauded. One or two whoops and whistles followed.

Emily sank slowly into her seat, a flush rising past her collar. She reached up and gave Olivia a friendly shove against her shoulder. Olivia felt herself sliding, and reflexively pushed back against the wooden floor with her feet, but over-compensating, she managed to fall across her lap. The small crowd of friends succumbed to fits of laughter.

5

11:15 p.m.

It had been a good evening. The best. They made their way out to the car park.

The night air was reviving, breezy and fresh, but not as cold as expected. The wind rustled through the balding canopies of the surrounding trees. Most of their leaves now lay on the ground, brown, withered and sodden with the recent rain. The pot-holed tarmac was littered with puddles, their surfaces rippling in the breeze, reflecting and scattering the array of coloured lights from *The Clubhouse*.

At the car, they waited for Julie to unlock it, then for her to climb in and reach over to unlock the other doors.

Inside, Julie waited for the engine to warm up and for the air vents to de-mist the windows. Emily again sat in the rear seat, behind Julie this time.

Julie engaged first gear, and they started to roll towards the exit. Spots began to appear on the windscreen, multiplying and running into veinous streams on the outside of the glass as it began to rain again. Julie flicked a switch to turn the wipers on. The blades throbbed back and forth methodically.

'Great,' said Olivia, looking out. 'Hope it stops in good time before the morning, Ames.' She glanced over her shoulder to face her.

'Me too,' smiled Emily from the gloom of the back.

'Well, Ems,' said Julie, looking momentarily into the rearview mirror at her friend's reflection, 'That's it. Eight months of engagement over. All downhill after tomorrow.'

'Ha,' she replied.

Julie smiled back at her.

'What's the time?' asked Emily.

Olivia looked at her watch, rotating it to catch the light of the passing streetlights. 'Hm, twenty after eleven,' she reported, stifling a yawn.

'I wonder if John's back yet,' she said, suppressing her own urge to yawn.

Her fiancé, John Hudson, an electrical engineer, was staying at her house. It wasn't traditional, but circumstances had dictated. His parents would be coming down from Cambridge early the next morning for the wedding. He was out with a few of his own friends tonight. They had sworn to stay away from the popular spots in Eldonbridge to avoid the two parties clashing.

'He'd better get a move on,' said Olivia, turning to face Emily again. 'It's unlucky to see the bride on the day of the wedding – well, you know – before the ceremony.'

'Neither of us is superstitious. So we'll see each other on the morning of our wedding – so what? Anyway,' she added, 'it couldn't be helped.'

6

The road out of town quickly left behind the comforting glow of streetlights as it snaked out into the oily blackness of the countryside. The car's air vents now poured out sufficient heat to keep the front windows clear, at least.

The warmth and the monotony of the surrounding darkness began to induce a feeling of drowsiness. Dark hedgerows whipped by hypnotically outside. Emily blinked, and found herself yawning again. Leaning to her left a little, she could see out ahead through the windscreen.

On the horizon, three miles away, the stubby peak of Blaxton Hill stood out with fuzzy relief against the inky blackness of the overcast night sky. Occasional pinprick shafts of light floated lazily up and down its face, fading and re-erupting further along their paths – cars that were negotiating the steep, winding and tree-covered scarp-slope of the hill. Home lay on the other side of this natural barrier. All three girls were from the Haltham area – Emily and Julie in Haltham itself, and Olivia from just down the road in Fordham. The church was prepared and waiting for them, also in Haltham, just ten minutes from Emily's house.

'Turn the radio on will you, Julie?' asked Emily. 'I'm nodding off back here.'

Julie leaned forward in her seat to reach for the radio panel beneath the centre of the dashboard. Fumbling for the switch, she dropped her eyes momentarily. The others felt the car lurch as it moved out of line, spraying mud and leaves from the soft verge.

'Julie!' shouted the other girls in unison.

Julie corrected their course immediately, braking to reduce speed to take the next bend slowly.

'Sorry about that,' she said, shaken. She glanced at Olivia, and then into the mirror at Emily. 'Sorry.'

Emily exhaled slowly. 'Okay, okay. But I could do without getting killed right now,' she said flatly. Olivia forced a smile. They were all alert now, the drowsiness evaporated.

Another car whizzed by in the opposite direction. It was sheer good luck that nothing had been coming around that bend at that instant. They settled down again.

Silence reigned over them for a few moments. Then it seemed that Olivia was fidgeting. Emily saw what she was trying to do.

'Aw, no. Come on, forget the radio, Olivia,' she said impatiently. The half-skid had unnerved her to the extent that she didn't need the radio to keep her alert. 'There's not long enough now to make it worth worrying about.'

Olivia ignored her, and continued to fumble for the switch.

'Which one is it, Jules?' she asked.

Julie ignored her, concentrating on her driving, her eyes cast rigidly in front.

'Ollie ... ' Emily began to protest.

'It's the black one ... ' started Julie.

'I can't see it in the dark, silly,' said Olivia.

'Let me finish,' snapped Julie. 'It's the one on the right of the panel; the tuning knob is in the middle.'

Olivia's hand fumbled in the near darkness. 'Oh yeah, got it,' she said. The radio blared into life. A deafening, jumbled cacophony of static and music filled the car.

Olivia frantically tried searched for the volume control. Emily shouted above the din. 'Ollie, *please* ... '

Julie was momentarily unable to offer Olivia any help. She

continued to concentrate on the road, which was just straightening out to reveal the crossroads at the bottom of Blaxton Hill, three hundred yards away.

It occurred to neither girl in front to simply turn the radio off. Was that what Emily was shouting from behind?

Checking her mirrors for any sign of other traffic, Julie relaxed her concentration just long enough to reach down herself, brushing past Olivia's hand to find the volume control, and turning it, reduced it quickly to a tolerable level. Then she had both hands on the wheel again.

'Phew! Thanks,' said Olivia.

Julie looked at her. They were approaching the crossroads, starting on the slight incline towards it. Her features were illuminated feebly by the light from The Bull, a public house on their right, at one corner of the junction of this, the Haltham Road, where it crossed the roughly east-west running Valence Lane.

Olivia, now able to see the panel through the dancing shadows, found the tuning knob of the radio, and began flicking through channels as Julie braked, dropping through the gears to edge up to the Stop line across their route.

The crossroads provided the last opportunity for traffic travelling north to abort the arduous one-in-nine climb up Blaxton Hill. While it was a little unusual to have a main artery such as the Haltham Road give way to a minor cross-route, the position and history of the junction dictated no other action.

Following a natural bench here at the foot of the scarp, Valence lane descended steeply from the village of Frickley to the east to emerge abruptly at the crossroads. The gradient gave little opportunity for traffic coming this way to stop safely had a give-way situation been in operation. A history of accidents tragically showed this to be the case. So, it was decided to reverse priorities: traffic travelling up or down

Blaxton Hill was to give way. In addition to the interest of safety, the staggering of traffic up or down the hill during peak hours because of the Stop situation on the crossroads had also proven beneficial.

Julie brought the car to a stop short of the line – not quite far enough to see much along the road to her right. She tried to catch the car's weight on the clutch to avoid engaging the handbrake, but over-revving the engine, the car lurched and stalled, rolling back a little before she stamped on the brake.

'Well done,' said Olivia.

Julie huffed as she pulled on the handbrake, and fiddled with the ignition key to restart the engine. Emily sat quietly in back, her patience tried somewhat by Olivia's antics with the radio.

Engaging first gear, Julie released the brake and edged closer to the line. Olivia resumed her tuning through several more spluttering channels. Overshooting one she liked, she began to backtrack to locate it.

Seeing nothing in either direction through the gloom, Julie allowed the car to pull out over the line. At the same moment, Olivia found the track. 'Got it,' she said. She reached quickly for the volume knob, turning it up.

Julie gave her a disapproving sideways glance.

Immediately, Olivia's expression changed, to one of wide-eyed horror as it filled with the bright light from a rapidly growing source that emanated behind Julie's right shoulder. *'Oh my God!'*

A sharp screech of brakes tore through the music – the music that had masked the approach of the car. Julie turned just in time to see it bearing down on them, headlights blazing.

There was a sudden, sickening jolt as it impacted. All went black. The roar of crumpling and tearing metal continued for a half-second as the Consul was shunted sideways down the lane, to come to rest with the other car buried in its side. Glass and fragments lay everywhere about.

The commotion subsided to leave only the sound of the radio, continuing to play amongst the carnage, and the anguished but slowly ebbing cries of a single female voice in the darkness.

Already, people were milling from the pub, running over to help.

It was 11:27 p.m.

TWO

Charlie Pemberton was a veteran officer with the County Constabulary. So veteran, in fact, that he had been retired for a decade. Unlike most, he had been one that couldn't simply leave the life behind when he retired as a Chief Inspector, much to his wife's chagrin, and he spent a few days in every month working with the Division as a mentor and advisor, coaching younger officers from his long experience, and serving on a panel for community relations.

With over thirty years of service behind him, he – not proudly, he would say – had seen everything in his time: road accidents, house fires, crime, violence, murder. That was all the bad side, anyway. There had been a lot of good too. But as he, and other officers might tell you, if people made order and peace their business, the Police would be out of business.

Tonight was another RTA, a road traffic accident, only this time he found himself caught in the jam caused by it as he headed home out of Wellstone. Up ahead, a police car and an ambulance, beacons pulsing, sat in line against the verge beyond the crashed vehicles.

Two officers seemed to have it under control. One was talking to four people by the vehicles. On the other side of the nearest car, a Ford Fiesta, a paramedic, by the looks of it, leant into the passenger window. The other police officer waved traffic past the scene in single file in a slowly moving procession in the outer lane of the dual carriageway.

He waited in line until he got closer. He glanced at his dashboard clock. 10:05 p.m. He had promised his wife that he'd be back before ten. No chance of that now.

He recognised the two officers. As soon as he was through the jam, he pulled over and parked his car out of the way, two wheels up on the nearside verge. He got out, slipped on a hi-viz vest, and walked back to the scene of the accident.

The traffic officer spotted him and began to protest, then recognising who he was, acknowledged him simply with 'Sir'.

'Everything under control, Tony?' he asked.

'Pretty much, Sir.'

'Just Charlie now, Tony... just Charlie,' he replied, but he was appreciative of the gesture of respect.

He looked over at the car wreck. 'What have we got?'

'Four walking wounded; one of the drivers already transferred to Eldonbridge General with minor injuries and shock; one still trapped in the Fiesta; female; suspected fractured hip and leg, but conscious and communicating.'

Pemberton gazed at the damaged vehicles and their occupants, who stood around the other officer. The Fiesta, with its crushed bonnet, sat askew behind them.

'Cornflakes boxes ... ' he said to himself absently.

The crumpled remains of most vehicles betrayed their frail construction and with it, the false sense of personal protection they provided. Sheet metal, he thought, fared little better than the thin cardboard of a cereal packet when crashing even at moderate speeds.

'Sir?' asked the traffic officer.

'All youngsters,' he observed. 'They know one another?'

'It seems so,' replied the officer. 'Out for a bit of joy-riding, if you ask me. Could've turned out a lot worse.'

Pemberton nodded. His very first attendance at a road accident had been only a little north of here, on what was then the main route between Eldonbridge and the towns on the other side of Blaxton Hill. As bad luck would have, it had also been one of the more graphic of his career. He was twenty-four at the time, and it had left a lasting impression on him regarding the fragility of life.

He looked back at the slowly moving line of traffic. 'Well, it seems to be flowing okay. I guess you won't be needing the diversion.'

'No, not this late, Sir.'

A peak time incident would almost certainly have meant diverting the northbound traffic off four hundred yards back, where a slip road led to a roundabout option for the original Haltham-Eldonbridge Road. Since the modern dual carriageway had been built it had become a bit of a backwater route, providing access to the surrounding villages, or as a turn-around opportunity for traffic heading back to Eldonbridge. And it permitted traffic to proceed northward on the old road to where it could re-join the new road half-a-mile up Blaxton Hill.

Charlie Pemberton avoided that route if he could. Especially at night. Especially alone. Ever since that night many years ago now, but not very long after the death crash at the crossroads outside The Bull public house that was the first fatal RTA he had attended.

He heard sirens approaching and turned to see a fire-engine at the base of the hill, firing out shards of blue light. Near the car wreck, the other officer evidently had finished taking statements and had stepped away.

Pemberton stepped over. 'Hello, Joe.'

The officer was taken aback. 'Charlie! What are you doing here?'

'On my way home and got caught in this. Anything I can do?'

The officer looked over at the traffic control and shook his head. 'Thanks, but no. Fire's here now to get the girl out.

There are a couple of flatbeds lined up after to recover the vehicles. Should be out of here in an hour or so, hopefully.'

He looked up to the sky. Droplets of rain streaked past, glowing like meteors in the flashing blue lights of the police car. He pulled his yellow waterproof jacket around him. 'No reason for you to get wet too'. He smiled.

Pemberton nodded. 'Right. okay. Good job. I'll check with the other services, then get on my way.'

THREE

A coin dropped into the Jukebox. The man walked away before the track started. He passed a table in the corner where a young woman sat, then stepped aside to permit a young man to pass him with a pint in one hand and a glass of something else in the other.

'Thanks.'

The young man set the drinks down and slid into the seat facing the young woman.

'What's this?'

'A drink. Tomato juice for you.'

'You only went to the loo?'

'I know. But I thought we could have another one while we waited for the cab.'

The woman sounded exasperated. 'You mean *you* could have another one?'

'Sally, I'm alright. It's just *two* pints.'

'Plus the bottle of wine with the meal.'

Richard Wentworth sagged in his seat. 'I'm not driving. I thought we'd be able to, you know, chill out and enjoy your birthday.'

'It *has* been nice,' replied Sally. 'Just you and me for a change. Without your friends. But it doesn't mean you have to drink every we time we go out.'

Richard was taken aback. 'We agreed we'd get a taxi tonight – you know, so I didn't have to worry about driving?'

'So *I* didn't have to worry about you driving.'

Richard fell quiet.

'Sal –'

'Don't 'Sal' me,' she replied. She raised a finger to wipe a tear from her eye.

He fell silent. A couple seated nearby glanced over. Richard stared back.

'What you have to realise, Richard, and what upsets me more than anything, is that you don't care – '

'Of course I do.' He reached for her hand, but she tore it away.

'No you don't. Not really. You don't listen to me, even though I have only ever had your best interests at heart. You don't care about us, about the extra strain it's putting on our relationship – goodness knows we've had enough of that already this year.'

Richard sat there, looking sheepish. He nodded. Finally, he spoke, and his manner was calmer, subdued.

'Yeah, look. I'm sorry. I don't know … it's been a tough couple of months.'

'Of course I know. But that just makes things worse, doesn't it? It means that you've just gone off selfishly, drowning your own sorrows without a care. But it hasn't just been about you, Richard,' she said in a less animated tone. 'I know you know that. But I think you can get so wrapped up in your own concerns, you forget that sometimes.'

'Has it really been that bad?' he asked.

'Yes!'

He swallowed hard. 'Why didn't you say something earlier?'

'I did. But not to begin with. I felt you needed that release, to deal with it, to come to terms with it in your own way. Besides, when something like that happens, a woman will naturally look to herself for the blame.'

She looked at him with a kind of vacant, tortured expression.

Guilt descended on Richard heavily. 'What? No. You didn't blame yourself? Why?'

Sally simply nodded, then burst into tears.

Richard was around the table in an instant, holding her, hugging her, as she sobbed against his side. He pulled her away to plant a kiss against her wet forehead, and gently wiped the tears from her eyes with his thumb.

A female voice called out: 'Hi, are you alright?'

Sally looked up with puffy eyes to see the woman at the near table looking over. She nodded. 'I'm okay,' she said.

'Sure?'

Sally nodded again.

Richard nodded at the woman more kindly. 'We're fine. Really.' He looked at Sally, then back at the couple. 'Thanks.'

Sally reached down to pick up her handbag, perching it on her lap, where she opened it to pull out a tissue.

'You're not blaming yourself, are you?' Richard asked softly.

Sally shook her head. 'Not now. But I did at first.'

'But why?'

'Because it was me who started that argument the night before. I shouldn't have been pushing you. It was my fault.'

'Your fault? How could it be your fault that I had cold feet about getting married?'

'Because I got scared. Pregnant and paranoid, I suppose. I was scared you might leave me. And when you said you didn't want to marry me, I took that as proof you didn't really love me.'

'I ... ah, I was just scared myself. Too much happening too soon, you know? And a lot of responsibility on the way. But you know the real reason – the hospital told you. There was nothing anyone could do.'

'I know. But I didn't know that at the time. And anyway, then there was that thing with my dad. None of that would have happened except for me. You can see how it all added up.'

'Yeah, well,' he smiled. 'I think that was coming anyway. At least it got it all out in the open. But we're alright now, aren't we?'

Sally just looked at him.

'Well, you know what I mean. Your dad and me are fine now. We're – you and me – are getting the house, making real plans to get married. Looking up, right?' he said, trying to sound as if everything had been plain sailing ever since.

'Hm,' said Sally.

Richard sighed. 'Okay, point taken,' he said. 'Fine birthday celebration this has turned out to be. I'm going to make it up to you, I promise. What is it – six weeks or a bit less 'til the house is completed? And another two after to Christmas. By then – by Christmas – you'll be looking back on this night thinking that was the best birthday you ever had ... '

'How d'you figure that one?'

'Because by then I'd have proven that this is the night you got the real me back for good.'

'Well, you know what they say: actions speak louder than words. We'll see.' She smiled thinly.

Richard leant in and kissed her. 'Now, why don't you pop into the toilet and freshen up a bit?'

'Why, what do I look like – has my eyeliner run?'

He looked at the murky smudges beneath her eyes. 'Oh, just a little bit. Hardly notices,' he said. But the woman opposite gave a small affirming nod.

2

Sally emerged from the toilet feeling calmer and more composed. She turned the corner at the end of the bar, and unexpectedly almost ran into Richard, who was at the fruit machine. One hand repeatedly hit the spin button, which was rewarded each time by a flashy pattern of lights and flutey mechanised chimes; the other remained motionless, clutched around a pint glass. She bit her lip, before realising it wasn't a fresh one.

'Oh, there you are,' he said. 'You've been in there a while.'

Sally glanced at the clock behind the bar. Ten-fifteen.

'Are we ready to go?' she asked.

He shook his head. 'Half an hour,' he said.

'Really?'

He shrugged. 'Friday night. They're busy.'

Sally, expressionless, stepped around him to return to their table.

'Sally,' he called after her. 'I – '

The fruit machine made a shrill sound, which looped as a cash prize clunked into the tray. 'Wait a sec,' he said. He popped his glass on the bar behind him before scooping out a handful of coins and pocketing them without counting. He stabbed the spin button again. 'Last one,' he said to himself, and had turned to retrieve the remainder of his drink before the wheels came to a rest and the display went dark.

He drained the rest of his drink, replaced the glass on the bar and walked back to the table. The couple from the other table had gone. He remained standing.

'Aren't you going to sit?' asked Sally.

'I need to pay a visit.'

'I thought you pre-booked the return trip?'

'I did. For ten-thirty. When I phoned to see if they can get here any earlier, they said forty minutes. The barman gave me another number. I'll be back in a minute.'

3

A gust of wind buffeted the window nearest her. The weather

was surprisingly mild for the time of year. Rain ran down the outside of the glass in serpentine streaks, catching and redirecting the light from the car park's lights and car lights in a changing array of colours.

The lights caused the swaying branches of trees to cast eerie shadows of twisted limbs squirming and shifting outside the window.

'Boo!'

Sally jolted back in her seat. 'Don't do that!' You scared me,' she said.

'Cab's here – just saw it pull up.'

'Good. About time.'

Sally picked up her handbag and walked ahead of him along the side of the bar to collect her coat from the stand.

The main door opened and the cab driver stepped inside.

'Cab for Wentworth?'

The barman pointed at Richard, who stepped over.

'Won't be a second.'

'Take your time,' the driver answered. 'The clock's already running,' he winked. 'I'll be outside.'

Sally slipped on her coat. A calendar hung on a post at the end of the counter. The picture was of a bronzed female in a white bikini wading in the gentle surf of a white sand beach under a cobalt sky. She stared at it for a moment before realising it was the empty backing of a packet snacks card.

Beneath it was the calendar itself. She noticed that the disposable tear-off date slips were not up to date. The red-inked print read OCTOBER, MONDAY 23. The small-print below, the daily proverb, read:

Our greatest regrets are for our lost opportunities

She was on the verge of leaving it, walking away, but couldn't help herself; a pet hate. She reached out and tugged at the slips, balling them up in her hand until it showed the correct date: OCTOBER, FRIDAY 27.

A good companion on the road is better than a carriage

Sally stared at it with some satisfaction before picking her bag off the counter and hurrying over to where Richard waited for her.

'Ready?'

'Hm-hm.'

4

Outside, the rain was easing a little. They trotted over to the idling cab and hopped in the back.

'Eldonbridge, wasn't it?' the cabbie asked.

'Yup. Clinton Avenue, off Archer Street?' replied Richard.

'I know Archer Street.'

The cab pulled out towards the exit. Richard glanced through a hole he had made in the misty condensation on the window. Sally reached over and placed her hand on his knee. Her face, illuminated by the orange glow of the streetlamps, showed a hint of a smile. He returned it.

Soon, they were travelling down the dark country lanes behind the pub. Little was visible in the gloom besides the hedgerows and trees bordering the road, and the cats eyes that flared as starbursts marking the centre line of the road.

Perhaps cabbing it home wasn't such a bad idea after all, thought Richard. Except that it would mean getting another cab back down over the weekend to collect his car.

The rain was intensifying again, causing a grey haze to form beyond the headlights. The driver slowed to take account of the deteriorating conditions.

'Rotten evening, ain't it?' he said.

'Yes,' agreed Sally, 'The forecast said it would probably remain dry for most of the evening, turning to showers later. Wrong again.'

'Yep,' the driver said. 'It's caused some problems tonight – a crash on the motorway, and one at the bottom of Blaxton Hill.'

Up ahead, two bright green orbs moved from side to side, fading and re-igniting as they reflected the headlights.

The driver was already on his brakes. The car slowed, twitching on the wet road surface. All the while, the form ahead did not move. As the driver regained control, the headlights fixed on the creature, now scurrying away. A fox.

They passed over the spot where it had stood and Sally peered out the side window to see the animal look back, its eyes glimmered faintly.

'Sorry about that,' the driver said. 'I don't like to hit 'em if I can avoid it.'

Richard hadn't reacted throughout the incident. Sally turned to him. 'You awake?' she asked.

'I am now,' he muttered quietly, 'Dozing. What happened?'

'Just nearly smeared a poor fox, that's all,' she said.

'Oh,' he replied nonchalantly, stifling a yawn, and propping himself up in the seat.

A blaze of light appeared before them. A car travelling in the opposite direction swept around the bend. The glare backed down as the other driver stepped down his main beams.

When it passed, the orange glow of streetlights came into view, marking the edge of the town. Sally reached down between her feet to locate her handbag.

6

The cab pulled up outside a smart detached house at the end of a cul-de-sac, set back and raised above the turning bowl there. Sally's home.

'C'mon, sleepy head,' said Sally, nudging Richard as she opened the door.

The cool, damp evening air hit him. He pulled himself upright.

Sally closed the door as gently as possible after her, a gentle clunk as the lock connected. At least there was a break in the rain for the moment. The street was deserted. She made her way around the back of the car to the curbside where Richard had wound down the side-window.

She leaned in and gave him a quick kiss. 'Ring me when you get in,' she said. She kissed him again. 'Goodnight.'

'Night,' Richard answered as Sally stepped back away, turning toward the house. Richard turned back to find the cab driver's eyes on him in his rearview mirror.

'You not getting out here then, son?' he asked.

Richard glanced out at Sally who, having fumbled in her handbag for a moment up at the door, resorted to ringing the doorbell. A silhouetted figure peered from between the curtains of the front bay windows of the living room. He returned his attention to the driver.

'Er, no. I ... ' He glanced back up to the window. The figure had retreated from the window. 'Can you drop me off in Haltham?'

'Haltham?' repeated the driver, shaking his head. 'My brief

was for two to Eldonbridge. I'm supposed to be knocking off after that.'

Richard frowned. 'Oh.'

Shit. What now?

He peered up to see Sally suddenly lit by warm yellow light as the hallway lights blinked on. The door opened for her and she gave a quick, sheepish wave before stepping into the house. He returned it almost unconsciously, his thoughts preoccupied by his predicament.

The door clanked shut and, almost immediately, the light snapped off, breaking his train of thought.

"I can drop you back in the town?'

'Sorry?'

'I said I can drop you off in the town, if you like? You can pick up another cab from there, or I could call ahead and have one waiting for you?'

'Er, okay, yes, thanks,' said Richard. 'Drop me in town.'

'Right you are,' replied the driver.

Within a minute, he had turned the car in the bowl at the end of the cul-de-sac, and coasted down to the road junction. He indicated left, and made the turn towards the main road.

'Actually, on second thoughts,' said Richard, 'could you drop me here?'

The driver frowned, but acquiesced. 'I could, but … '
Richard answered the cabbie's as-yet unspoken question.

'I'll phone home. My brother'll come down and get me'. He tipped his head in the direction of Sally's house. 'Don't want my girlfriend to worry, you know?'

This wasn't quite true. His brother didn't actually own a car, or drive, in fact. Not many twelve-year-olds do, he thought.

'Whatever you say,' said the driver. He pulled in at the first available space.

'Perfect,' replied Richard. 'Thanks.' He hopped out, paid

the driver and then watched as the cab pulled away and vanished out of sight at the bend. He glanced at his watch. 10:48 p.m. It was beginning to rain again.

He pulled his collar up and turned and made his way back along the road, crossing the side-road to Sally's house, and pulled his keys from a pocket. He thumbed a button on the fob and his car's sidelights flashed in response a dozen yards away.

Sally's words echoed in his mind. He had promised that he would take the cab home.

Then again… as far as she was concerned, he *had* gone home by cab. She had seen the cab pull away. He wasn't to know that the cab driver couldn't go up to Haltham tonight.

It was getting late. His car was right there, and it was only a twenty minute journey home at this hour. Much better to risk the short journey than have to arrange to get down here in the morning to pick up the car.

He fumbled for his car keys amongst a pocketful of loose change, and lurched around to the driver's side. Within a moment, he was behind the wheel.

7

The road out of town was fairly clear, thankfully, but its surface was slick and reflective, throwing up a kaleidoscope of images and colours in the rain-streaked windscreen, which he struggled to make sense of through his already glazed vision. Perhaps it wasn't such a great idea, after all.

A car horn screeched its agreement, shaking him alert as he realised he had begun to drift over the dividing line. The burst of adrenalin from the near-collision cleared his head and he corrected his course. Another mistake like that and he'd be crippled, or dead.

Just concentrate, he told himself. Keep within the lines, keep the speed down. Just drive naturally, and you'll be okay.

When he was sure it was safe, he reached down and fumbled for the radio. A burst of noise erupted above the drone of the engine, and he quickly adjusted the volume to a more tolerable level. Background noise, but hopefully sufficiently distracting to help keep him awake and alert.

8

Shortly, the traffic picked up again as he passed through the roundabout system that held options for the local villages and the approach to Blaxton Hill and he began to feel a little better.

The cold air from a half-opened window had cleared his head. Feeling more confident, he accelerated to match the speed of the other vehicles starting the climb on the dual carriageway that would take him up and over Blaxton Hill and home.

There seemed to be a greater volume of traffic than normal for this hour, but the poor conditions would explain this, he thought. The glare from the southbound traffic meant he did not immediately notice the lengthening string of brake lights ahead. Just beyond lay the reason. He could see the pulsing of blue lights.

'Shit. Shit!' he said aloud. The traffic was slowing at the scene of an accident. He could just make out a sign indicating the closure of the inner lane of the carriageway, and a police officer waving the nearside traffic over to join the outer lane.

He made a quick appraisal of his situation, but there really wasn't any choice but to follow in line. He slowed, glancing in his rearview and side mirrors. There was no traffic behind him at the moment. There was no reason why he should be stopped. The police would be interested in keeping the traffic moving. But he didn't want to take that chance.

But wait. Two hundred yards ahead, just coming into view, he could see the slip lane that led off the dual carriageway some way before the police cordon, that led down to join a roundabout below Blaxton Hill. One vehicle had already left the slowing queue onto it.

Impatiently, he stayed in line, gradually moving closer to the exit, until finally, he signalled and followed it off the main road. The beauty of the manoeuvre, he mused, was that the roundabout gave opportunity to completely bypass the queue. And the police presence. In fact, he was surprised that few other motorists seemed to have had the same idea, and that the police hadn't set up a formal diversion. Then again, the traffic was flowing smoothly, if slowly, through the lane restriction, and most other drivers probably had less cause to fear than he. It would certainly be quicker by the main road once it opened out again.

The noise of the traffic died away along with the light as his route led him down the incline. At the bottom he could see the tail-lights of the other vehicle, then its brake lights as it paused at the roundabout before turning left and vanishing from sight. He could relax a little, if only for the few minutes it would take to climb the hill.

His headlights lit up the sign before the roundabout. The first option, at nine o'clock, was for Broadford and Nedworth. Straight over, the slip lane that led back onto the dual-carriageway for Haltham. Can't take that one. The accident bottleneck looked like it was a little way north of where it re-joined the main road.

The third option, the one he intended to take, at the three o'clock position, was marked for Frickley and Knowlworth. And Haltham, he thought, as he signalled right.

On completing the turn, the underpass beneath the dual

carriageway came into view. At this point, it not only preserved this, a section of the old Valence lane, as a through-road linking Frickley and Broadford, but bridged Milburn stream, which originated from higher up on the scarp face of Blaxton Hill. A little further downstream, it was a quietly meandering flow on its way to river status, but here it burbled and chattered energetically over the rocks of the stream bed, which ran beside the south side of the road.

As he emerged from the underpass, the patch of light that marked the location of the pub up at the crossroads came into view; the pub itself hidden below the rise of the road. He started up the low gradient that gave the stream its energy towards the crossroads, where he would make a left turn on to the preserved stretch of original road that had linked Haltham with Eldonbridge before the construction of the new carriageway.

Unlike the new road, whose gradient and sinuosity had been reduced by blasting through the upper face of Blaxton Hill, the older route negotiated a steeper, sinuous path.

As he levelled out at the top of the section of road, the pub came fully into view. Occupying the southeast corner of the crossroads, its lights, supported by a solitary lamp-post, created a little, comforting oasis over the road.

A shifting, flickering glow above and behind the building announced the approach of a vehicle from the steep section of lane out of Frickley, a village a mile and a half beyond.

As he came onto the crossroads, left indicator flashing, the car emerged around the sharp bend and sped straight through the junction. It passed Richard and disappeared down the dip towards the underpass, its brake lights flaring in his side-mirror.

Another car appeared from the left, edging out over the STOP line, checking left and right carefully. It waited for

Richard to start his turn before driving straight over, heading down towards the carriageway intersection bound for Eldonbridge.

Richard glanced through the windows of the pub as he turned, deliberately keeping his speed low, briefly noting the throng of people dotted around the bar. It looked inviting and safe in there. For some reason, he felt suddenly uneasy. He wished he were in there.

He tore his gaze away and started up the darkened lane ahead. Between second and third gear, the car began to cough and jerk, the battery light on the dashboard and headlights flickering like a candle flame. He dropped back into second and pumped the gas pedal to try to prevent it stalling. But with too much gas and a high clutch, it lurched forward and stalled anyway. He stamped on the brake pedal before the car could begin to roll back.

'Shit,' he said aloud, reaching for the ignition key to restart. As he did so, he glanced through the windscreen. And stopped.

There was something a little further up the road, on the left, on the verge. A person? It looked like a girl, but there was no movement. Just waiting there. He stared at it for a moment, but without adequate lighting, he couldn't be sure what it was. He had more pressing concerns.

He switched his attention to the starter, turning the ignition key. In reply, he heard only the suffocating groan of the engine, refusing to draw breath.

Probably flooded it.

He stared at the board for a moment.

The radio continued to crackle. Not only an annoying distraction at this moment, it was also an additional drain on the battery. He reached down and turned it off. Sometimes it seemed to help.

Again, he tried to restart the car. This time, the engine began to cooperate, gurgling and then catching, roaring into life again.

Relieved, he eased off the gas pedal slightly. His eyes fell to the readouts on the dash, momentarily distracting his attention. The headlights burned brighter, providing a little more illumination of the road up ahead. The object was still there.

He could see now that it was a young woman, standing just outside the range of his dipped lights. It was impossible to judge her age or appearance with certainty. He glanced around him, looking to locate someone or others in the grounds of the pub behind, whom she might be waiting on. No-one there.

If that were the case, though, why not stand within the lit forecourt itself?

No matter. He selected first, then second gear, and slowly and tentatively climbed towards the figure, enabling the closer range and better illumination to reveal more detail. As he drew closer, he shifted in his seat, unable to shake a growing uneasiness.

On the face of it, she appeared normal enough. Perhaps in her early twenties, wearing a light blouse and skirt, somewhat ill-dressed for the conditions.

But where had she come from? He could have sworn she wasn't there as he completed his turn. And what was she doing just standing there?

Pushing away further speculation, he pulled up beside her. Oddly, she didn't appear to react to his presence.

He glanced behind him again, towards the pub, to doubly ascertain that there was no-one there whom she might be waiting on.

No, she – they – were alone.

He felt a sudden and almost irresistible urge to drive off, as fast as possible. The muscles along his spine were twitching;

the hairs on his neck and forearms bristling as if in response to a strong electrostatic charge.

He fought back the sense of alarm, trying to overpower the primitive, fight-or-flight response of his nervous system, to regain rational command.

Maybe she was in trouble or frightened and in need of assistance. Yes, that must be it. Why else would she be here and not back at the pub?

He pressed a button on his door rest and the passenger side window wound down to half-way. He hesitated for a second, then wound it all the way down.

I don't know what you're so spooked about, he said to himself. She's the one out here alone.

He leaned over the passenger seat in order to see her properly. Damp green air flowed in around him.

'Ah, are you alright?'

No reply. Didn't even look his way. Her gaze was somewhere over the rear of the car, towards the pub and the crossroads.

'Do you need a lift anywhere?'

Again, no response.

It occurred to him that she might be ill, or in shock. The latter seemed the more likely. She did look a little gaunt and dishevelled.

As he pondered what to do next, she began to move, slowly, turning towards him. She took a faltering step forward and bent towards the window. A sweet fragrance wafted in on the breeze. Lilacs?

His initial estimate of her age stood up: early twenties. Her attire was smart but casual, a light blouse with (brown?) skirt. Her hair, light-brown or mousy, was swept back and fastened behind the ears by two plain gold hair-clips. The rest fell to shoulder length. The light drizzle formed beaded droplets on her fringe.

He repeated his question.

'Look, if you need a lift, get in, but I'm only going as far as Haltham.'

Her expression began to come alive. She smiled slightly, her eyes indicating acceptance of the offer.

His uneasiness abated somewhat. Put it down to the conditions. And the drink.

He pulled the lock-release on the door, but the girl made no effort to open it. Instead she stepped towards the rear passenger door, waiting there without comment.

Richard was puzzled by her action but decided to make nothing of it. After all, from her point of view, a lone female travelling at this hour, it was probably a sensible decision. He released his seat belt and reached over to unlock the door. Without sufficient leverage, he was unable to push the door open more than a few inches for her, but she made no attempt to catch it before it swung back.

She appeared to fumble for the handle as if unfamiliar with its design. Richard was on the verge of getting out to assist her when she managed to open it wide enough to get in. The car's internal light came on, then snapped off again as she more ably pulled it closed, robbing him of the chance to make a detailed evaluation of her condition. But he had noticed she appeared a little pale. Even in the poor back-light, he could see that her expression was mute, almost expressionless. Almost. There was something there, especially around the eyes, a somewhat pained, mournful expression. Or was it simply disorientation, or shock? He began to feel concern again.

'Where is it you'd like to go, then?' he asked, framing her reflection in the rearview mirror.

The girl's eyes met his. Sad eyes. But she didn't speak. Instead, she raised her right arm, index finger pointing ahead through the windscreen.

Chills struck him again. This was too weird. But, fighting the resurging discomfort, he concentrated on re-securing his seat belt and getting underway, convinced by now that there was something wrong with her, mentally perhaps.

On the face of it, while a little ruffled, she didn't appear to be injured. But unless he could get an address or telephone number from her, he might have little choice but to take her to the hospital. Or to the police. They could at least take responsibility for her.

Actually, no, not the police. Might think he had something to do with her being in this state. He hoped neither course would be necessary. He was beginning to wish he hadn't stopped at all.

He glanced into the mirror again. The girl was staring back, her eyes locking with his own. His heart skipped a beat, and he looked back to the road.

'Er, what were you doing out there on your own? Were you at the pub?' he asked, trying to induce conversation.

No reply. His eyes were drawn inexorably back to the mirror, though he tried to resist doing so. But he had to. It was like trying to avoid glancing through the gates of a graveyard whilst walking past late at night, as he had once. You just *had* to look, even though what you might see might drive you mad.

He quickly dismissed the association from his mind. She continued to just sit there, staring ahead. He could just make out her features in the mirror.

Enough. He glanced over his shoulder.

'What's your name? Mine's Richard.'

Still she stared blankly forward. Shaking his head, he returned his attention to the road, checking on the vehicle's course. He was not anticipating an answer.

After what seemed an eternity, he heard her shift in her

seat. He was more than surprised to hear her speak, for the first time, though slowly and without inflection.

'I ... I've been in an accident,' she said uncertainly. 'I need to get home.' She seemed puzzled, as if her own words were a surprise to her.

The pieces suddenly fell into place. Now he had no choice but to go to the hospital, regardless of where she wished to be taken. She must have been in that car smash on the dual carriageway, and somehow wandered away in a dazed, possibly concussed, state.

'Look, you seem like you need to be looked over. I'll take you to Knowlworth Hospital. Then, if you give me your name and phone number, I'll ring your family. How's that?'

'No.' She seemed confused, hesitant. He decided not to pursue it. Best get her out of here as fast as possible.

He accelerated, moving up through the gears, achieving fourth at thirty-seven mph along the darkest section of the lane, at the bend at the top, where thick hedges pressed in on the road.

A murmur from behind attracted his attention.

'Are you alright?' he called out.

'Please, take me home. I must get home,' she pleaded.

'But,' Richard said as sympathetically as he could at this hour, 'you haven't told me where home is, have you?'

Silence.

He glanced over his shoulder again.

'I ... ' His senses collapsed into immediate and utter horror. Gone. The girl was *gone*.

Where? How?

In his state of shock and confusion, his grip on the steering wheel tightened, pulling it round in his desperate attempt to find the girl in the rear of the car. The left-front tyre crunched into the kerb as the car veered to the left on the bend and mounted the narrow strip of pavement. In a blind panic, he jerked the wheel back, which sent the car into an uncontrollable skid. It smashed side-on into the hedgerow on the other side of the road, finishing up in a ditch. After a few seconds, all was silent.

The impact was not as severe as he feared. Remarkably, he found himself supported by the door frame and the edge of his seat, with little sign of real injury. He realised he was holding his breath, which he released abruptly through clenched teeth. His heart was pounding with the combined shock of the girl's disappearance and the accident. His mind was reeling. A cold sweat soaked his back and thighs.

After resting for a moment to calm himself, he pulled himself upright. He released the belt-strap with a trembling hand, and tried to shift his weight over to the passenger side, where the door was free. He winced in pain as he tried to move. The steering wheel, he figured, had made some impression on his ribcage. But his fear and determination provided him with the motivation to get out. The door opened with no difficulty. Before pulling himself free, he felt compelled to re-check the rear seats again. Nothing. He opened the rear passenger door and placed his hand where the girl had been sitting. The seat was damp.

Despite the pain, he ran… he ran as fast as he could, down the hill, away from the car.

The lane was in total darkness. There was no sign that anyone had been alerted to the crash, despite the piercing screech of his brakes on the damp road surface. The only response was the occasional and distant whine of traffic on the major road a hundred yards or so away on his right.

He trotted back along the road to gain a clear view of the road in both directions. No sign of his passenger.

But she must be around here somewhere. People don't just

disappear from cars, not at forty miles an hour, and not from the rear seat.

His breath began to come in short, sharp bursts again as his head began to swim. At the bottom of the hill, he could see the comforting glow from the pub's windows. He made for it as fast as possible, clutching at his now-screaming ribs, keeping to the middle of the road to avoid stumbling over the kerb in the darkness.

FOUR

'Time, ladies and gentlemen. Drink up please!' called the barman, a stout, balding man in his late fifties.

It had been another good evening. Despite the establishment's relative obscurity, on this backwater country lane, it was popular with many inhabitants of the local villages. Now, at 11:15 p.m., most had gone home.

He had just started his glass collection and clear-up routine in the bar, when the main saloon doors burst inward. The remaining people in the bar stopped their conversations to look.

A young man stood in the doorway, superficially wet, his breathing rapid and shallow. He clutched at his ribs with his left hand, and stood there, looking around anxiously.

The customers looked from him to the barman, as if expecting that he, their host, should make some initial comment or gesture. Meanwhile, the man had gained his bearings, and made his way over to the bar.

The barman's eyes narrowed at the sight of him. 'Sorry, lad,' he said. 'We're closing shortly.'

The young man, still panting, just leaned against the bar. His face was drawn and pale, his expression wide-eyed and fearful.

'You okay?' asked the barman. 'Sit down.'

Richard slid onto the nearest barstool. 'Has … has a girl, maybe twenty, twenty-one, been in tonight – I mean, in the past few minutes?' he gasped.

The barman eyed him curiously. He exchanged glances with an old man who sat on the next stool, who had taken special note of Richard's entrance.

'We've had a number of young women in here tonight, lad. But you're the only person to come in for the last half-hour or so. Is there a problem?'

'I ... '

The old man, Jim Eddowes, a regular and personal friend of the barman, leaned towards him.

'You alright, boy? You look like you've seen a ghost.'

Richard flinched, then looked the man in the eye. He looked serious enough. On impulse, Richard decided to risk the ridicule and tell the truth. He was too scared, too weary to think of anything else.

'I ... I think I just gave one a lift,' he said flatly.

Eddowes and the barman exchanged glances, a knowing contact that was not lost on the frightened young man before them.

A young woman tittered behind his back. He decided to ignore it, though he could feel a number of eyes now burning holes in his back.

'Hold tight,' said the barman. 'I'll get you a drink. You look like you could use one.'

Richard nodded. His eyes darted about the bar nervously.

'Er ... I don't have any money on me.'

'We'll worry about that later,' replied the barman

Richard tried to force a smile, but couldn't break the suffocating sense of fear and disorientation that engulfed him. The bar seemed to be in a different time frame, slow and lethargic. Unreality washed over him. His mind raced and whirled in a waking nightmare.

2

The barman brought him a double scotch, which he downed in a single shot. He almost coughed but managed to contain it. As its acid warmth spread throughout his body, his tension eased. Slowly, he seemed to regain his sense and composure. The barman refilled his glass with another slug.

'You know something about this?' he asked, glancing from the barman to the old man and back. Several people on the other side of the bar now were focused on him.

He made his way to the base of the stairwell out back. 'Sheila!' he called. 'Sheila, come and cover down here, will you love?'

3

In the upstairs lounge, an open-hearth fire glowed invitingly. The barman, who Richard learned was named Cyril King, took Richard's jacket, and gestured for him to sit in one of the armchairs. After assurances from Richard that he was alright (although he continued to clutch his bruised ribs), the barman and the old man allowed him to relate what had happened.

He paused frequently to sip at his drink, to moisten his mouth and to fortify him as he relived his experience for the two men.

4

'You don't seem surprised,' said Richard. 'I got the impression downstairs that you knew more than you were letting on. How come you seem to know about her?' he asked.

After a pause, the barman spoke.

'It must have been forty-odd years ago. There was a fatal crash at the crossroads out there. Two or three young women died. A few months after that particular accident, motorists began to report picking up a girl on the way up the hill, just beyond the crossroads. When I took over here, ten years ago, I heard that one fella came running in here in a panic after he met her, just the way you did tonight. Scared him stupid, it did. His story runs pretty much the same as yours, so I gather.'

Jim Eddowes nodded in agreement.

'Personally,' he continued, 'I always thought it was a load of rubbish – y'know, a bit of a yarn ... which I'd still feel inclined to believe. Well, I did, perhaps, until you came in.'

Richard felt his stomach begin to churn again. 'And the girl disappeared from the car further up the hill?' He was slowly shaking his head.

The barman nodded. 'So it goes,' he said.

'Y'know,' said Richard, 'I still can't believe it. When I saw she was gone, I ... I don't know. She was so *real*. My first thought was that I must be going nuts. But where she was sitting, it was wet. She opened the door herself ... she said she was getting married tomorrow.'

'She spoke?' asked Eddowes beneath a raised eyebrow. He seemed impressed by this particular detail.

'Should I report it? I mean, just in case ... '

'Why?' asked Eddowes, interrupting.

'Just to cover myself,' answered Richard.

'Why?' Eddowes asked again.

Richard frowned.

'What Jim is asking you,' said King, 'Is what would you tell the police? The truth? I think you'll find they've probably heard of the story before. The tale is well known around here. If I were you, I'd accept it, and save myself the embarrassment.'

'Well, I'll have to tell them something, won't I? My car's in a ditch up on that bend.'

Jim Eddowes spoke again. 'Listen. That fellow Cyril mentioned, he used to be a friend of mine and another regular of this place. I'll confess that when he took me aside one day to tell me of his experience, I didn't believe him. He eventually moved away, after suffering months of personal and public ridicule. The press had a field day.

'To me, he was as honest and reliable as could be, but even I doubted his story, until later reports featured in the local papers. Of course, the story died down in time, but it took its toll on him.

'Your experience is the first for a number of years, as far as I'm aware. Do yourself a favour, and don't mention it to the police when they get here. It'll only get out.'

'But ... what if she was – is – real? I'd have a duty to report it to them in case she is wandering about injured out there.'

'Do you really believe that?' asked the old man.

'No,' said Richard quietly. 'Oh, I don't know ... '

He dropped his face into his cupped hands.

5

11:55 p.m.

The pub had been clear for fifteen minutes. Cyril King peered out of the upstairs window at the sound of tyres crunching on gravel.

'It's them,' he said.

He wandered over to Richard and sat opposite him.

'Remember what I said. You came in here looking like death warmed up. I gave you a drink not knowing you'd been driving. okay?'

Richard nodded.

While they had been waiting the barman had told Richard that he had been able to tell that he'd been drinking almost as soon as he walked in. And out here, he knew it was likely that he was driving. But he had purposely not asked that question.

He could see that Richard had needed the drink. Not that he approved of drink driving, of course. Not at all. But he guessed Richard could do without the additional hassle.

'Consider yourself lucky that there'll be no point in them breathalysing you now,' he'd said.

Richard had thanked him, acknowledging his stupidity.

'I'd probably have lost my job if I got a conviction, but I didn't plan to stack the car,' he said. 'Then again, I can't just make driving off a clear road an excuse to take a drink. You're supposed to stay by the vehicle. But there's no way I was going to do that.'

'Just say you swerved to miss a fox or something, and was shaken up by the crash,' said Eddowes. 'That's all. Don't mention ghosts, missing persons, or even hint at it.'

FIVE

He had just returned from an assignment, interviewing a local councillor about proposed increases in public transport fares. Not the most inspiring afternoon's reporting. He stopped to hang up his coat, fumbling in its inside pocket for his phone and flip-notebook, then marched across the busy open-plan office.

Peter Pumfrys exchanged pleasantries with colleagues as he zigzagged between desks on his way to his own. He switched on his own terminal and set his notebook down beside the keyboard, opening it to the correct page with one hand, already scanning his shorthanded notes, mentally constructing the write-up he was keen to complete as quickly as possible. A glance at the clock indicated he did not have a great deal of time. He was taking a lady friend to London to see a show.

He fiddled with the mini-cassette, trying to get it to fit the variable-speed playback deck. All of his colleagues had long since traded up to electronic devices for their interviews. He preferred the old methods, notebook, shorthand and backup tapes – the trappings of a real journalist, as he kidded his younger colleagues.

His eyes fell on a note left by the deputy editor. He read it with disdain:

Pete,

Sorry to land this on you. A two-column half-page will do (Steve's pix are in the day folder). It's only a filler, but Bill said he thought you wouldn't mind and would be able to get it done quickly. Steve has been sent out on an urgent photo job, anyway. Ready for six?

Cheers,

Robin

He sighed. But he picked up the brief. He hated picking up other people's notes. Too much room for error, and he could never be sure the details were as accurate as he would make them. But Steve was a good young reporter who sometimes doubled as a photographer when situations dictated.

He scanned the material, and his eyes widened. He could see why Bill Jensen, an old friend as well as the editor, had suggested asking him to take it on. The material was familiar. Very familiar.

But, did he really want to get involved with it again after so many years?

He picked up the phone and dialed 263. It rang for a few moments before it was answered.

"Lo, Hayes.'

'Robin, about this ghost piece. I don't –'

'Yes, I'm sorry, Pete, but Bill heard about it and thought you wouldn't mind taking it. Look, I was just on my way out.'

Pumfrys could mentally see him looking at his watch.

'See if you can put something together? If something more newsworthy turns up late, we'll pull it anyway.'

'Yes, but what about this fares interview?'

'Mm, we definitely need that.'

'But, I'm going out tonight. I was supposed to be leaving early myself.'

'Oh, yes. Sorry. You did mention it,' he said disinterestedly. 'Well, if it's going to be a problem, give it to someone else. It's not important. Look, I've really got to be off. I'll leave you

51

with it. Catch you tomorrow, okay?' and he hung up.

Pumfrys replaced the receiver and studied Steve Baker's notes for a moment. It wasn't the best-researched story. Then again, this type of thing never was.

As far as he could see, the witness hadn't even been interviewed. There wouldn't have been much time for that, though, admittedly.

But there was enough to write what was required. And, he could write it up quickly; almost blindfolded, in fact.

He put it aside for the moment, turning back to the fares interview. Priorities first. He told himself that if he ran out of time, he would give the ghost article away. But, deep down, he knew he wouldn't. It belonged with him.

SIX

Richard heard first the clatter, then the masked thump as the newspapers hit the floor in the hall. They had the *Daily Mirror* delivered every day, plus a copy of the *Courier* every Friday.

He made his way to the hall from the kitchen to rescue the papers from the dog, a cocker spaniel called Ricky, who alternately yapped and gnawed on the corner of the folded bundle. He picked up the papers and two items of post, gingerly, avoiding any undue stress on his ribcage, and shooed Ricky away with his foot. The dog promptly switched to one of his loose slippers, pulled it off and marched off victoriously with it into the kitchen.

'Little git,' muttered Richard, and gingerly followed him back through to the warm surroundings of the kitchen breakfast bar. He had elected to go sick for the remainder of the week.

Sitting, he put aside the *Mirror*, while he unfolded the larger format *Courier* to reveal its front page.

The headline read: COUNTY SCHOOL MEALS SERVICE UNDER THREAT.

He was about to flip the page when he saw something familiar, a photo of his own car, centre-right of the page. It was a total surprise.

His eyes switched to the title-caption:

THE HAUNTED HILL
Haltham Man has date with Phantom Hiker!

Chapter Six

By Peter Pumfrys

> On Wednesday evening this week, a lone motorist venturing up the old Eldonbridge-Haltham Road at Blaxton Hill came face to face with the notorious female hitch-hiker said to haunt that stretch of road.

> The driver, Richard Wentworth, 24, of Claygate Road, Haltham, crashed his car when he realised that the girl for whom he'd stopped to offer a lift had vanished from his car.

'My God,' Richard said aloud. 'Where did they get my name?'

He dropped the slice of toast and marmalade that comprised his breakfast onto his plate. The hand that held the paper dropped into his lap as he tried to take it in.

The *Courier*, published on Friday, reported on the news for the region for the past week. His encounter apparently rated as one of the main stories of the week, despite its brevity; a short, two-column piece supported by a photo of his ditched car.

Taken in daylight, the photo had clearly been taken near to first light before the tow-truck had pulled it out. The police had decided that it posed no immediate obstruction to other traffic that evening. Evidently, it had provided the paper with a tangible focus for its story.

Getting over his initial surprise, he read on:

> When the police arrived at the scene, they found Mr Wentworth in The Bull public house, where he had hurried for a stiff drink following his horrifying encounter.

> The incident is the latest in a series of similar reports over the years, the last around twenty ago, when another motorist stopped near the same spot to offer a lift to a young woman, who promptly disappeared when he spoke to her.

> Motorists who claim to have met the girl are traditionally male,

alone, and tend to meet her on wet evenings at around eleven-thirty p.m.

The reputed source of the tale is found in a motor accident on the hill in October 1978, in which three young women perished.

The ghost is rumoured to be a bride-to-be amongst the party who, tragically, never made it to her wedding, scheduled for the following day.

Meanwhile, as of yesterday, Mr Wentworth was still unavailable for comment.

2

Despite the sensational headline, the article appeared to be essentially accurate. But how the story got out was a mystery. He looked at the article again.

The car's registration, or the fact that he'd been checked over at the hospital might have provided some intent person – one Peter Pumfrys for instance – with a means of obtaining this information.

He had also been aware from his conversation with Cyril King and Jim Eddowes at The Bull of the basic story behind the haunting, but was impressed with the insightful detail given by this reporter – the details about witnesses always being alone, and the time of the incidents, around 11:30 p.m. The time of his encounter would have been ... hm ... around ten past eleven.

The immediate association between his experience and the hitch-hiker tale by Pumfrys suggested that the story was well known, as Cyril King had indicated. It wouldn't have taken much research to make a meaningful connection.

By its recurrence, independently experienced by himself on

that same stretch of road, and in obeyance of the story format, it also hinted at a fundamental reality to it all – something he had begun to question over the past day or so, simply because it, by all accepted standards, it could not have happened.

But here it was, some evidence to the contrary. And, thankfully, it didn't mention his drinking beyond the scotch he had had in the pub. The public would be even less likely to offer belief or sympathy for his experience if they had known that he had been drinking prior to his experience. Naturally, the first thing the police had intended to do that night was breathalyse him. Thank God for the drink Cyril King had given him. He had vowed secretly not to put himself in that position again. The breathalyser test had been duly abandoned.

As it was, he was going to have to suffer quite enough ridicule from friends and colleagues, not to mention what he would hear from Sally.

3

He had decided to go along with old man Eddowes's recommendations regarding the incident. As he neared the bend, something had scurried out in front of his car. Swerving, he missed the object – a fox – and crashed the vehicle. Shaken up, he had made his way to the pub, where he had ordered a drink. Only after he had downed a couple had he told the barman that he had been in an accident. The barman had dutifully telephoned the police so that arrangements could be made to clear the obstruction caused by the vehicle.

The story was fine, or so he thought. The two police officers had seemed suspicious. One had stated that his obvious anxiety was not in proportion to the relative harmlessness of the accident. He had had no answer for that.

It was when they had suggested that he accompany them

up to the vehicle that his cover-story fell apart. Wide-eyed, he had vehemently refused to go.

Puzzled, the officers left him at the pub while they drove up there. When they had returned, one sat opposite him and said simply: 'Now, do you want to tell us what really happened?'

He had begun to defend his original version, but the same officer interrupted with the observation that his car had not swerved in the manner described, and that made them a little suspicious regarding the rest of his story.

Of course, he had forgotten the swerve onto the kerb on the left as the girl had vanished. It was only after that that the vehicle had veered across the road and tipped into the ditch.

Seeing his original story as transparently false, he decided to tell the truth – well, about the incident at least. 'Look, you're not going to believe this … '

4

The recalled memory of the incident brought a now-familiar chill. He tried to shrug it off, to rid himself of this feeling. The dreams – nightmares, really – had kept his memory alive. Indeed, they had made it worse. He had dreamt about the incident every night since.

The first had been almost a repeat performance, up to a point. When he had finally arrived home and found sleep in the early hours of Thursday morning, he dreamt that, having picked the girl up, he continued up the lane, aware of what was going to happen, but in the fashion of dreams, totally unable to do anything about it. At the point he discovered the girl had vanished, he had felt the same alarm and sickening jolt of the crash.

The dream had not ended there, though. Out of the car, he

had begun a frantic effort to get away from the spot, but despite the downhill path, he felt the slow-motion drag weighing him down, as if he were trying to run through liquid honey.

And when he rounded the bend, which should have brought him in sight of the pub at the crossroads, there she was, standing in his way.

He had awoken with a start, his sweat drenching his sheets.

The following night – last night – he had looked into the rearview mirror to see her staring sadly and intensely at him before she vanished. Again he had jolted awake, and had lain awake for some time, light on, fearful of going back to sleep, before finally electing to go downstairs to make some coffee.

5

He looked at the paper again, unable to believe his experience had really made the paper, especially its front page. It had really dropped him in the poo, so to speak, not just with Sally, but with work as well. He had lied to both, not to be deceitful, but to avoid the complications and questions that would have come out had he told the truth.

Sally usually bought a copy of the *Courier* on Friday mornings on her way to work. It was a betting certainty that she would ring him this morning. It wasn't a call he looked forward to.

On the night of the accident, he was supposed to have texted her when he reached home – their standard arrangement for reassuring they were home safely. It should have taken fifteen to twenty minutes at most for the cab to reach Haltham.

Sally had texted him, then called his mobile when he had been twenty minutes overdue. Despite the knowledge that he must surely be there, probably soundly asleep, she couldn't shake the feeling that something was wrong. And so she rang his landline, and was about to hang up, when Richard's mother had answered. It was obvious from her tone that she was a little annoyed at having been woken up, but Sally registered none of this. His mother's reaction had turned to concern when she had checked his room to find it empty. The outside light was still on. Always, when he was out, she would leave it on for him, and when he got home he would turn it off and lock up. When she returned to the phone and recognised the concern in Sally's own voice, she tried to reassure her, promising to get him to ring her as soon as he got home.

She had waited up another hour. Concern had turned to anger. She couldn't rightly phone his house again. She continued to wait.

Finally, at 1:50 a.m., her mobile buzzed. Richard was at the hospital, where he had had his ribs examined and strapped. The damage was not severe, heavy bruising; nothing more, fortunately.

In truth, he had forgotten to text her, and only when he had phoned home to inform and reassure his mother did he find out that Sally was waiting up for him. He had called her immediately. For someone concerned for his safety, she was pretty mad when he told her where he was and how he had ended up there.

He had felt it diplomatic not to mention the disappearing girl. He still really wasn't convinced himself on that one. Although he had no strong feelings on the paranormal – in fact, he had given it little thought in the past – Sally was openly against it, a stance she had likely inherited from her father, a hard-nosed skeptic. Well, no. To be fair, she had formed her own opinions, but like many people, this had been out of fearful rationalism and, he could see now, ignorance.

He was already in enough trouble with her over his driving. Now this. He couldn't tell her about this part over the phone, more so to convince her that it wasn't an excuse for or result of his drinking – although she must have known he hadn't had nearly enough for that.

As for work, he would be expecting calls later from one or two of his workmates. Terry Andrews would be the lead candidate for this. Of course, they would want to know if it was true or not. Wouldn't everyone?

Yesterday morning, he had called in to say he wouldn't be in for the rest of the week. His boss had not been very sympathetic. They were short-staffed and under pressure just weeks before Christmas.

The newspaper piece would not only make him look ridiculous; it would make a liar of him as well.

6

As expected, it wasn't long before Sally called him from work. She hadn't been best pleased at having been lied to, but agreed that discussing it over the phone wasn't right.

He knew that she wasn't so much concerned with the reason for the crash, as others might be, but that he had broken his promise to her. The business about the ghost could be discussed later.

And it would have to wait until later. Sally didn't drive, and it was unlikely he would be able to drive comfortably for a couple of days, even if he had a car. His was in for repairs. There was quite a bit of damage, but it wasn't a write-off. Goodness knows what the Insurance people will make of it now, he thought.

Perhaps it was just as well. Grounded, he could concentrate on recovering, both physically and mentally. His ribcage was still as sore as hell from the crash, and his back and neck ached, and he felt drained from the past two nights' dreams. Now, with the newspaper's involvement and Sally's reaction, he was feeling pretty beaten up.

Sally had offered to cab it over after work, but he had turned her down. It would be too much trouble for her. And he really didn't feel like talking. Time to himself might enable him to make some sense out of the whole thing. He'd call her over the weekend. They could sort something out then.

7

He spent the remainder of the afternoon pondering the encounter. Had it really happened? With the dreams confusing his recall, he found it hard to believe. But something had happened. It couldn't all have been in his mind, surely?

He found an unused schoolbook his younger brother seemed to have abandoned, and set about making notes on his encounter, forcing himself to mentally study it for all of its detail and impressions, for anything that would provide proof of it as an objective experience.

The alternative, the thought of it being a product of a mental aberration, scared him more than the idea that he may actually have met a ghost.

When John, his brother, came in from school, he had just noted down the telephone number of the *Courier*. The article had already caused him some trouble. No doubt it would open him up to some ridicule. He wanted to talk to this Pumfrys, to find out how he could have published an article without talking to him first. But, if he were honest, he had to admit that Pumfrys was also the most promising source for further information. He had read that much between the lines of the article.

8

Richard awoke the next morning to two surprises.

Firstly, his mother showed Sally into his room, where he still lay sound asleep at ten-to-eleven. He winced, coming awake sharply, as she pressed lightly on his right shoulder to stir him.

His tension subsided when he saw who was standing there. Her defensive smile disarmed him. It meant, at least, that the time apart had worked. He had been forgiven.

The other surprise, which dawned on him as he spoke to her, was that he had had a dreamless, restful night. He breathed a mental sigh of relief.

When he had washed and dressed, they discussed Wednesday night's events over a cooked breakfast, prepared by Sally while Richard's mother took John out shopping.

She understood now why he had felt compelled to take the car, but extracted a promise that it would never happen again. He had no problem with that. He had already made this promise to himself after his close shave with the law.

Her reaction was a little cooler over his claims about the ghost. Oh, she listened intently but, when he finished, she brushed it off almost casually.

Though disappointed in her reaction and, hurt by it, if the truth be told, he realised it was going to be a source of some measure of conflict between them. For he couldn't just sweep it aside. He had already made up his mind to find out what he could, starting with the *Courier*.

SEVEN

November 6

Richard phoned the *Courier* offices in Eldonbridge at ten, asking for Peter Pumfrys. He was placed on hold before the receptionist came back on. Mr Pumfrys was out.

Richard asked if he could leave a message, and she grudgingly, it seemed, noted his name and number. He hung up thinking that that would be the end of it. But a little under two hours later, his phone rang and when he answered, it was Pumfrys.

'Mr. Wentworth?'

'Yes,' Richard answered.

'Sorry I wasn't available earlier.'

'You know what I was calling about, of course,' said Richard flatly.

'Uh, yes. For that I apologise. In fact, I meant to try to contact you before the paper came out. I'm really sorry about that.'

He sounded sincere. The gesture was disarming. He had meant to take Pumfrys to task over his article. It wasn't what he expected. Nor was the impression he had of the man himself. His voice was refined, somewhat nasal and relaxed. Richard formed an immediate mental picture of someone in his late fifties or early sixties.

'I have a couple of questions,' said Richard.

'Naturally,' the voice said.

'Well, obviously, for one, I'd like to know where you got your information.'

'Quite. And the other is what else do I know?'

Richard hated being anticipated, pre-empted like this. He frowned at his end of the line. 'Yes,' he said.

'Ah, in answer to the first question, I have to say that I wasn't responsible for the research. It came to me on top of another assignment. I only wrote it up,' he added.

'As for how we came by the story, it's routine to phone around the police stations a couple of times a day for interesting news items.'

'You got it from the police?' asked Richard. 'I thought statements were supposed to be confidential.'

'The contents of statements are,' answered Pumfrys. 'But the essentials of a report are not. The police are quite free to give us material without betraying confidentiality. It works both ways, you see. We are of service to the police whenever a situation demands. Obtaining the specifics is just good journalism.'

'Well, 'good journalism' has caused me all sorts of problems, with work, with my girlfriend. Doesn't someone have the right to veto something like this, using names and so on without permission?'

'Well, if you feel strongly about it, you could write to the editor, or there are other channels to lodge a complaint.'

'No, I don't want to do that,' replied Richard.

'Well, thank you. Look, again, I'm really sorry for the way it came out, but if we can get on to your second question, you might find I can help you.'

Again, Richard was disarmed. He had hoped Pumfrys might indeed be able to provide some answers, and here he was volunteering it. Or so it seemed. He decided to shut up and listen.

'As it happens, this type of thing used to be an interest of mine. I really would be interested to hear your story first hand… for my own personal interest, I should add. Nothing for publication, I promise. And, in exchange, if you are interested, I'm sure I can fill you in on some of the background to this story? It really is quite fascinating.'

'Um, sure, that'd be good, Richard heard himself saying.

'Hm, what's the time now? I tell you what, how about tomorrow? Over lunch, if you are free? All on me.'

'Er, yes, okay. Where? What time?'

'Well, if you can get here, around twelve-thirty or one? I know a good little spot around the corner. I'll bring along some material I'm sure will interest you. Just ask for me at the front desk.'

'Okay.'

'Good. See you then. Nice talking to you. Bye.'

And that was that.

2

The newspaper offices were located on the outskirts of Eldonbridge. The building was a four-story affair, fronted with silvered glass that reflected its surroundings like a polished mirror.

The entrance sat at the top of a low, semi-circular flight of steps. Above the lintel, in gold-embossed lettering:

THE COURIER
The County's Favourite Newspaper

Richard made his way up the steps and into the shadow of the entrance. Automatic glass-doors slid back and he passed a man and a woman on their way out. A down blast of air from the air-curtain ruffled the woman's hair as she crossed the threshold.

The reception lounge was broad and spacious. The main desk, semi-circular in plan, sat against the back wall between two sets of lift doors, which opened periodically to disgorge their passengers.

He glanced at his watch: 12:45. He approached the desk. A young, blonde woman sat behind it. She glanced up at Richard's approach, but carried on talking into her headset. He waited until, finally, she looked up with a small smile.

'I'm here to see Peter Pumfrys.'

'Is he expecting you?'

'Yes, he is.'

'I'll see if he's in. And your name is?'

'Richard Wentworth.'

'One moment.' She rang a number.

He could hear the faint burble of the telephone ringing at the other end. She allowed the phone to ring for a few moments more. But, at last, her hand moved to sever the connection.

'There's no-one answering. He's probably at lunch.'

'But I'm supposed to –' He turned to see what had caught her eye.

A bespectacled figure was approaching the desk from the main entrance.

'Ah, Peter...' started the girl.

The man looked past Richard to the receptionist.

'Yes, thank you, Jacquie.'

He switched his attention to Richard, proffering his hand. 'Mr. Wentworth – or can I call you Richard? Peter Pumfrys. Pleased to meet you.'

Pumfrys did not quite look the image conjured by his voice. He was a small man, quite thin, with rather aquiline features, topped with a thinning, peppery mop of hair that seemed to have a mind all of its own. He wore a scuffy pair of well-worn black shoes, and a light-tweed jacket over a cream shirt and a green tie. He pumped Richard's hand with a surprisingly firm grip.

'Shall we off?' he said.

The two of them started toward the entrance.

'If anyone wants me, I'm following up a story, okay, Jacquie?' Pumfrys said over his shoulder.

Richard shot him a glance.

Pumfrys waved it away. 'Don't worry. Just fending off any interruptions for a bit.

'There's a nice restaurant just across the road from here,' said Pumfrys. 'But we won't go there,' he added, looking to Richard and enjoying the puzzled frown that crossed his brow. 'There's another one just around the corner; less crowded, not so many newspaper people at this time of day. Hate talking shop,' he said.

3

Ye Olde Farmhouse Kitchen strived to be just that. Polished old oak tables and chairs were arranged around a central red brick column decorated with old-fashioned bellows and iron tongs. The bar and kitchen lay beyond. The doors to the kitchen and the bright, sterile light that poured through their glass ports, were the only aspects to the restaurant that spoiled its faux nineteenth century ambience, barring the presence of obviously twenty-first century clientele.

They took a table in a corner. Richard slipped in behind the table beneath wall-mounted sepia-prints of old Eldonbridge and outmoded modes of transport. Illuminating these, the low-key yellow light of imitation oil lanterns helped to create a suspension of time that seemed appropriate to the discussion of a ghost story.

'One plaice?' asked the waitress.

'Yes, here, said Richard.

The waitress set the plate before him, and turned to Pumfrys. 'And one steak, medium.'

Pumfrys thanked her, at the same time making room on the table top, an unnecessary gesture that caused Richard's beer glass to slop precious liquid onto it and into his own drink, a tomato juice.

'Dear me.'

Richard and the waitress exchanged amused glances. The girl handed Pumfrys a clutch of paper napkins to mop up the spillage.

'Thank you, thank you,' said Pumfrys. 'I'm so clumsy at times.'

Despite this air of clumsiness, Richard suspected that some of it was, in a way, deliberate, that he made use of it to some extent when it suited. After a few moments, Pumfrys bundled the napkins into a moist ball on the table, and indicated towards Richard's untouched plate. 'Please, don't wait for me.'

Richard picked up his knife and fork. 'Thanks.'

'Don't mention it; the least I can do after the apparent trouble I've caused you.'

'I'll get over it. I think,' said Richard. 'Besides, I didn't think that that would be a concern of yours – you're a journalist, aren't you? It's good copy. It sells newspapers.' He reached for his drink.

'Hm, a cynic!' replied Pumfrys with mock surprise. 'But, no, seriously,' he said as he started on his own meal, 'believe it or not, I still see my role as a reporter, to report the facts. That's what I entered journalism to become, and that is what I strive to uphold. And,' he added, 'surprisingly perhaps, so do the majority of journalists.

'Of course, you can't help a certain amount of personal bias, and you can't help error caused by pressures of deadline. And, yes, there is also the responsibility to make the news interesting, if not entertaining, in order to sell the product. Unfortunately, in my opinion, this has also encouraged a growing trend towards sensationalist reporting, even to publications *making* the news rather than simply reporting it. It's all a far cry from my early days in the profession.'

'Well, to be honest, I don't see the difference between what you wrote and what you've just said,' said Richard.

Pumfrys considered the remark for a moment. 'Yes, it's true that this type of subject receives a more frivolous treatment than ordinary items of news. I don't know why that should be, really.

'Well, in fact, no. I think I do. It's because even newspaper people don't like to get egg on their faces.

'While the item in question may be considered newsworthy – and in your case, to get on the front page, it plainly was – it's always going to be a difficult one in terms of presentation. On one hand, you can't afford to wholly endorse it as true – it can easily backfire. And you're on that marshy ground of belief, not accepted fact.

'Then, again, you shouldn't dismiss it out of sight either, since it *might* be true and then, what a scoop!

'But above all, it makes interesting reading, and that's what we're in the business for. What was it Mark Twain said, 'Interesting, if true, and interesting anyway?'

'So, what you go with is the 'safe' treatment, the cautious approach.'

Richard took a sip from his drink. 'From the newspaper's and the reporter's point-of-view, perhaps. But what about the poor sod, the witness, who, without a choice, ends up at the butt end of the joke? It's the witness who pays for the safe line, don't you think?'

'Often so,' agreed Pumfrys. 'It's unfortunate. Some reporting does go over the top. But I put it to you that if you're going to report these stories to a general audience accustomed to hard reporting on everyday matters, there's really no other way to go – if you really think about it,' he added.

Richard frowned.

'Let me ask you a question: Did you come away from your experience in full belief and yet later begin to question its reality?'

'Of course. I think anyone would.'

Pumfrys nodded. 'Then how is the public to view it, if you, the witness, aren't yourself certain? As I said, the style of presentation doesn't advance understanding or acceptance of the said phenomenon with the general public, but it does permit it to be met while protecting all concerned – the paper, me, my editor, the public; even you.'

'How me?' asked Richard.

'Because anyone can be wrong. And if someone can be seen to not have committed too strongly to a particular belief or interpretation, by not taking it too seriously, the truth, if or when it comes out, will prove less damaging.'

'The best way to protect me would be to have left me alone.'

'But then if we did that with everyone, we would have no news at all, would we?' said Pumfrys.

'Anyway, before we lose track of why we're here, can I remind you that I've yet to hear your story? Then I will share what I know.'

Richard realised that this was true. He paused and set himself, then told Pumfrys the story he had by now repeated several times.

When he finished, he said simply, 'What do you think?'

The reply, when, it came, was unexpected.

'Quite remarkable.'

'So, you believe me?' Richard studied him carefully.

'Well, I've no reason to disbelieve you. What you've described tallies well with the Blaxton Hill story as I know it, and in character with other examples of this category of ghost, and of apparitions in general. The real question is: what, precisely, did you experience?'

Richard looked at him quizzically.

'I mean, was it really the spirit of a young woman killed on the hill? If so, why has she come back? What for? How? How can she apparently manifest to a degree where she could manipulate a door handle, for instance?

'And, if not, what was 'she'? A figment of your imagination? You say you hadn't heard the story beforehand? How then could you so precisely replicate an account at precisely the right spot without any prior knowledge of the case? Perhaps you did it unconsciously, having heard the story before, subliminally perhaps, and recreated it out of your unconscious? But then, why would it come to the surface now, and what triggered it? If it was hallucinatory in nature, how could it achieve such a degree of reality that it could fool you so completely? And again, *why*?

'When you look at a lot of these so-called 'fringe' subjects, you find levels of detail and unanswered questions that make the issue of whether it is real or not a far from simple matter.'

Richard was beginning to regard Pumfrys from a fresh perspective. He had not expected anything near a sympathetic attitude.

'You seem to have more than a passing interest.'

Pumfrys nodded. 'Although the article might suggest otherwise, I actually have — well, I used to have — some genuine interest in the paranormal, partly through personal experience, but mainly through background reading. When I heard your story, I was already familiar with the history of events on the hill – which was the main reason I was handed the write-up.

'There's a book on the subject,' he said, reaching down to a black leather articles wallet at his feet. Finding it, he placed it on the table top in front of Richard, rotating it so that Richard could see the cover the right way up. Richard passed his dinner fork from left hand to right, and drew the book closer.

'The only book to make more than passing mention of the Blaxton Hill ghost, which you'll find detailed in chapter three, if memory serves.'

Richard looked at its faded cover. *Highway Horrors: Phantom Hitch-Hikers and other Road Ghosts*, by James E. Wetherby. The cover picture showed a faintly transparent figure of a young woman standing, thumb cocked, in the path of an oncoming vehicle, headlights blazing, on a dark stretch of road. He found himself shudder. He picked it up, turning it over to scan the back cover, then back again, flicking the front cover over to check the publication date: 2005.

'That's what these ghosts are called, is it – phantom hitch-hikers?'

Pumfrys nodded. 'Or the 'Vanishing Hitchhiker', in the United States.

'Can I borrow it?' asked Richard.

'Of course. That's why I brought it along,' replied Pumfrys. 'Plus a few others, if you're interested?'

'Sure.'

Pumfrys stooped to retrieve a plastic bag-wrapped bundle. 'Keep them as long as you wish. All I ask is that you take care of them – particularly that one – and return them safely afterward. There's an address label inside the cover. I'd rather you deliver rather than post them, to either my house or to the office, it doesn't matter.

'That one,' he said, nodding towards the Wetherby book, 'will obviously be of most interest. In the back is a list of newspaper and book references that include some on Blaxton Hill. They are probably worth following up.'

'Thank you,' said Richard, genuinely interested.

'My pleasure.'

'I suppose the fact that this kind of ghost has its own name suggests some level of reality to it all?' asked Richard, seeing in this some reassurance.

Pumfrys's expression, though, was noncommittal.

'I mean,' said Richard, 'These kinds of encounters are obviously more common than you'd think.'

'Actually, they're really quite rare. And yours, quite frankly, is virtually unprecedented.'

Richard simply looked at him.

'What *is* common about them is the folklore that underlies them, as you'll find if you read the book – the ubiquity of the tale, the same pattern of events you yourself described, repeated again and again around the world – which raises all kinds of questions about the 'reality' of the events.'

'Having studied the subject, what do you think it is?' asked Richard.

Pumfrys smiled.

'You've pinpointed the problem: what do I believe? The honest answer? I don't know. No-one can truly know. The whole subject is too under-studied for anyone to hold anything more than an opinion on it. At the same time, it's also too ambiguous for that opinion to really mean anything. What it is, or seems to be, depends on a number of factors, not least the personal beliefs of the witness and the person documenting the account. The evidence, if you wish to call it that, can guide one's opinion in a particular direction, but all one can say for certain is that some people – frequently ordinary down-to-earth people – do occasionally undergo very peculiar experiences which, together, do suggest a genuine phenomenon at play. What that phenomenon really represents is the real question.'

'What else could my experience have been – if it wasn't a ghost?'

'By inference, the spirit of a deceased person?' clarified Pumfrys.

Richard nodded. 'Yes. I mean, she seemed totally real; I couldn't see through her; she spoke to me; I felt her weight as she got into the car.'

'I don't know. It does sound like a strong case for Survival,' admitted Pumfrys. 'But what can you prove by it? It could … it could be a particularly vivid hallucination, as I suggested earlier, that came about as – '

'I didn't imagine her, Peter.'

'I didn't say you did. But powerful hallucinations can and have been demonstrated, by something as familiar as stage hypnotism, for instance. I'm only pointing out the possibilities to highlight the inherent difficulties of the subject.'

'I'd rather believe it was a real ghost than I was prone to hallucinate like that,' said Richard. 'If I was to fabricate a ghost, I would have made it a transparent-looking thing, not something so solid-looking, so *real*?'

'Most apparitions appear to be exactly that: opaque, and in full colour. But I was referring to hallucinations as a mechanism – a medium, perhaps – for the experience. But I take your point. It would be a sorry state of affairs if people randomly hallucinated in that manner when driving. But, as you discovered for yourself, many of these events are not randomly distributed; they tend to be focused on certain areas, which suggests something else is at play, doesn't it?'

Pumfrys glanced at his watch. He raised an eyebrow.

'Look, I'm afraid I'm going to have to make a move in a minute,' he said. He raised a hand to attract the attention of the waitress. 'All I can say is it's been good of you to share your story with me. And don't worry, you won't see it in the paper!'

Richard grinned.

The waitress arrived at the table.

'Can you make up the bill, please?' asked Pumfrys.

The girl nodded and left.

'And,' continued Pumfrys, 'should you wish to discuss the subject further after you've read the books, or you have any questions, or anything I can help you with, don't hesitate to get in touch.'

Pumfrys stood up, offering his hand again. Richard got to his feet and the two of them shook hands. And just as suddenly, he was off.

Richard sat back to finish his drink as Pumfrys walked over to the bar where he met the waitress to pay the bill. A few moments later he made a final wave goodbye, and was gone.

5

Richard started on the books even before he arrived home. Unpacking the bag containing the books on the bus back into town, he noticed that, in addition to the Wetherby book, Pumfrys had included three others, two of which seemed, on first inspection, to be serious and scientifically-based studies of hauntings and apparitions, which he quickly decided were a little heavy for his taste. The other appeared to be more palatable – the bestseller by American author John Fuller, *The Ghost of Flight 401*. Its back cover described repeated appearances of the ghosts of a pilot and flight engineer whose

Tristar jet had crashed in the Florida Everglades in 1972, with a loss of over a hundred lives.

But it was the Wetherby book, as Pumfrys suggested, that was going to be of greatest interest. Turning to chapter three, 'The Phantom of the Hill', he became immediately engrossed, so that he almost missed his stop.

At home, he quickly made himself a coffee and, with some hours before he had to get ready to meet Sally, he retired to the warmth of the living room to read.

The book began with a short history and setting for the location:

Geologically, Blaxton Hill is composed of sandstone. The quartz-sand sediments of outwash deltas 120 million years ago now form a gently-inclined, north-dipping slab of rock, 500 metres thick. The exposed 90 metres or so has been denuded over time to produce a rounded ridge or escarpment that stands elevated above softer, more easily eroded, rocks to the south.

The hill is a high point along this ridge, which overlooks the River Eldon and the market town of Eldonbridge below. Once considered a source of iron ore, the hill has been quarried in the past for its concentration of precipitated iron oxides, which formed along the discontinuities in the rock, giving it a veined appearance in cross-section. Where the rock surface has weathered, concentrations of iron leach out to stain the rock face. Hence, the name Blaxton, contracted from the original Blackston(e). Where the colour is less intense, the sandstone takes on a ruddy complexion.

As might be expected, the hill has its share of folklore and legend. The blood-red colour of the rocks is rumoured to preserve for all time evidence of the ritualistic killings of hundreds in sacrifice to some obscure and incompassionate god. Sounds of their death-cries are said to be heard on some nights, though many claim the unearthly sounds are simply the screeching cries of foxes.

The most significant marker in the hill's history was the introduction of the Roman road that laid the straight route that later became the single most important means of traversing this densely afforested countryside. This same route was to later become the Eldonbridge-Haltham Road, which took a steep, winding course where it negotiated the escarpment at Blaxton Hill. The portion of this road's path remaining today is known as Old Haltham Road.

As a significant artery for millennia, it is hardly surprising that the road at Blaxton Hill should support its own coterie of ghost: a bedraggled band of Roman soldiers spied along the old road on dismal winter evenings; the re-enactment of a grisly murder in a field behind the site of an old inn, which itself burned to the ground in 1901. But no-one has seen or heard of either haunting for many years.

There is, however, one ghost that is both recurrent and contemporary in origin. Furthermore, in this tale, we are treated not only to a ghost story, but the interaction of the spirit with our physical environment in a fundamentally real manner, since the ghost hitches lifts from passing motorists!

The story of the phantom hitch-hiker is pervasive in the local area. A poll conducted by the author revealed that the basic structure remains remarkably consistent, though the detail that would potentially support such a tale is, of course, missing.

An example of the essential story is recounted by a member of the general public:

> 'Drivers sometimes stop to pick up a girl on the Blaxton Hill. It's late and she is alone, and wishes to be taken to an address in Haltham. But before they get there, the driver finds that she has vanished from the car. The people at the address later inform the driver that he must have met the ghost of a girl who died years before at the spot he picked her up.'

Variations on the theme include the girl's wish to be taken to Nedworth, not Haltham, or that the girl states she is to be married the next day. But irrespective of such variations, all the expected hallmarks of the hitch-hiker legend remain: the ghost is initially regarded as a normal flesh-and-blood human being (until her disappearance), the apparent lack of motive and logic in the whole experience, and the lack of identifiable first-hand witnesses available for interview. It is this latter point that fails to separate the story from established folklore.

In the folklorist tradition, the lack of personalised detail is precisely what we would expect if the claims to sightings were spurious. We almost invariably have a lone, unidentified motorist of the opposite sex to the ghost's gender. We hear that the ghost has given an address to which this anonymous individual proceeds, only to find his erstwhile passenger has not been alive for years. In fact, she/he died on the very spot on the anniversary of that fateful day.

To combat the strong case of the folklorist, we have

to confront a fundamental question: What came first? Is it a case of fact imitating fiction (if not in reality, then in the mind or subconscious of the experience – a process known to folklorists as *ostension*) – or does the perpetuation and ubiquity of the little-known hitch-hiker myth owe itself to 'real' encounters?

Of course, if there was a ready answer to this question, we would not have to pose it.

The Blaxton Hill case is unusual and stimulating since it evokes new questions which offer to separate the bipartite elements of the fundamental question. If only a myth, why does this ghost persist into the twenty-first century, reportedly encountered by otherwise sober and reliable witnesses?

Conversely, if this case demonstrates that the basic hitch-hiker myth is being somehow temporally relocated and modified, we have to answer how it intrudes into the lives of ordinary people with such consistency and impact, particularly those uncaring or ignorant of its tradition. Furthermore, we have to identify what such a fictitious encounter might mean on a symbolic level in our technological age, and how our perception of 'reality' can be so readily altered to allow for the victim to believe so utterly in his or her experience.

In the best evidenced encounters, the elements as related by the driver conform strongly to the idealised tale of the hitch-hiker encounter – something that supports the contentions of the folklorist and debunker. However, this does not necessarily hold true. The basic story, when overlain with specific details, can serve as a reinforcement of the validity of the encounter.

Such is the case with published, checkable facts concerning the Blaxton Hill case. Contrary to the claims of the folklorists that a source is never identified with confidence, the stories concerning the haunting of the hill have been related to a real motor accident that occurred in 1978, on the very stretch of road that later gained its terrible reputation.

The original accident, involving two vehicles, was covered in detail at the time by regional press. Covering front pages of two local newspapers, one having county-wide circulation, the facts are clear:

TRAGEDY

The Courier of 3 November 1978 details the tragic deaths of three young women, when their Ford Consul was in collision with another car at a crossroads on Blaxton Hill. The occupant of the other vehicle escaped serious injury.

According to the newspaper account, the accident occurred at around 11:30 p.m., in changeable conditions. The driver of a Morris Minor, rounding the bend of Valence lane on the approach to the crossroads, failed to see the stalled Consul until too late.

The cruel and premature termination of young life was made increasingly tragic because of its timing. It happened the evening before the wedding of one of the young women. Indeed, the crash happened on the homeward journey after an evening of celebration with her friends.

A later inquest found no fault with either driver of the vehicles involved. A verdict of accidental death was given by the Coroner in February 1979.

SPECTRE

Two months after that accident, a newspaper article in *The Herald* brought rumours of an alleged hitch-hiking ghost on the hill to the attention of the public. Remarkably, the author of this piece made no connection with the accident at that spot. The article, a minor column-filler, seemed just another mildly interesting curio at the time, although perhaps not for the alleged subject of the encounter.

Two months on, another encounter on the hill brought wider interest to the case, not least since it involved an officer of the county constabulary. The story broke following – incredibly – a further experience by a third lone motorist only two days later. This time, the journalist assigned by the *Courier* lost no time in linking the appearances with the accident. The police officer, incidentally, remains anonymous.

The article served to bring together the common elements of the encounters for the first time, and no doubt sparked the widespread public awareness thereafter.

According to a local researcher, in ten claimed first-hand encounters collected over the next decade, all involved lone males travelling up the hill from *The Bull* crossroads. Half took place in the autumn. Seven occurred at or around 11:30 p.m. (the others, for sake of completeness, occurred at 8:10 p.m., 10:35 p.m. and 12:40 a.m.), and four of the ten actually on the anniversary of the original crash (27 October). A staggering correlation, and a true anniversary performer, if these sources are to be believed.

However, since I have not been able to interview

this researcher, or study his notes, I cannot vouch for the veracity of the information nor, of course, the reliability of the witnesses. The 'evidence', then, permits no definite conclusions to be drawn.

As far as I am aware, the last reported sighting occurred in 1998. The ghost, real or imagined, appears to be fading from popularity, destined, it would seem, to be lost in the misty realms of folk tradition once again.

Richard's eyes nearly ran off the edge of the page. He looked up and around at the room about him, and then he lowered the book, slowly, placing it face down, spreading the pages so that the spine creased along its length. His right hand found his forehead. He was surprised to find a light beading of sweat there.

Somehow, seeing in print a version of what was essentially his own experience made far greater impact on him than he had expected. It provided corroboration for his story, which he had, subsequent to his experience, come to question. After all, these things couldn't happen, could they? Not really?

He had half-convinced himself that he had suffered either an alcohol-induced hallucination, or was simply flipping his lid. If true, it challenged his entire worldview on life and the hereafter which, on the latter point, in truth, amounted to little.

He got up and placed the book face down on the middle shelf of the inglenook bookshelf behind the television. Stretching and stifling a yawn, he made his way out to the kitchen to grab something to eat. It was ten-past seven.

His mother and brother were visiting his aunt down the road, while he and Sally had arranged to meet a group of friends at the pub a bit later.

He changed then drove over to Sally's in his mother's car. His own car, quite badly dented, but not beyond repair, was in a local garage awaiting his insurance company's final go-ahead to begin the repair work.

His journey took fifteen minutes longer than usual. He consciously avoided going via Blaxton Hill, despite the fact that he would keep to the main, well-lit dual-carriageway, well away from the old road.

6

At Sally's house, he honked twice and waited in the car. The living room curtains shuffled as Sally peeped out, and then made her way to the door.

'Hi,' she said, as she got into the car. She slammed the door after her and leaned over to give Richard a peck on the cheek. 'You okay?'

'Yup,' he replied, trying to sound as normal as possible. 'Where are we going?' he asked.

'The pub,' she replied. 'Like we arranged'.

'That was before all this, you know, this business with the paper,' he said. 'I can't go there. I'm supposed to be out sick. Besides, you know what they're like; what Terry's like. The last thing I need is for him to carry on about it in front of a pub full of people.'

'You can't blame them for being curious.'

'I know, but –'

'Well, I told Alice we'd be there. We can't just not turn up. And, anyway, wouldn't it look a bit like running away?'

'I don't care about that. I don't want to talk about it. And I know you don't. If we go, there'll only be one subject on the menu.'

'Well, we'll just have to steer the conversation away. Come on, we've got to go. You know that.'

7

The pub was only moderately full. Still, it was only eight-thirty. Richard and Sally quickly located their friends in what they regarded as 'their' corner – the same bay window where he and Sally sat the night of the ... incident.

They were the last to arrive. Seated from left to right were: Terry Andrews and his girlfriend Alice; Jennifer, a friend of Sally's, with her boyfriend, Tom, and finally, Gary, a workmate of Richard's and Terry's, and a friend of his friend, Craig, something of an outsider to the group.

'Evening all,' said Richard with as normal an air as possible. He conducted Sally to her seat by the window, next to Alice. 'Sorry we're a bit late. Anyone for a top-up?'

'Ah, go on, then,' said Terry, who drained the last of his lager and held the glass out to Richard. Same old Terry.

'Anyone else?' asked Richard, looking from one to another. Everyone, with the exception of Gary, declined. He made his way over to wait his turn at the bar.

Terry leaned across Alice to address Sally. 'Where's his other girl tonight, then?'

'Terry!' Alice shot him a disapproving look.

'Just asking,' he said impishly.

'Well don't,' replied Alice. She turned to Sally. 'I'm sorry, Sally. He's already had one more than he should. He can be such a prat at times.'

Sally smiled weakly, but alarm had already settled in her stomach. 'It's okay. I know what Terry's like. So does Richard. In fact, he was wary of coming along tonight for that reason.'

'Why? asked Alice. 'We're all friends. Richard knows he doesn't really mean it. Do you?' she asked, looking at Terry.

Terry sat back. 'Course not,' he said with a twinkle in his eye. 'Just a bit of ribbing.'

'I know. It's just that.. I.. oh, I don't know, Alice. I'm a bit worried. He's never reported anything like this before, and he seems to be taking it quite seriously. I –'

Sally started to say something else, but noticed Richard was on his way back. Terry noticed him too.

Richard set the drinks on the table.

'I was just saying, Rich,' said Terry, 'good job you didn't bring your other girlfriend… because they don't serve spirits in here.' He cackled.

Alice dug him not unforcibly in the ribs.

Richard glanced from Terry to Sally then back again. 'Cut it out, Tel,' he said.

Terry's well-oiled grin faltered momentarily at his friend's cool reaction.

'You're a bit touchy, aren't you?'

'Yeah, well,' said Richard. He took his seat, facing the others across the table. A moment of awkward silence fell.

'How are you, Richard?' asked Alice.

'I'm okay, thanks. Up and about, as you can see. Still not fit for work, I should add. Not for a couple of days, anyway.'

'It must have been frightening … er, even without the er … you know?'

Richard found himself smiling. Here they all were, all eager to hear the story from his own lips, but all scared to broach the subject. Well, with the exception of Terry, of course.

'Even apart from seeing the ghost?' he said, completing the unspoken part of her sentence.

Alice smiled feebly.

Richard settled in his chair. 'I should have known this would be unavoidable. But first, I can tell you I'm not going nuts, so there's no need to treat me with kid gloves. I'm not that touchy about it – not yet anyway,' he said, glancing deliberately in Terry's direction.

You haven't seen Hargreaves yet,' replied Terry.

'Who's that?' asked Jennifer.

'Our boss,' answered Gary.

'Here, listen to this,' Terry continued. 'When Hargreaves came into the office on Friday morning, we all thought we were going to get roasted for standing around, but all he did was walk up with a copy of the *Courier*, and said, 'I see Wentworth has graduated from misplacing tools to losing passengers.' It was so funny.'

He looked at Richard, whose face was marked with disdain. 'Well, you know,' said Terry. 'You had to be there.'

Richard sighed, glancing at Sally.

'He was quite sympathetic, then?' said Richard sarcastically. 'Okay, the ghost,' he said after a moment's pause. He sat upright. 'I'll tell you once in my own words what happened, and that'll be the end of it, okay?'

'Okay?' he repeated.

Nods came from around the table.

'Right,' he said, taking a deep breath. 'Here goes.'

He went through the whole story again, trying to tell it without waver or lingering reflection. When he finished, he sat back, taking a sip from his glass.

'To be honest, I always thought this thing about the ghost of Blaxton Hill was a load of rubbish,' said Jennifer. 'After all, nobody has reported anything for years.'

Richard looked at Terry, who just sat there, saying nothing.

'The last encounter apparently took place in 1998,' said Richard.

Sally turned to him with a questioning look.

'Er, I've er… been reading a book about phantom hitch-hikers.'

'And it has something about this ghost – Blaxton Hill?" asked Sally.

Richard nodded. 'A chapter.'

'What does it say about it?' asked Terry.

'Well, basically, it says that the girl I met the other night is probably a myth.'

'I could have told you that without the book,' joked Terry.

'It's also supposed to be unlucky to see one. Anyway, according to the book, or at least as much as I've read so far, there's never actually been a named witness before, suggesting that it probably is a load of rubbish – a tale that is somehow relocated from place to place as it catches on. That's what folklorists believe, anyway.'

'I suppose these stories must start somewhere,' conceded Alice. 'There must be some factual basis to them.'

'Where did you get this book?' asked Sally a little suspiciously.

'From the journalist who wrote the article.'

'What?' said Sally. 'When?'

Richard hadn't mentioned it before now.

'Today. I went to see him at the *Courier* offices. It turned out he knew a lot about the subject. And he loaned me some books.'

'Why?' asked Sally.

'Why what?'

'Why did you go to see him? What's the point? What will it solve?'

The others looked on in quiet embarrassment. Richard, aware that this could get out of hand, said quietly, 'Because it might help me understand what I experienced, that's all.'

Tom decided to break the awkward silence.

'This story relocation bit, Rich. It reminds me of that story about the rabbit – you know the one about the rabbit that's found dead in its hutch?'

Richard nodded, although more out of politeness than

familiarity. The others looked suitably vague.

'Anyway,' said Tom, 'I was told this by someone I used to work with. The story goes that one day his dog strolled into the kitchen with his neighbour's pet rabbit in its mouth. The rabbit was definitely dead, and caked with mud.

'Well, he panicked and grabbed the rabbit from the dog, scrubbed it clean in the sink, and blow-dried it, and returned it to its hutch in the neighbour's garden. Well, later that afternoon, his – Pete's – neighbour knocked on his door, and told him that he had just found his rabbit in its hutch, stone dead.

'Embarrassed, thinking he'd been caught out, Pete feigned ignorance, and just generally said, y'know, he was sorry to hear that, all that.

'But,' said his neighbour, 'I only buried it in the garden this morning after I found it dead!'

The group found themselves laughing, and the mood lightened considerably.

'The point is,' continued Tom, 'that the same story appeared on a letters page of one of the national papers some time later, from a different area. I think they're known as urban legends, or something – stories that are told as true, but can't possibly have happened to so many people.'

'Yes,' agreed Richard. 'That's probably true for most phantom hitch-hiker stories, too. Except, in this case,' he said, getting to his feet, 'this one really is true.'

8

An hour later, and they were ready to leave. Richard dropped Sally off at home. Then, he made his way home nervously through the dark back lanes the way he had come. And with the darkness, returned the fear.

EIGHT

That night his dream returned. It was familiar, and yet significantly different from the nightmares that had comprised the others.

At first he was not sure where or who he was. Soon an inkling of self-awareness allowed him to realise he was experiencing common identity with the girl.

2

Her existence was a timeless one. It had no meaning, no pattern, no logic. There was seemingly no beginning, and no ending. It had all the qualities of the dream state – dark and fragmentary, punctuated with flashes of unconnected scenes and images.

She seemed to remember a life in the light, but it was distant, detached and impersonal, like looking through the wrong end of a telescope. But that half-remembered joy and security was gone, replaced instantly with the suffocating darkness and confusion that had surrounded her ever since. In this state, there was no reference to physical space or time, no sensory experience; just feeble states of emotion.

She was lost, trapped in a limbo, unsure where or even who she was. She was only aware that there was something she had lost, something she endeavoured desperately to remember, something to do with a wedding and a man she would never marry. Whatever it was, it somehow held her here, preventing her from evolving, moving on; preventing her from finding peace.

The darkness slowly drowned its victims. Like a

preternatural venus fly-trap, it absorbed the personality and conscious identity of the individual. She had little of that remaining.

Occasionally, though, she experienced a resurgence of energy; briefly, fleetingly. Where it came from, she had no way of knowing, but it evoked familiar images... of her fiancé, driving a car?

Yes. Yes, that was it. Images of him in a vehicle, on a hill. He had found her. At last! Why hadn't she been able to remember – the wedding, her family and friends, the accident?

During these moments of illumination, everything came back, though still she remained detached and removed from it, like watching herself in filmed slow-motion. Joining her fiancé in the car, they would start out for home, away from this nightmare space.

But wait! The driver isn't her fiancé. As the vehicle pulls away, she realises she is accompanying a stranger. Fear and panic meet in her again as she feels herself slipping ... slipping away, the scene around her fading until she finds herself back in the darkness, and its nightmarish cold seeping into her soul again. And gradually again her sense of self and awareness of what had transpired would wane.

But, this time ... this time, there was a residue of recollection. The disruption of the darkness was startling, the imagery powerful. She found herself waiting on a roadside. It was raining, and she could almost feel the clammy coldness of the night. There was no third-person perspective here, but a personal involvement that rivalled reality, whatever that really was.

The car had pulled up the hill, and stopped beside her. There was no sound. The driver, she could see, was peering through the windscreen, and then the side window. He wound the window down halfway, and was speaking to her. The voice was hardly audible, fading in and out like a poorly-received radio signal. Was he offering her a lift? Yes. She found she had the ability to react, and nodded slowly.

The next thing she was really aware of was sitting in the rear of the car. She seemed to be steadily gaining energy and personality, and weight and substance, as her exposure to this situation continued. She could now hear and feel the idling of the car engine. Her senses began to come alive, like the tingling feeling one gets as blood returns to a hand that has gone to sleep.

He was asking her where she wished to go. She had no power of speech. Instead, she raised her right arm and pointed up the hill.

Here, at this moment, she could recall the other occasions she had found herself in a similar state, but none of these had the lucidity of this experience. She felt increasingly stronger with their progression up the hill, soon finding she could talk, if a little disjointedly at first. Her memory was largely a blank. How she found herself here alone was a mystery. She knew she had been in a car accident, but there was no sign of another vehicle, nor her friends. Confused, she asked to be taken home.

Her trust in this man with the strange car was unjustified. She didn't know his name, or anything about him, yet he made her feel safe and secure. She felt a tingling flow of force emanating from him, an energy that was increasing steadily.

Still, there was something not quite right. It wasn't just the strangeness of her situation, or the unfamiliarity of the vehicle. For one thing, she couldn't remember where she lived, or her parents' or fiancé's names. She began to feel frightened. Her vision began to break up in a slow explosion, sending shards all over. She felt despair as the fragmenting view before her began to fade, losing detail and colour. Then, after wavering for an instant, it blinked out.

Noooooooooooooo ...! her mind screamed as the shadowland reclaimed her.

3

He felt the utter despair of the void.

'Emily! *Emilyeeeeeee!* he cried out and was suddenly awake. He sat up in bed, his eyes moist. The luminous dials on his bedside clock read 03:20. All was still.

'Richard?' a voice asked quietly.

He looked up. His mother was at his door. 'Are you alright?'

'Yes, mum. Yes. Just another bad dream.'

'The second in the past week. If this keeps up, I think you should see someone. For your own good, love. Okay?'

'Mm,' he replied, nodding.

'Well, if you're okay, I'll say goodnight, then.'

'Okay. 'Night.'

She left. He could hear her return to her room, and the bedsprings squeak as she got back in. Then, the glow from her room blinked out and there was silence.

He hadn't told her about the second nightmare.

4

He lay awake for some time. The strong emotion of the dream was still with him. But it felt more than simply a dream. Then he remembered the name. Emily. Where had that name come from? He couldn't be sure, but he didn't think he had read it in the book, or heard it from any other source; Pumfrys, for instance.

5

He found he couldn't get off to sleep again. He got up quietly, anxious not to disturb his mother and brother, and made his way downstairs.

Ricky, in his basket, lifted a heavy eyelid, and then dozed off again.

He lit one ring on the gas stove to warm the air in the kitchen, then put the kettle on for a cup of coffee.

He fetched the book and the copy of last week's *Courier* from the living room, and returned to the kitchen. The paper first, being quicker to check, revealed nothing new. It did mention an approximate date for the accident, but little else; certainly no names.

He turned to the book. Turning first to the index, he began to scan the list. It seemed a trifle ridiculous to go on nothing but a dream, looking for a name that probably wasn't there anyway, but he continued all the same. Shortly, the kettle came to the boil, and he stopped to make his coffee, placing the book face down on the counter.

After a few minutes, he was able to confirm his suspicion – there was no listing of an Emily. He flicked the pages back to chapter three and began to quick-scan the material he had been through the previous evening. Again, nothing, no name.

At least it proved he couldn't have read it. Just one of those things, he thought.

He looked at the kitchen clock. 04:18. There didn't seem to be much point in going back to bed now. He was sure he wouldn't be able to sleep anyway. Instead, he decided to read on, flicking through the book until he found the references section.

Listed there, under Chapter Three, were newspaper references for the two local newspapers going back to 1978.

The first in the chronological listing related to the car crash of that year. The article referred to in the text he had read earlier was first: *The Courier* of 3 November, 1978; front page; by Charles Scrimpton. The caption read 'Eve of Wedding Tragedy'.

Another, in the *Herald*, of 30 October held a similar headline: 'Wedding Eve Crash Horror Claims Three'.

He glanced at the other entries, ten in all:

3. Hill tragedy: an 'accident', 5 February, 1979. THE HERALD. Page 6.
4. Mystery of the Hitch-hiking Ghost, 25 January, 1979. By John Sheriton. THE HERALD. Page 8.
5. Ghostly Girl Seen Again, 19 March, 1979. By Keith Prescott. THE COURIER. Page 3.
6. Ghost Girl has them Spooked! 25 March, 1979. NEWS OF THE WORLD. Page 2.
7. Phantom Girl Rides Again, 13 September, 1982. THE HERALD. Page 3.
8. Have You Met the Female Hitch-hiker?; 15 August, 1984. THE NEWS. Page 5.
9. Reappearance of the Disappearing Hitcher, 17 August, 1984. THE COURIER. Page 3.
10. Phantom Hiker on the Road Again, 11 June, 1990. THE HERALD. Page 5.
11. The Ghost of Christmas Past? 17 December, 1997. By Cynthia Jackson. THE NEWS. Page 8.
12. 'Haunting' Encounter on Blaxton Hill, 28 August, 1998. THE COURIER. Page 10.

They all had titles relating to the ghost reports. No, number three seemed to describe a report, an inquest verdict, on the 1978 accident.

He sat back. Well, these articles might provide him with some kind of answer as to why he was dreaming about this girl so frequently. It didn't make any sense to him, but it was worth a try. Pumfrys must have looked at them at some point.

Perhaps it was best to contact him first…

No, it really might be better if he read them for himself.

6

The town library was a smart but incongruously placed building, nestled as it was between buildings of much greater age. Richard had never set foot in the place before. The doors were automatic, the usual down-blast of warm air from air-curtains blasted him as he crossed the threshold, relieving the sting of the cold wind on his face and hands.

The interior was warm and brightly lit by natural light that flooded through huge panes of lightly-tinted glass. Despite the modern appearance of the building, the air was tinged with the faint but musty smell of books, old and new that held a certain familiarity, a nostalgic aroma of school classrooms and textbooks. He glanced around to gain his bearings. Main Library. Children's Library. A post-board advertising local features, charities and events. Reference Library. Yes.

He mounted the steps and made his way over to the reception counter. No-one there. He turned and surveyed the room. There were perhaps a dozen people at the six wood-topped reading desks. Most were youngsters, working, perhaps, on a school assignment or project.

The walls were faced top to bottom with shelves of books: history, local history (these kept behind lockable sliding glass-doors), biographies, arts, travel, politics, business, economics. The open geography of the room was broken up by free-standing shelves. Books, books, books.

A woman appeared from the double doors at the back of the room that displayed a 'No Entry to the Public' sign. She had a book in her hand, which she carried over to an elderly gentleman who sat in front of one of the large windows. He looked up, smiled, and whispered words of thanks.

She turned and headed in his direction. Her eyebrows arched inquiringly and a faint smile formed as she approached. 'Can I help you?'

'Yes, please. Is it possible to have a look at some back-issues of the *Courier* and the *Herald*?'

'What year did you have in mind?'

'1978 and 1979. To begin with.'

Her expression paled. 'Did you make a reservation?' she asked, reaching for a diary on her desk.

'Er, no. I ... I didn't realise that was necessary,' he replied.

'Well, you see, the *Courier* and the *Herald* before 1990 are still in bound hard copy. They're kept in the basement and are therefore normally only made available with twenty-four hours' notice.'

'I see.' There was a brief, awkward silence.

'Look,' the woman continued, 'We're not that busy right now. I'll see what I can do.'

'Thank you.'

'Do you have any specific references you're interested in?'

He handed her his scribbled copy of the reference list. 'Can I have the first two, and the fourth, if possible?'

She glanced at the paper, and visibly flinched. He smiled. He could read her thoughts – was he really going to ask her to fetch all the titles – all ten?

'Er, it may take a while. I'll have to find them and get them to the book-lift. If you take a seat, I'll do what I can.'

'Thanks again,' he said. 'Sorry to put you to any trouble.'

'Not at all,' she replied.

Not entirely true, he thought.

He found a seat near to the double-doors. If they were volumes, it would be less far for the librarian to carry them. From this vantage point, looking back towards the entrance, he could see a recess to the left, behind the counter. Lined up were three microfilm readers. One of them, right in the corner, was being used. A middle-aged man was flicking through screen after screen at the touch of a button on a mouse-like contraption. His concentration was complete; every so often he stopped and made a brief jotting in an open notebook.

The time ticked by. 10:40. His fingers tapped unconsciously on the table top. He would allow himself an hour or so. His eyes drifted across the table again, this time settling on a tray containing scrap paper and assorted pencils. His gaze lifted again to acknowledge the entry of a man and a woman who made their way to the reception desk.

He began to feel a little embarrassed when a further five minutes passed and the librarian had not reappeared. It was his fault that the reception desk was unattended, and now another man had arrived there.

'Excuse me, sir.'

It was the librarian. 'There are four volumes just inside the lift. Would you mind fetching them yourself, only they're a little heavy, and I see I have some other customers?'

'No. Not at all,' he said, getting to his feet. 'Thanks very much.'

'You're welcome. Oh, mind your clothes. They're a bit dusty.'

'I will. Thanks again.'

He sat down with the books. *Books* was the wrong term, really. They were volumes, huge and heavy, particularly those of the *Herald*, an old broadsheet format the size of the *Times*. He made a brief mental apology to the librarian who he saw was now scurrying around in attendance to the couple. Still another person, a young woman, entered the section.

Selecting the earliest volume, the *Courier*, for October-December 1978, he placed the others on the chair next to him.

He reached into his jacket pocket to remove a tissue and wiped away most of the dust from the volume cover.

With his hands now on the volume's cover, he paused. A tingling sensation, of trepidation, coursed through his fingers and on up to his heart and throat. Even though his accident had been real enough, he had come to regard the cause as something less than real with time – partly because his recollection of the incident had become fused with his dreams, so that his better judgement tended to view the whole thing in light of the latter. Now, though, the information contained in these records threatened his new-found sense of reality by offering verifiable facts relating to his experience.

He took a deep breath, and opened the volume about a third of the way through, to early October. He flicked through the pages, turning them over in careful arcs so as not to crease or tear them. As each page fell, a gentle waft of dry, musty air tickled his nostrils and throat.

Then, suddenly, he was staring at the front cover of the *Courier* of 3 November, 1978. The first thing he noticed in the momentary jumble of words and pictures was that the paper was called the *Eldonbridge & County Courier*, issue no. 1728 – not simply *The Courier,* as it is now known. He scanned through the headline titles. It took but a second to skip from the main headline to the second. His eyes fell on the accompanying photograph of a two-car crash. His heart jumped as he recognised the scene of the accident – the crossroads at Blaxton Hill.

He read on:

EVE OF WEDDING TRAGEDY

By Charles Scrimpton

THREE young women died tragically last Friday evening in a motor accident on Blaxton Hill, near Eldonbridge.

The incident occurred at approximately 11:30 p.m. at the Valence Lane – Haltham Road crossroads, when a Ford Consul carrying three young women out on a wedding-eve celebration, was hit side-on by a Morris Minor travelling down Valence Lane.

Two women, including the bride-to-be, died instantly. A third from the Consul, died on the way to hospital. The driver and passenger in the Morris escaped serious injury, but were detained in Eldonbridge hospital, suffering from shock and superficial injuries.

A police spokesman said after the incident: "There have been a number of serious accidents on this treacherous stretch of road in the last few years. The bend in Valence lane west of *The Bull* public house provides little warning to vehicles passing north or south along the Haltham Road. We hope that the completion of the dual-carriageway parallel to this route will remove this danger, once completed in the next few years."

It is thought that the driver of the Consul, Julie Cabot (22), of Kean Avenue, Nedworth, who died in the accident, stalled the car on the crossroads whilst attempting to pull away up the hill. The Morris, driven by Mr. Peter Kilmer (30), of Lark Rise, Kenton, said later:

"We were on our way to Broadford, where my girlfriend lives. We rounded the bend on Valence Lane towards the crossroads at *The Bull*.

"It was dark and visibility was poor due to a steady rain. By the time I noticed the vague shape of a vehicle straddling the crossroads, it was too late. We hit the car with force.

"The next thing I could remember was an ambulance man pulling me out of my car. The other car was a mess."

The families of the other dead girls, Olivia Evans (21), of Church Road, Fordham and Emily Reynolds ...

Emily. Emily Reynolds? No, he thought. It can't be. Coincidence. It must be a coincidence. I must have seen the name before.

He looked up to see someone looking at him. Had he made a sound, or said something? He didn't know, or much care. His gaze dropped again, and he forced himself to read the rest of the article:

... Emily Reynolds (22), of Harefield Road, Haltham, were being consoled earlier this week.

Emily Reynolds had been due to marry

Mr. John Hudson the following day at the Church of Christ the Saviour, in Haltham. Mr. Hudson is said to be distraught after hearing of the death of his fiancée in the early hours of Saturday, just hours before the wedding. He is currently staying with Ms. Reynolds' parents.

Mr. Kilmer was discharged from hospital the day after the accident, while his girlfriend, Joyce Devereux (26) was allowed home on Monday.

The coroner's verdict will be heard at the conclusion of an inquest in February.

He left the page open, and reached for the volume that contained the *Herald* for 30 October. Finding the appropriate page, he read through an article that was virtually an identical copy of that in the *Courier*. The photograph here was from a different angle, but in all the article added nothing to what he had already learned.

He found page 8 of the *Herald* of January 25, 1979 in the third volume with no trouble, but try as he might, he could find no trace of the 'Mystery of the Hitch-hiking Ghost' article. He turned back to the front page and began to work forward, reading off the headings. On page 6, his eyes found the article, tucked away at the bottom of the page, partially obscured by the tight fold against the spine of the volume.

The article was but a short, one-column piece. It was vague in detail, but interesting, not least because it was likely the first reference to the sightings of a ghost on Blaxton Hill.

Mystery of the Hitch-hiking Ghost

by John Sheriton

LONE MOTORISTS driving up Blaxton Hill between Eldonbridge and Haltham have over the last few weeks, been reporting giving lifts to a female hitch-hiker.

Nothing particularly unusual about that, you might say, other than that she hitches lifts late at night, alone. But, this girl has demonstrated a habit of vanishing during the journey!

After flagging down traffic on Blaxton Hill, she directs the motorist to take her to her home in Haltham. At some point in the journey, the motorist discovers that his passenger has disappeared from the rear seat of the vehicle.

A thorough search of the vehicle and surrounding area shows no sign of her. Carrying on to the address the girl has given him, he finds that he has given a lift to a girl who died in a road accident on the hill.

After some investigation, *The Herald* has been unsuccessful in tracing anyone who claims to have actually picked up the girl, although the rumours suggest these include a taxi-driver and a motorcyclist.

Richard began to feel like he was losing his grip on reality again. There were no specifics in the article, but the general description of the encounter with the girl he furnished with images from his own encounter. He shuddered. It was becoming harder to deny his own experience.

He looked for the volume he felt contained the inquest article. He reached for it with some apprehension, and began leafing through the pages. After all, this article would confirm in print for sure what the hypothetical witness of a disappearing hitch-hiker soon discovers – that the girl is, in fact, dead.

The article, another brief piece, reiterated the general details of the earlier crash reports. The verdict was Accidental Death. In fact, there was an interesting discrepancy. He pulled the first article over and re-read part of the text:

> Two women, including the bride-to-be, died instantly. A third, from the Consul, died on the way to hospital. The driver and ...

Then he went back over the inquest article.

> All three women died in the crash. The coroner heard that one woman, Emily Reynolds (22), of Harefield Road, Haltham, died instantly. Olivia Evans (21), of Church Road, Fordham, died on the way to hospital, whilst the driver of the car, Julie Cabot (22), of Kean Avenue, Nedworth, succumbed later during emergency surgery at Eldonbridge General Hospital.

If the inquest details were to be trusted over those of the original crash coverage by the *Courier* and the *Herald* – as it should – then it appeared that Emily Reynolds was the only one to actually die at the scene of the accident.

He glanced at the clock over the reception desk. 11:50. He had been here little over an hour, but the time he came in seemed long ago now. How he had known the girl's name through his dreams was now evidently less to do with his own imagination than with something operating outside his consciousness. Not only to find that he had the name right, but that Emily Reynolds was the only one of the three to actually die on Blaxton Hill was too much.

It seemed that something was keeping her tied to the spot, perhaps her peak emotional state caused by the imminence of her wedding, and the sudden trauma of the loss of life and love and happiness? Then what did she want with him? And what could he do about it forty years after the event?

He picked up the first volume and approached the reception desk, where the librarian was now seated.

'Is there somewhere I can make a few photocopies?'

The librarian regarded the volume in his hands. 'I'm afraid original newspaper copies are still bound by copyright. You'll have to contact the newspaper offices themselves.

'Sorry,' she said with an apologetic smile. 'But there are pencils and paper at the reading desks if you wish to take notes?'

'Okay, thank you.'

He returned to his seat, and pulled a few sheets of paper out of the tray. Finding a pencil (no ink near original newspapers, please), he began to copy each article, word for word. But after a couple of minutes of this, he quietly slipped his phone out of his pocket and, when he was sure no-one was looking, he snapped photos of each article.

NINE

Three weeks had passed.

In that time, Richard had experienced only one more dream of the girl. In it, he again experienced her loneliness and despair, but there was a feeling of reduced involvement, as if she were a weakening radio signal. He had awoken with a fading image in his mind of her saddened face, but in the light of reality he began to forget.

There was really too much else going on. Christmas was even closer, and the house was in its final stage of completion. Sally had been taking regular photos of its progress – window frames in; walls plastered and painted; kitchen and bathroom fitted. In the next week or so, the final contract would be signed and the furnishings could be moved in, shortly to be followed by Sally and himself.

He had finished the books Pumfrys had loaned him. The hitch-hiker book had been interesting beyond its Blaxton Hill coverage. The book covered a dozen or so other hitch-hiker encounters, some convincing, most not. The more convincing ones involved first-hand witnesses, people who could give their own accounts in their own words. What these accounts had in common was their very pointlessness – the hitch-hiker vanished before the journey was completed. Only in very rare cases did the passenger give personal details whereby the driver could fulfil his, or her, traditional function of following up the encounter by inquiring at the given address or with relatives.

His own experience fell into this 'convincing' category. The girl had vanished, in contradiction of the convention, before he'd had a chance to discover any pertinent details. He was sure by now, though, that he had not heard the girl's name or read it in Pumfrys's book. If it were not for his knowledge of this through his dream, he probably would by now have written it all off as a vivid by-product of stress, tiredness, or drink.

Still, despite the evidence he brought away from the library that day, Sally was still skeptical. Much of the blame for his dreams she lay at the feet of Pumfrys for loaning him the books, which had encouraged him to make more out of it than he may otherwise have done. It wasn't that she disbelieved him exactly, but it was most likely a case of mistaken identity, an hallucination, or some form of subconscious suggestion. Something. Just not a ghost.

Now, though, things were settling down again. The normal routine had returned. Sally was at his house. With their own new home nearing completion, they had to tighten their belts somewhat. The nights out had been cut back and Richard was doing more weekend overtime to help make ends meet. Not that they were badly off – they just needed the extra in reserve in this initially expensive period. Things should quieten down after Christmas, and then the serious saving would begin for the wedding. Thank goodness, he thought, that they had planned for the autumn.

'We have an invite to go bowling tomorrow night,' said Sally, setting the mugs of coffee and the biscuit barrel on the low coffee table.

'Who's going?'

'Jennifer and Tom. They go quite regularly. Tom plays at regional level, did you know?'

'Yeah, ah, I mean, no,' Richard replied.

'Well, shall we go or not? If we are, I've got to let Jennifer know tonight.'

'How much?'

'Twenty pounds.'

'Each?'

'No, for both of us. Excluding drinks,' Sally added. 'Jennifer said Tom will give us a lift.'

'Well, that sounds like a plan.'

'I thought it might do us some good, after... you know.'

'Have you played before?'

'Yes, a couple of times. Why?'

'Okay, on one condition – don't make me look bad.'

Sally smiled. 'As if I would.'

'What time will Tom get here?' he asked.

'Seven o'clock. The alley is booked for eight.'

'Okay. Tell Jennifer we'll come.'

2

The day had not gone well. His workload had been fine in the morning, but after lunch, a recalcitrant boiler had sprung a leak at what should have been a routine service. By the time he had repaired it, he was exactly an hour behind schedule. He had shelved lunch in an attempt to get his remaining jobs done so that he might get away a little earlier to get home and change for the night out. Sally was getting the bus up from Eldonbridge by six, and they were to have a bite to eat at his house before Tom arrived.

That was the plan, anyway. But when he called in to check for any last jobs (as was his duty on the extended hours shift), he was not happy to hear he had been given a final job six miles away in one of the satellite villages of Eldonbridge.

John Egerton, an overtime vulture, had agreed that morning that he would take any overflow jobs. Now, Hargreaves was telling him to get on with his work. Where was Egerton? he had protested. Didn't know, didn't care. It wasn't Egerton's turn on cover, and everyone else had gone home, so he would just have to get on with it.

3

As it happened, the job hadn't proven too bad, a reported domestic gas leak identified and sealed off with no problem. He arrived at the house a little after five o'clock, and was near completion of the work by five-forty. Meaning he should still be able to get home by six-fifteen.

Instead of taking the same route back through Eldonbridge, he made a right turn out of the village and towards the motorway junction two miles to the north. His home was only a three or four minute drive into Haltham from there.

He got as far as a few hundred yards from the junction with no trouble at all, despite the rush-hour traffic and the onset of rain. But then he saw ahead the rotating beacons of police cars and an ambulance and the tail-lights of queued traffic.

'Blast!'

He braked and joined the back of the queue. There was nowhere to go. From his vantage point, he could just make out the cause of the hold-up. A juggernaut lay at an ungainly angle, straddling the two lanes of the roundabout. Beneath the rear axle was the crumpled remains of a car. He looked away. Someone was going to hear some awful news tonight. He was immediately sorry for his own impatience at the hold-up. At least he was alive. What had he been complaining about – being late for a bowling date?

There was no choice but to sit tight, to watch, wait, and obey until he could get through or find an opportunity to turn around.

Other motorists in the hold-up, and a small gathering crowd of pedestrian bystanders, looked on in morbid fascination. Morbid, yes, but, at the same time, understandable;

a rare individual confrontation with the reality of personal mortality, and a reminder that a life of three-score-and-ten-years was not a guarantee.

Perhaps the driver of the car there had plans to go out tonight too. Here one moment, vital and full of life; the next, gone.

Hadn't that been the moral of the Fuller book, the Flight 401 ghost story? A routine flight of a Lockheed Tristar L-1011 from New York to Miami that had ended tragically when it crashed without warning into the swamps of the Florida everglades, killing a hundred passengers and crew. It occurred in the Christmas holidays, just before New Year, 1972. The total unexpectedness and horror of the impact of this 'fail-proof' aircraft, one capable of fully automatic flight and landing, seemed to have impressed itself into the very beings of the captain and co-pilot, whose ghosts were reportedly seen after their deaths on various other Eastern Airlines L-1011s.

What was particularly intriguing about many of the apparitional forms was their lifelikeness. Until they vanished, they appeared to be completely solid, three-dimensional forms, for all intents and purposes, normal human beings. The shock of the crash, their own personal feelings of responsibility, and that the crash investigations seemed to place fault for the disaster at the feet of the flight crew (which was actually due to a combination of factors, not least technical in nature), it was conjectured, provided a means by which these two men had been unable to rest.

Richard's thoughts switched naturally to Blaxton Hill. Could this really be a viable comparison to the situation in Flight 401? Unexpected violent death, coupled with a strong emotional tie to life, leading to a continued existence in this realm in a manner we can't comprehend? The descriptions of the apparitions, as ostensibly normal people (up to a point) were not a stone's throw away from the classic phantom hitch-hiker.

He interrupted his thoughts, bringing his attention back to the situation at hand. Traffic was likely to be held up here for some time. Already, a queue had formed behind him, but the tailing vehicles were using their room at the back to turn their vehicles around. Twenty yards ahead of him on the left was a turning; one car was performing a three-point turn in its mouth. Once he was clear, the next vehicle repeated the action. The two vehicles remaining ahead of him edged forward, but remained in the queue. As soon as he was able, Richard turned in and spun the van around and indicating right to go back the way he had come. The car behind flashed to let him out, and Richard raised a hand in thanks.

When he had completed his own quick turnaround, he realised that his quickest route to Haltham was to go back down and through Eldonbridge. It was already five past six, and he would likely have to crawl through the town's one-way system until he emerged on the dual carriageway on the north side of town that led to Blaxton Hill.

It would be only the second time he had ventured up or down the hill since his encounter. The first had been an unavoidable journey, although in broad daylight. Now, on a dark winter evening, it would be a different matter. But, with the tail-end of the rush hour traffic making its way home along this route, it should be safe enough. Besides, this time he wouldn't be venturing off the dual carriageway.

As he expected, there was some queuing in the one-way bottleneck through the town, but at least it was moving. He was through within ten minutes, and making his way through the outskirts of the town on the Haltham Road. Presently, the roundabout at the foot of Blaxton Hill came into view, with its option for the motorway. Most of the traffic was picking the motorway option. Traffic coming off the motorway generally headed into Eldonbridge, or in the opposite direction, towards Blaxton Hill. He still had plenty of company on his route, and he felt reassured by this fact.

Starting up the hill, he felt comfortable enough. Being framed on three sides by other traffic using the up-lanes of the carriageway made it virtually impossible for the world of the supernatural to intrude into the technological twenty-first century. Or so he thought. He, of all people, could attest that the gothic setting was not a prerequisite for an eerie experience.

His van had windows in its rear doors. Visibility through them over the length of the van, though, was not great. He tended to make more use of the side mirrors.

A vehicle approached from behind, momentarily flooding the van with shifting light before pulling out to overtake him. Richard glanced into his rearview mirror, and gripped the wheel. A dark shape momentarily blocked out the some of the glare. Then, as the other car passed, it melted back into the gloom.

Richard swallowed hard. He fixed is gaze ahead, avoiding the mirror while he tried to rarionalise it. Some of the equipment back there could have caused it – there were old blankets covering old gas fires, and a grill, plus some dirty overalls. Yes, that was probably it.

Reflexively, he glanced in the mirror again, long enough to tell that the rear windows were unobstructed. Some of the junk *could* have shifted – but if it had, there should have been some noise. In fact, had they not been strapped and cushioned, they would have creaked and rattled like mad. Then again, the sound of the engine would have disguised any minor movement of equipment, and the shifting light sufficient to magnify and distort the assorted shapes in the junk-pile of tools and fittings back there.

Just a case of the jitters, then – understandable, as he approached the slip road turn-off that led to the old, steeper section of Haltham Road up Blaxton Hill – the one he had taken that night. He pushed any further thoughts from his mind. He couldn't always avoid Blaxton Hill. It was the most direct route between Eldonbridge, where he worked, and Haltham, his home town. Facing his fear was a necessary part of vanquishing the ghost.

Another car approached the van from behind. This time, Richard made a conscious effort to identify the cause of the shape in the mirror. It had to be an effect produced by the interaction of light with objects in the van – or, something as simple as the shadowed side of his own face reflected in the mirror as he moved his head. It had happened to him before, but only rarely had it the ability to spook him; usually when he was off his guard, when lost in thought or just plain tired.

His van followed the road into a sweeping arc that brought his forward vision in line with the glaring headlights of the opposing downhill traffic. Light again began to fill the cab of the van. He squinted against the glare and distracted his attention away momentarily to check the rearview mirror again. Through fading red and green spots, what he saw in the combined front and back-lit interior of the van stopped his heart cold. Staring back at him was the reflection of a female face.

4

Sally glanced at the clock again. Seven minutes past seven. Tom had been there for a few minutes, and they both sat in the living room, coats on, waiting for Richard.

'He must be delayed by the accident,' said Sally, referring to the one Richard had run into at the Kingswood roundabout. Local radio travel reports had detailed it as an area to avoid, and Sally knew it to be the route that Richard would now normally pick to get home. Not so long ago, he would have come straight up Blaxton Hill.

'Normally he'd text or call,' commented Sally, unconsciously rubbing her chin.

'Maybe be can't.'

Sally shot him a glance.

Tom winced. 'I meant he might not be able to – you know, if he's in slow-moving traffic or something.'

'He could pull over, Tom. He hasn't answered my calls or texts.'

'Look, I'm sure he's alright. We'll give him a bit longer. It doesn't matter if we're a bit late. We just cut into the time we have to play.'

'We can't wait too long, else it won't be worth going at all. If he isn't here in five minutes, you go on. Richard can always drive us up there as soon as he's –'

They both looked up at the sound of a key in the door.

The strain in Sally's face melted away. She stood. 'Ah, good...'

Then the door to the living room opened, and she caught her first glimpse of Richard. Her jaw dropped.

5

Richard stood there, unmoving, his face gaunt and expressionless. Well, almost. There was an expression there, only Sally had never seen it on his face before – of shock; dissociation? She almost ran to him.

Tom was on his feet in a flash, coming to help Sally bring him inside.

Sally looked to Tom and said one word. 'Coffee.'

Tom immediately left for the kitchen.

'Richard, what is it?' asked Sally. The tremor in her voice betrayed the calm she was trying to project. Richard was shaking, but he responded to her voice to look her in the eyes. He shook his head, as if to say 'not now'.

Apart from seemingly being unable to talk, he seemed to have his wits about him. She took his hand. It was pale and cold to the touch. As was his face, the skin tight, drawn about his eyes to give a stark, staring look. She guided him to a chair. All thought of the bowling evening had left her mind. It was obvious from looking at Richard that it was far from his own at this moment.

After a few minutes, Tom returned with three mugs of coffee. Richard's was black, and he took it from Tom's proffered hand and held it between his own. He managed to thank him, and lifted it to his lips and took a sip. He winced at the hot bitter taste. It was a good sign. He hated black coffee.

'Are you alright, Rich. What's up? What happened?' asked Tom, sympathetically.

Richard nodded. He let out a long sigh. 'Yeah, I'm Okay,' he said at last. 'I think.' He made a faltering attempt at a smile.

'Are you up to telling us what happened?'

Sally's concerned gaze flicked between Tom and Richard.

'Er, no, thanks. I'm alright,' Richard replied, this time more positively. 'Are we still going bowling?' he stammered.

Sally almost laughed in relief. Tom nodded. He's alright.

Tom squatted before Richard. 'Maybe that's not a great idea right now, mate. Listen, Richard. You've got to tell us what's happened. If you've been in an accident, we'll have to contact the police, may be take you to the hospital.'

Richard looked at Tom. At last, he seemed to have regained his composure. He took a deep breath and another sip of his coffee. 'No. I haven't been in an accident. And I haven't been drinking – 'though I could do with one now.

'Okay … ' He went on to recount his late finish at work, and his rushed journey to get home. As he described the scene of the accident over at Kingswood, it was apparent that it had affected him quite deeply, perhaps more than he realised himself at this point.

As soon as Richard mentioned Blaxton Hill, Sally and Tom could both see where this was leading. Richard described how he had looked into the rearview mirror. His immediate recognition of the face had stunned him completely. He shuddered at his necessary recall. For an indeterminate amount of time he simply sat, staring ahead, as if faced with a vicious dog, where any sign of movement might instigate an attack. It seemed an eternity before he lifted his eyes back to the mirror, although it was probably only a few seconds.

Nothing there. Thank God.

He had a clear view of the traffic behind through the rear-door windows. Shifting light danced around the van interior again. Although he tried to convince himself that what he had seen was a product of this light and shadow effect, he knew deep down that it was not. Whatever had been there had appeared solid, or at least opaque; it had reflected light, and was undeniably human in form. The expression was again one of sadness. She said nothing, or if she had, he had heard nothing above the noise of the engine.

The thing that had puzzled him, he explained, was that where the girl had appeared, there was really no room for a person to be. Junk piled up just there prevented that. Still, skipping over this little snag, he decided that the girl might have been on eye level if she were on her knees.

Sally was seriously concerned. Tom seemed less than comfortable. They looked at Richard warily. He seemed to be rational enough now, on evidence of his manner of speech, at least. But it was the content that was most disturbing. His claim of another sighting of the ghost was unsettling enough, but he wasn't even consistent in his own fantasy. He seemed to fail to see the contradiction here: for one, he regarded whatever he had seen as a ghost, but at the same time failed to attribute traditional ghostly abilities to where she had 'appeared'. Here, he was thinking in terms of a real flesh-and-blood person, and the physical restrictions of the space involved. This is what was most disturbing – if he really believed he had seen a ghost, this shouldn't have been a concern. Sally tried, as sensitively as possible, to point this out to him.

'Don't bloody patronise me, Sal!' he exclaimed. She jumped. 'Don't you think I know that? Can't you see all I'm trying to do is see how and why this happened.'

'But, Richard. This ghost thing of yours ... ' began Sally.

'Ghost thing? What's that supposed to mean?'

'Ah ... '

'Look,' said Richard, 'I know you didn't believe me the last time ... '

'I didn't say that.'

'You didn't have to.' He sighed and sat back. 'Anyway, I *do* know how this sounds. And I don't expect you to believe me. All I'm asking is for your support. I *know* I wasn't seeing things, or hallucinating, or any other rational term to explain it away. I wanted to believe that when I first thought I saw something back there. But if you'd seen what I saw the second time, close-to and in that detail, you'd be saying the same thing.'

He turned to Tom. 'You're quiet, Tom. Do you think I'm going nuts?'

'Of course not. I believe you saw something tonight, it's

just that we don't know what. I mean, you look up and see the reflection of what you thought was a girl in the back of your van. You look again, and there was nothing there.'

Richard's eyes tracked from point to point around the room, mentally biting on his tongue, as Tom spoke. 'You'd not long before witnessed the aftermath of a probably fatal accident... which could be a factor. I think you should sleep on it, and reflect on it tomorrow. It's just possible you might find a normal, rational explanation after all?'

'So you're saying I'm irrational?' asked Richard defensively.

'Come on Richard,' said Tom. 'You know what I'm saying. You know you have to look at all possible explanations before considering the supernatural.' He looked Richard in the eye. 'Yeah?' he asked.

Richard nodded feebly, his eyes blinking slowly in agreement.

There was an awkward silence. For a moment.

'Anyway,' said Tom, getting to his feet and glancing at his watch. 'I'd better get off. Jennifer'll be wondering what's happened.'

'You still going bowling?' asked Richard.

'It's a bit late now. And I don't think you'd be up to it anyway?'

Richard shook his head. 'Sorry, Tom.'

'No problem.'

Sally saw him to the door. 'Thanks Tom. Tell Jennifer I'll ring her at work tomorrow.'

'Sure.'

'And sorry again about the bowling.'

'Some other time, perhaps,' said Tom.

TEN

Sally closed the door and came into the living room. Richard had switched the television on and was staring at the screen, sound down. Whatever was on played silently to his unseeing eyes. She reached past him to retrieve the tray of mugs, and then, without speaking, returned to the kitchen.

Richard's mother was quite fussy about petty things like unwashed cups lying around, Richard had explained once. She had buried herself in the housekeeping since she and his father had separated, and finally divorced when Richard was eleven, and John had been just a baby. It had become habitual; something concrete to focus on. She worked on the checkouts at Tesco – she was at work now. It paid the bills, and kept John fed and clothed, although Richard contributed a great deal more than he was obliged. Part of the responsibility he felt to the family in the absence of a father.

Sally returned shortly with a fresh mug of coffee and a sandwich. He had managed to turn up the sound on the television, and was now staring at another channel. She sat in the armchair opposite, and they sat there for a while without speaking.

She felt an undue sense of guilt, for doubting him, she supposed. Ever since Richard had first reported seeing this ghostly girl, she had felt uneasy. She didn't believe in ghosts as such, and his preoccupation with the subject had begun to disturb her. She had tried to be as sympathetic as possible, but it was something she couldn't relate to. For this reason, she felt that he was growing away from her, and that scared her.

Although, in reality, there was no concrete reason to believe this. The best policy, she had found, was to simply avoid the question wherever possible.

And, now, when things had settled down, Richard was starting it up again. Why? What psychological need was he fulfilling by enacting this fantasy? The first time he might very well have invented the ghost story as a cover for his drink-related accident. But what reason could he have for this second incident?

As always, there were more questions than answers. Surely he might have picked a more plausible explanation than the one he offered – one that would be more believable to the police, for instance, and one which would attract far less attention from the media.

Sally found this last point all the more disturbing. She was aware of this particular ghost story – had, in fact, grown up with it, like many people locally. But Richard had only moved into the area a few years ago. Although they had never discussed it themselves, it was possible that he had come across it sometime, perhaps unconsciously. But she doubted it. And that being the case, she would have to face the almost equally frightening prospect as Richard's possible mental breakdown – that what he claimed to have experienced might just be true.

2

Almost inevitably, Richard relived the incident again that night in his dreams. He found himself watching the incident from outside his own body. The point of view suggested he might be looking through the windscreen of the car from the driver's seat, and looking in through the side of the van, all at the same time. He was in both and neither place at the same time. The

119

effect was much like the three-quarter sets seen in television soaps, where one wall of a room is missing to allow access for cameras and personnel. The physical structure of the van presented no obstacle to his sight. What he saw was himself – it took a moment to actually recognise himself. Behind him was the girl. it sent chills down his spine to see her there, staring ahead. He felt he had to warn himself – his body –that she was there, but he – the driver – seemed unaware of anything but the road ahead.

The girl reached out and touched his other self on the left shoulder. He twisted slightly in his seat. The girl removed her hand suddenly, as if she were surprised that she should elicit any response at all. He noticed a curious thing – the girl, while appearing opaque, was surrounded by a very faint bluish-grey glow. It did not illuminate her surroundings, the fittings in the rear of the van, and was really only visible in the shadows and spaces between the passing overhead carriageway lights. He felt it to be more than an illusion that the glow seemed to increase in intensity after her brief contact with his body, only to diminish once she removed her hand.

He watched as she reached out again, tentatively, to replace her hand. He was not mistaken – there *was* a boost in this glow; it increased gradually until the whole cab began to fill with this light. The girl appeared to be coming to life; her movements became more fluid, her skin colour began to take on a more natural hue, even in the monochrome of the eerie glow. Finally, she turned to face *him* – the autoscopic self – through the side of the van. A tear was balanced on her cheek, poised above a timid smile that expressed hope or joyous relief. She began to speak: 'The ring … ' when he felt himself yanked back into his body with force. His eyes locked on hers in the rearview mirror. *'Take the ring,'* she said, withdrawing her hand. Her image dulled and faded rapidly, before blinking out.

3

The next day he skipped work, phoning in with a report of the flu, a virus. He felt drained and lethargic, despite having slept through the night. His memory of the previous night was again fogged by the subsequent dream. The stuff of real experience and of dreams, he was discovering, had the same quality in memory. Subsequently, he was again experiencing difficulty in separating the two versions in his mind.

It didn't help that the dreams seemed more real (if that was the appropriate word) than normal recall. Maybe this had something to do with one's perception of reality.

He, like most people, grew up with a steadily reinforced idea of what the real world is like. And in most cases, this held no room for the existence of ghosts and other fringe phenomena. But in dreams, there is rarely no perceived conflict between the familiar forms of the material world and the fantastic, which tends to be accepted uncritically, and is therefore capable of eliciting a forceful emotional response that may be carried into wakeful recollection.

He didn't tell Sally about the latest dream or his skipping work. He put the dream and his lethargy down to plain exhaustion. Although disturbed by his dreams, he was not about to advertise their repetitiveness to anyone, even Sally.

He made the most of the day by resting, watching television, and reading through the notes and photos he had taken at the library.

That evening, he met Sally from work and took her home, instructing her to get ready to go out. When she protested, he had hushed her up, simply saying that he felt they deserved it. That this was Richard's placation following the previous evening went without comment.

He sat quietly while she got ready. Sally's mother passed

little more than the time of day with him, as he sat in the living room. Sally's father was out. He was not sure he would have sat there had he been home. Still, if Sally and he were determined to live with one another, and to eventually marry, it would be best if he and Sally's father came to some settlement at some time. After all, they didn't have to necessarily like or respect one another, but to simply get along whenever their paths crossed – the wedding, inevitably, but on other occasions too.

The special treat, a meal Richard had hastily arranged at a newly opened bar-restaurant in Eldonbridge, went well for both of them. Neither mentioned the ghost; the conversation was light, but underscored with a discussion centred on the buying of the house, now likely only days away from completion. Richard was thankful of this chance to patch things up a little with Sally. She was pleased that Richard appeared to be his same old self. Whatever questions that remained regarding his underlying mental state were conveniently ignored.

For the moment.

But, as he made his way home, by the circuitous route through Kingswood, his thoughts returned unwillingly and inexorably to the girl on the hill, and the long night of dreams ahead.

4

December 8

Moving-in day. The day was filled with the usual triumphs and tribulations of a move of house and belongings, but since there was very little in the way of personal possessions coming from their respective houses, the occasion was one of marked joviality.

The house, completed only the day before when square sods of grass had been lain over a thin layer of topsoil, had been carpeted and furnished before it was even legally theirs. What they had was a small, first-time buy of a place, comprising a step-in porch, barely large enough to turn around in, which led immediately into a square, plain-painted living room. At the rear right corner of this room, rose the staircase, flanked by two diagonal runs of light-varnished wooden bannister. Upstairs, turn right for the main bedroom, left for the smaller, front ancillary bedroom and bathroom/toilet, situated between this room and the stairs.

The kitchen, situated behind the living room, through a door in the left side of the rear wall, was spacious in proportion to the other rooms of the house, second only to the living room.

The completion of the house naturally included the turning on of the utilities. All that Sally and Richard really faced was the sorting of their transferred packages, and waiting on the delivery of the fridge-freezer and washing machine.

The actual moving-in ceremony, if you will, aided by Richard's friend, Terry, and Sally's parents, went well, and, after serving coffee and biscuits at eleven-thirty or so, they had been left alone to enjoy the peace and the prospect of forming a home for themselves. Both had booked holiday for the following week to enable themselves to settle in and sort through their belongings.

Richard was surprised to see Sally's father show up; even more so to find he was being spoken to amiably. Indeed, they got into a discussion on boxing, which turned out to be something of an ice-breaker. Sally had seemed impressed with Richard's ability to find this common ground with her father, and offered him an approving smile over her father's shoulder.

It was great that Sally felt more relaxed in face of this apparent detente between him and her father, but he knew, as he suspected that the old man knew, that they could never become friends. Boxing as a subject for discussion was ironic, almost comically so, considering the altercation between them of not so long ago. He suspected that Sally's mother had something to do with it all, as mediator and diplomat.

That night, they celebrated with a drink out with a few of their friends, but returned home earlier than normal. They sat watching television for a while amid boxes and assorted items, drinking coffee, and generally relaxing in their new-found independence and privacy.

While it was not the first time they had shared a bed, this night they could do so without fear of discovery, in the security of their very own home.

5

December 22

Christmas was almost upon them.

Richard had managed to get out of work a little earlier than usual, a small concession granted in the Christmas spirit. The early release was especially welcome since he had warned Sally earlier that he had been nominated to cover until ten p.m. as part of a skeleton service for the holiday. Thankfully, someone else had wanted the overtime.

He detoured on the way home at the supermarket to pick up a couple of extras, a small bottle of VSOP Cognac for himself (a prospective remedy for the cold he felt he was falling for), and a bottle of Southern Comfort for Sally.

He parked near the house. The afternoon was quiet and still; the sky above, purple-grey. A chill tainted the air; the fading light cold and heavy around him.

He stood there for a moment by the car, taking brief opportunity to observe the view. From the estate's elevated position in the south-east of the town, a large part of Eldonbridge stretched out below like a golden spider's web as its streetlights flickered to life.

The sun had already set, leaving a rusty stain on the horizon. A little to the east, almost lost in the gloom, stood Blaxton Hill, its wooded crest just breaking the uniformity of the escarpment to catch the last light. A moving thread of red, amber, and white filaments traced the course of the dual carriageway on its face.

He exhaled sharply, his breath dissipating in a whispy effusion that curled into the air.

Shit, it's cold!

He turned to make his way up the path, glancing back momentarily for a last view of the hill.

6

He stepped into the porch and closed the door behind him. Kicking off his shoes, he lowered the white carrier-bag containing the bottles to the carpet, holding them upright with a strategically placed foot while he shuffled to remove his overcoat.

He heard Sally's footsteps thumping down the stairs and peered around the door jamb to see her launch herself into the middle of the living room, a wide grin on her face.

'Hiya. What do think?' she asked, sweeping her arm in a wide arc. The room had been transformed by Christmas decorations: all kinds of foil and paper streamers, mobiles, a wall-mounted card holder, and, of course, a tree, although artificial and small, which dominated the scene with its red and white tinkerbell lights and silver and gold tinsel.

'Very nice,' he said. 'How much?' he added, then wished he hadn't.

Sally's expression faltered for a second, but bright mood prevented her from succumbing. 'Don't be such a Scrooge,' she said cheerfully, reaching up to kiss him. 'As well as a Rudolph,' she added, pulling away.

'Huh?'

'You've got a red nose,' she replied.

'Oh', he replied.

'I'm just making some tea.' She started towards the kitchen.

'Don't worry. I've got something.'

She stopped in the doorway. 'What?'

He went back out to the porch and returned with the white carrier. The sound of clinking glass drew her attention.

'A little winter warmer.' He pulled out the bottle of cognac with a flourish.

Sally's eyes locked on the bottle. She looked at him uncertainly. Then, suddenly self-conscious of her reaction, she forced a small smile. 'I suppose it is Christmas.'

But he couldn't miss her dismay. And it was understandable. It must have evoked some unpleasant memories for her. His own smile faltered for an instant, but giving neither of them any more time to react, he pulled out the other bottle.

'And this is for you,' he said quietly. It was still wrapped in soft paper. He handed it to her.

Deftly, she twisted the neck of the bottle in the paper so that it slipped out easily. Her reaction this time was positive. She seemed genuinely pleased.

'And how much did this little lot cost, then?' she asked,

mischievously echoing his own earlier sentiment.

'About the same as your spend, I reckon,' he said, casting his eyes around the room again.

Her tone grew serious again. 'You're not planning on overdoing it on Boxing Day?'

They had invited friends and relations over for a proper house warming.

'Of course not. I'll be driving my mum and John home, remember?'

'I know, but that'll be fairly early in the evening. I don't want you and Terry getting... '

'Don't worry,' he said, cutting her off. 'I'll be Okay. Have a bit more faith in me now, eh?' He lifted her chin so that she looked him in the eye.

'Hm?'

She nodded.

'Besides,' he added. 'A bottle this size is hardly going to make much difference.' He tossed it a few inches in the air, and snatched it back, the broad side slapping against his palm. Walking over to the glass cabinet, he placed it there.

'Anyway,' Sally said, changing the subject. 'You're home earlier than expected. I haven't got anything out the freezer for dinner yet.'

She started for the kitchen.

He followed her. 'Yeah, 'thought I'd surprise you with something else,' he said. Her back was turned and he threw his arms around her midsection. She yelped in surprise. 'Richard!'

He nuzzled her neck below her ear, and kissed her. Her perfume was the one he liked most on her. She squirmed a little. 'Hey, come on. I've got to get the dinner on.'

'We'll eat out,' he said, pulling her toward the living room.

'We can't afford that,' she said.

'There are no 'can'ts' at Christmas.'

He pulled her closer. She was dressed in casuals, with no make-up, but he liked her that way. She exuded femininity and grace even through slacks and the styled but light roll-necked pullover, an expensive cashmere sweater in pastel pink and green that he had bought her for Christmas the previous year.

'We won't get a table anywhere. Not tonight.'

'We'll find somewhere.'

He slid his hands behind her back, bringing them up to caress her shoulders as he bent to kiss her again.
As they parted, he began to pull at the hem of the sweater, raising it.

Her mood became more measured as she realised his intention. She began to protest again, though unconvincingly. 'No. Not in here. Not now ... '

He didn't answer.

She allowed him to pull her over to the sofa.

7

Richard returned to work on December 29, the last day of work before the New Year. New Year's Day was for visiting – Sally's parents first, for a Christmas-style dinner, then Richard's mother and brother later in the afternoon. Sally didn't question the longer drive out to the Kingswood roundabout, which from Sally's parents' house, described a hairpin route through Eldonbridge, and back out to Haltham. Neither needed to articulate or outwardly justify the manoeuvre.

Richard's mother looked a little weary. It turned out that she had been putting in some overtime at work, mainly to make Christmas worthwhile, with the extra expense this necessarily incurred. Richard's absence from the household was a saving of a kind, but Richard had really paid for more than his share of the housekeeping while living there. Though reluctant to have to do so, Richard could no longer help with his family's finances. His mother recognised this fact, and never made any comment about being short of money. She was simply doing was she had to. Still, Richard felt some guilt over it.

Richard's brother, John, greeted him with the interested but tactless sense of a twelve-year-old. He asked, even as they removed their coats, whether they had seen the ghost on the way up Blaxton Hill. Richard answered awkwardly, trying to change the subject by leading the youngster into the living room. This diversion seemed to diffuse the situation, but the boy followed up with more questions about Richard's meeting with the girl. Evidently, he had seen the *Courier*, or perhaps discussed it at school. Richard found himself telling him that it was all a mistake, and finally, to shut up. Snivelling, John backed off, but not before demanding of Richard why, if there was no ghost, did he look so scared?

Richard was speechless. And angry. Angry not at his brother this time, but at himself. It was true. He *was* scared. He had deliberately avoided coming up Blaxton Hill, the most direct route to Haltham. Certainly, he believed he had good reason to feel the way he did, but it was extremely difficult to impart this reasoning to others. Looking at it all objectively, ghosts could not exist, and therefore didn't. Therefore, his fear had no foundation. That was the theory anyway.

They left around eight, after a quiet tea. It wasn't far to the roundabout that gave them options for Eldonbridge, and Kingswood. On the approach, Sally noticed that they were in the wrong lane. Instead of the right-hand, westbound approach for Kingswood, Richard kept the vehicle to the left. That meant he was intending to go straight over the roundabout towards Eldonbridge via Blaxton Hill. She propped herself up in her seat, and had half opened her mouth to speak as she turned to face Richard, but then thought better of it. He half-glanced in her direction, but did not make eye-contact.

Within a minute, they were on the slip road that took them onto the dual-carriageway that descended the hill. The carriageway was still busy. As always at these times, the glare from the oncoming uphill traffic was intense. Richard kept the car pointing down the middle of the lane, avoiding peering into the rearview mirror.

In his peripheral vision he could make out, to his left, shafts of light that flickered and soon died. He recognised these as coming from a vehicle heading up Old Haltham Road, its headlights playing through the bare branches of trees. Whoever the driver is, he thought, I hope they're not travelling alone.

Thankfully, soon, they were in Eldonbridge, sailing through the outskirts towards home, and they both relaxed, the tension melting away.

ELEVEN

Richard had agreed to pick Sally up at ten p.m. She was at a friend's house for a cosmetics and coffee evening.

The whole of January had been normal; drearily, boringly uneventful. Which was just fine. Richard was working some overtime most evenings, plus an occasional Saturday, enough to keep them afloat in the initial stages of higher expenditure. Actually, the additional money was not that crucial right now; it simply gave them a bit of a safety net.

An occasional extravagance was permitted, hence this evening out for Sally. He pulled up at the house at five-to-ten. The driveway was full, and the road outside the house was crammed with parked cars. He glanced again at the clock and sat back. He would give it ten minutes or so. Sally would be aware of the time, and had promised to look out for him around ten.

But by quarter past, he began to feel a little restless, a little annoyed. He didn't mind waiting a few minutes over, but having to be up early for work the next morning, he didn't want to be out too late. It was a twenty minute drive back. Then again, he didn't want Sally to feel pressured into leaving – he wouldn't like that himself. But when his dashboard clock reached ten-thirty, and Sally hadn't so much as looked out, he decided he would have to do something.

He got out of the car, and made his way up the drive. As he reached towards the front door, it opened, spilling warm light across the path and flower beds. Shadows, then shimmering silhouettes filled the aperture, as some of the guests pulled coats around them and stepped out into the night. One girl, turning from the brightness of the doorway, shrieked in surprise as she lurched into him. She recovered, then backed off, apologising and giggling to a friend at her reaction. Richard smiled.

The girl standing just inside the door he recognised as Sally's friend, Karen, who was hosting the party. She recognised him immediately, and invited him in to wait for Sally.

'Wait for her? What's she doing?' he asked.

'Oh ... it's alright,' said Karen. 'She's just having a reading done.'

'A what?' he asked.

'A reading,' she repeated awkwardly, surprised at the sharp reaction it had evoked.

'That's what I thought you said. You mean Sally's having her palm read. By a *medium*?'

'She prefers to be called a *spiritual advisor* ... '

'I don't care what she calls herself,' he said. 'Why is Sally having a reading? I thought you were holding a coffee evening?'

Karen looked from Richard to the few women in her hall and back again. 'Look, Richard. Why don't you come in? She won't be long,' she said with a conciliatory smile.

Richard hesitated, then said simply, 'Okay.' He edged past several women in the hall, passing the kitchen door, which he noticed was closed. He had been here twice before. There was a female voice behind the door – not Sally's – which proceeded in a calm, practiced manner, although what it said was not intelligible. The medium.

He stopped at the living room door at the sound of Sally's voice. It came from the kitchen. It momentarily rooted him to the spot, as if he hadn't believed Sally was really in there with this woman.

Karen's voice sounded behind him. 'Please, Richard,' and he turned and stepped into the living room. 'Have a seat. I'll go and check.'

He sat in the armchair in the nearest corner, beside the fireplace. Across the room, the TV was off. Two of Karen's guests were seated on the couch, chatting quietly but intently about something, unmindful of his presence.

As he sat there, he became aware that the two women were discussing their own readings.

When she said my mum was there, I looked round. I couldn't help it. She told me mum wanted to warn me about my spending. I only ordered two new sofas last week…

He looked up and around. What kind of crap was he listening to?

Karen was there again. He thought she knew what it must look like to him. 'It's not what you think,' she said.

'Really?' he replied.

'No. This,' she said, sweeping her arm to indicate the room, '*is* a cosmetics and coffee evening. Stephanie is one of my guests. She also happens to be what you call a medium. On learning this, one of the girls asked her for a reading, which is something she does occasionally for friends. Free of charge, I might add. Anyway, with the cat out of the bag, it sort of took over,' she shrugged. 'It was only supposed to be a bit of fun. I had no idea you were so sensitive about it all.'

'I'm not, as a rule. I'm just surprised at Sally for going along with it. Did you know she once had a bad experience with a so-called medium?'

'No, I didn't.'

'Well, I thought she knew better. What convinced her to go in?'

Karen looked uncomfortable. 'I suppose we twisted her arm a little.'

Richard looked disgusted.

Karen continued. 'But not a lot. Once she saw that it was basically harmless, she went along with it. She seemed concerned about you, for some reason.'

'You mean she was asking questions about me?' he asked incredulously.

'Well, I only know that she was concerned about you. I didn't ask for details.'

He got to his feet. 'Ah, it's about time we were off. Sorry for being rude, but ... ' He strode towards the kitchen. He paused for a second, then opened the door.

He was momentarily taken aback. For some reason, he had envisaged a clichéd sitting: dim light; a cloth-covered round table; a dowdy middle-age woman seated opposite her subject, hand clutching the palm of her subject.

Instead the normality of the kitchen environment, fully lit, confronted him. Sally and the woman, Stephanie, looked up simultaneously from the polished wooden top of the breakfast bar. He noted casually that he had one part right – Sally's left hand was positioned palm-up on the bar, Stephanie's hand supporting it, forefinger and thumb light gripping the wrist.

Sally looked surprised and embarrassed. And scared? She pulled away from Stephanie's grasp. Her brow was creased, her eyes wide.

'Richard ... ' Sally began, then the woman looked at him. Her eyes, crystal blue, stared out of a powdered, rounded face, framed by a cup of blonde hair; sixty-something in age. She looked startled. 'Does anyone know a… an Emily?' she asked. 'I'm getting powerful signals from a troubled young lady.'

No-one replied. Richard's face had visibly blanched. All of his forthrightness had waned. If he had been able to take notice, he might have seen Sally's expression of fear deepen. She had never learned the name of the Blaxton Hill girl; had never read the copied articles Richard had made; had never been interested in encouraging Richard in his belief.

Now, not only was she betraying her own good sense in sitting here, but she had been caught red-handed, as it were, by Richard. In the instant he had appeared in the doorway, the thoughts had piled up on top of one another so quickly that they ceased to be coherent thoughts at all, becoming rapid equations – questions and fears posed and answered in an instant. There could be no more plea to Richard to maintain a sense of sanity and balance in the event of any future experiences he might claim.

No matter what she believed personally regarding the paranormal, and the hereafter in particular, she had regarded fortune-telling as a gimmick, the experience of a few years previously aside. She had rationalised that away as cruel advantage taken by a scare-mongering charlatan. However, with Richard's new predisposition towards acceptance of much of this, her presence here could create a drastically wrong impression – that she had, in effect, mocked his experiences, then herself had dabbled behind his back, under the cover of a coffee party.

All of this was exploded in an instant. The intrusion of the woman's voice, which seemed suddenly different, threw her off balance. Seeing Richard stop dead in his tracks as if on the receiving end of a stiff jab, she found herself plunged into confusion, and the disorientation that comes with a sudden shock.

Richard's expression said it all. The name did have meaning for him, that was obvious.

'What did you say?' asked Richard.

The lady, Stephanie, looked puzzled, and a little worried. 'I can hear the voice of a woman. She's asking for you.'

Richard felt his heart jump.

'How can she be asking for me? You don't know who I am.'

Stephanie looked him in the eye. '*She* does.'

Richard felt a chill. 'No, you must be… imagining it.'

'Take the ring. She's saying that you must take the ring?'

'Ring? What ring? What are you talking about?' he asked, the panic rising to constrict his words.

'Her … mm … her wedding ring?' she replied, frowning. 'Wait,' she said with some urgency, as if addressing someone else. She looked up. 'She's gone.' She slumped in her seat.

2

They were still sitting around the kitchen table. It had been fifteen minutes since the 'contact' had been broken. Fortunately, most of Karen's guests had left, some reluctantly.

Karen remained with a friend of hers, who was staying the night by prearrangement. The medium, Stephanie, looked a little pale, seemingly drained of energy. She sat, staring into her cup of tea, spoon absently stirring as she listened to Richard's explanation of the significance of her message. His voice showed the same strain and detachment as Stephanie had demonstrated.

'It … she … was a strong contact, Richard,' she said. 'I've had some unusual communications in the past – you know, odd images and voices – but they have been too ambiguous and too rare to treat seriously.'

She shuddered. 'I don't think I'm going to do this anymore. It's not that I feel I mislead people. I do believe I have some genuine ability, and I read as honestly as I can, as I did tonight. But ... but when something intrudes into your mind like this...'

'What do you think is going on here,' asked Sally. 'If this... ghost really exists, why is she trying to reach Richard?'

'I really don't know. I can only guess that the girl's death coming in what should have been the happiest hours of her life means she has been unable to rest.'

'Did you get any impression of what I'm supposed to do about this ring? Why me?' asked Richard.

'All I can tell you,' said Stephanie, 'is that a ring is important to her, perhaps linked to her release in some way.

'"Why you?" Well, I would imagine you must be special in some way, someone she can identify with. Personally, I would say you probably have the gift.'

'I don't think so,' said Richard flatly. 'If that was true, I'd have heard her myself, wouldn't I?'

'You did better than that,' replied Stephanie. 'You met her.'

Richard looked from her to Sally, to Karen.

Karen spoke for the first time in some minutes. Like many potentially embarrassing situations, she had chosen to stay out of the conversation initially in case she might offend.

'Richard, have you had any other experiences, before or after your, er ... experience?' she asked.

'Such as?' he asked, shifting in his seat with some impatience. Or was it uneasiness or vulnerability?

'Well,' said Stephanie, 'a recent history of stress or depression, or disturbing dreams or other ghostly or poltergeist activity?'

Richard shifted again. A skip in the rhythm of his breathing betrayed his denial.

'Are you sure?' asked Karen.

'Look,' said Richard firmly, 'I've had enough.' He got to his feet. 'You seem to be leading to a suggestion that I either imagined it all, or I have a spirit trying to get me to go on a special mission or something. Whatever it was,' he said, sweeping a hand over the reading set-up on the kitchen table, 'this is just exploiting the situation. And me. C'mon Sally, let's go.'

Sally started to quietly comply. Karen looked at Stephanie, who appeared far from hurt or rebuked. She had looked Richard squarely in the eye all along. It was he who could not hold the eye-contact in what was essentially a personal attack on her.

'It's not over, Richard. And, please, don't run away from it. I really feel this girl needs your help – more than you know.'

Richard started towards the door.

Sally stalled to offer something in way of an apology to Karen and Stephanie.

'Goodnight Karen,' muttered Richard as he allowed her to take charge of the open front door.

Sally felt a slight tug on her sleeve. She turned, lowering her gaze to the still-seated Stephanie.

'See if you can talk to him, Sally. It's scared me, I can tell you. If it's still going on, whether in his mind or not, he must be worried, and frightened. Try to be understanding, love. Meanwhile, I'm sorry that I seemed to have stirred it up for you again. If there's anything I can do to help, let me know.'

' I will. Thanks.'

'And, I'd be interested to hear the full story when it comes out.'

3

They arrived home a little after midnight. Little was said about the events of the evening. They stayed up to drink some hot chocolate, then went up together. Sally collected a towel and went into the bathroom, while Richard hunted around for fresh underwear and clean overalls for work the next day.

Shortly, Sally returned and Richard took towels, intending to shower. When, twenty minutes later, he emerged into the cool air of the hallway, he saw that the bedroom was illuminated only by the pink cast from the headboard lamp. Sally was curled into a foetal position, facing the wall. He climbed into bed gingerly, so as not to disturb her, and then fumbled for his book, which had slipped down between the bedside cabinet and the bed.

He had been reading for some fifteen minutes or so before he realised that he had taken in little of the previous couple of pages. He paused, bringing his hand to his face to massage the bridge of his nose. He placed the book face-down on the cabinet top, and settled down under the covers. Since his thoughts had distracted him from his book (or was it the book that had been unable to distract him from them?), he gave into them and allowed his rather vivid memory to replay the events of the evening.

What occurred to him only now was the possibility that this Stephanie had prior knowledge of the case. This was the problem with much of this type of material – you could never be certain if you yourself ,or others claiming to be witnesses, were not unconsciously fabricating experiences out of pure imagination or confabulating them from buried information.

In this case, there were a few possible sources of information. The story of the girl hitch-hiker was well known. Someone making their living as a medium in this area would likely be aware of popular local phenomena. And, of course, with his own tale in the papers only a couple of months back, it was entirely possible that Stephanie had been able to rig a contact that would appear convincing. The setting for the séance, Karen's kitchen, hardly had the traditional ambience, but it would have developed its own atmosphere, which would increase believability for the subject matter.

And then, there was Sally. How much had she told Stephanie?

But wait, there was another feasible explanation, albeit one that was almost as hard to accept as ghosts: Extra-Sensory Perception. ESP. Another book (and he had been reading a great deal about paranormal abilities and events lately) described the progress made into psychic research, particularly in Russia and the United States. It was somewhat ironic that the scientific community that had studied this phenomenon was actually more open-minded than the general public – a consequence of being better informed. Much of this research described proof in terms that few could rescind. If it were not so, why would either government invest in such research? The rewards in terms of espionage could be huge. If this were the case, where individuals can communicate without apparatus over many miles, then surely such a receptive mind – a sensitive, a medium –could pick up thoughts, or at least, an emotional impression that could allow them to 'read' a train of thoughts?

It sounded incredible, but assuming Stephanie had no specific information on this case, how else could she be so accurate in her reference to the ring? Apart from, that is, having been given this by the spirit of the girl herself.

He shuddered, his skin crawling as his mind spontaneously recreated the girl's features.

'You really need to resolve this thing, Richard,' said Sally out of nowhere.

Richard almost jumped out of his skin. He exhaled sharply. 'I thought you were asleep.'

Sally propped herself up. 'I was. You managed to wake me up when you came to bed. Since then, I've been lying awake, listening to your thoughts ticking away.'

'I can't help it. You really surprised me tonight, Sal.'

'Stephanie?'

'Yeah.'

'Whatever made you go in there? Especially to talk about me?'

'Who told you that? I suppose that was Karen?' asked Sally, no longer on the defensive.

'Is it true?'

'Look, despite appearances, I didn't go in there with any intention of quizzing Stephanie about you, the ghost, or anything in particular.'

Sally hoped that this partial truth would not be questioned by Richard. He stayed silent.

'Richard,' she said, losing some patience, 'I went along there tonight for an innocent get-together. I hadn't even met Stephanie before tonight. When most of the girls had decided what they wanted, one of them – Claire, I think her name was – got talking to Stephanie. When some others found out she was a medium, they persuaded her to do a few sittings. That's all.'

'For free?'

'She doesn't charge. She said she'd only do a few short readings for those who wanted them. I gather she was quite accurate.'

'What do you mean? Couldn't you tell that from your own reading?'

'I didn't have one.'

'I *saw* you!'

'What you saw was only the start. Before you came barging in, nothing much was happening.'

'What do you mean?'

'It's true. Stephanie only began ... picking up things when

you came in.'

'That doesn't... ' He frowned as her last sentence sank in. 'What are you talking about? You're telling me that Stephanie only went to work when I came in?'

'Yes,' she replied truthfully.

'But she was chatting away before I came in. I could hear her through the door.'

'Yes, but she was really vague, searching, not very specific – until you came in.'

He evaded the implications that Stephanie's reaction had brought out. Despite all that he had gone through, he chose the least painful course, denial rather than confronting the issue. Which brought him back to his initial irritation at Sally's involvement with a fortune teller.

'That doesn't take away from the fact that you were in there of your own will.'

'Yes. But you know how these things are. Everyone was having a go. It was hard not to.'

'Even after the reading you had years ago?'

'That was a long time ago. I've learned that it's mostly a load of rubbish. None of it came true.'

Richard stared ahead for a moment. 'About tonight. Did you know the girl's name before this evening?'

'No, of course not,' replied Sally.

He turned again to face her. 'And her ring – have you heard me talk about that?'

'Again, no. What are you trying to say?'

'I've been having dreams about a ring. Just as Stephanie described – the girl telling me to take the ring.

'Don't you see? Stephanie picked that up, and I don't even know if there was ever anything special about a ring in the case. She got her name right too.'

'Surely all that has been documented?' said Sally.

'No! No, it hasn't. Not all of it. I only found her name when I went to the library.'

'The library? When?'

'Never mind. The ring, though… the ring has only featured in a dream I had.

Sally was a bit quiescent. 'Have you er… dreamt about her since we've lived together?' she asked timidly.

'No, I … ' Then it dawned on him what she was thinking. He looked her, astonished. 'You're not actually jealous of a dead person, are you?'

'It's not that.'

'No?'

'Please, Richard. Don't start it all off again.'

' Well, what were you thinking?'

'I didn't realise you had involved yourself so deeply with all this stuff. When did you go to the library?"

'A few weeks ago.'

'And you didn't tell me? Richard, you've got to leave it alone. *Please?*'

He shuffled down under the covers, sighing. 'I don't know if I can. *It* doesn't seem to want to let go of me. I'm scared, Sally.'

Against her impulse at this point, she cuddled up to him. Richard reached out and flicked off the bedside lamp.

4

The next morning, Richard forced himself to get up for work. He was finding this more and more of a struggle. The late nights, like last night, he could handle. Weekend overtime also – no problem. Tiredness and fatigue were not new or unexpected experiences. He expected to pay his dues in order to reap the benefits and rewards that a new home and his life with Sally would provide. Plenty of people were in the same boat. It wasn't this that made him feel so uneasy, so insecure. It was the restless nights, the thoughts and fears he carried with him after his experience on that hill. He recognised this mental burden he carried was just that – something his mind suffered, but something he should be able to rationally offload just as easily – in theory. But the suggestion that he could relieve the problem simply by not becoming preoccupied, or too emotionally involved with it, was easier said than done. He felt like Jacob Marley, weighed down by a tangled and knotted mass of chains that was slowly crushing him under its insufferable weight.

He knew he was experiencing mental aftershocks from a totally unexpected event. What he was experiencing was, in effect, a shattering of his perception of reality. And he was finding that he was struggling to deal with it, unable to shake it off and continue with his routinely mundane, comfortable, and understandable life.

At the table, he sullenly regarded his breakfast. He struggled with his thoughts to try to find a way of explaining to Sally – or to anyone – how he was feeling.

Until recently, things had seemed so clear: you worked for a living because it was the thing to do if you wanted things in life. There was no questioning the steady cycle of existence. You were born, you grew up, worked, formed friendships, perhaps married and had a family, and then descended into the twilight of retirement, and the eventual darkness of death.

Now, the comfortable ordering of life had been interrupted. He had been forced to confront the possibility of a greater reality beyond the material world –something he had never seriously considered before. That was the domain of old people, to whom it was perhaps an increasingly important issue, and of various believers, philosophers, and assorted weirdos.

But he had caught a glimpse of something that made any semblance of a normal life at the moment impossible. He *had* to find some meaning, some explanation for the events of his recent past. He couldn't go on without finding some order, some framework for understanding what was happening to him. If he weren't actually losing his mind at the moment, he feared that it might well come to that if the problem was to remain unchallenged.

He looked up to see Sally turn away from the sink. 'I think you should go and see a doctor,' she said flatly.

'A shrink?' he replied.

'A psychiatrist.'

'I don't think they'd do any good,' he said calmly, getting up from the table. 'I've decided to go and talk to Peter Pumfrys again.'

'How can *he* possibly help?'

'I'm not sure. But at least he seems to be sympathetic. Besides, I need to return his books.' He gave her a peck on the cheek. 'See you later.'

Sally didn't reply. She heard the front door clunk shut.

The last thing he needs is for someone to encourage him in this, she thought. Please God, don't let him go to see Pumfrys.

TWELVE

Pumfrys lived in the village of Caldwell, twenty miles east of Eldonbridge. Richard had purposefully left it a little late, thereby avoiding getting caught up in the rush-hour traffic. He arrived on the outskirts of the village at seven-thirty, and then spent the next quarter of an hour trying to find Pumfrys's house in the gathering darkness.

It was no fun – in fact, it was downright spooky – crawling around the lanes, the car headlights picking out grotesque shapes in the trees and hedges. Eventually, he found the lane off which it was located. Hoppers' Lane. The sign-post was partially obscured by an overgrown hedgerow. The lane itself was narrow, a single-track, accounting for how he had managed to drive past it once already.

He started down the lane, its pock-marked and cratered surface reminding him of a bombed-out runway. Backwater country lanes were not on the council's priority list for sure. The car rocked gently from side to side as its tyres found the holes, scrunching on the gravel they always seemed to contain.

Presently he rounded a bend, and there, at last, was Pumfrys's cottage, on the right, set back from the lane. The beams of his headlights picked out the building's flaking whitewash façade. The windows stared back blankly. It seemed as if no-one were in. The small upper windows – bedrooms, or bedroom and bathroom – were dark eyes that silently acknowledged his presence.

Adding to the effect was the absence of any street lighting near the cottage, and no outside light. Isolated houses invariably seemed to have these little beacons, bathing them in their protective glow. This did not.

He pulled up below the high stone retaining wall of the front garden. There was no obvious way to drive closer to the cottage. From here, he could just see above the ragstone wall and into the gloom of the front garden. He could make out the close-cropped stems of plants silhouetted against the cottage, now illuminated by the back-scatter of light from the car's headlights. On a sunny spring afternoon, the garden would likely become a blooming delight, but in this unearthly glow, it looked drab and uninviting.

He decided to leave the engine running, with the headlights on, while he made his way up the path to the front door. Six feet forward of his parking position, he could see a set of stone steps in the gently curving bank of the retaining wall. A shallow recess to the right of the steps contained a simple woodcut sign the name of the cottage: Windmill View. Seven or eight steps negotiated the five feet of the wall itself.

He switched the car's hazard lights on before shuffling over to the passenger side – he had inadvertently parked too close to the wall. As he did so, he detected movement in the lane, at the foot of the steps. Pumfrys stepped into the beams of his headlights, glowing green, the colour of the tracksuit he was wearing. He had managed to get out of the cottage, and down the stone steps unnoticed..

As Pumfrys approached the car, squinting into the light, Richard noticed that the cottage had taken on a more welcoming appearance. The door, post-office red, stood ajar, spilling warm yellow light. He sat in the passenger seat, feeling a little foolish. He waited for Pumfrys to reach the side of the car. He wound down the window.

'Evening,' said Pumfrys cheerfully. 'Welcome to my humble abode.

'Is there somewhere around here I can park?'

'Just what I was about to show you,' said Pumfrys. 'You see there,' he said, indicating down the lane, 'on the right, just before the bend, that narrow right-turn, where that red post is, just this side of the trees?'

'Huh-huh,' acknowledged Richard.

'Take that right, and it'll bring you up to the back of the cottage. It's a back-to-front kind of place. I tend to make more use of the rooms at the back.'

He immediately set off up the steps again. 'I'll meet you in the kitchen.'

2

'Coffee, tea?'

''Tea, please.'

'Have you eaten? I can rustle you up a sandwich or something.'

'No, thanks,' replied Richard. 'I had something before I left.'

'In that case, if you'd like to go into the living room and make yourself comfortable, I'll be right in.'

'Sure,' said Richard. He made his way into the room, from which he could hear the strains of classical music playing.

Pumfrys lit a gas ring with a match, and turning it down a touch before placing on it a scorched and battered kettle. 'Turn that down, or off, if you like,' he called out.

The room was warm and comfortable-looking. A gas fire with an imitation log stack glowed beneath the mantelpiece. The main source of illumination was a tall lamp standing in the corner of the room opposite the door. Two smaller and dimmer lights shone through the glass of a large dark wood bookcase, which took up most of the wall opposite the fireplace. A similarly dark-stained wooden armchair with worn and faded cushions sat in the corner in front of the lamp. Sepia prints of local scenes were arranged in stepped fashion on one wall, while the space above the mantelpiece showed a framed two-feet by three-feet map of the county as it had been around 1820.

On the other free wall was an original oil painting, an attractive summertime depiction of the cottage itself. In the picture, a young man dressed in army uniform leant in the doorway of the cottage, seemingly talking with an old man who was seated and apparently mending shoes on a wooden shoehorn. Richard got up to examine the signature on the painting: Peter David Pumfrys 1989. He raised an eyebrow, impressed. The scene appeared to be set in wartime, WWII. Relatives?

He saw why Pumfrys chose to live here, in this isolated spot, and in a house whose style seemed out of step with the times. A family home, perhaps, host to a lot of good times, family times, and a lot of memories, representing timeless stability. It had the feeling of having been a happy home. Therefore, it perhaps held strong emotional bonds to a man living alone, with no evident family; one with a due sense of nostalgia.

Richard approached the bookcase. The number of books was what immediately struck him, around five hundred works, of assorted sizes, and subjects: politics, history, biography, religion, philosophy, local history, art and architecture, computers. By far the most numerous, though, were those that might be termed fringe subjects: ghosts & apparitions, UFOs, Psi, Remote Viewing, Ancient Mysteries, Earth Mysteries.

'Ah, I see you've discovered my collection,' observed Pumfrys, tray in hand, which he carried to a low coffee-table. On it, two mugs of tea and a plate with a selection of biscuits.

'Yes – which reminds me,' said Richard, 'I've brought your

books back. Except the one on road ghosts, if that's Okay?'

'Yes, of course. No rush,' replied Pumfrys. 'Please take a seat.'

He waited for Richard to get settled before he spoke again. 'So, tell away.'

'Mm?'

'Well, I know you didn't come all this way just to return those old books.'

'Well, now that I'm here, what I was going to say seems ridiculous, but ... well, I'm not sure what I thought I'd achieve, really. Your opinion, some advice, I guess?'

'About?'

Richard sighed. 'Blaxton Hill; the ghost. I need to find out whether I'm overreacting to that first encounter, making more out of it than I should, or if I'm going nuts. Or if there might be more to this thing than it first appeared – that it wasn't just some random event where I just happened along at the wrong time, but something that seems, for some reason, to have a definite interest in *me*.'

'Well,' said Pumfrys, 'Perhaps you should begin by bringing me up to date. Has something else happened?'

Over the next twenty minutes, Richard updated him on recent events, at first self-consciously, then, as he saw that Pumfrys was listening intently, without judgement, simply nodding periodically without interrupting the flow of his story, he found himself able to relax. He sensed a sympathy and a definite knowledge in Pumfrys, which made the telling of even the most difficult or nebulous aspects of his experiences easier than he expected. Here he was telling Pumfrys about the dreams he had had and about the séance night – something he hadn't discussed in detail even with Sally.

'So,' said Pumfrys, as Richard finished. 'It seems your situation is a little more involved than I believed.'

'Do you think it could all be real, then?'

'All I can say is I believe as much as you do,' replied Pumfrys. 'You are the only one who can make any reasonable judgement as to what's been happening to you. If you feel that you are not misleading yourself, becoming overly preoccupied with your initial experience, then that's good enough for me. To begin with.'

The relief showed on Richard's face. 'When the dreams started, I began to think I was losing my grip.'

'If you can recognise that as a possibility, then it's usually true to say that that's not the case.'

'And the dreams – getting her name; this thing about a ring? What do you think?' asked Richard.

'Names are usually a matter of public record,' replied Pumfrys. 'But I'm fairly sure that a ring has never featured even in tales of Blaxton Hill's ghost – although Emily Reynolds was about to married, of course.'

'Peter, I'm *certain* I didn't know her name before the library. I even rechecked the book you loaned me – there's no mention of it.'

'Perhaps you heard it sometime – perhaps I mentioned it in passing, or you heard or read it at some point in the past? The brain is remarkable instrument, capable of unconsciously retaining often the most trivial things.'

Richard seemed suddenly uncertain, even a little exasperated.

Pumfrys picked up on his reaction. 'Just playing Devil's Advocate,' he said reassuringly. 'It's just hard to be certain, that's all.'

He sighed. 'But encountering the dead in dreams is well established in the literature, even to their imparting important information to the living – although an interpretation often applied is that it is the dreamer's own subconscious bringing something to conscious attention.'

'That doesn't make much sense to me,' replied Richard. 'Why would I be reminding myself about something that I don't even know about? And then there's Stephanie, when she mentioned the ring?'

It was Pumfrys's turn to looked puzzled. 'Stephanie?'

'Oh, yes, sorry. That was the medium. Stephanie... um. Blast,' he said, tapping the arm of the chair with his fingers. ... can't recall her surname...'

'Caulson, perhaps?' ventured Pumfrys.

'Yes, that's it,' said Richard. 'You know her?'

''Know of' would be more accurate,' replied Pumfrys quietly.

'Well, she was spot on with the ring,' said Richard. 'Doesn't that suggest I didn't imagine it?'

'Perhaps,' said Pumfrys noncommittally. 'Many of them are convincing because, if nothing else, they are very good – practiced – at leading their clients into belief that the ability to contact the dead. In your case, it does seems unlikely. She couldn't have known that she might run into you, and I can't imagine what motive the lady might have, but let's face it, there is a certain amount of information available on the Blaxton Hill girl, and you had only recently been featured in the papers. People, alas, are even less predictable than the machinations of the spirit world.'

'I don't think so,' said Richard. 'She looked too scared to be faking. And she knew too much about my dream about the ring.'

'Well, yes, there is that,' conceded Pumfrys.

There fell a natural pause between them.

'So...' said Richard, 'what would you do in my place?' He didn't wait for Pumfrys to answer. 'There's a nagging thought that I should just drop it – you know, try to dismiss it all as a product of an overactive imagination or something. That's what Sally thinks, anyway. But what if it won't let go of *me*?'

'The 'Why Me?' Syndrome,' said Pumfrys.

'Sorry?'

'It's natural to try to make sense of an unusual experience such as yours: 'Why did it happen to me?'; 'Was I simply in the wrong place at the wrong time; or was I somehow singled out for the experience?'

'It may be tempting to believe there is something personal about it, but if we accept that genuine paranormal events sometimes *do* occur, we must also accept that they occur neither according to logic or schedule. They simply happen.'

'But that's not always the case, is it?' asked Richard, a trifle defensively.

'Isn't it?' asked Pumfrys.

'Well, some people seem to be especially sensitive and things can happen fairly frequently to them, or around them, at certain locations.'

'That's true,' agreed Pumfrys. 'But rarely on cue. It's always the phenomenon itself that determines whether it is experienced or not. But yes, all we can be sure of really – and this, of course, applies to Blaxton Hill too – is that some locations seem to be a particularly prone to anomalous events. So, we have houses that are said to be haunted, and haunted rooms and roads, and battlefields and churchyards.

'And in those places, descriptions of apparitions can be consistent across time and different witnesses.

'But really, it's people who are haunted, rather than places, if you think about it. The question is whether the phenomenon is truly objective and independent, or in a large degree dependent on the presence of a witness in order to manifest?

'Shirley Jackson's classic novel about a haunted house, *The Haunting of Hill House* – it's on the bookshelf if you'd like to borrow it – has a wonderful opening paragraph that ends with, 'And whatever walked there, walked alone'.' He gazed into space as he quoted, before bringing his focus back to Richard. 'But does it? When no-one is in the house, does it? *Can* it?'

Richard listened without comment. It was obvious that Pumfrys was a man who could get carried away with this type of conversation. Well, conversation was a misnomer, really. It was a bit one-sided, but Richard decided to allow him to continue. He probably didn't get a chance to chat like this very often.

'What defines a haunted location, of course, is that the ghost appears to be bound there, by some force or principle that we do not understand… actually, I do have some ideas about that, but more on that another time. But it is often assumed that emotional attachments formed in life, or at the moment of death, particularly violent death, tie them to the location.

'But like all systems, ghosts need energy to operate materialise or to move things. There is good evidence that electrical devices fail, batteries are drained, and people feel a numbing cold at these spots. This 'psychic cold' is the mind's way of sensing the depletion of energy. So when a sympathetic soul happens along, like a psychic battery, the witness may unwittingly provide some of the energy it requires to materialise or to move things.'

'I don't follow,' said Richard. 'Are you suggesting that ghosts may actually draw energy from people?'

'Some paranormal activity suggests that quite strongly. Poltergeists, for instance, the so-called 'noisy spirits'. Some research links this mischievous activity – things removed or thrown around the room – with the emotional flux of adolescence.'

A psychic battery? Could that possibly be why this girl was

trying to reach out him? Was she *feeding* off him? Richard shuddered, momentarily appalled.

'Do you recall feeling cold or in some way drained after your experience?' asked Pumfrys.

'No. Just very scared,' replied Richard, his mind still half on his train of thought.

'There is no reason why contact with a ghost or spirit shouldn't continue away from the 'haunted' location, to susceptible, sensitive or suitably attuned persons. Like you, and Madame Caulson, perhaps.

Richard squirmed in his chair. 'I'm not psychic,' he said.

'Perhaps some latent talent,' suggested Pumfrys.

'Some people, witnesses and investigators, report picking up attachments from haunted locations, so that activity may continue in their homes – but usually at a less intense level than at the haunted location itself.'

'So you think I have an attachment?'

'It's a possibility,' admitted Pumfrys.

'That makes me feel better,' said Richard.

'They tend to fade away with time.'

'Okay,' said Richard, 'what do you suggest I do? What if it happens again?'

'My advice is: don't force it; don't encourage it. But also, if it happens again, don't fight it. Perhaps it will resolve itself that way. And try not to dwell on it. I don't believe that's too healthy. Curiosity is one thing, but if you're to never know why or how it all occurred to begin with, then simply accept that and get on with your life.'

Pumfrys excused himself. When he returned, he offered Richard more tea. Ten minutes later, he was back with a fresh tray.

Richard checked his watch. Nine-forty. Later than expected. He felt suddenly guilty for leaving Sally for so long, then immediately pushed that out of mind.

'You seem very knowledgeable about this subject,' commented Richard.

'I try to be informed,' replied Pumfrys

'Did you gain your knowledge from the books?'

'Mostly, but the opinions I expressed are my own. I did some of my own research a few years back. I have an aborted book draft around here somewhere. It was to be an in-depth discussion on the nature of ghosts, but with a strong local flavour.'

'*Was* to be? What happened?'

'Hm. Well, I couldn't resolve my feelings about the subject, and I was becoming busier with my regular work. It was intended to be published by the newspaper's own publishing house, but it more and more seemed to be a waste of time. It wouldn't have done my credibility any good. Not that that matters much anymore.'

'Did you ever experience anything yourself?'

Pumfrys smiled. Everyone expects the investigator to have a personal story to tell. 'No. Not exactly. Of course, it was during that phase that I found out as much as I know about Blaxton Hill. No, the only personal experience of any note I had was with a group of colleagues at work, when we experimented with a ouija board.'

'You what?' asked Richard. Even he knew it wasn't wise to dabble with the things, real or purely psychological in nature. Either way, they were bad news.

'Indeed. It was part of my research at the time, and none of us were very well informed back then. My only lasting regret is that I involved other people who were ignorant of the possible consequences.

'But,' he reflected, 'the only way you learn of the dangers of fire is to be burned a little. I knew of the dangers, but I never intended to use the device for information gathering; simply out of curiosity as to the way it operated.'

'Did it work?'

'Oh, yes. It operated true to form. What happened to us I later read has happened to other people. The planchette – not the type with a vertically-set pencil in it, but one with a small window in it that allows you to see the letters on the board – it began to glide around the board, tracing letters and numbers in lazy circles. Of course, we asked the usual questions of one another. There were five of us – you know, who was pushing the device with their finger? Of course, each of us denied it.

'But ... once the first coherent word – a name, actually – was spelled out, it commanded our attention, and once it had that, of course, it started to gain pace. That's when I first became a little alarmed. I had difficulty in keeping my finger poised on the planchette as it raced across the board. Names and personal details flew at us. Many were true details; a few sort of came true later, but the vast majority were either inaccurate, misleading, or outright lies.' He sighed heavily.

'When it slowed a little, it developed a definite style of language, as if a dominant personality was in control rather than a confused gathering of minds.

'Anyway, this personality, for want of a better term –the one that dominated on this occasion – claimed to be the recently deceased father of one of the sitters. This man was a down-to-earth type, and he had grieved hard over the loss of his father, which had occurred only the year before. But, instead of the personality giving assurances about his state of well-being on the other side, as you might expect, it indicated that he was far from happy.

'Naturally, we were all very disturbed. We were about to break off the contact, but the er... friend I mentioned beat us to it by pulling away, escaping from the room. He was really quite traumatised.'

'And you?' asked Richard. 'It was after that that you decided to give up the research on the book?'

'Yes,' said Pumfrys quietly. 'It was a factor. I gave up the ghost on the book idea.'

Richard smiled at the attempted humour. 'How long ago was all this?'

'Hm, let me see. It must have been 1985. Around June of 1985.'

'I noticed, said Richard, 'that most of your books on the paranormal are more recent than that. You obviously didn't lose your interest entirely?'

'Oh, I did,' Pumfrys replied firmly. 'I got rid of the few books I owned at that time. I suddenly felt very wrong, tainted somehow. I needed to gain some lightness in my life. It was a number of years later, around 2006, before I revived my interest. After I moved in here, as a matter of fact.'

'Why then?'

'My brother and I arranged for our father to be admitted to a residential home that year. He just wasn't capable of looking after himself, and we were both unable to commit much time to him. But, rather than sell the house, which has been in the family for generations, I decided to move in myself. It seemed the best thing to do, considering my wife had just divorced me and was intent on living in our home in Eldonbridge. I wasn't prepared to argue about the house at the time. Clean break and all that. I threw myself into my work.'

Richard was a little embarrassed to be listening to this man's personal history, but perhaps Pumfrys, like himself earlier, had discovered the need to talk. And, he seemed to be taking his time building up to something.

'Well, a few months later, my father died. It was, I suppose, another two months or so after that that something happened to change my mind about the paranormal.'

Richard continued to listen intently. He felt goosebumps begin to break out on his arms and torso. Curiously, he had no similar reaction during his own experiences. They either happened too quickly to react properly, or gave him a feeling of nauseating disorientation. It was different being the protagonist in the drama.

'I went up to bed late, around midnight,' recounted Pumfrys. 'I read for a while, then turned off the lamp and was off to sleep in no time at all.

'Around two o'clock, as I recall, I woke suddenly with a feeling of unease. Someone was in the room with me. I knew it.

'I lay there for a moment, on my left side, facing the window. Most nights it would be dark as pitch – no street lighting around here – but this night, light from a tree-top moon streamed obliquely into the room.

'Then I heard a shuffling sound at the doorway behind me. My heart skipped a beat. I listened intently for a moment longer, then turned over slowly. I could just make out in the gloom the outline of a stooped figure entering the room.'

'What did you do?' Richard asked.

'Momentarily, I thought I had a burglar. But I quickly acknowledged the truth. Although I was almost frozen by fear, I was also fascinated. Was it a genuine phantom, or a hypnopompic illusion? The figure seemed unaware of me. It paced slowly from the doorway to the window, and back, apparently looking for something on the floor. Its slippered feet made a shuffling sound like leather on exposed boards – although the room has been fully carpeted for some years. As my eyes adjusted to the scene, I could make out a little more detail. I was keen to see its face, if it had one.

'I waited for it to turn from the window and pass by the

bed again. As its face came into view, illuminated by the moon's reflected light, I discovered that I knew him. It was my paternal great-grandfather. He died in 1953, here, in this house.'

Richard's eyes were drawn to the painting on the wall, focusing on the elderly gentleman sitting outside the cottage.

Pumfrys followed his gaze. 'Yes, that's him, with my grandfather, during the war. That painting was based on an old photograph I found in the loft after moving in. I'd never seen it before. On the back it read simply: 'Windmill View. Father and Son, 1942.' I decided to reproduce it as a painting.'

'It's good,' remarked Richard.

'You think so? Thank you.'

'Well, what did you do – about the ghost?' asked Richard.

'As I said, I was afraid. But also interested. It seemed to intend me no harm and, besides, it wasn't exactly a stranger. He was a relative, albeit one who died before I was born.

'I was aware that to make any sudden disturbance could break the spell and the figure would likely vanish. However, without some action, I couldn't possibly find out any more about the figure, or be able to ignore it and get some sleep.

'So, I reached out carefully and fumbled for the switch on my bedside lamp. My hand was shaking quite badly ... '

'I can imagine,' said Richard. And he could. He could see it in his mind's eye clearly. All too clearly.

' ... and I had some trouble finding it. After what seemed an eternity, I found it and with a dull click, the room was flooded with warm yellow light... and the figure was still there!

'That surprised me. I was simultaneously horrified and pleased. I can't accurately describe the feeling. I had fully expected it to vanish. Instead, it reflected the light like a normal human being, except its clothing was dull in colour – the mute tones of working clothes of seventy or eighty years ago.'

'If you recognised it as your great-grandfather, why do you continue to refer to him as 'it'?' asked Richard.

'Do I?' asked Pumfrys, genuinely taken aback. 'I suppose,' he reflected, 'it's because I can't accept the idea that it *was* great-grandfather. I mean, phantoms are generally pathetic things, repetitive and uncommunicative. What sort of existence would it be if, when we die, we simply grind out mundane and trivial tasks for all eternity – pacing up and down, hitching lifts from motorists – for no evident reason?

'What happened to the idea that a released spirit is enlightened and enriched beyond the senses of the flesh? No, 'it' is the correct descriptive term. 'It' was and wasn't my great grandfather. It had his likeness; his general appearance and mannerisms were there, but there was none of his personality, none of the essential spark that made him the kindly man I'm told he was. It was something else.'

'Such as? What does a ghost have to be?' asked Richard.

'Most, I would say, are recordings. Extremely convincing, three dimensional recordings – holograms, really – but recordings all the same. Under certain conditions, they replay. Until the source of their power dies down, at least. I mean, ghosts dating back as far as Roman times and beyond are very rare. They seem to wind down over time.'

'But others, started Richard, 'might appear to be actual ghosts of the dead? Ghosts with intelligence and purpose?'

'There is that possibility, of course. You certainly can't rule it out. But you have to remember, even these ghosts seem too often be very limited in ability, and are seemingly here only to trivial ends. There is nothing very informative or even imaginative about what they say or do.'

Richard didn't know what to make of that last remark. 'What happened to your ghost?' asked Richard.

'Great Granddad? Oh, he busied around for another minute or so, and then left the room.'

'What did you do?'

'Oh, I followed. I searched the entire house, but couldn't find a trace. Naturally. There had been nothing real there in the first place, not as I understood the term.

'But, it's interesting. You discover that you can accept the idea of a ghost, but you still go through the motions of searching for a physical human being. I mean, I was actually a little surprised to find that all the doors and windows were still locked, just as I had left them. That was somehow more disturbing than actually looking at the phantom.'

'Because it provided some external corroboration for the experience?' said Richard.

'Exactly. Whatever it really was, it wasn't a real person. That's when it hits you. But, you would be aware of that, wouldn't you? I sat up in the kitchen for the rest of the night, lights on, radio on, until daylight, when I made another quick inspection of the place.'

'Have there been any other times since?' Richard asked, by now stifling a yawn. It was getting late.

'Twice. A few years later. Same M.O. I don't know if it's mere coincidence, but there hasn't been a sign of it since the painting has been on the wall.

'But, what was interesting was at that time, just following the death of my father, I would have guessed that I'd have seen him standing there, not my great-grandfather – if it were all a mental projection, that is. Why his image should have appeared, I have no idea. They both lived here most of their lives.

'I can only say that I am no longer frightened by the whole thing. I'll go to bed tonight just as calmly as any other. If he appears, I'll ignore him. If he does something different than before, if he reacts to me, we'll sit down and talk.'

3

Richard finally left Peter Pumfrys at midnight. Before he left, Pumfrys had offered him the choice of selecting a few more books to take with him. Richard found he couldn't help himself. He realised he was hungry for anything to fill the gaps in his knowledge, anything that chipped away at his sense of isolation. He picked out four books. He looked at Pumfrys for approval, who said he could take as many as he liked; same arrangement as before.

Richard watched Pumfrys disappear in the red fog of his tail-lights. In a few minutes, he was on open road again, sailing back to the comforting oasis of Eldonbridge. His thoughts followed Pumfrys as he re-entered the house, and locked himself in. Alone. Perhaps.

It had been a worthwhile evening, although it was apparent that Pumfrys didn't hold the same view as himself regarding the general nature of ghosts. But then, he had seen a more-or-less traditional ghost. What if he'd witnessed the Phantom Hitch-Hiker, and the girl looking him in the eyes. Would he feel differently?

4

Back at Windmill View, Pumfrys was not quite as composed as he had convinced even himself. He had enjoyed the evening's talk with Richard, but this subject always hyped up his senses, and he often found it difficult to relax afterwards.

He put a saucepan on the stove, and filled it with half a pint of milk. He went into the living room again to collect the tray of cups and biscuits, and a bottle of whisky he kept in the slide-base of the bookshelf. A milk-and-whisky nightcap was one he had learned from his mother.

He stooped to retrieve the bottle, and his eyes fell on a black leather-bound album on the bottom shelf. He slid it out, and opened it to the first page.

His abandoned book. And in here, information about the ghost of Blaxton Hill that Richard Wentworth would have found very interesting. Had he pushed for details on that case, would he have allowed Richard to read it? He couldn't answer that. Some of it was confidential. He had given the witnesses his word. But it was all a long time ago. Perhaps he had a right to know? Perhaps he had a genuine need to follow it up, for his own peace of mind. If he was really determined to pursue it, he'd be back.

But this was not the main reason for his somewhat troubled thoughts tonight. His own behaviour was becoming of some small concern. First, the newspaper article, raking the subject up again after years of dormancy.

What need had the action fulfilled in him? More importantly, he had bent the truth – lied actually –about the ouija board session. Goodness only knew why he had told that story at all. It dredged up some unsettling memories. Why couldn't he tell Richard that it was *he* that had fainted away that evening? When his deceased mother had come through, asking to speak to him.

THIRTEEN

When he arrived home, Sally wasn't there. He found a note in the kitchen that read simply, 'Gone home to my parents. Phone me at work tomorrow.'

He considered phoning her right away, but quickly decided against it. It would only cause a row, and it could wait until the morning. She'd be back in the evening, anyway, he told himself.

But she wasn't. When he called her, she'd told him in no uncertain terms that he had to give her more consideration or forget the whole thing. This ghost thing was turning into an obsession. The wedding was set for 21 September. That gave him six months to get a grip. Meanwhile, she was going to stay at her parents' place for one more night. 'Use the time,' she said, 'to think it through.'

And he did use the time, some of it. The rest of his spare time he used to read and mull over the conversation with Pumfrys.

An attachment? A psychic battery?

Had the Blaxton Hill girl somehow formed a connection with him? Was he somehow providing her with the energy to appear, in his dreams, and in a more tangible fashion near the site of her demise on Blaxton Hill?

Worse still, was he (as he suspected many people thought) deluding himself? Did the ghost girl really exist outside his own imagination? Was it – as some had suggested; as had even been hinted at in Pumfrys's article – that it was a guilt-excuse for his drink-driving that night? If so, that would mean his mind was covering up for him by sending him the subsequent experiences, especially the dreams.

The only snag with all of this, though, was that he *did* still trust his own judgement and soundness of mind. For now, at least. And, the experience with Stephanie Caulson was pretty difficult to dismiss.

The only way to test the objectivity of the entire experience was to do as Pumfrys had, and face it; come to terms with it. If it was real, he'd know sooner or later. If it was rubbish, nothing would happen, and he would be able to put it behind him.

He decided he would need some verifiable facts from any future experience – things he could be sure he or Pumfrys could not possibly know.

There were ways of challenging the phenomenon, of course. He could try to reproduce the meeting with the girl by approximating the conditions of the first night of contact – but without the booze, that is.

Having said that, another book had suggested that a little alcohol, with its ability to relax and strip away preoccupation and inhibition, might actually be conducive to paranormal experience. When the mind is not distracted with everyday concerns, it is actually more receptive to more subtle stimuli. It was one possible explanation why so many pubs and inns seemed to be haunted. A combination of history and alcohol, perhaps an ideal mixture for ghost-spotting.

One other method was to go back to Stephanie Caulson. He quickly dropped that idea. It could get back to Sally too easily. He had made some commitment to her about getting himself back on track. Actually, there was another – the one that had apparently scared Pumfrys all those years ago, the Ouija board. But he ruled that out. It was dangerous instrument; dangerous and unreliable.

No, there was really one way to go about it. And it meant going back to Blaxton Hill.

Pumfrys's voice broke into his thoughts again, the voice of his conscience.

Don't force it; don't encourage it.

He pushed the thought away. Sorry, Peter, you also said if it happens again, don't fight it. Well, I won't, but I also can't just wait for it to happen again. I need to find out if this thing with the ring really means anything or not. If not, then I'll give it up, with relief. But, if it does... well, that would be another question.

2

February 10

Sally got back at seven. Even before she put the key in the lock, she knew Richard wasn't home. The house was in darkness, and his van was nowhere in sight.

Inside, she found everything in order, apart from an empty coffee mug stack of books on the living room table that she didn't recognise. From that Pumfrys fellow? She hoped not.

She went into the kitchen and took a pair of ready meals out of the fridge's freezer compartment, removed their outer packaging and popped them into the oven before turning to put the kettle on. She took a fresh mug from the cupboard and dropped a teabag into it. While she waited for the kettle, she stared at the crumpled note on the kitchen table – the one she had left Richard the other evening. Had she overreacted? Maybe. But she had to make a point; he had to realise the effect his actions were having on her.

The kettle clicked off. She made her tea and took it into the living room. She placed it on a coaster and sat to check her phone. Nothing; no messages. For a moment, she considered calling him. But no – she had been forthright with him yesterday. It was up to him now.

But when eight-thirty came and went, she decided to call Terry. Maybe Richard was with him, or at least he might know where he was.

After a couple of rings, Terry answered. No, he hadn't seen Richard since work and didn't know where he was. He and Alice were in London for an evening out. He was sure Richard would be Okay, though.

So that was the end of that line of hopeful reasoning. Sally thanked him and hung up.

She tried calmly to sit it out. In fact, worried as she was, it was anger and betrayal she felt more than anything.

Finally, at nine-twenty-five, she heard Richard's key in the lock. Then the front door as it swung inwards, scraping on the bristle doormat. A slam announced its closure, and then, there was Richard, entering the living room, pink-cheeked from the cold.

'You're back,' he said with mild surprise.

Sally's anger and frustration melted into relief, but she tried hard to not show it. 'I was getting worried, she said.

'Emergency job,' he replied. 'Took longer than expected.' He dropped his gaze.

'Oh. All sorted?' she asked gingerly.

'Um, yeah,' he replied, slipping his jacket off.

'Good. I ah … did something to eat for us. It'll be cold now. If you'd called, I could have done it a bit later.'

'That's Okay. I couldn't. Sorry,' he replied. 'Have you eaten?'

'No, no. Didn't feel like it in the end,' she shrugged. She decided not to push it. She heavily suspected he had been up to something else, but closed her mind to it, even though in so doing, she felt as if she were somehow condoning his actions, aiding and abetting him in a conspiracy of sorts against herself.

She knows, thought Richard. She probably checked with Terry or someone and discovered there was no emergency tonight. But he couldn't admit the truth – that he'd spent a thoroughly cold and miserable two hours sitting on Blaxton Hill, willing the appearance of a girl dead for four decades? No, transparent as the lie was, he knew she'd rather live with that than upset the uneasy truce they had. At least, until the mistruths became impossible to accept or ignore. But, he hoped to be done with it all long before that became a possibility.

He didn't really know why he had decided to go up the hill tonight. It felt like the right thing to do, like he was drawn to it. A couple of weeks down the road might have disguised it better, but that was the nature of impulse – the sudden inclination to act, without thought for the consequences, as the dictionary put it. And, because it was action without forethought, it allowed one to actually do that something before better sense prevailed.

So, he just went. Thought of what he might meet, what he might see and do were pushed aside, and so after work, he found himself parked up along the darkening back lane at Blaxton Hill.

After a half-hour or so, the traffic overspill from the rush hour that had to use this route subsided, and he could safely turn off the engine and his hazard lights. Leaving side-lights on, he sat there, waiting.

He had done it! It was like landing on the Moon, he thought with a dramatic flair. And, in a sense, he was on a journey of experience not dissimilar to that of those pioneer astronauts. Both were journeys into the unknown, both providing a feeling of extension of self, tethered to conventional reality only by the most tenuous of threads.

But, now, perhaps the Moon was better understood than the field in which he found himself becoming more deeply involved.

Captain Kirk tells us that Space is the Final Frontier. But really Death is the ultimate unknown, the absolutely final frontier. He supposed that it had its place in the natural order of things; 'useful' even, in the same way as fire – dangerous and yet servile – as a merciful end to pain and suffering, and a saviour of the living who were released back into life through its taking of a totally dependent relative.

But, in its awful generality, it was darkness itself, a black hole that sucked into its maw all life with a relentless and insatiable hunger, consuming ideas, and dreams, and potentials, crushing them into nothingness.

But, could the human spirit transcend the apparent finality of death, either going on to a new sphere of existence, or be somehow held back from the void to walk again with the living?

Could it be that the Blaxton Hill girl, Emily Reynolds, had been prevented from crossing over by her sudden and cruel demise, just hours before her wedding? What was she in search of – and why had she seemingly singled out him as the means of pursuing it?

Bridge over troubled water.

The thought occurred to him naturally, not at all forced, and he now believed he understood the purpose of this visit this evening, where it was leading. This girl had fallen into troubled waters. He was the only one who had heard her cries for help and he was obligated to do something about it. But she was drifting further and further downstream all the time, her cries growing ever more faint.

And yet he felt inadequate. No-one truly believed he had

seen and heard her, with the exception of Peter Pumfrys and Stephanie Caulson – two strangers – and even Pumfrys had offered alternative explanations.

Of course, he had his own doubts at times. And yet, he sensed that a real life was at stake here, perhaps until now not elucidated, but it had been there all along. He recognised it as a motivating factor in his dreams and in his voracious appetite for related reading material following his encounter. He was being asked to conduct a rescue mission of sorts, and he lacked the basic know-how and experience. Not that he could have been taught it exactly, but he needed more support than he was getting from friends and relations – probably the reason he had turned to Pumfrys so readily as someone who might guide him a little along the way. And yes, he felt he might be wading into his own troubled waters; there would be little understanding and sympathy ahead. Who would lay down the bridge for him?

He sat there until the coldness had seeped deeply into him. He came awake, and looked at the dashboard clock: 21:09. Time to go. Nothing had happened, not a whisper. Well, what had he expected, really? Still, he wouldn't make judgments on the basis of one visit. It wasn't even late. He had met the girl at around eleven, a couple of hours away yet. And, he reflected, a watched pot never boils.

He started the engine, and turned the driver's side directional air-vent towards him, blowing a warming stream of air into his face and hair. He had already decided not to mention any of this to Sally, at least for now.

FOURTEEN

Sally reached across the dining table, collecting a growing stack of plates and cutlery. Richard stood to help her, but she shooed him away. 'Go on. Go and sit down with the others. You'll only get in the way.' There was a relaxed air about her, worlds different from the quiet unemotional Sally that came home to last night. If it wasn't for this dinner party, a belated house-warming planned weeks ago, he wasn't sure she'd have come back before the weekend. As it was, little was said between them regarding recent events. Sally, for her part, preferred to concentrate on the final arrangements for the party, which included a shopping list of last-minute items. Playing his part, Richard had helped to clear up, to rearrange the living room furniture, and otherwise act and communicate in the carefree, easy manner of one half of an ordinary, contented couple.

And this evening, so far, had gone very well. The group of friends here really were the best. With the exception of Craig Mountford, they were the regular gang, who tended to meet up every few weeks or so, usually on a Friday evening, at their favourite pub. But there hadn't been a meeting with everyone present for some time – months – since the meeting immediately after Richard's encounter had featured in the newspaper.

Again, with the exception of Craig, they were all couples. Even Gary, to whom concession had been made with regard to Craig as a friend who had accompanied him to an occasional pub meet, had found himself a girlfriend in the meantime, Chantelle. Consequently, while the invitation to Craig would not have been revoked, no-one had really expected him to turn up.

The conversation, before and during dinner, had been light and fun, refreshingly free of any mention of the ghost, much to Richard's (and, he could tell, Sally's) relief. That, coupled with the fact that Sally had really surpassed herself with the cooking and layout, no wonder she seemed to be full of beans. While the girls took over in helping clear the table, retiring to the kitchen together ('for a bit of a girls' natter,' said Jennifer), he and 'the boys' settled into the living room around the television, which Richard flicked on, sound low, to a Sky Sports channel while they waited for the girls to return.

Presently, Terry got up and headed upstairs to the toilet. Watching him go, then looking round to see both Gary and Craig engrossed in the TV, Tom turned back to him.

'How are things going, then, Richard?'

'Yes, Okay, Tom.'

It was the first time Richard had seen Tom since the night they were due to go bowling. As Sally's friend Jennifer's boyfriend, he didn't have as much contact with Richard as Terry and Gary, who worked with him and therefore saw him on an almost daily basis. It should, then, have come as no surprise that Tom should be curious, especially after the state Richard had been in when he last saw him.

'I mean, about the ghost thing,' he said quietly. 'Anything else happened since?'

'Yeah, I know what you meant, Tom. No, nothing. Nothing of interest,' he added, diminishing the lie. He looked around at the kitchen door, which stood slightly ajar. Laughter emanated from there. He looked back, then over to Craig and Gary, sitting nearby, then back to Tom again.

'Look, Tom,' he said a little defensively, 'can we drop it, at least for tonight? I don't want Sally hearing me talk about it.

There's really not much to add. Maybe I'll tell you some other time.'

'Okay. I was only curious. And, you know, after last time, a bit concerned, that's all.'

'Yeah, sure. Thanks, Tom.'

'What last time is this?' said a voice behind them. Shit. Terry.

Richard looked up. 'Hm?'

'Tom just said something about last time. What's that? Seen your ghost again, Rich?'

'No. No. We were talking about something else.'

Terry stooped to retrieve his glass and slumped into the armchair opposite, sensing Richard's unease. 'You hiding something from us, Richie?' He had an annoying habit of referring to Richard as 'Richie' when he sensed a bite.

'What are you talking about?'

'You are. I can tell,' he said. 'C'mon, you can tell me.'

'Look, Tom was just asking me about the book I was reading last time. Right, Tom?'

'That's right,' he agreed.

'Oh,' said Terry. 'Give us a run-down, then.'

Richard was beginning to feel impatient. And a little angry. 'You wouldn't be interested.'

'Of course I would.'

'No, you're just looking to take the piss again. So, forget it, eh?'

Terry smiled. 'I'm not, honestly. Besides, you were telling Tom anyway, weren't you?'

'I...' Richard cut off as, peripherally, he saw the kitchen door open, and the girls coming back into the room, brandishing two metal trays bearing coffee and biscuits, which Jennifer and Alice set down on the coffee table. Sally, following up behind, noticed the television was on. 'Turn that off, Gary. We're going to play Trivial Pursuit.'

'Hold on, Sally,' said Terry. 'Richard was just about to update us on his ghost.'

Sally stopped in her tracks. She glanced at Richard, and he could immediately see the disappointment, the hurt, in her eyes. She looked suddenly deflated. After a moment that to Richard seemed like an eternity she said simply, 'Was he now?'

But despite her intention to sound as matter-of-fact as possible, she hadn't been able to disguise her true feelings, the tone of her voice in distinct contrast to a few moments before, which was lost on none of their friends.

Terry, inquisitiveness in his eyes, looked expectantly from Sally to Richard, then back again. Her face showed the same disquiet – or was it fear? – that he had sensed in Richard's reaction.

Richard's jaw dropped open, as if to speak, but the words failed to appear.

Finally, Tom spoke into the awkward silence. 'Sorry, Sally. It's my fault. I er… I brought it up.'

Sally looked at him, but said nothing.

The newest face, Chantelle, looked on with interest. 'What ghost is this?' she asked innocently, if not tactfully. 'I love that stuff.'

'Ask Richard,' said Sally coldly, before turning and heading for the stairs.

'Where are you going?' Richard called after her.

'Going to look for the game,' she said without looking back.

Jennifer hesitated for a moment, then followed her.

Richard stood up. 'Thanks a lot, Terry,' he said shortly, and went after Sally.

2

'Sally,' called Richard, looking past Jennifer. 'Sally, wait.' She paused on the stairs.

'Um, I'll just wait in the kitchen,' said Jennifer. 'Give you two a minute'.

'Oh, Okay, Jen. Thanks,' said Sally.

Jennifer stepped back and Richard stepped past her to follow Sally up the stairs.

In their bedroom, Sally flicked the light on and moved to the built-in wardrobe and opened one door. She didn't look his way.

'Sally, don't be like this. I didn't bring it up. What Tom said is true. It was Terry. Again.'

She turned to face him. 'Neither of you seem to be able to let it go.'

Richard frowned. 'What's that mean?'

Sally didn't reply. Instead she turned and reached in to the top shelf space of the wardrobe to retrieve the game.

'I can't control what other people might say.'

She turned back and took a deep breath. 'I know,' she sighed. 'We're only in control our own actions, aren't we?'

It was Richard's time to fall silent.

'We've left our guests unattended,' said Sally. 'Go down... tell them what they want to hear, if you need to, and let's get on with our evening.'

'You're coming back down, though?'

'Soon. Take this.' She handed Richard the Trivial Pursuit box. He took it and headed back down.

The atmosphere in the living room was quiet, a little tense.

'Okay, everyone.' He pushed the game onto the corner of the coffee table. 'Can someone clear some space?'

Alice, seated next to Tom, whispered, 'Is everything alright?'

Richard nodded.

'She coming down?' asked Alice, mouthing the words rather than speaking them.

'Shortly', replied Richard. He took a seat. 'Right, first, let's get this out of the way.'

He turned to Terry first, who, this time, paid sober attention. 'No, I haven't seen anything else. I've had some dreams, nightmares, that's all.' He stole a glance at Tom that he hoped Terry wouldn't notice. Then he turned his attention to Chantelle. 'The others have heard this, so it's only fair that you should too – if Gary hasn't told you already.'

Gary shook his head.

'But afterwards,' he said, looking around, 'do you mind if we drop the subject, at least for tonight?'

Back to Chantelle. 'It's about Blaxton Hill. A few weeks ago.'

Chantelle's expression flickered with recognition. 'Oh, that was *you*? I read about it in the *Courier*.' She looked at Craig, aware that he wasn't one of the core group of friends, who was watching the television, sound turned down. 'Have you heard this?'

'Yep,' he said without taking his eyes off the screen. 'I don't believe in that stuff.'

'*Craig*,' said Alice.

It's alright Alice,' said Richard. 'It's hard for anyone who hasn't experienced it to believe it. I can hardly believe it myself, so I don't expect anyone else to. Including you guys.

'Okay, final time, then,' he said.

3

Sally stayed in the bedroom, holding back while Richard told his ghost story. She went to the window and closed the curtains. When she turned back, she saw that Richard had left some clothes on the floor on his side of the bed, a crumpled shirt and some socks. She didn't know how many times she had to tell him – one of the things you only learned about one another once you live together. She stepped over to pick them up, when her attention was diverted to his bedside cabinet. The bottom drawer wasn't completely pushed in. Something was stopping it. She pulled the draw open, revealing the corner of a book cover, then the rest of it.

The cover picture struck her first: a gaunt female figure; fair hair, dressed in white, standing on the roadside, glowing in the glare of a car's headlights. The title, in bold white letters surrounded by a subtle blue haze, hovered above the figure:

ROAD GHOSTS
From Resurrection Mary to the phantom bus of North Kensington.
Strange encounters on our highways and byways

She glanced at the door before picking the book out. She turned it over, then opened it and started to flick through it. A scrap of paper fell out at page 134. On it were a few crude scribbles in Richard's handwriting. The numbers 22, 63, 83 appeared to be page numbers. The notes, at least those she could make out, were quite meaningless to her: B & H folk, time slips, fpps. None of them made any immediate sense.

She started to put the book back, but hesitated. There were a few other books – paperbacks – in the back of the drawer. And a smaller book, black cover, thin, with a faux leather finish.

A diary.

She stared at it for a moment, a flurry of thoughts crossing her mind. For one, she felt wrong somehow, just in finding Richard's notes, as if it were an invasion of privacy, of sorts. Or was her disquiet due to the discovery of something that could destroy the fragile understanding they had at this point?

She opened the diary and thumbed through it. More notes. A few related to personal events – the date of his M.O.T.; his younger brother's birthday; their moving-in date. But most of the recent entries were related to Blaxton Hill: summary notes of his meetings with Peter Pumfrys; his trip to the library; notes on Stephanie Caulson; and… just yesterday: *Blaxton Hill – Day One, 7:30 p.m. – 9:10. p.m. Impressions: zilch.*

Sally felt her heart thud. She fought back conflicting impulses – to cry, to shout. Her hands shook as she replaced the diary and the books back in the drawer and closed it. She sat on the edge of the bed and dropped her head into her hands.

4

'And that's it, really,' said Richard as he finished his story.

'That's amazing,' commented Chantelle. 'I've heard of the ghost, but never met anyone who's actually seen it.'

'You still haven't,' chuckled Craig.

Richard smarted. 'And how would *you* know, Craig? What makes you the expert?'

Craig shrugged. 'I'm not. Just there's no such thing, that's all. When you're dead, you're dead. The rest is all bollocks. That's what I think, anyway.'

'Ignore him, Rich,' said Gary. 'He's a few over the top.'

Richard stared at him for a moment.

'And the nightmares?' asked Chantelle.

'Just dreams,' replied Richard distractedly. He glanced at the stairs. He thought he heard movement there. He looked back at Chantelle. 'Replays, really. I'm not sure they mean anything.'

'They might,' replied Chantelle. 'They can come in your dreams as well, you know.'

Richard's nostrils flared.

'Yes. It happened to my mum, when she was young. There was something in their house. They all saw it, some sort of brown haze. They all had nightmares too. It wanted them to leave. Perhaps yours is trying to tell you something?'

Richard was momentarily speechless.

'Have you been up there since?' asked Chantelle.

'Er, no, I haven't.' A lie.

As he said it, Richard noticed Sally on the stairs. Her eyes looked red. 'Why don't you tell everyone the rest of it?' she said.

Richard was confused. 'What?'

'Oh, about what Stephanie Caulson told you? About what you saw in your van the night we were supposed to go bowling? What you *didn't* see last night?'

The others fell quiet. Even Craig and Gary took their eyes off the TV.

'What are you doing, Sally? Why are you carrying this on?'

'Because you *are*, Richard!'

She came down the remainder of the stairs and went into the kitchen. Jennifer and Alice followed her out.

Terry waited for the kitchen door to close. Then he said, 'Are we still playing Trivial Pursuit?'

Craig laughed.

'Give it a rest, Terry,' said Richard. He slumped into an armchair.

'What was all that about?' asked Gary.

Richard shrugged. 'Wrong again, clearly.'

Chantelle, sitting next to Gary, said, 'Stephanie Caulson – the psychic medium?'

'Yes,' said Richard.

'You had a reading with her?'

'Not exactly,' replied Richard.

'But she gave you some information about Blaxton Hill?'

Richard exhaled and nodded languidly.

'She's supposed to be good. What did she say?'

Richard looked at Chantelle, then at Gary. 'I'm not sure I want to talk about it right now.'

Tom spoke for the first time in a while. 'It might help,' he suggested. 'A trouble shared is a trouble halved, and all that?'

Richard glanced at the kitchen door. It remained closed.

'Hm. Actually, it was Sally who was having a reading –at a friend's house. I'd just gone to pick up her. When I walked in, she – Stephanie – asked if anyone knew an Emily. Then she told me that she was asking for me.'

Chantelle squirmed in her seat. 'You see! She *is* trying to tell you something. Was there anything else?'

Richard hesitated. 'No, nothing. The connection was lost.'

Tom glanced at him.

Chantelle's face was alive with interest. 'We should go up there! Tonight.'

'Don't be daft,' said Gary. 'It's getting late. I'm not traipsing around somewhere in the dark. Besides, you saw how Sally was about it.'

'But if she is reaching out to Richard, it must be for a reason. Perhaps she needs help. Sometimes spirits don't realise they're dead and are just calling out for help like anyone else.'

It was a thought, of course, that had occurred to Richard. In fact, it was spot on, the same conclusion he'd come to himself.

'Perhaps we can help?' continued Chantelle.

Instead, Richard heard himself say, 'Look, if you want to go up there, feel free. I'd be happy to show you where it happened another time. But not tonight.'

It was Terry's turn. 'Rich, can I ask you a question?'

'Sure'.

'You don't have to answer this, but were you up there last night?'

Richard wrinkled an eyebrow. 'Why'd you say that?'

'Something Sally said.'

'You noticed that?'

'Yeah. And... she rang me last night asking if you were with me.'

'Thought she might,' replied Richard. 'What did you tell her?'

'The truth – I hadn't seen you since knock-off time. Anyway, all I wanted to say is: when I rib you about the ghost thing, you know I don't really mean it?'

'I know, Tel.'

'I don't know if they're real or not. But, as a mate, I can say you have gone a bit weird over it all lately.'

Despite himself, Richard laughed. 'Thanks... *mate*.'

'Anyway, so you don't get into any more trouble, let me know what you're up to next time – not so I can lie for you, but so someone knows where you are. I might even come with you sometime.'

Richard nodded slowly. 'Thank you.'

'That's it,' added Tom. 'At least if someone else saw it – her – as well, you'd know it wasn't all in your head?'

It was true. It's what he wanted, wasn't it – some independent corroboration?

'The last two times you've been up there, you've seen her,' said Chantelle. 'There may be no better time.'

Richard said nothing, but his eyes betrayed the thoughts

that fluttered behind them. Finally he said, 'Not last night. Anyway, who would go – *if* I agreed to go, that is,' he added hastily.

Chantelle glanced at Gary. 'Um, we would, wouldn't we? It's on our way home anyway?'

Gary looked at Richard, then to Chantelle and Craig. 'We could stop off for a bit, if it's not too late... and if Craig's up to it.'

Gary had given Craig a lift there, and was to drop him off home later.

Craig looked over. 'Better than sitting here listening to this.'

5

'Shouldn't we be going back in?' suggested Alice. 'They'll be thinking we've disappeared over the garden fence.'

They had been in the kitchen, just talking, for thirty minutes now.

Sally nodded. She dabbed the corner of her eye with a knuckle. 'Thank you both. It's been good to talk.'

'Sure,' said Jennifer.

Jennifer in particular had been able to provide Sally with some perspective on her situation – that both she and Richard were trying to deal with it as best they could. Sally was reacting instinctively out of fear. She couldn't accept that Richard's sighting was supernatural; that somehow it was symptomatic of his drinking and Sally was expressing her concerns over that – and, possibly, a deeper fear that he was on the brink of delusion or suffering from an uncommon mental affliction. Richard's second claimed sighting hadn't involved alcohol, which deepened that fear.

On reflection, the preferred option, ironically, would be that he had seen a ghost.

So, what if Richard really had encountered something supernatural? How would he feel, especially if it kept happening? Frightened, of course. But bewildered, his worldview shattered. How would he feel if no-one believed him; if the closest person to him also couldn't understand what he was experiencing? It might make him secretive; send him to elsewhere for understanding and support. He may need some time to work through it.

And so she and Richard had found themselves in their own little bubbles, carefully revolving around one another. If they didn't make an attempt at some common understanding, it could begin to spiral out of control.

6

The kitchen door opened and Alice led the way out, Sally sandwiched between her and Jennifer. Richard looked past Alice to gauge how Sally was. She met his gaze, looking a little sheepish. Richard stood and, once Alice had stepped past, he moved to her and they embraced.

'I'm sorry,' they said in unison, and smiled at one another at the coincidence.

Seated behind them, Tom caught Jennifer's eye and nodded. Good job.

Alice checked around the room. 'Anyone for coffee, tea?'

'Got another beer?' asked Craig.

'I'll get you one,' Alice replied. 'Anyone else?'

Sally moved to the table and picked up the Trivial Pursuit. 'Are we still playing this?'

The question was met with a few blank looks.

'Um… ' began Chantelle.

'It's okay. We don't have to,' said Sally.

Chantelle let the moment pass.

'Yes, come on,' said Tom, rising from his seat. 'One game, anyway.' He winked at Sally and shuffled over to help set it up. He looked around, finding Alice. 'I'll have a coffee, if that's alright? No sugar.'

'Great,' said Sally, visibly relaxing. As everyone (except Craig) dragged themselves around the coffee table, Sally thought perhaps they might still pull together the frayed strands of the evening.

7

'Well done, Rich.'

Richard sat back. 'What can I say?' he said.

'He's played this before,' said Terry, pushing himself back into his seat.

'A couple of times', conceded Richard.

'I meant you know all the answers,' said Terry, deadpan.

'Ha, ha,' Richard replied flatly.

Sally glanced up at the clock, raising an eyebrow in mild surprise at the time. Jennifer's eyes followed her. 10:40 p.m. That had come around quickly.

'Does anyone want another drink?' asked Sally. 'There are still some snacks left in the kitchen.'

Everyone shook their heads. It was clear that that moment had arrived, when everyone has fallen quiet, the conversation replaced by restless shuffling and stifled yawns. The unspoken acknowledgement of the end of the evening.

'Thanks,' said Jennifer, 'but I think we'd better be off shortly.' She looked at Tom, who nodded.

'Us too,' said Gary, stirring from his seat. 'You two ready?', addressing Chantelle and Craig.

'We still stopping off for your ghost hunt on the way back?' It was Craig.

But Chantelle chimed in as well. 'What do you think, Richard?'

Sally bit her lip. She glanced at Richard, who suddenly looked defensive.

'I didn't say I'd go,' he said. 'Nothing to stop you going, though.'

'You did,' belched Craig.

'Craig, I didn't. I –'

'Yeah, you did. You wanted to know who else was going.'

Richard's jaw clenched. Gary glanced between Craig and Richard and Sally, who hadn't said anything as yet.

'I know it's late now, Rich,' said Gary, stepping in front of Craig. 'But you did sort of give the impression you were willing to take a run up there.'

'Well, I didn't mean to,' said Richard.

There was that awkward silence again. The girls remained quiet. Jennifer and Alice stood there, coats draped over arms. Sally began to collect up the cups, but kept looking up with a nervous eye.

Chantelle looked at Sally. 'Um, we were just musing earlier that if we went up there with Richard, and we saw something too, it would prove that he didn't imagine it all. Just an idea,' she added into the silence.

'Or, he just got spooked by a road-sign or a stray punter from the pub,' snorted Craig.

Richard gave Craig a hard look. 'It was just an idea,' he said, looking at Sally, who stood with cups and plates in hand. 'But it's too late,' he said to the others. 'We all have things to do tomorrow.'

'Wuss,' said Craig under his breath.

Richard rounded on him, taking an unconscious step towards him. 'What's your *problem*, Craig?' He stood there, silently fuming. He had a dark stare at these times. If he could have seen himself, he might have thought the whole situation ludicrous: two people, one drunk, surrounded by five others, facing up over – wait for it – the existence of ghosts, or at least, one particular spook.

'Leave it, Rich,' said Gary. 'You can see he's pissed.' He turned to Craig and said through his teeth, 'What are you up to?'

Craig shrugged, blinking over glassy eyes.

Richard stepped back. Put it down to the hour, or the fact that by now he took the subject very personally. Until now, he had been able to brush off the occasional jibe, but tonight was the proverbial last straw. Or was it just that Craig was one of those people who unfailingly push your buttons, without even trying very hard?

'That's no excuse, Gary,' said Alice. 'I know he's your friend, but he's never really fitted in, has he?'

Terry placed a hand on Alice's arm, as if to say 'don't make it worse'. 'Just get him home, Gaz,' he said. 'We're all going now anyway.'

'It's always about that freakin' ghost lately,' protested Craig, 'which we're supposed to just accept like it's real or something. I just tell it the way it is, that's all.'

'Hey ... ' started Richard.

'Ah.' Craig swiped the air dismissively.

'For heaven's sake, just go, if it will save arguing!' exclaimed Sally.

Richard stared at her. She felt his eyes on her and met them with her own. 'Yes, I know. But you need to get this out of your system. If this will help, then do it.' Perhaps if he were up there with others, it might prove cathartic.

Then, an afterthought: 'You haven't had a drink, have you?' she added quickly.

'No... well, one bottle of beer earlier. I'm okay.'

It was Ladies' night, their turn to have a drink if they wished; the men's turn to drive. Richard, even though he was home, hadn't felt in the mood to drink this evening.

Sally forced a taut smile. 'Alright. But don't do anything silly.' She had almost added 'like last time'. She turned to Tom. 'Tom, you're going?'

'Er... yes, okay,' he replied. He looked at Jennifer.

'Is that alright, Jennifer?' asked Sally. 'Would you stay?'

Jennifer nodded. 'Of course. If they're not too long.' She could hardly refuse after encouraging Sally to give Richard the room to work it out in his own way.

'Okay,' said Richard. 'Who's coming?' He looked at Chantelle, then at Gary, who, seeing Chantelle's enthusiastic nods, shrugged his agreement.

Richard pointed at Craig. 'And you are coming.' It wasn't a question. Not that he had much of a choice if Gary and Chantelle were going.

'We won't. We're going to have to push off, mate,' said Terry. 'But you be careful.'

'Are you really going to go?' Alice asked timidly. 'Just for him?' she said, indicating Craig. Craig returned her glance icily.

'No, not just for him,' replied Richard. now quite awake. 'But we'll do our best not to disappoint.'

FIFTEEN

The five of them could have all squeezed into one of the cars, but if they were to park and try to replicate what Richard had tried last time, they would need the back seats to be empty. Richard drove, with Tom as his passenger. Gary took his car, with Chantelle and Craig.

The plan was simply to have a look around, particularly at the spot Richard had picked up the girl. And maybe, afterwards, to do a couple of drive-by circuits of the location. It would be the first time he had ventured outside his car on that stretch of the hill since the night he had fled from there as fast as he could. At least on this trip he would have some company.

But on the approach to the darkened lane, Richard felt some of the bravado melting away. He was glad he was here, though, for the chance to test things from within the protective shell of company. But if he were alone at this hour, he wasn't sure he would be able to handle it. There was something different than the previous night. Perhaps it was merely due to the later hour. The Bull had closed, its lights dimmed; just one car in the car park, idling, readying to go. But there was something else tonight about the darkness that chipped away at this resolve; a faint charge of something else.

The cars pulled up one behind the other on the verge a short distance up from the crossroads. In the lead car, Richard extinguished the headlights, leaving the sidelights on. The shrubbery and grass along the verge lost their bright hue, fading to grey.

Leaving the engine idling, he nodded to Tom to get out.

Tom undid his seat belt and opened the passenger door. Dank air poured into the car, washing over them, carrying with it the somewhat fetid smell of damp undergrowth.

Richard's stomach churned. The dark was a blank slate upon which the imagination sketched all kinds of fears, or made previous experiences suddenly more vital again, covering the bare bones of memory with new flesh.

He tried to push thought aside as he got out of the car and eased the door to, careful to not let it clunk shut. No unnecessary noise. There were a few isolated houses perched on ledges about the hill. Even the noise of traffic on the nearby dual carriageway had fallen at this hour to an occasional hum. Sound would carry well in the late night stillness.

He breathed deeply, then watched the exhaled air curl away and up, dissipating into the night. The atmosphere of the place was intact, he thought. But somehow not so vital. It had lost something. Perhaps it was because he was with company this time. Or was it that any aura he sensed might be due simply to the evening's discourse, and the vagaries of a tired mind?

Whatever the reason, he felt able to function. They walked over to the other car, where Gary and the others were getting out. Gary held a torch.

He noticed that Gary had turned his engine off; the only sound was the mumbling purr of his own car's engine behind him. He realised now that leaving the engine running had been a mistake. The sound it produced was unnecessary. He glanced back. What had he left it on for? A quick flight, if need be?

Gary swept the beam up the lane, picking out the hedgerows on either side.

'Keep it down,' said Richard. 'There are houses round about.'

Gary lowered the beam to their feet. 'Well, what are we going to do?'

Tom was staring up the lane, not that he could see anything of significance in the gloom, only the bend to the right, just picked out as a shade of dirty grey on black. 'Up there,' he said, nodding in that direction. 'It was up there, wasn't it, Rich? Your crash?'

Richard glanced up the lane. 'Yeah, just around the bend.'

'Someone is,' chuckled Craig.

'Well,' said Tom, ignoring Craig's comment, 'Shall we start by taking a walk up there?'

'No,' said Chantelle. 'Oughtn't we go down to the crossroads? I mean, that's where the original accident happened.'

'I can't see the point in doing either, really,' said Richard. 'Right where we're standing – right here,' he said, 'is where I first saw the girl.'

He shuddered, he hoped, imperceptibly. 'I picked her up here, and pulled away. Then ... '

His words trailed off. He looked up the lane, which was dimly lit by the rusty glow of Eldonbridge behind them. The others followed his gaze. It was odd how one's estimates of time and distance could be so far out. He could've sworn that, on that night, he had driven much farther and for much longer before she vanished.

'You okay, Rich?' someone asked. 'What do you see?' came another question, more measured.

'Oh, nothing,' he replied. He detected the defensiveness in his voice, and immediately softened the tone. 'I was just thinking.'

Here, right at the scene of it all, his friends could be forgiven for thinking that he might be the key to any novel experience that might unfold. He decided to file away the train of thought that had caused his falter until later, when he could consider it more carefully. It nagged at him, though. How could he possibly trust his recall of the experience if parts of it were so distorted? It was obvious now that he hadn't got so far as he thought. The bend in the road was the most striking feature of the lane, where it bent and began to level out at the same point. It was barely two hundred yards ahead. Barely enough distance to have had the length of conversation with the girl that he remembered.

He shook his head gently. He was aware that all eyes were on him again. 'C'mon,' he said, starting off. 'Let's go and have a look.'

He stopped at his car, retrieving his key and killing the side lights. Twin pulses of amber light lit up the hedgerows as he locked it with his key fob.

They walked up to the bend together in a little oasis of torch light, the sound of their footfalls on the asphalt path loud in the quiet night air.

'Is this it?' asked Chantelle.

'Yes,' said Richard.

He became aware that Craig wasn't with them. Then he spotted him down the lane a bit, a shadow that had merged with the dark foliage, where evidently he had stopped to relieve himself.

'Er, yeah. I'd just turned into the bend, when I noticed she had fallen quiet. I turned to check on her...' He shuddered involuntarily. It was surreal being here again, at this exact spot. '... and she was gone. And I hit the kerb...'

A pin-prick of white light appeared at the foot of the lane, distracting them. It started up the lane towards them, the intensifying glare of the car's headlights picking out Craig's outline as he rejoined them. The group unconsciously bunched together as it approached. Through the glare they could make out one driver, a man, who slowed the car perceptibly as his headlights illuminated the group. He was craning his head forward, in effort to see them better. Once he had identified the grey mass for what it was, his engine burred as he changed down in gear, and accelerated past them. Richard's mouth shaped itself into a bemused expression at the driver's reaction – one of surprise, then evidently of relief as he passed them.

Richard walked up the lane a little further. 'I hit the kerb about here.' Gary shone the torch at the spot. 'And I ended up over there,' he said, pointing to a black smudge that ran alongside the opposite verge.

They walked on a little further, to where a break in the hedgerows afforded a view of the countryside below, which spread out like a great undulating sheet of black velvet studded with twinkling tiny jewels of amber and white.

Through the dark silhouette of trees at the foot of their view, the studded orange trail of lights of the dual carriageway snaked down the hillside towards Eldonbridge.

They stood there for a while, the breeze picking up and ruffling their clothes, bringing a chill as it carried away the dampness of the night. There wasn't much more to say. Or do.

At last, someone spoke up. It was Gary. 'What do we do now?'

Beside him, Craig yawned.

'No point in staying here getting cold. Shall we?' said Richard.

No-one disagreed. It was all rather anti-climatic. Silently, they made their way back down the hill.

'Are we still going to do the drive around?' asked Chantelle.

'You still wanna do that?' asked Gary. 'It's getting late now.'

'We said we wouldn't be out too long,' said Tom. 'It's… ' He checked his watch. '… eleven thirty.'

'We haven't been here very long. Just a couple of loops, then we just drive on home like we agreed,' suggested Chantelle. 'We've got to go up the hill anyway.'

Gary shrugged. 'I'm easy. Up to Richard.'

'Tom?' said Richard.

'You're the driver,' replied Tom.

It was true. They hadn't been here for very long. Twenty more minutes wouldn't make much difference.

'Okay,' said Richard. 'A couple of circuits. Up to the Frickley roundabout at the top, then back down the dual carriageway; off at the slip to The Bull and back here. Repeat, then stop.'

'Alright,' said Gary. 'Let's go.'

'Wait,' said Richard. He pointed at Craig. 'You're coming with me.'

'Me?'

'Yeah. You're not afraid?'

'No.'

'Good.' Richard turned to Tom. 'If you go with Gary, we'll swap back afterwards.'

'Okay … ' replied Tom. He looked puzzled but went along with it. He followed Gary and Chantelle to their car. Craig walked around Richard's car and got in.

'Are they going to be alright together?' asked Chantelle.

Gary unlocked his car. 'Yeah. Richard probably has something in mind to put the wind up Craig a bit. They'll be alright.'

2

Richard pulled away ahead of Gary. He drove slowly up the lane, giving Gary time to get started up and follow, but by the time they rounded the bend near the top, there was no sign of following headlights. Richard eased off the accelerator and changed down into second gear, looking into his rearview mirror.

'Where is he?' he said aloud. He brought the car to a stop. 'Get out will you, Craig, and trot back and take a look?'

Craig looked at him suspiciously. 'What?'

'I said run back and see where the others are.'

'Why? Just carry on. We've only just left them. They'll be coming.'

'Because there's something wrong. I can feel it.'

''I'm not getting out,' said Craig. 'Just reverse back.'

Richard's voice showed some irritation. 'This shitbox doesn't have a reversing light at the moment. I'll probably ditch it if I try.'

Craig realised he was being backed into a corner. He suddenly decided that this was a set-up, designed by Richard and involving the others, to get back at him for his behaviour earlier. Why else had Richard insisted he ride with him? In any case, he wasn't about to get out of the car and walk down in the dark alone, if only for a hundred yards or so.

'*Please* Craig,' said Richard. 'I'm not going to drive off, if that's what you think?'

But it made no difference.

'Just go around,' said Craig.

Richard was about to answer him when, in his mirror, he detected a greyness forming in the dark. It intensified, and flared through the hedgerows on the bend of the lane. A car. At last.

He put the car back in gear, and pulled away, trying to gain speed before Gary rounded the bend and ran into them. As Richard made third gear, the glaring headlights of the following car were joined by the orange flashing light of its indicator as it pulled around them and sped past, leaving him with the streaky red afterglow from its tail-lights to go with the patchy green reaction of the headlight glare on his retinas.

'That wasn't Gary,' said Craig, voicing the obvious.

Richard didn't reply. He slipped the car into fourth, and increased speed along the final stretch of the lane towards the roundabout interchange.

3

Gary tried again, turning the key and pumping the accelerator. 'It's just not catching.' The starter motor whirred lazily.

'Watch you don't flood the engine,' remarked Tom.

'I know,' said Gary. He gave up momentarily, giving the steering-wheel a clump with the heel of his hand. 'I don't know what's wrong with it! It hasn't done this before ... '

'Flip the hood,' said Tom, undoing his seat belt. 'Let's have a look at the engine.'

Gary started to protest. 'There can't be anything wrong.'

'Let's take a look anyway,' replied Tom.

Gary sighed resignedly and reached for the bonnet release. The front of bonnet popped up with a dull clunk.

'Where's your torch?' asked Tom.

Gary found it and handed it to him. Tom got out and went around to the front of the car. He fixed the bonnet up and Gary and Chantelle watched the light from the torch play back and forth beneath it. After a few seconds, Tom appeared beside the driver's side and tapped on the window. Gary wound it down. 'Keep turning it over,' said Tom, and then he disappeared behind the bonnet again. Gary continued to turn the key. The starter stuttered, slowing with every second. Then, as he was about to give up again, it caught, and the engine roared into life.

'Yes!' said Gary. 'Well done, Tom.'

The torchlight dimmed, as it moved away. It sprung up again by the open window. Tom stood there. He held out his hands and shrugged.

'Well done,' repeated Gary. 'What did you do?'

'I didn't do anything,' replied Tom. 'I wasn't touching anything when it fired up. There's nothing wrong with it as far as I can see. Well, whatever it was, it's okay now,' said Tom.

'I'll get it checked out later,' said Gary. 'Let's get out of here.'

4

By the time Gary and the others reached the roundabout at the top of the hill, Richard and Craig were well on their way back down. They took the first slip road off to Valence lane and turned left and then left again opposite The Bull back onto Old Haltham Road. The road was dark and empty. Too late. Gary had evidently managed to get away after all.

'Okay,' said Richard. 'We'll wait here for a few minutes. If they saw us turning off, they'll follow.'

'I reckon they've gone on to your house.'

'No, they won't,' said Richard. 'They know we were going to do a couple of circuits. Give them a call. Tell them we're here.' He stifled a yawn.

Craig patted his trouser pocket. 'My phone. I think I left it in Gary's car.'

Richard reached into a pocket and retrieved his. He unlocked it and handed it to Craig. Richard moved the car closer in to the kerb while Craig dialed.

The phone bleeped. 'No signal', reported Craig.

Richard frowned. 'Give it here.' He selected Gary's number and pressed the call button. The phone showed the same message. He tried Tom's number. Same there. 'That's odd.' He'd never tried calling from this location, but there was no reason he should have any trouble. The signal strength on the display showed medium.

'Head up the road a bit,' suggested Craig. 'You might get a better signal.'

Richard shook his head. He placed the phone on the dashboard and sat back. 'They should be here soon. Let's give them a few minutes.'

5

'Shit. Not again. I don't believe it!' remarked Gary as the engine first faltered, then cut out. The car coasted into the top of the slip lane off the dual carriageway.

'Pull it in,' said Tom. 'Let's have another look. Must be a loose lead or something.'

'You didn't find anything before,' said Gary.

'The light is better here,' replied Tom, knowing that the torchlight earlier had been sufficient to make a thorough check. And yes, there hadn't been anything obviously wrong. 'Let's take a closer look. Do you have any jump leads?'

'No.'

'Maybe Richard does. If he saw we moved off, he might have gone around again? He can't be far behind us,' said Chantelle.

'Go up and see if you can see them,' suggested Gary. They were around eighty yards from the entrance to the slip road. The road there was lit by the carriageway lights. 'Here,' said Gary. 'Try calling him.'

6

Richard shifted in his seat. He shuddered perceptibly.

'What is it?' asked Craig.

'Probably nothing,' answered Richard. 'But I still feel there's something wrong.'

'Don't start that again.'

The hairs on the nape of Richard's neck bristled. The purring engine faltered momentarily as if its heart had skipped a beat, and the headlights dimmed noticeably before flaring back into life.

Richard looked at Craig. In the reflected light, he could see that Craig also felt it, a feeling of building electricity. His eyes showed a little more white than usual.

Richard wondered if Craig could also feel the dull ache that had begun to work its way up his spine. It had started at the same instant as the engine falter, but continued to grow even when the engine had corrected itself. It felt like cold fluid had been injected into his spinal canal, and was creeping up his back.

Something was beginning to happen.

'Let's get out of here,' said Craig nervously.

Richard seemed not to have heard him.

Craig started to panic. It showed in his voice. He pushed Richard on the arm. 'I said, let's get out of here!'

But Richard didn't respond. Instead, his eyes darted to the rearview mirror. Craig saw his expression change from puzzlement to surprise. The engine began to splutter again, before cutting out altogether. Only the rusty glow of Eldonbridge behind them and the spilled light from the dual carriageway below kept them from total darkness.

Then Craig noticed another source of light. It came from behind them. Richard's transfixed eyes were illuminated by a horizontal bar of reflected cool grey light. He froze. He knew there was someone else in the car with them.

The atmosphere in the car was charged with electricity. It wasn't his imagination, and he was suddenly quite sober and completely petrified. And it was *cold*. As he exhaled – hyperventilated – he could see his breath frosting the windscreen before him.

His rationale dissolved in his fear. His instinct was to flee, but his legs felt like warm jelly.

There was a sound like material stirring behind him. He shuddered, and with shaking hands, he managed to find the door handle and pushed the door open. He tried to launch himself out, but something tightened around his neck and he was pulled back into his seat. He yelped before realising what it was. Without thought for Richard, and blocking further thought from his mind, he fumbled desperately for the seat belt's clasp. The car door swung back to.

He tried not to look to either side for fear his peripheral vision might catch something he'd rather not acknowledge. With a trembling hand, he depressed the red plastic button on the clasp and the belt loosened. He threw it across his chest and its metal flange cracked against the window.

He came out of the car so fast he pivoted off balance. As he steadied himself, he stole a glance at the rear seat of the car. There was a shadowy form there; not very distinct, but vaguely human in shape. It gave off a smoky blue light.

'Richard?' he burbled. Then his nerve broke, and he found himself stumbling down the road to the crossroads.

'Dammit,' he said to himself. He'd left Richard's mobile on the dashboard. But no way was he going back there. He looked back. The car appeared abandoned. The front passenger door stood agape. All was dark and still.

7

Chantelle came back to the car.

'Anything?' asked Gary.

'It rang, but then went to messages. I left one to say to call back.'

'And you didn't see them coming down the road?'

'Oh, yes, and I waved at them as they flew past,' replied Chantelle sarcastically. 'How's it going?'

Tom sighed. He lifted his head clear of the bonnet. 'Nothing. Again. It all looks fine – leads, battery, everything. I don't know what's wrong with it. Perhaps we can bump start it on the slope?'

'We can try,' said Gary. 'If that fails, though, we'll have to call someone out. Chantelle, help Tom push.'

'I can't push a car!' protested Chantelle.

'You don't have to; not much. It's on a slope,' said Gary.

He stepped past her. 'Get ready,' he said. He got behind the wheel, and set himself. He simultaneously called 'Okay', dropped the handbrake and turned the key. The engine started crisply, immediately. Gary stamped on the brake.

From being set to push, Tom and Chantelle found themselves suddenly brought up against an immoveable object.

'Sorry', called Gary. The engine idled contentedly. He raised an eyebrow.

Chantelle and Tom rejoined him in the car. 'Righted itself again?' said Tom.

'A bit spooky, wouldn't you say?' commented Chantelle.

'Let's get Tom back while it's okay,' said Gary.

'Aren't we going to see if Richard's still here?'

'He must have gone back by now. It's been too long. We would have seen him.'

'Shouldn't we check, though, to be sure?'

'Just hold it here,' said Tom. He pulled out his phone and dialed. A moment later, it was answered.

'Jen, it's me.'

'Where have you *been*?' asked Jennifer. 'You've been ages.'

'Yeah, a bit of car trouble. Look, are Richard and Craig back there?'

'No. Why?'

'We got separated. Thought he might have headed back.'

Jennifer was saying something, though not to him. He heard Sally's voice nearby.

'How long ago?' asked Jennifer.

'I don't know. Maybe twenty minutes. We're still up here. We'll have a look around again. If he shows up, let us know, eh?'

'You too,' replied Jennifer.

'Yes, okay.'

8

Gary turned at the crossroads. There was The Bull, holding in its own dim inner light behind its closed doors. And there, in the burnished gloom of the uphill lane, sat Richard's car. The interior was dark, with no sign of exhaust emission, and no signs of movement within. He and Tom exchanged worried glances.

They pulled up behind Richard's car. The passenger side door was ajar. There was something definitely wrong here.

'What the ... ' began Gary.

'Hold on,' said Tom. 'Let's find out what's happened.'

They got out of the car, and immediately they heard the sound of scurrying footsteps behind them. They turned as one, and were shocked to see Craig stumbling towards them. He was breathing heavily and was clearly relieved to see them.

'Craig, what happened?' asked Tom.

'I ... I don't know.'

Tom looked back towards the pub. All the lights, except a small sentry light in the bar, were out. Evidently, he had not been in the pub itself. Goodness knows how long he had been standing over there.

'Where's Richard?' asked Gary.

'Still in the car,' said Craig. 'I think,' he added.

Tom walked around to the driver's side. Even before he opened the door, he could see Richard in there, slumped to one side. He breathed a sigh of relief. At least he was still here. That was something. He pulled the door open, and tentatively shook Richard by the shoulder. Thankfully, he stirred, muttering and pulling himself upright.

'What ... what?' Richard murmured groggily.

'It's okay, Rich. It's Tom. What're you doing here, mate?' he asked sympathetically.

Richard shook his head, reaching up to massage his forehead. He opened his eyes. 'Ah, Tom. It's you. I thought ... '

'C'mon, get up.' Tom helped Richard to sit up. He looked at Gary, who was peering at Richard over his shoulder.

'I think we should get him to hospital,' Gary said. 'Get them to check him over.'

'And tell them what?' asked Tom.

Gary shrugged. 'A near accident? Shock,' he offered.

'No!' Richard gripped Tom by the shoulder. 'No hospital,' he said in a calmer, more collected tone. 'It's alright. I mean I'm alright.' He exhaled sharply.

'What happened, Rich?' asked Tom.

'I'm not sure at the moment,' he answered slowly. 'I must have fallen asleep. I feel so tired.'

Tom looked around, searching for something. No, *someone*.

'I think I've been dreaming,' added Richard, yawning.

'Leave it. He's not really with it,' said Gary.

'I can see that,' replied Tom. He looked around again, then spotted what he was searching for. 'Craig!' he called in a voice as loud as he dare. 'Craig, come over here!'

Craig was in Gary's car, his face lowered into shadow in the back. Tom made his way over and opened the door. Craig looked him in the eyes, and dropped his gaze again. Tom was about to speak, but in the light of the interior bulb, he saw the dark stain in Craig's jeans. He stepped back out of earshot, leaning closer to Gary. 'Something happened here. We can make guesses about what, but one thing's for sure: he's scared. And he's pissed himself.'

9

Tom and Gary quickly put a plan together. Tom would drive Richard back in his car, while they would leave Craig in the back of Gary's. Craig was staying at his house tonight anyway. Gary gave him a plastic carrier bag to sit on, which he accepted without protest. There was no evidence of injury to either Richard or Craig (aside from Craig's damaged pride), and so the best course was to take them home, put it out of mind, and review the whole thing in the cold light of day. It was too easy for tired minds to misread perfectly normal and logical events, and come to invalid conclusions about them.

As for Sally, they would tell her that they found them both asleep. Craig had been drinking, accounting for his state. They would keep Craig in the car until Gary came out, and so the fib, for her sake, could be perpetuated at least until morning when Richard could tell her what he would.

For themselves, they were too tired to care much for the detail right now. But, tomorrow, they would want to know what had happened. Richard would, no doubt, tell them if he were willing, or able. Craig, though – yes, Craig's reaction was a clearer indicator as to what might have occurred. They would have to get to him first.

But not tonight.

SIXTEEN

The phone rang at ten. Tom turned in his sleep. The ringing continued, and he came suddenly awake. He glanced at the bedside clock momentarily before picking up his phone.

'Hel... lo,' he croaked, sleep still fogging his mind, his throat dry. He swallowed, and cleared his throat. 'Hello?'

'Tom, it's Gary. Sorry, did I get you up?'

'Hm,' replied Tom. 'It's okay.'

'Sorry, mate. Thought you'd be up and about by now. I got your number from Terry – I should've got it off you last night. It's about last night ... it's Craig.'

It all came back in an instant. Tom pushed himself up against his headboard. 'What about him?' he asked curiously.

'I think he saw something last night. Well, that's what he claims.'

'What do you mean?'

'He told me he saw something appear in Richard's car.'

His words hung in the air.

Goosebumps formed on Tom's arms and legs. *'What?'* he said.

Gary sounded somewhat embarrassed. 'Mm, a girl, he said. Can you believe that?'

Tom didn't reply right away. Finally, he said, 'You haven't told Richard yet, have you?'

'No. Not yet.'

'Well, I wouldn't. What did Craig say, exactly?'

'Well, when we got to my house last night, I was ready to go straight to bed. But when I came out of the bathroom,

Craig called to me from the spare room. That's when he told me what had happened.'

'Where is he now?' asked Tom.

'I've just come back from dropping him off home.'

'You said he said he'd seen the girl?'

'Yeah. Apparently, he pissed himself when he heard something rustle in the car behind them. After that, he got out and ran. But, just before that, he looked back and thought he saw someone in the back of the car.'

'Didn't he wait to find out for sure? What about Richard? He just left him there?'

'He said Richard didn't move; seemed to have gone blank or something. He didn't answer. He got scared and decided he didn't want to be there.'

2

Wednesday

Richard came in at five-thirty. Sally was sitting quietly, staring at the television. A nature programme was on – not her usual choice of entertainment. She showed no acknowledgement of him.

A plate of picked-at food sat abandoned on the single-stand coffee table by her side, fork and spoon askew, a curry of some kind that had since cooled beneath a gravy-like skin. He looked from the plate to her face. Her hair was dishevelled, as if she had been running her fingers through it. Her eyes were slightly red and bloodshot, and her cheeks showed a trace of run eye-liner.

'You okay?' he asked, removing his jacket and flinging it across the back of the settee.

'Suppose,' she said without inflection. Then she sighed.

He approached her, perching himself on the arm of her chair. It creaked beneath him. He reached around to cup her neck with his left hand and attempted to pull her close. At first she resisted, holding herself taut. Then, slowly, she relented, allowing her head to fall against his hip. She began to cry again. He held her closer.

'Sally, you think I'm flipping, don't you?'

She didn't reply. He continued. 'Well, until today at work, I really wasn't sure myself.'

She looked up for the first time.

'But now it turns out someone else has seen her.'

There was no need to explain who he meant by 'her'. At times she felt like a wife hearing from her husband's own lips the sordid details of an affair with another woman. Only somehow ... somehow this was worse.

'Who? Do you know who?' she asked, both puzzled and a little more frightened.

'Gary told me. He said he and Tom decided to keep it from me at first, because they weren't sure how I'd take it. Anyway, in the end, this afternoon, before we left work, he told me.'

She sat up. 'Who?'

'Craig. Gary's friend.'

She was immediately suspicious. 'Richard ... '

'On Saturday night. He thought he saw her in the car, in the back.'

'Are you sure?'

'About what – what he saw?'

'No. About Craig – how reliable he is?'

'Gary phoned Tom on Saturday morning. He – Gary –and Craig stayed up the night before. Apparently, Craig was pretty shook up.'

Sally just looked at him. If the story was true, which she doubted, it was fuel to Richard's fire.

'What if Craig was just trying it on, to get back at you in some way?'

Richard shook his head. 'No. Gary told Tom he was just too scared to make it up. Even wet himself.'

Sally swallowed. There was an awkward pause.

Richard's voice was calm and controlled. 'Don't you see what this means, Sal? It means that the phenomenon is objective. It's real.'

Sally blinked slowly and exhaled. 'But you said that Craig only thought he saw someone in the car. That's not the same as knowing he did, is it? He was drunk. That could explain all of it, surely, even the wetting himself?'

He got up from the chair arm. 'That ... well. Look, it's a start, alright? I need to talk to Craig.'

'A start?' exclaimed Sally. 'A start to *what?* No, Richard, this has to end.'

Richard stared at her, wide-eyed, nostrils slightly flared.

She still doesn't believe me. Not really.

She knew what he was thinking, but her own pain was too deep now to spare much sympathy for his feelings. His behaviour was now beginning to threaten their relationship. And that made her begin to feel resentment. No more tiptoeing around the subject. Time to bring Richard down to earth before it was all too late, before he ruined everything.

'Promise me, no more. It's getting out of hand now. You're scaring me. I don't know you anymore,' she said. She sat on the edge of the chair, hands clasping.

'But Sally, please. Don't you understand? I have to try to help her.'

'*Help her?*' She glared up at him, wide-eyed and exasperated. 'Richard, how can you help her? She's not up there. She's *dead!*'

He couldn't fail to notice how Sally had weighted the 'she' in each phrase.

'Please, you've got to let this go. You can't really believe that you are communicating with a dead woman? Honestly ... ' Her voice wavered, and she began to sob.

He left her there, face cupped in her hands.

After some slamming around upstairs, she could hear water running. Sally sat up, wiping her eyes and blowing her nose with a tissue from her skirt pocket. Her thoughts were racing over what to do. Richard needed help. Her thoughts returned to Sunday morning, to when Richard had told her everything over breakfast. She had listened without comment then, trying to not let her expression reveal the worry and turmoil beneath.

He had recounted how the air in the car had turned cold. The light, what there was of it, began to falter, and then the car's engine had stalled. The next he knew, he found himself alone in the car. He must have passed out. Craig had gone.

The contact, he described as having the same quality as a freshly recalled dream. Following the closing in of the darkness, she had suddenly been there. From that moment, he was aware only of his own self and the girl. Everything outside the immediate environment of the car itself had ceased to exist. There was no significant sight or sound to offer distraction, only a peculiar faint crackling sound that wavered like electricity.

Craig had been there for some portion of the encounter. He knew this on a subconscious level, but he was not sure for how long or how much he perceived. All he knew was that he was only peripherally aware of him, and at some point he was no longer there.

After his initial fear, he noticed that the girl seemed as frightened as he was. In his rearview mirror, he could see her, pale and bewildered. Her eyes were misty and wide. He had felt her anguish and confusion. And then something even more peculiar began to happen. He thought he could see, momentarily in flashes, his own face illuminated weakly in the mirror, as if seeing himself from her point of view.

'Where... where am I?' she asked feebly.

He didn't know how to answer. He was still trying to get over her appearance and determine how she communicated. Had her lips moved? He really couldn't decide. All he knew was that he could hear her voice, light but broken.

She repeated the question, gathering strength. As in his dreams, she seemed to be drawing strength and substance from him. He felt increasingly cold, a little light-headed. He first put it down to the rush of adrenaline he had felt at her appearance. True, his heart was beating rapidly, but the energy drain was unmistakable.

What was she asking him now? His name?

It was his turn to feel confusion. His thoughts became woolly. He was unable to articulate. He compared it to a feverish or drunken deliriousness. He started to shiver, feeling the cold seep into his marrow so that he felt he might stand it no longer. The glow from the girl seemed to grow in proportion. With his growing debilitation and confusion came renewed fear. He felt as if he were drowning.

Suddenly, on the verge of passing out, the feeling lifted, as if he had burst through a membrane. Coincidentally, the glow from the girl stepped down, and her skin tone took on a more natural and wholesome appearance. She suddenly seemed more real., while his own physical self-awareness was diminished. He felt numbed and detached. Was she somehow more real, or had he become less substantial? Whatever the explanation, he felt that some essential part of himself had crossed a boundary. He felt he was meeting her on common ground, a place between their two worlds to which neither properly belonged.

All the panic and disorientation evaporated, as if this were a side-effect of the transition. He turned to face her. Her features were clear. Her expression was melancholic, but her complexion positively radiated health and vitality. She looked beautiful.

'Who are you?' she asked in a frightened tone.

He had planned a series of questions for her should he ever manage to make contact. Now, he found it almost impossible even to speak. He struggled to put together a reply. 'Er,. ah ... Richard,' he replied.

'I ... I thought you were someone else.'

Was this really happening? All the time a deeper part of his mind was trying to force its way up to find conscious acknowledgement of this meeting.

I'm face to face with a dead girl. A ghost.

He pushed the thought away.

She looked unsettled again. 'Where are the others – my friends?' she asked, looking around her, frowning at what she saw. He followed her gaze. His eyes widened with surprise. The last he had been aware of his surroundings, they had faded into darkness, just before he had been launched into the state in which he now found himself. Now, he could see that the hedgerows and trees had returned.

No, they were different somehow. The image they presented was somehow wrong; soft-focused, unreal. There was no sound.

He didn't know what to say. Did she realise she was dead? How could he possibly tell her? What effect would it have on her?

He decided to avoid a direct answer. 'Friends?'

'Yes ... ' She fell quiet, her expression quizzical. He could see that she was struggling to recall their names.

'Emily?'

She looked into his eyes. He felt a trifle uneasy again. The sorrow that resided there was disturbing.

'Your name is Emily. Emily Reynolds?'

A glint of recognition flickered in her eyes. 'Yes,' she replied quietly. Then she looked afraid again. 'How ... how do you know my name?'

'Never mind that for the moment.'

Evidently, the other meetings, the dreams that he felt were instigated by her, meant nothing to her at this moment. He tried to be sympathetic.

'Look, you've been involved in a bad car crash.'

She just stared at him at first, then she began to shake her head.

'I'm sorry to have to tell you,' said Richard, 'but your friends are dead.'

'No! That can't be.'

'Yes, Emily. You've just forgotten. Try to remember,' he said gently.

She dropped her eyes from his. In this state, the physical barriers of the car's interior didn't seem to exist. She raised her head again, and proffered her hand, as if she instinctively sought his energy as well as his support. He hesitated, finding himself repulsed by the thought of touching her. His heartbeat fluttered in his throat.

Slowly, tentatively, he reached out and placed his hand in hers. It was firm, a little cool. A tingling feeling flowed through his hand and into his lower arm. Her hand was warming in his. Where their skin touched, hers also became warmer in colour. One small area of contact was slow to warm. He looked down to see a band of gold, a ring. *The* ring?

She closed her eyes. He could feel her concentration. He gazed at her for a moment, then closed his own eyes. Almost immediately images began to form on the dark screen before him. He – they – were searching through a succession of unconnected events from her life.

Then, one scene began to form, growing and coming into focus before him, eclipsing the others. It depicted the inside of the car on that fateful night. He viewed it from Emily's vantage point, from the rear seat of the Consul. He had read of the circumstances of the crash from newspaper reports of the time, but somehow in striving to recall the events of that night for herself, Emily was showing him what had happened. No sound accompanied the images.

The car was approaching the crossroads at The Bull. Despite knowing what was going to happen, he was unable to react, to warn.

The girl in the front passenger seat, whom he knew to be Olivia Evans, was fumbling with the radio. The car stalled as Emily's other friend, Julie, failed to hold the car at the STOP line.

There was an exchange of words, then the car sprung to life again, and the lane ahead was lit by the car's rekindled headlights.

Julie started to pull out, glancing towards Olivia as she did so. From the rear seat, he could see Olivia's startled features turned towards a source of suddenly intense illumination. Horror was written over her face. Her mouth articulated something inaudible.

He felt his line of vision wrenched away, in the direction of the oncoming vehicle. Emily had turned her head in the very last moments of her life. There was a burst of light, followed immediately by a tremendous jolt, and then a dizzying blackness from the impact.

The blackness gave way to a new scenario. He was standing off from the wreckage. Well, no, not exactly. He realised that the vantage point was elevated above standing height above the scene. He looked down on the scene dispassionately from her point of view.

How could she possibly have been aware of all this? How could she have witnessed events immediately following her own death? Then he realised he was judging the situation from the limited point of view from which most would proceed. The fact that she had been appearing to him, as she did now, confirmed that her personality – her spirit – had survived bodily death.

He looked around. Two police cars were parked outside the pub, off to the right. A fire engine and ambulance were parked closer. Two firemen were engaged in cutting through the wreckage. The front passenger door of the Consul had been removed. There was no-one in the seat.

A young policeman stood nearby, watching with a pained expression on his face. He seemed unmindful of the steady rainfall.

Richard noticed that the operation was not hurried. It was carefully coordinated, but there seemed to be no urgency. That could mean only one thing. He knew that Emily's and Julie's deaths had been instantaneous.

He wondered if Emily herself was taking all this in. At the thought, darkness closed in again, as if she were aware of his thoughts, and backing away from the truth.

Slowly this time ... slowly, a new scene developed. It was once again on the hill. He sensed it was some months later. He somehow also sensed that Emily did not recognise the temporal shift as he had.

In this scenario, he felt the close identity he had with her weaken and begin to break apart. He was no longer seeing things from her point of view.

He saw her standing on the roadside, very much as he had seen her when he first picked her up. Waves of anguish and loss and an intense feeling of frustration struck him. Fading images of futile attempts to stop vehicles and frightened motorists impressed themselves on him.

Then he felt the link dissolving. Slowly, he opened his eyes. The girl had withdrawn her hand from his. He looked at her face. At the broken contact, she had weakened, her vitality and the hue of her skin paled. Her eyes were moist with welling tears.

She understood.

It was clear that it was the first time she had really comprehended the fact of her own death and the cause of it. She looked at him.

'Emily ... ' he began, but she shrank away from him. Tears began to spill down her cheeks.

'I'm sorry,' he said gently.

'*No.*' She was shaking her head. And suddenly, she was no longer there. He had been looking right at her.

He jolted upright in his seat. He found he had been slumped over the wheel of the car. Cold air fought its way around him. He turned his head to see Tom and Gary standing over him, concern written on their faces.

He glanced from them to the rearview mirror. Nothing. He quickly turned around in his seat to look directly into the rear seat of the car. Empty.

3

Sally's thoughts were interrupted by a muffled thump from upstairs; she came back to the present to the *schtickking* sound of the shower curtain being drawn back. Richard had finished his shower.

Last night he had stayed out until the early hours. So much for Valentine's Day. He looked cold and drawn when he finally came home. She had waited up for him, seriously concerned, but he had said very little other than to say where he'd been.

He hadn't even eaten his – admittedly dry – dinner before falling into bed. She scraped it into the bin along with the card she had bought for him.

What could she do, really? Leave him, like last time? What would that achieve? She could approach his doctor, or a psychiatrist, but they could do nothing without Richard's cooperation. Unless he was a danger to himself or others, of course, but there were no signs of that.

Despite hating herself for sitting back, she realised she could do little else. She could only hope that he would give up and return to some semblance of normality.

The overriding question in her mind now was no longer whether the ghost was real or not, or what it really meant to Richard, but whether their relationship could survive intact through this. *Unblemished* was a term that could no longer apply. It was by now too tainted to be fully as it was, but it was not irreparable. Not yet.

February 23

Richard had waited eagerly for this evening to arrive. Ostensibly it was just another meet-up with their friends, but really everyone (with the probable exception of Sally) was keen to hear Craig's own story. Gary was going to bring him along, and Richard was hopeful that it would permit Sally and the others to finally accept that there was something more to it than his own overactive imagination.

But when Gary and Craig hadn't appeared by seven-thirty as arranged, Richard's hopeful mood began to wilt. Then he noticed that Terry was holding his phone in his lap and shaking his head furtively at Sally. Sally frowned and silently mouthed *What?* back at him.

Richard caught all of this. His lips parted as he was about to ask Terry what was going on, when one of the main doors opened and Gary – only Gary – walked in. He clutched at his car keys unconsciously with one hand as he approached their table. Richard stood to greet him, but Gary was looking past him to Terry, who repeated the same head shaking gesture to him.

Richard was suspicious. 'What's up?' he asked, his eyes narrowing on Gary. 'Where's Craig?'

'He ah… he's not coming,' replied Gary. 'Wouldn't come,' he added, dropping his gaze.

'But he… he said he would. Why not?' asked Richard.

'He just said he'd had time to think about it since then,' replied Gary. 'It was dark and he admitted he was pissed. He er… thinks now he just saw the trees reflected in the car's rear window.'

'What about the rustling sound. I know he heard that. I remember…'

'Just the wind, in the trees. Nothing,' said Gary.

Richard looked at the others, his house of cards instantly demolished. He turned from Gary. '*No,*' he said, shaking his head. 'I *know* he saw her. That's why he ran!' His jaw clenched and he brought a hammer fist down on the table with a resounding thump. A wine glass jumped and toppled over, spilling its contents in a curdling swirl with the sloshed beer of two full pint glasses.

'Richard!' exclaimed Sally into the awkward silence that followed. She stole a glance at the bar, where the barman looked on warily. He wasn't yet doing anything, but his expression indicated he was closely analysing the situation and readying himself for a possible escalation. Her eyes darted back and forth. She placed a hand on Richard's hip, trying to get him to sit back down.

He glanced down at her, but just stood there for a moment,

taken aback by the force of his own reaction as thin streams of liquid poured over the table's curved perimeter in half a dozen mini niagaras.

The others were taken aback. Richard's eyes shone with an intensity he had never before revealed. Alice and Jennifer found napkins from somewhere and started to mop up the spillage.

He felt a hand on his shoulder and turned to find Terry there. 'Richard, forget it. It's not important.' His voice showed a degree of concern that was genuine, something as uncharacteristic of him as Richard's outburst had been.

He chose not to acknowledge Terry, although his mind formed and repeated the response he found he was unable to articulate. *But it is. It is!*

Last week, they had all heard Craig's story, admittedly through Gary. The last two minutes had shattered all that, when a refreshingly cheerful Richard had been stopped cold by the news of Craig's blunt denial.

Tom stepped in, speaking carefully and, he hoped, sympathetically, appealing to Richard's sensibility and intelligence. 'Come on, Richard. We were up there to sort of tempt fate, don't you think? We were hoping to see something. When you're feeling spooked, your imagination can play tricks on you. You know that.'

It probably wasn't the right thing to say.

Richard bit on his lower lip. His eyes tracked around his friends, looking into their own for any sign of understanding, for their belief. But all he saw in them was fear and embarrassment, verging on pity.

Gary dropped his gaze, his own expression a reflection of his embarrassment at the situation, or possibly his own feelings at the betrayal of Craig's volte-face.

When Richard's eyes came to rest on Sally's, her face

218

showed the same flickering dismay. She said nothing. But what hurt most of all was when her eyes also fell from his.

Deflated, defeated, Richard turned away and, without looking back, he marched out the door, ignoring even Sally's plea to him to wait for her.

4

Gary and Terry came back inside the pub. 'He's gone; just drove off.'

'Arsehole!' said Sally. But the tears were already in her eyes.

'What's happened to him, Sally?'

Sally wiped the moisture away with her fingers. 'I wish I knew, Jen,' she replied with quivering lips. Then she broke down.

5

Richard drove around aimlessly. He had left Sally behind. Not good, but the flight impulse had simply taken over, and he fled the pub. He couldn't go home – well, that wouldn't look good either. He replayed the scene in the pub in his head. Although Craig wasn't there, he could see his smug expression in his mind's eye. And he could see, and was smarting from still, his friends' looks of wariness and disapproval, especially Sally's.

He wasn't surprised when he found himself on the run up Blaxton Hill. He made what was becoming a customary circuit of the haunted stretch before pulling up outside The Bull on the final turnaround towards Eldonbridge.

There was still a fair amount of traffic about, on both the main road and on this backwater route. Valence Lane here provided a means of passage to the villages for workers heading home from work in Haltham and Knowlworth, and a homeward conduit from the industrial districts to the east, below the irregular flank of hills of which Blaxton Hill formed a part.

Here was part of the reason he felt little sense of atmosphere. With vehicles whizzing by frequently, it was very difficult to achieve the relaxed state of mind necessary to making genuine contact.

It also made a mockery of book and newspaper coverage that claimed this older part of Blaxton Hill was an isolated rural spot. Perhaps that was true when they were written, but did the authors ever drive by during the day? Then again, in a while, the traffic flow would dry up miraculously.

He glanced again at the dashboard clock: 19:58. Not late. Not yet. The evening was dry, mild for the time of year. A quick pint, maybe? He had time to kill and played the thought around in his mind. He'd walked out on his spilled drink, a tall shandy, back at the pub in Eldonbridge.

He started the car and drove it into The Bull's car park. Entering the pub, he looked around to see a moderate crowd. He headed for a gap at the bar. It wasn't long before he was served.

The bar lady served him a pint of draught lager, *sans* lemonade top. Richard took the frosted glass from the drip-tray and downed half of it in three gasps.

A figure stepped before him, a large man. He hadn't recognised him immediately through the froth-clouded curvature of the uptilted glass, but his mind had retrieved the man's name before he was in a position to articulate it. He lowered his glass, and nodded a greeting. 'Cyril.'

The barman eyed him suspiciously for an instant before returned the greeting, and they exchanged a few words, both avoiding the question as to why Richard was here.

The barman looked at his glass. 'You driving?'

'Hm,' Richard nodded. 'Just the one.'

'Okay, then,' he replied. 'You know the score.'

6

Leaving the pub, he parked at his usual spot a hundred yards up from the crossroads. There were a number of other cars parked every which way outside the pub, overflowing the small car park onto the verges of the lanes at the crossroads.

He sat there, waiting, trying to clear his mind; pushing away images of Sally and the others from his mind's eye, focusing on Emily Reynolds.

How long he sat there like that, mentally searching and calling ... *willing* her to appear, he had no idea. He saw in his rearview mirror that some of the parked vehicles by the pub had gone. However long it had been, it had proven fruitless. In trying to force the contact, he realised, he was inadvertently blocking it. He was too tense, too eager in thought, not receptive.

He glanced up the lane. Through the trees and shrubs bordering the lane twinkled lights from far-off houses and streetlights up on the other side of the dual carriageway where it finally won out its climb over Blaxton Hill. A light wind sent mauve clouds billowing across the sky.

Relax... relax.

He closed his eyes again. Presently, his breathing settled unconsciously into a regular, easy rhythm.

He had explained to Sally that he had to help Emily, but what did that really mean? When he really thought about it, he realised that he hadn't a clue how he knew she needed help, or how to achieve it. None of the contacts had included a specific request for help from her. Not as such.

He shivered. His willingness to help was strong, but while it was seemingly a blind, thoughtless motivation, it was also disturbing. It hinted that things were not entirely under his own volition.

He raised his head from its slumped position. The back of his neck ached, cricking as he moved it. Wincing, he noticed that forty minutes had passed. Through the misted windscreen, the foliage of the verge quivered in the breeze and the dim light from The Bull. Then he saw her emerge from the deep shadows.

7

Sally stirred. She reached over to Richard's side of the bed. Her hand hadn't travelled far before the coolness of the sheets and the undepressed mattress told her what she already suspected. He wasn't there. Hadn't been there tonight. Her troubled thoughts resurfaced unbidden, forcing her to full wakefulness. She reached out to find the lamp on her night-table, and warm, rosy light flooded the room. She squinted at the clock on her bedside cabinet. 03:20.

She sighed and turned onto her back. She just didn't know what to make of Richard's behaviour any more. He had changed – deteriorated – and she no longer knew what to expect from day to day. Absurd as it may seem, she found relief in sleep. Her concerns were temporarily lost in the void, although sometimes they found her there and chased her back to consciousness.

Finally, she propped herself up. The bedsprings creaked beneath her, joining the faint morning chorus outside as the only sounds in the house. Then she could discern the sound of his snoring from the living room.

8

Terry and Alice had given her a lift home the previous evening. Richard wasn't there when they arrived. After seeing her inside, they had offered to stay until he returned. Knowing of Richard's new-found penchant for trips to Blaxton Hill, Terry had even offered to drive up there, but she turned them down on both counts. She just wanted to be alone.

She had fallen against the door as it closed after them, tears welling in her eyes, which she wiped away with the cuff of her sleeve. Slowly, her composure returned and she made her way into the kitchen, reaching for the kettle out of unconscious habit.

She had stayed up until eleven and then went to bed, where she lay awake until, finally, she heard Richard's key in the lock. The relief seeped through her, bringing on a fended-off drowsiness. But after the door closed, he neither called out or started on the stairs. She wasn't going to call out or go down to *him*.

Instead, she mentally followed him into the kitchen, where he opened a cupboard and retrieved a plate. Then the sound of the cutlery drawer. Then he left the kitchen for the living room, and she heard the creak of the sofa as he sat down. Then it was quiet. After a while, the faint aroma of something spicy met her nostrils as she drifted off to sleep.

9

When Sally rose at seven-thirty, all was quiet. Halfway down the stairs, the lingering smell of Richard's takeaway became mingled with the sour odour of alcohol. She experienced a sudden and stark vision of him sprawled on his back, choked on his own vomit. She quickened her step, but as she rounded the bottom of the stairwell, the vision evaporated. Richard was sound asleep and breathing deeply and rhythmically on the couch.

He had kicked off his shoes and socks beside the couch and lay otherwise fully dressed. His face was turned away from her, into the cushions. On the coffee table beside him was a clear rectangular plastic tub that contained the remains of his meal – some kind of noodle dish – and a fork; and beside that, lying on its side on a small crumpled white carrier bag, a glass hip-flask bottle of whisky. It was empty.

Cold fingers of alarm gripped her heart. He hadn't had a real drink, at least to her knowledge, since his crash last year.

'Stupid! Stupid… selfish… bastard!' she whimpered. She retreated to the kitchen. She remained there for a while, seated at the kitchen table. A mug of coffee, untouched and growing cold, stood on the table before her. She had poured one for Richard, black, but had left it on the table. It too would be nearly cold by now.

'Is that for me?'

Sally jolted upright. Startled, her jaw dropped, but no words came out.

Richard stood in the doorway. He looked terrible, his features drawn, his eyes dark circles beneath a scruffy mop of black hair. He held onto the door frame, as if for support.

She nodded.

Richard picked the mug up and drank the coffee down without pause. He didn't seem to notice or care that it was cold.

'I'll make another one.'

He shook his head. He went to the sink and rinsed his mug, then refilled it with cold water and drank that down too. When he finished, he placed it in the bowl and leant against the sink unit.

'Why did you leave me at the pub last night?'

Richard didn't answer. He pursed his lips, looking at her.

'*Why?*' repeated Sally. 'Why would you do that? Do you have any idea how I felt; how it looked? Did you even *care?!*'

'I just had to. I didn't think,' he finally replied.

'That's no answer. Terry and Alice had to bring me home.' Sally paused for a moment.

Richard stared at her.

'I don't need to ask where you were – at least, I hope I don't. But the booze – you've never drunk spirits before. When did that start? Where does it end?'

Richard raised a hand to his temple. 'Sally... not now.'

Sally spoke slowly and forcibly, although her voice trembled. '*When* then, Richard? We keep going over this. I've tried to be sympathetic. But you just wallow in self-pity; that you're not understood and all that. And all the time you don't seem to notice or care about the effects on others – *me.* I can't stand it! You just act like a child and storm off, and drown your sorrows. And risk throwing away all you have. If you can't get yourself together, I'm going back to my parents, and you can get on with it.'

Richard responded defensively, callously. 'Fucking go, then!'

'I beg your pardon?'

'I said, *'Go, then.'*' He stared unblinkingly at her, until she broke eye contact and turned and ran upstairs.

So, he had made his choice. Taking him at his word (she had never been sworn at in that manner by Richard before), she wasted no time in beginning to pull together some things. From downstairs, she heard Richard calling out, 'Sally. Sal. Sorry. I didn't mean it. Just got a thumping headache...'

She hoped Richard wouldn't come up and try to stop her before she could ring her father to come and pick her up.

But, coming out of the bathroom a short while after, she paused on the landing. It was quiet. She crept down the stairs cautiously, not knowing what to expect, half-expecting him not even to be there. What she saw instilled in her a mixture of sympathy and further alarm. Richard was just sitting there despairingly, head forward, his face cupped in his hands. She had taken a step down towards him before deciding against it, and retreated back to the bedroom.

Presently, her phone buzzed to indicate her father was outside. Permitting herself no further thought, she took up her bags and made her way downstairs and marched towards the front door. She became aware of Richard raising his head.

'Don't go,' he said quietly, pathetically.

Sally swung around to face him. 'Grow up, get sober, and decide what you really want. Call me when you've decided.'

And at that, she was gone.

SEVENTEEN

'His car's still not here,' she said as they pulled up outside the house.

It had been six days since Sally left. In that time, she had phoned a couple of times, and dropped by once. On none of these occasions had Richard been in – or, at least, he hadn't answered. A neighbour had confirmed on the visit day that Richard had been about, and yes, he had seemed Okay, if weary-looking and in need of a shave. The house itself had looked untidy – the bed slept in, and the living room and kitchen a bit of a tip, but there was no evidence to suggest that Richard hadn't been looking after himself.

The turning point had been this morning, when she had phoned Alice, and had learned, through Terry, that Richard had, in fact, been out sick from work since the pub bust-up, and hadn't been heard from since. They had tried calling him, with no luck, and had, in fact, been discussing whether they should call round. They were surprised, of course, to learn that Sally herself hadn't been there herself for that time.

The door open, Sally and her father stepped into the small porchway that led directly into the living room. Her father had been seething when she had first gone home nearly a week ago. With her wedding only months away now, they could all do without the disruption and uncertainty Richard's behaviour was causing. Sitting at home that morning, crying, Sally had had some difficulty convincing him that Richard had not been abusive towards her. Her mother knew better, thank goodness, and calmed him down.

She hadn't been able to give them the precise reason for her walk-out, at least not while they were together. It was better that he didn't know that his prospective son-in-law seemed to be losing his mind. So, she was forced to leave her father with his preconceived notions and basic dislike for Richard, explaining that they had argued over money. She still didn't really understand while he had so little time for Richard, although she could see how his view could have become discoloured by her falling pregnant only a month after they'd met. She had miscarried in her third month after Richard had crashed the car with her aboard when a dog had ran out in front of them. Her father had not spoken to him for some time afterwards.

She had later told her mother the full story. Her father had guessed that there was more to it when he saw that Sally intended to stay more than a couple of days. She finally told him on the way back over.

This time, the state of the place was much worse. In the living room, empty bottles and cans lay about the waste bin, which had been placed on the floor at one end of the sofa. In the kitchen, the draining board was stacked with washed crockery, but the sink was also full.

'Bloody hell!' exclaimed her father, as he surveyed the place. He stooped by the sofa to pick up a grey lever-arch file. As he did so, loose sheets of paper fluttered out. He caught a handful of them and, replacing them, bent to gather together the others. He read some of the scribbled notes on some of them, looking up guiltily to see Sally's disapproving stare.

'What's there?' she asked.

'Well, it looks like he's done a fair bit of phoning; a lot of these are photostats of old newspaper reports.'

Sally frowned. She made her way back out to the kitchen, to where she had seen a small pile of mail. She set about sorting through it, picking out those addressed to her only, then opening those that were jointly addressed, or those she recognised as bills. She left two items unopened that were addressed to Richard, one apparently from his work. Clearly he hadn't examined the post when it arrived; simply shuffled it together into a rough pile on the side.

She found a pen and used one of the envelopes to scribble a short note, asking him to get in touch with her, ostensibly about payment arrangements for some of the bills, but she really wanted to find out just how he was.

2

Richard got home at eight-fifteen that evening. He immediately knew that Sally had been back. He could detect a trace of the perfumed carpet-cleaner in the air. His pulse quickened momentarily at the thought that she had returned, but the darkened rooms and the silence told him otherwise. He sighed, closing the door behind him, and took the few steps into the living room, reaching round to flick the lights on. He blinked with surprise. The room had been straightened, the furniture rearranged as Sally preferred it, and all his rubbish cleared up. It looked as tidy and neat as it ever had, as it had every Friday evening at least, when Sally would hoover and tidy, in order to leave much of the weekend free.

Except, there was something not quite right about it. He stared at it awhile, then started to turn to the kitchen, before stopping in mid-stride.

Folder.

He felt a momentary stab of concern when he couldn't locate his notes. Then he saw the grey plastic folder on the sideboard behind the sofa. He breathed a sigh of relief. He set his carrier bag down on the sofa and went over to examine it.

In it was his diary notebook. He had been writing in it quite a bit of late. It was his way of sorting and justifying his actions and providing some feedback and comment. It was almost possible to analyse the material objectively, and so, he found, it was a useful tool for self psychoanalysis – a means of keeping tabs on his own sanity, which he believed he still possessed – although the litter of spent cans and bottles might have suggested to otherwise to Sally.

He hoped she hadn't read any of the diary, though, for the lengthy notes he made following each contact could easily be misconstrued. He flicked through it, content it hadn't been tampered with, and replaced it.

Why, Sally? he thought. Why couldn't you just try to understand? He pushed the thought away. The Craig episode, and Sally's attitude immediately afterwards still stung a week later. That last night she was here, he had simply stared at her as she issued her ultimatum. Until he had sworn at her, that is.

Why had he done that? That wasn't ordinarily like him. Why, then? Perhaps because he had felt wrung out, emotionally spent. He had finally reached that point of defencelessness, of literally having nothing to say. He had become just as weary about it as they. And so he had fallen back on the drink; it had seemed the only thing to do right then, but its depressive effects had deepened his emotional low to a point that had really begun to scare him. Sally's reaction, of leaving him again, showed that it had unnerved her as well.

He wandered into the kitchen, not surprised to find it also cleaned and tidied. He took a bottle of milk from the fridge when he noticed Sally's note. He picked it up, and wandered into the other room and sat down. The note really said nothing. He had hoped for a real conciliatory flavour to the wording, but it was direct and impersonal. Sally was as stubborn as he, neither prepared to offer the first olive branch. He threw the note casually in the direction of the coffee table.

And stopped.

He found himself looking back across the room, in the direction of the kitchen. It struck him what had bothered him about the room on an unconscious level when he first came in.

The cushions on the sofa. They were never specifically arranged, but they were never crowded into the corner, one over the other, like that. He knew of only one person who arranged them this way. Sally's father. He had a lower back weakness which he supported by wedging cushions behind him. On a sofa, he preferred to sit at one end, arranging the cushions across the corner. It annoyed him that Sally had brought him along, or had he insisted on coming? Then again, how else would Sally have got here?

No matter, it was enough that he had been here. Sally's father had seen the state of the place, and would now be working on Sally to convince her to keep away from him, to stay home. And, noticing where his folder had been left – just behind that end of the sofa – he just knew that he had looked at his notes.

Suddenly, he didn't feel quite so hopeful about Sally's intentions or the outcome of her impromptu visit. He sat down on the sofa and eyed the carrier bag next to him. Presently, he reached inside and withdrew a bottle.

EIGHTEEN

He stepped out of the house with a sense of purpose he had not known for a while.

The air was a little chilly. A dull overcast shed grey light over the town, portending rain later. The walk into town would take a while, but he had all day. And, frankly, he had the time. The fresh air and exercise would help shake off the cobwebs, and any preoccupation over some depressing news he had received that morning in the post.

He shouldn't have been surprised, really. He'd been to work only for a few days over the past weeks, which had seemed aimless, pointless even. The letter from his employer informed him he would now be placed on statutory sick pay and referred for a medical assessment. Weeks ago, he'd had to concede to their writing to his doctor, who had suggested stress as the root cause of his depressed state and dragging tiredness. He would have expected no less considering the nature of his job, where safety of the public was of utmost importance.

One of his friends, Terry or Gary, might have warned him about it. But they had, hadn't they? Well, they had tried to. He had ignored one of Terry's calls, and when both had called round one day, he had hid behind the curtains, pretending he was out until they left. That night at the pub had soured him more than he realised. When he had felt most vulnerable, even his friends had turned against him. Or, so he believed.

The letter might easily have been made worse, but for the incident in the kitchen the night before.

It was funny how the mind could dredge up or connect bits of information or snatches of conversation weeks or months later when the time is right. While half-heartedly throwing together a sandwich in the kitchen, his thoughts had been idly tracing the events that had led him to this point when something Pumfrys once said came back to him, and it had sent him scurrying from the kitchen into the living room to find his notes.

Checking through the assorted notes and photocopied newspaper articles, he found what he was looking for. But to be sure, he would have to go back to the library. It was there he now felt sure he would find a key piece in this ghostly jigsaw puzzle, which might lead him on to resolve this whole incredible business.

And it had everything to do with Peter Pumfrys.

He retired to bed feeling hopeful and content for a change, not even consciously missing Sally's presence, which had become a nightly ritual. But he found he wasn't able to sleep for very long, and what he did manage was occupied by a delirium of images, of musty newspaper pages and scribbled notes.

2

He had made his way through the streets purposefully. The clock over the entrance to Benton's, the jeweller in Webley Street, read nine-twenty. The doors to the library would open precisely at nine-thirty, yet his pace did not slow. He marched on, oblivious to the vibrant hum of traffic and to the pedestrians who bustled about on their way to work.

Where I should be, he thought.

3

He stared at it, it seemed, for ages before he broke off and started to read. Here it was. As he had anticipated, whether from intuition, or special guidance, it didn't matter. It was here.

It took him a full five minutes to read the article and captions, spread over the centre pages of the 7 December 1984 issue of the *Courier*. At one point he gasped audibly, looking around quickly and self consciously.

When he finished, he stared at the screen of the microfilm viewer while thoughts raced through his mind. He leaned back in his chair, muttering to himself. Bastard. The *bastard*.

Another patron sitting nearby – an elderly man – stole a condescending glance at him.

The dimly-lit facsimile waited patiently, indifferently. He turned his attention back. Squaring and re-focusing half-page segments one by one, he hit the green COPY button. The screen went dark momentarily as the viewer's printer function cranked out hard copies. He held each of them up to check them before rewinding the film onto its spool, and switching off.

He left the library with the familiar headache he always had after scanning the papers for a number of hours. It didn't help that the weather had brightened considerably.

4

Back home, he poured himself a coffee and sat down to go over the article once more. He read it again slowly, as if for the first time, studying the pictures, taking it all in. One inset picture showed a much younger Peter Pumfrys, with slicked black hair (and more of it), and thick-framed glasses.

He had mixed feelings over his discovery: triumph turned to anger; hope tainted by further betrayal.

The article provided a great deal more than he had expected. It was been a wonder it existed at all, really. As a review of Pumfry's ultimately unpublished book, it offered reasonable explanation as to how he had come up with additional detail on the Blaxton Hill case. Anyone researching with any degree of diligence could achieve that.

It was no surprise to find that the case might feature in the book and in the review article. What *was* totally unexpected was that it was the principal subject of both.

A SPIRITED ENDEAVOUR: Our Man's Investigation into the County's foremost Stories & Legends of the Supernatural

This week, *The Courier* presents a special preview of the soon-to-be-published book by reporter Peter Pumfrys.

Exploring our region's rich ghostly heritage, the book will be the culmination of several years' research and investigative effort.

Combining the better known historical and legendary tales and more up-to-date reports of encounters with spooks and spectres, Mr. Pumfrys hopes the book will appeal to a wider readership:
'Historic accounts of hauntings and apparitions are too far removed from us or have become so folklorised that we cannot relate to them other than as a form of entertainment.

'Unfortunately, nowadays, it is the media services that are largely responsible for this by treating the subject irreverently.

But, if the evidence is studied, an inner consistency soon becomes apparent that suggests that, although poorly understood, it is a valid area of study. The Paranormal may prove to be an important but long-neglected aspect of human experience, and of Nature.

'Of course,' he added, 'although the book will have serious intent, I also hope that the material will be enjoyable and add to people's appreciation of their heritage.'

Although having had a long term interest in the occult (he will no doubt wince at the use of this term, preferring 'Paranormal', which is increasingly used these day) – although he told me it really only means 'hidden' or 'unknown') – Peter began his quest shortly after joining *The Courier* in 1979, when he became fascinated by the then fresh story of the ghost of Blaxton Hill, first reported by the late John Sheriton ...

The article went on to describe additional background to the book, identifying some of the county's other famous haunted sites. But much of the body of the text covered the Blaxton Hill haunting. Described even then as 'promising to become the region's best known ghost-story for its poignancy', there was a wealth of information here. In spite of his own research efforts, Richard had not turned up anything to compare to some of the information in this article, most notably its photographs. There was one of the 1978 crash scene, which he had seen before. But it was the first time he had seen a photograph of Emily Reynolds herself. It was this that had caused him to gasp in the library.

The photocopy quality was not as faithful as the microfilm copy (itself not particularly good) but her features were recognisable, if not her expression, from his hill encounters and his dreams. It was the first piece of objective evidence supporting the reality of his experiences.

He felt an air of sadness as he stared at her picture. Emily smiled naturally and easily from the paper, her features seeming to stand out with relief. It contrasted with his mental picture of her, one of hurt and loss and longing. He swallowed hard.

Pumfrys had clearly conducted some in-depth research. The article described the encounters of various people with Emily, which included a police officer 'of notable rank' who was one of those present at the scene of the accident.

Evidently, he had also approached Emily's fiancé, John Hudson, for a prospective interview, which was apparently declined, though the article failed to mention just what kind of reception he may have received.

Pumfrys was a man whom he felt, in spite of being a journalist, was basically reserved and sensitive. If he had pursued his research as far as approaching Hudson, knowing full well what distress it might cause, then he must have had very good reason, or a strong compulsion to do so.

Tracing Hudson was something he had considered himself. He had established that he had married in 1980 and set up home in Haltham, but when records indicated he had moved in 1983, he hadn't tried very hard to locate him. What good could come of it?

Now he could see that Pumfrys had contacted Hudson some time in 1984, with unknown effect. It meant he just might have Hudson's address, assuming he hadn't moved again. And if he had, it was just possible that he had kept track.

Despite his reluctance to have to do so, he had to find John Hudson. Emily had asked for him.

5

His eyes widened in surprise at the deterioration in Richard's appearance since he had last seen him. He was unshaven, somewhat bleary-eyed, and in need of a haircut. They stood facing one another over the doorstep for a few seconds before he remembered his manners and invited Richard inside.

Pumfrys led him into the living room, familiar from the night of his last visit. From appearances, it might have been that very same night, save for the lighting – it was not quite dark outside, and a single lamp was sufficient to make up for the deficit in natural light.

Everything else was the same as last time – except for the faded and bloated manila folder, held together with two thick elastic bands, on the arm of the chair he was guided to sit in. Richard looked at it and then at Pumfrys.

'What you came to see.'

Richard nodded. 'Yes,' he replied quietly.

Earlier in the afternoon, he had phoned Pumfrys at the newspaper offices. Perhaps it hadn't been the right moment. It had been a spur-of-the-moment kind of thing. And perhaps he had let his feelings colour his tone and his language. 'I think you have a bit of explaining to do,' he had said.

In the time remaining, and during the drive to Caldwell, he had regained his composure and his sensibilities. He knew that he needed Pumfrys's help.

Sitting opposite one another again, Richard sat quietly, the fire in his belly all but extinguished.

Pumfrys tried to ease into the conversation. 'How have things been?' he asked, as if Richard's appearance hadn't provided ample evidence.

'Oh, really fine,' Richard replied facetiously. His tone during the brief telephone conversation earlier with Pumfrys had carried more than a suggestion of blame for his current situation. Although, if he were to look at it objectively, he might have admitted that this was not entirely fair.

In a way, Pumfrys had started all this by writing the article last year. Richard hadn't asked for the publicity. He hadn't asked for the encounter to begin with.

Pumfrys, he had discovered, had withheld a great deal of information that could have saved him months of torment, of false leads and dead ends. And what had he lost as a result – his fiancée, his job (almost), his peace of mind?

Yes, Pumfrys was to blame for some of this. But he had not forced him to start his own investigation. He had neglected his personal life, wasted time and energy, first to try to make sense of his experiences and then, with his eventual conviction as to the reality of the encounters, to find a way to help Emily.

Emily – her fate – played constantly on his mind. He knew he wouldn't be free to continue his life until he had helped her achieve her desperate goal of reaching out to contact those she had left behind and escape the withering darkness of her entrapment at the scene of her physical demise.

His conscience wouldn't allow him to walk away as his friends – as Sally – had urged. Emily had become too real. He had come to know her; had felt her pain and despair. He felt obligated to help.

But his actions and intentions had been misjudged by everyone who knew him. The only one left with some knowledge of the events, and who hadn't, so far, formed a negative opinion, was Pumfrys. And he had hardly encouraged him to be sympathetic. If anything, his tirade over the phone could only count against him, reinforcing any doubts that might exist regarding his stability.

After all, Pumfrys had been out of touch for some time now. He couldn't possibly know how far the contacts with Emily Reynolds had advanced since their last meeting. And there he had been, prattling on in a confused and agitated manner, about how he had been directed by a ghost to contact the man she had been cheated of marrying.

To tell him… what? Er, that he didn't know. It hadn't looked good.

There was an uneasy silence.

'How is, er – I'm sorry … '

'Sally,' said Richard.

'Yes, of course. Sally,' Pumfrys acknowledged. 'How is she?'

'Good,' replied Richard. 'As far as I know,' he added with a sense of bitterness. He saw no point in hiding anything. He looked at Pumfrys, who looked a little embarrassed. But, he must have guessed anyway. But he gave no indication that he had heard Richard's mumbled afterthought.

'She's … gone back to live with her parents.'

'I'm sorry,' said Pumfrys.

Richard nodded. 'It'll sort itself out. Just as soon as I get… my obsession out of my system.'

'Is that what she thinks it is – an obsession?'

Richard's expression provided the answer.

Choosing his words carefully, Pumfrys asked, 'Do you suppose she may be right?'

Richard's eyes narrowed on him. The question hung in the air, unanswered.

Pumfrys got to his feet, taking the fall of silence as opportunity to offer Richard a drink.

When he returned, he found Richard engrossed in the contents of the folder. They lay before him, spread out on the low coffee table that he had pulled over. Soft ruts in the carpet traced its path.

He said nothing as he set the mugs down on the table, pushing aside some of the papers to make room.

Richard looked up only to acknowledge Pumfrys. He felt unapologetic about opening the folder without permission.

In the few minutes he had had to examine the contents, he realised that Pumfrys had been more deeply involved in the Blaxton Hill story than even the newspaper article had suggested. On some points it seemed he had been deliberately evasive, if not misleading.

Pumfrys noticed that Richard had been sorting the Blaxton Hill material from the rest of the ghost research. He sat opposite, immediately picking up his own drink.

Richard looked up at him over the newspaper centre-spread he held out in front of him, hands wide to spread the paper. He lowered it.

'It's so much better to see the article in original form,' said Richard. 'Much easier on the eyes.'

He looked expectantly at Pumfrys, waiting for his response like a man holding a trump card in a game of poker. It was a guarded attack on his secrecy.

It had taken him weeks to pull together the small amount of material he had on the case. And all the time, Pumfrys had an extensive dossier on the subject. Stacked beside him was a variety of maps, notebooks, handwritten and typed notes, and numerous newspaper cuttings, now yellowed and fading.

'You could have told me you had been heavily involved in the case. Why didn't you tell me when I was last here?'

'I had my reasons,' answered Pumfrys.

Richard frowned, momentarily thrown, too tired to fight the evasiveness of the answer. He waited for Pumfrys to continue.

'I did give you a clue,' he said. 'When I mentioned my

research notes for my book. Remember?'

And now he did. His eyes darted about beneath his creased brow as he retraced the memory.

'You didn't pick up on it at the time. I suppose I rather hoped that you might,' said Pumfrys. He looked a little drained, a little distant himself.

'But,' said Pumfrys, sitting up straight, 'I knew that anyone with more than a passing interest would likely be back. You found the article in the *Courier*. And here you are.' He smiled gently, sympathetically. 'What led you to find it?' he asked.

Richard folded the paper. 'Well, y'know, I never really asked myself how you were always so well informed.'

He reached for his mug of coffee.

'It occurred to me that you didn't seem surprised by anything I said. Not really. I suppose I'd accepted it because you were knowledgeable about the subject, and that Blaxton Hill just fit in easily with all that. You admitted to having done some research on it for your book. What I didn't expect was just how much you'd done.'

'So what prompted you to go looking for it?' asked Pumfrys.

He seemed genuinely interested, but Richard was aware that he was stalling, sidestepping. But Pumfrys was also wiser than that. Richard realised that he was probably making his own assessment of his character and stability from the conversation.

'Okay,' replied Richard. 'Late yesterday afternoon, something just clicked. 'I don't know why I didn't make the connection before. *You* are the local researcher mentioned in the Wetherby book, aren't you?'

Pumfrys pursed his lips. 'What makes you think that?'

'On reflection, I thought who else could it be? To have researched and drafted a book yourself, you must have had more than a casual interest in the case.

'Then, in your article last year, you give the time for the encounters as 11:30 p.m. – about the time the 1978 crash occurred. Only none of the ghost articles I've seen mention actual times ... '

'Perhaps I took it from the Wetherby book?'

'Which credits the 'local researcher'... So,' continued Richard, 'when you told me you'd abandoned your book draft in 1985, it occurred to me, being a journalist for the *Courier*, that you just might have written something back then about it.

'And I was right.' He held up the paper, shaking it unconsciously. 'And there is more here than I could have expected – photos of Emily; her grave.'

He paused, realising he had allowed the tempo of his speech to pick up, to become too animated.

Pumfrys nodded slowly, and smiled. 'Very good.'

'Only I don't know how Wetherby could have missed it.'

'Because I chose not to give it to him,' said Pumfrys. 'He didn't do a lot of his own research for the case. He contacted the paper, and someone at the office told him about me. I'd given up my own book aspirations, so I assisted him as far as he needed for his project, but no more.'

Richard exhaled. He looked Pumfrys earnestly in the eye. 'I gambled on that article being there. And tonight, I'm gambling that you still have more to tell.'

Pumfrys shifted in his seat.

'I think you would have put me off over the phone if that wasn't the case,' continued Richard.

The words led into stillness. He had brought Pumfrys back around to his original question, and to the point of the repeat visit.

Pumfrys's response was measured. He nodded. Slowly. Thoughtfully. He cleared his throat before speaking.

'You know, apart from Wetherby, you are the third person

to seek me out over the years about this story.'

A quick exchange of glances reminded Pumfrys that it had been *he* who had initiated the contact with his article on Richard's crash.

'Including yourself – here, now – all three meetings have come as a consequence of *that.*'

He pointed at the article that Richard had now replaced on the table between them.

'One – in fact, both previous meetings have taught me to be very careful about opening up about the case. It... I didn't fully appreciate at the time how hurtful it might be.'

'You're trying to tell me that one of them was John Hudson?'

Pumfrys nodded. 'When I was researching the book, I traced him to his... to an address back in Haltham. I thought five years or so might have enabled him to get over the tragedy, and I was discreet about the attempted interview. Or so I thought.'

Richard noticed that Pumfrys looked strained as he recalled the incident. The fingers of his left hand slowly clenched and unclenched around the arm of his chair.

'I wouldn't have dared approach him, you understand, not without good reason, but ... '

Richard's heart skipped. He was suddenly sure Pumfrys was going to say he had had a message to relay from Emily. His tenseness evaporated as Pumfrys continued.

'There were a few convincing encounters that I felt justified my action.

'One was by someone very reputable – which Hudson already knew about. It concerned the anonymous police officer mentioned in the newspaper article. In fact, that report was the reason for my initial interest in the story. I had only been with the newspaper a short while when I accompanied Keith

Prescott to interview the man for the *Herald*, a sister paper to the *Courier*, who stressed that he didn't want to be named.

'It was the first time I had seen a man literally quiver with fright as he recalled the incident. He was the first individual I had ever met who had claimed a close encounter with a ghost. Perhaps that was why it made such a big impression on me, prompting my growing interest in the case in later years.

'The officer was driving home after a late night at the station in Eldonbridge. It was a winter evening, dark early; dry and very cold. This was in the years before the new road was built.

'As he approached the crossroads at The Bull, he pulled over for a young lady who waved at him to stop. For some reason, he felt uneasy even as he came to a stop. She looked vaguely familiar.

'Then it dawned on him. It was one of the women whose bodies he had seen cut from the wreck of a car only a few months earlier. He was certain of it.

'His reaction was instinctive. He sped away, almost colliding with another vehicle in his haste.

'The following day, he pulled the police accident report and the newly completed inquest report. He hadn't been mistaken. All three passengers of that vehicle had died. He therefore chose to believe, at first, that he had been mistaken. It *couldn't* have been the same woman. It was impossible.

'A few days later, much troubled, he felt compelled to contact the family, not as a police officer, but as another human being.

'John Hudson, then still grieving, had apparently been more understanding then. He had met the officer a couple of times; been interviewed by him following the fatal crash, and on those occasions the man had been properly detached and officious. Seeing him in such a troubled state impressed

Hudson. It was the first time he had been told that Emily was the candidate for the Blaxton Hill ghost, rumours about which had been circulating for a little while.

'So, when I came to approach him to give fair notice of the article, and my book, before it came out, I didn't quite expect the reaction I received.'

'He was upset?' asked Richard.

'Very upset.'

Richard nodded.

'Unfortunately, the write-up for the *Courier* was already in. I had wanted to hold off on it for a while, but my editor refused. He wanted it for the lead up to Christmas.

'I've regretted ever since the level of detail I allowed to be included. I believed it would help promote the book.'

'But the book was never published?'

'No. I received a phone call from Mr Hudson after the article was published. He was still angry about the whole thing. He wanted me to take out the Blaxton Hill material. At first I refused. I'd put so much work into it, you know. It was too much to give up. The heart of that book *was* that case.'

'So it wasn't the ouija board episode that made you give it up?'

'Hm?' said Pumfrys. 'Oh,' he said, as he recalled the white lie he had fed Richard. 'No. It wasn't that. But that incident is largely true,' he said.

'So. you dropped it,' said Richard.

'Yes. I gave up the ghost on the book – or the book on the ghost, whichever you prefer.'

The feeble play on words fell into empty air.

'You have to understand,' said Pumfrys, 'the man was very upset. It was still all too raw back then. It turned out it had also hurt the mother of the bride-to-be. She hadn't long buried her husband, early in 1984. It was too much. What else could I do?'

'Mmm,' agreed Richard.

'And then,' continued Pumfrys, 'Not long after, I betrayed that promise by revealing too much to someone else, a young woman who came to me with what seemed a genuine interest and sympathy for the case. That,' he reflected, 'was probably my biggest mistake. And greatest regret.'

'She contacted Hudson?' asked Richard.

'Yes. But it was also worse than that.'

Pumfrys took a deep breath. 'Her name was Stephanie Caulson.'

Richard visibly blanched at the name. He sat upright. 'What? Are you sure?'

Pumfrys nodded ashamedly. 'Quite sure.'

'Then all she told me ... ' said Richard. His speech fell away as doubt and confusion surfaced again.

'It's possible she was telling you the truth, but you must bear in mind that she knows a good deal about the case. Why she would mislead you is more to the qu–'

'When was this?' asked Richard, still reeling.

'A couple of months after I agreed to drop the book.'

'Bloody hell, Peter.'

'I know. But in 1985, she was a young teacher with what I thought was an honest interest in the subject. She was supposedly going to present the story to a class of English students as an example of how modern myths develop. After a couple of visits – really no more than the degree to which I've come to know you – I agreed to let her borrow my notes. Only, I naively – stupidly – left my address book in there. She phoned Hudson.'

'She *what?*' said Richard.

Pumfrys sighed. 'Yes. And what I didn't know was she was a fledgling clairvoyant, a medium. She said she could put him in touch with his fiancée, and you can guess the further anguish that must have caused. Although she didn't mention my name, I still felt responsible when she told me.

'So, you see, I couldn't be too free with what I knew thereafter. I had no idea what your intentions might be. Your experience would naturally make you curious. I understood that. But I couldn't risk the same thing happening again.'

Richard looked away for a moment, thoughts tumbling in his mind. 'So why did you write the article last year?'

Pumfrys sat back. 'Actually, I was given that piece by my editor. He knew about the book research from years before, and knew I could write it up quickly. He took it from a junior reporter to give to me.'

'Did you protest?'

'A little. But it would have been written anyway, and I knew I could deal with fairly, if superficially, without making too much of it. Besides, it wasn't as if I had initiated it. The story had become somewhat impersonal by now, regarded as little more than folklore. It couldn't do any great harm after all these years.'

Richard was startled by the way Pumfrys had justified the action to himself. 'Except to me?'

Pumfrys looked awkward. 'I believe I've already apologised for that?'

'Yes, you did,' replied Richard. 'But my story gave you an excuse to get involved again.'

'If you want to put it that way. But only peripherally. When I heard the full story from you – at *your* instigation – then I can't deny it piqued my interest again, but only insofar as I could help you try to understand what had happened to you.

'Now,' said Pumfrys, 'let's get to why you're really here. You told me on the phone that Emily has asked for Hudson personally?'

'Yes,' said Richard. 'It's very important. I told her that I'll try to contact him.'

'I see. Even after what I've just told you?'

'I *must*,' replied Richard. 'And if I can convince you that I haven't lost my mind, perhaps you might agree to help me?

6

Pumfrys listened patiently as Richard described his ongoing encounters with the girl. In spite of the revelation about Stephanie Caulson, his doubts, like his fear, had receded with time, and he had wholeheartedly become convinced of her reality and the urgency of her message. From then on, he was able to concentrate his efforts on helping her – which was what she had been reaching out for from the beginning.

As he pointed out to Pumfrys – who had to accept it on faith, admittedly – the girl he had been meeting was the same pictured in the newspaper. And in those moments of lucid awareness when she was in his presence, she had been able to impart her desperate need to get off the hill, to break through the invisible barrier that held her there. Her living consciousness was tied to the home she was heading back to that night, and the fiancé she would never marry.

He had attempted to drive her home as she desired, but it always proved futile. Merely the conscious act of starting the car could be enough to break the spell and she would vanish. On the couple of occasions when he had dared to reach out with trepidation to take her hand, they had managed to venture a little way up the hill before she began to slip away, losing substance beneath his touch, even before cresting the hill. Her pleas for help cut into his own soul every time they were abruptly terminated.

Emily had repeated over and over the same message in his

dreams, and in the contact with Stephanie. *Take the ring.*

The inflection had always suggested to him that it had been incomplete, that there was more to the message. And then, one night, recently, in a meeting on the hill, she finally said it. Her expression and the way she said it induced a powerful sense of dejá vu. It was the first time she had managed to say it in any of the 'real' meetings.

In these situations, she would, at first, appear drawn and confused, unable to talk, not fully aware of where she was. Not even properly aware of him. Then, it was as if she began to thaw, to look around, to ask questions.

It was always the same, always frustrating. Rarely could she remember him immediately, as if her memory of the meetings was erased every time she vanished. And so, he had to spend time going through the same act of consolation and reassurance every time. And always too soon, she again vanished.

Consequently, it had taken a great deal of time, over frequent visits, to enable him to piece together the reason for her appearances – something that Sally, and his closer friends regarded as obsessive and worrying. And yes, it had led him into neglect of his personal life, and to his drinking again, out of sheer frustration.

Anyway, the night finally came when she completed her sentence about the ring. He even understood something about the means of accomplishing this. He suspected it was connected to this psychic battery thing that Peter Pumfrys had once mentioned. He somehow provided her with energy, which both enabled her to manifest and to communicate, and act as a kind of counter field to the force that trapped her here.

Superficially, the situation was akin to the gravitational fields produced by objects of differing masses. There was the dominant field created or sustained by the hill itself, and the girl's life force trapped in its orbit. His own psychic field had proven too weak to help her break free of the hill's powerful pull.

It wasn't a perfect analogy, but it worked well to illustrate the problem in his own mind. It didn't explain why, for instance, the hill itself could be so influential, but that was another story.

He sensed that the solution lay in what Emily had repeatedly projected to him. The ring must have some special power or significance. He assumed she meant her wedding ring. But he had only ever heard her speak of it in his dreams, and once through Stephanie.

When he first questioned Emily about it, she had looked blankly at him, and vanished shortly after. Each time thereafter, when she stayed long enough, she had no recollection of mentioning the ring, nor knowledge of its purported significance. It had been puzzling. It wasn't mentioned again, even though the duration of the encounters and her recollections and strength of identity increased over forthcoming encounters, so that there developed genuine two-way communication.

The quality of the meetings had also changed in that time, so that with concentration, he was able to feel the energy actually flow from him. It surrounded and protected them like a cocoon, a special oasis in which their states became equalised. On whatever level, he didn't know, but it enabled her to become more natural and easy.

But the higher state of concentration was more costly. He couldn't sustain the contact for very long, and it resulted in a more serious drain on his being.

For all his effort, and in spite of the gains in quality of contact, still the ring had meant nothing to her.

Until that evening, when out of the blue, she said, 'Take the ring… to John.'

He had looked at her and realised that time had caught up with itself. Somehow his dreams had been precognitive, focused on this one moment. His dreams – and even Stephanie Caulson, it had to be conceded – had picked up on events that belonged in the future, that hadn't yet happened, at least not in the accepted order of things. In Emily's state of existence, time meant nothing. She came to him from outside time. Would it be too farfetched to suppose he could have been relating to different aspects of her personality, dependent on how the streams of time flowed? It sounded like fantasy, but wasn't the whole thing beyond plausibility?

The significance of the ring had finally become clear. She had somehow realised long before he that more sympathetic energy would be required to save her, even if she had been unable to articulate that information to him.

She had held up her right hand to reveal the wedding band. It glittered weakly in the dim light of the dashboard. It was the first time he had noticed it.

She needed him to find her fiancé, John Hudson, and to get him to come to her. The ring, which she removed and proffered, would provide the proof he would need to convince him.

He had taken it from her, felt its weight and form and solidity. And yet, when she vanished, it had too.

7

'Do you realise that by now it would take something like that ring to convince Hudson of your story?'

'Yes, I do,' replied Richard.

'And you want to approach him without it?'

'I have to. There's not much time left.'

'What makes you think that?' asked Pumfrys.

'I've noticed for some time now that the strength of the contacts has been weakening. At first I thought it was because the seasons were marching away from the time of the accident – y'know that with some hauntings, the conditions are most apt for repeat appearances around the anniversary of death.

'I do think there's something in that, but there's also more to it. I think her energy and identity are gradually running down so that she will soon be unable to come through at all.

'I believe that when I came along, the conditions were right in every respect. It all came together – not only in the sense of the date being spot on, or my supposed sensitivity, but also that in her moment of lucid awareness, she realised that this might be her last chance and made an all out effort to make contact.'

Pumfrys looked on sympathetically. The story made sense within its own bounds. It had a structure and a sense of honesty and truthfulness. But still, he felt obliged to ask the final question. 'Are you sure – I mean, absolutely sure of yourself?'

Richard locked his eyes on him. They were dark, full of feeling. 'As well as I can be. If she doesn't make it soon, Peter, I think she's gone. She'll be beyond help; truly dead. And to tell you the truth, I don't think my conscience could live easily with that.'

He realised he had leant forward, his body held tense. He forced himself to sit back, to relax. 'You do believe me, don't you?'

Pumfrys nodded. His face conveyed belief and acceptance.

The argument was sold, although Richard didn't feel in a celebratory mood. There was still a long way to go yet.

'It's going to be more difficult than you perhaps realise,' said Pumfrys. 'I suppose you must have asked yourself why the

Emily you know is wearing her wedding ring? When she never got to wear it in life?'

Richard said nothing.

'I think you know. I suspect she was buried with it.'

Richard stared at him for a moment. 'Will you help me?'

Pumfrys got to his feet and started over to his cabinet. 'I can't guarantee that he's still living there, of course.'

'No, Peter. I guessed you might have his address, or could probably find a way to get it. I'm asking you: will you help me?'

'But –'

'I'm not sure I can do it all alone.'

Pumfrys regarded him for a moment, and returned to his seat. He sat there for a moment. Then he said, 'How long do you suppose we have?'

Richard smiled behind moist eyes. 'Not long. Weeks, perhaps days.'

'Then we can't waste any more time.'

8

Richard was as nervous as hell as Pumfrys rang the number from his landline. They waited as it rang at the other end. Two, three times. Four. Five. At last, Pumfrys straightened, glancing at him. His heart beat furiously in his throat.

'Hello? Can I speak to Mr Hudson, please?'

Richard could hear the faint but indistinct crackle of speech from the receiver.

'Hm-mm. Oh,' said Pumfrys. He shook his head at Richard, who visibly slumped. 'Er, that's right. I'm sorry for disturbing you. Thank you. Goodbye.'

He hung up, a look of resignation on his face. He said what didn't need to be verbalised. 'Moved. No forward number. An elderly lady; says she's been there for eight years. I'm sorry.'

Richard looked crushed, but there was still a glimmer of hope in his eyes.

'You've already checked the telephone books?' asked Pumfrys.

'Of course,' said Richard. 'And some of the Register of Electors. Nothing.'

'He may have moved out of the area. It's possible he may not even be with us by now.'

'No. Emily wouldn't have asked for him if that was true. He's still alive. I'm sure of it.'

He looked up at Pumfrys, who was still standing by the phone. He was flicking through the leather-bound diary which he had taken from the cabinet.

'What now?' he asked.

'Hmmm?' mumbled Pumfrys.

'I said, 'what now?''

'Your last chance,' replied Pumfrys, picking up the receiver again.

9

Richard listened patiently as Pumfrys spoke to the man.

Getting over the obstacle of introduction, Pumfrys explained how he had come by the former Chief Inspector's number via the *Courier*. He had interviewed him two years ago about a young man's claim that he had been assaulted by two officers while being arrested outside a nightclub in Eldonbridge. Did he remember?

Yes. What was his name again? Pumfrys?

Yes, Peter Pumfrys.

Pumfrys apologised for the late call, explaining that it was a matter of some urgency. He proceeded to ask if he also remembered briefly discussing another matter, a personal one, at the end of the interview, that they had spoken about nineteen years previously. He reminded the man of the details of his own encounter, in 1979. About how it had unnerved him, and why he had felt it his obligation to tell the groom-to-be, John Hudson about it? The Chief Inspector had indicated in their brief exchange two years ago that he had kept in touch with Mr Hudson. Was that still the case?

The line went quiet for a second before the man asked what this was about.

Pumfrys presented Richard's account sensibly, leaving out the more sensational items. But when he concluded with his request for Hudson's telephone number, if he had it, the man declined.

At least he hadn't said he'd lost touch, which would have been the easy option.

'Perhaps you should speak directly with Mr Wentworth?' suggested Pumfrys. 'As one close eye-witness to another?'

'Is the gentleman with you?' asked Charlie Pemberton.

'Yes,' answered Pumfrys.

'Then put him on.'

Pumfrys handed the receiver over to Richard. 'He wants to talk to you,' he mimed.

'Me?' said Richard, surprised and feeling off-guard.

10

Pumfrys went out to the kitchen to leave Richard to it. He had done all he could. Anticipating a negative outcome, he thought it best to absent himself and make a drink.

It wasn't long before he heard Richard hang up. He made for the living room, and almost collided with him.

'What happened?' he asked.

Richard smiled for the first time that evening. He held up a piece of paper. On it, Pumfrys could see a number with a Haltham prefix code.

'I just elaborated a little on what you said, but stressed the limited time factor. In the end, I had to plead with him.'

'But you convinced him all the same?'

'I don't know about that. I just asked him if his conscience would allow him to lose her. As mine won't.'

'Did he say anything else?'

'Yes. He asked for my name, address, and telephone number. For when Hudson rings him.'

'That won't be the only reason,' said Pumfrys.

Richard shrugged. 'It doesn't matter.'

'Did he offer to call him for you? That would be helpful.'

'No he didn't. And I didn't ask him to. I think he realises it should come from me. So do I.'

'But it will be more difficult. Don't build your hopes up too much.'

Richard gripped Pumfrys by the shoulders. He flinched. 'Don't worry. I know now that it'll be alright.'

'Well,' said Pumfrys, glancing at the kitchen clock. It's probably too late tonight now. I guess you'll have to call him tomorrow.'

NINETEEN

They planned to go away for the weekend, leaving later to avoid the rush hour madness around the M25.

John Hudson called down the stairwell. 'Em! Where've you put my electric razor?'

His wife answered, coming to the base of the stairs to call back. She saw him leaning over the bannister on the landing, stripped to the waist. He was still in pretty good shape for his age, as he occasionally reminded his wife, who had tended to put on a little weight over the years. His smooth head, girded by a ring of ash-white hair, obscured the single shaded bulb above his head.

'I've already packed it,' she said.

'Why? I need it. Can you get it for me, please?'

'Oh, John, it's right at the bottom of one of the bags.'

'Why didn't you leave it out?' he asked.

'I thought you could wet-shave for one night.'

'I ... '

The phone started to ring in the living room. Emily Hudson moved away immediately. She would get to it before he could get to the extension in the bedroom. He began to turn back to the bathroom. It was usually for her anyway. Hardly a day passed without their daughter, Karen, ringing for some reason or another.

He paused, frowning as he heard his wife's usually cheerful voice drop to a muffled, awkward tone. He felt that slight flush of adrenaline around the heart that comes when you sense that things aren't quite right.

'Emily?'

Carrying the phone out to the hall, cord wrapped around

her fingers, receiver gagged with the palm of her other hand, she called from the downstairs hall again, her voice sounding a little fraught. 'Ahem, John?'

'Who is it?' he asked, looking down on her again.

'Someone asking for you.'

He started for the stairs.

'No. Pick up the extension?'

Puzzled, he hurried into the bedroom and picked up the other phone. As soon as he did so, he heard a crackle as his wife replaced the receiver downstairs. Fine. No introduction, no clue.

'Hello?' he asked.

There was a pause, then, 'Er ... Mr Hudson?'

The voice sounded rather nervous.

'Yes. Do I know you?'

'Er, no. My name is Richard Wentworth. I'm er ... '

The voice suddenly became more positive. 'Look, I know how this is going to sound, but I'm calling in connection with Emily Reynolds.'

Hudson swallowed audibly.

He dropped the receiver from his ear. His body tensed, his heart skipping a whole beat. He was unable to respond immediately. He raised the receiver again.

The voice continued. 'You see ... '

Hudson cleared his throat. After what seemed an eternity, he was at last able to organise his thoughts and articulate a reply. An anger grown of defensiveness showed in his voice. 'Wait a minute. What's your name again? What are you –'

His wife was calling anxiously from the bottom of the stairs. 'John? Is everything alright?'

The man was talking in his ear again. He found himself trying to listen to what the man had to say, while at the same time trying to respond to his wife's question.

It was easier to placate his wife first.

'Yes,' he called. 'I'll be down in –' He whirled as he heard the bedroom door open. He hadn't heard her come upstairs.

Concern was written over her face. 'What's up?' she asked, miming the words.

He shook his head, waving her away. She took a step forward.

'Go down!' he said quietly but sternly.

She about turned and rushed from the room. He picked up the phone, and walked to the bedroom door, pushing it to.

She waited halfway down the stairs. She could hear John's voice, but not the content of the conversation. He seemed to be listening more than talking himself. Suddenly she heard him bawl, 'Emily Reynolds is dead! *Dead*. Do you know what that means? Just ... just leave us alone.'

She heard the phone slam down. She started to slip down the rest of the stairs as quickly and quietly as possible, expecting her husband to appear immediately. He did not.

2

He came down the stairs into the open-plan living room. The kitchen, through saloon-style swing-doors, was on the right. His wife, her back turned, was at the sink.

He sat heavily in the nearest armchair, suddenly feeling very tired. All enthusiasm for the weekend had drained from him. He brought his hands up behind his head, supporting its weight with his enmeshed fingers.

Emily strolled in, and sat opposite him. 'What was that all about?' she asked defensively.

'Nothing... nothing.'

'John, don't give me that. Please?'

'I said it's nothing!'

'*Tell me.*'

He sat forward, and sighed. He told her all the man had said.

3

Richard replaced the receiver without conscious action. He was himself in shock. His gaze wandered about the floor. He hadn't expected it to be easy over the phone, but the man's reaction had overwhelmed him, made him feel ridiculous, and awkward, and self-despising. He had put the call off for days, telling himself to expect just the kind of reaction he had just received.

What am I doing? Contacting a man whose fiancée died forty years ago. What for?

What was it about these experiences that so forcibly pushed him to disrupt people's lives? The idea that Emily Reynolds might be vital and trying to communicate? Could that concept, which had taken him so long to come to terms with, be assimilated by others: strangers, skeptics, friends, relatives?

The man's words played over and over in his head. *Emily Reynolds is dead! Dead. Do you know what that means?* His voice had cracked behind his anger before the line went dead.

The conflict he had tried so desperately to explain to Sally returned. Doubts about his actions were in pitched battle with his sense of compassion for the anguished spirit of this girl who was somehow ensnared at the scene of her demise.

How could he convince this man of the need – no, the sensed urgency of his participation in aiding his efforts to get her off the hill? He hadn't even been given the chance to explain this to him.

Emily Reynolds had sent out a distress call. He had received it, and his conscience allowed him no choice but to try to help. But, he knew he could not accomplish this alone. There was no choice either as to what his next action must be. Whatever the emotional pain he might inflict, he had to find a way for John Hudson to hear him out, and to assist him willingly.

4

Emily Hudson felt a little hurt by the mention of Emily Reynold's name. Of course, she knew the telephone call had concerned her in some respect, but to actually hear her husband speak it after so many years invoked a surprising degree of jealousy in her. He had only talked about her once, not long after they had first met, when he had emotionally relived the trauma of the night of the crash. That had been some six months afterward, when he was still very much in a depressed state. He came out of it fairly rapidly after meeting her, much to his family's surprise at the time, particularly in that they shared a first name.

He had told her then that she held full credit for his recovery, something in which she felt some measure of pride. But she also came to see that he had never truly gotten over his loss. Although she knew that he loved her, it was obvious he had loved the other Emily deeply —something, she thought, to do with his relative youth, twenty-two years of age at the time. At that age, in love, all is idealistic and romantic. To suddenly see all those dreams, all that potential, snatched away in an instant, could breed a certain cynicism in one's future.

What she suspected hurt him (and which hurt her in turn) was no matter how comfortable and fulfilling their married life together had been, and might be, there would always remain for him that gnawing uncertainty about what might have been if Emily Reynolds had lived. Reality seldom turns out to be a worthy successor to one's hopes and dreams, particularly those of youth.

Although he had never since spoken of Emily Reynolds, he had never tried to hide or destroy the personal items he had kept from those days, most notably his album of photographs and one or two ciné films of her, and she had never felt any sense of pain or disloyalty in this. So, why did she feel uneasy now?

'Is he the one who was featured in the *Courier* last year?' she asked.

'Eh?'

'It must have been October or November. It was on the front page.'

'I don't remember that,' he replied.

It was true that, on seeing the article, she had deliberately hidden the paper from him amongst the magazines and old papers in the newspaper rack. She hadn't thrown it out. He generally, but not always, picked up the *Courier* on a Friday evening. Of course, it was possible he had seen it. She knew, though, that he would not comment if he had. She had hoped he would forget about it, and apparently he had.

Now, though, after the telephone call, the cat was out of the bag. This Wentworth fellow had told him about his claim to have picked Emily Reynolds up on Blaxton Hill.

'Well,' she said sympathetically, 'do you suppose it's really possible? There have been so many stories over the years. And he wouldn't be the first to come to you – that policeman that time?'

'I know,' he replied. 'But I can't believe it.' He stood up. 'No, it's impossible.' He sighed. 'Well, we're not going to let this spoil our weekend. Go up and finish packing.' He forced a smile.

She returned the gesture. She reaching out to grasp his hand, then made her way to the stairs.

He looked after her, waiting for her to pass out of view. He mentally followed her as her footfalls mapped her ascent. He didn't feel very good about withholding some of what the man had said, but he needed some time to think.

Of course, he had seen the write up about Wentworth in the paper, but he had chosen to ignore it, like others over the years. And he would have dismissed the call as a tasteless intrusion – in fact, had been about to, when everything had been turned upside down.

The basic account as it was told was no different to the popular reports but then, in response to his growing anger, the man had said a few things that had sent him into a momentary shocked, confused, and defensive state. His immediate and natural reaction was to attack out of defence, and to slam the phone down.

He could still hear the man's words.

Does a ring mean anything to you? Together forever? Something about a pigeon, and ... a park?

He walked over to the walnut cabinet at the back of the room. He bent on one knee, one hand supporting the small of his back, and pulled the left-side door open to reveal his private safety deposit box. He reached for it, and rotated it so that its lock presented itself to him.

Reaching into his trouser pocket, he retrieved a bunch of keys. He selected a small brass key and inserted it into the lock, turning it until the latch popped open with a dull click. He lifted the lid to reveal layers of assorted, sharply-creased and yellowing papers: insurance policies, certificates, deeds. Removing these, he found what he was searching for. He picked it up gently with forefinger and thumb, bringing it out into the light – a broad-banded gold ring which was as bright as the day he had picked it up from the jeweller's four decades ago.

He tilted it. Engraved on its inside in light script was a

single word: Forever.

Together ... Forever

How could Wentworth have possibly known that? Only a select few knew of the matching rings made for himself and Emily. They had been paid for by his own parents, both now dead. The only others had been, of course, Emily Reynolds, and his own wife. Their two children had never been told. It was personal business that had been kept private. There was no way anyone else could know.

Together ... Forever was the full inscription shared across the two rings. Emily's ring, a lighter version of the one he held in his hand, and her half of the expression, was buried with her.

He had kept his, in spite of an offer by the jeweller to return it at full redemption.

He turned the ring over. Was it really possible that the essential part of Emily Reynolds had somehow transcended her death to communicate via this man? That was one of the few possibilities available as an explanation. He didn't want to even contemplate one of the others.

But that wasn't all Wentworth had said.

He heard movement upstairs. His wife was making her way downstairs. He hurriedly replaced the ring in the box, and replaced it in the cabinet without locking it.

When she re-entered the room, he was slipping on his shoes.

'Ready?' she asked.

TWENTY

The morning was bright but cool. He stood in the gateway of the cemetery, between its two huge and weathered stone pillars. Its painted black wrought iron gates were fastened back, anchored by drop-pin bolts into the tarmac of the path.

A light breeze ruffled the grass and billowed through the heavy foliage of the trees. It was so quiet, save for the chirruping of birds and the faint sound of far-off traffic. Nine-fifteen on a week-day morning, and you'd expect some sign of life. He almost choked on the irony.

He thrust his hands into his pockets and strolled through the gate. He shivered involuntarily, and not entirely from the coolness of the air. He surveyed the scene before him. The wide path on which he stood proceeded through the cemetery directly ahead, and continued on up to a building that was perched on an area of raised ground some hundred metres ahead. It looked like a chapel of sorts from here.

He met headstones immediately on the other side of the gate. These were clearly of an age. Some had been displaced to accommodate the relatively new path, which was a road-lane in width. Here and there, stones and markers abutted its tarmac perimeter. There was something distasteful about the laying of what was essentially a road through a graveyard, but how else would a modern hearse make its way to where it needed to be?

A large sand-coloured stone just off the path on his left caught his eye. It was the crest which drew his attention, a proper, albeit weathered skull-and-crossbones. It was the first time he'd seen one. He paused to examine it.

The name on it was barely legible: William French, 1776–

1823. Below the name, an inscription:

> STOP STRANGER, STOP AS YOU PASS BY
> AS YOU ARE NOW, SO ONCE WAS I
> AS I AM NOW, YOU SOON WILL BE
> SO PRAY PREPARE TO FOLLOW ME

The words seemed to speak to him personally, as was undoubtedly the author's intention. But there was something more. He shuddered, stepping away.

It – a rhyme, he thought, dating from the Middle Ages – summed up all he felt about cemeteries and what they represented. They were a tangible reminder of one's ultimate fate: that life, for all of its hopes and potentials, was ultimately a walk along a precipice.

More than anything else, they symbolised the common denominator to all human existence. We all share the grave as a common destiny, irrespective of belief, status, or personal differences.

It wasn't healthy, of course, to dwell on the inevitability and consequence of the death of the body, but he just couldn't help it. Not here.

2

He stood outside the building. He glanced at his wristwatch: nine-fifty. He had been standing here for nearly half an hour. The groundsman was supposed to be here at nine-thirty, according to the girl he had spoken to on the phone yesterday at the Council offices.

He stood about ten feet from the entrance to the small building. It seemed too small to be a chapel. It gave the impression more of a groundkeeper's repository – and that's probably what it was in addition to housing a copy of the cemetery plot-index that he knew was here and wished to view.

The entrance was a stone arch. A heavy-looking creosoted wooden door lay just inside, on the other side of a padlocked, iron-barred gate – a precaution against vandalism, no doubt – arched to fit the shape of the entrance.

He looked around, and his gaze once again surveyed the extent of the cemetery to the north, where it had been extended in recent years. At its farthermost northern boundary and to the west, some two hundred yards in each direction, it came up against a belt of woods and scrubland. To the east, it abutted a housing estate.

Somewhere out there lay the remains of Emily Reynolds, beneath a stone marker amongst countless others, arranged into semi-regular rows. They glittered in the morning sun, their rows reminding him of sharks' teeth, perpetual and threatening.

A sound behind him made him whirl. He saw a man approaching, pushing a bicycle. He breathed a sigh of relief. The man uttered a word of greeting.

Richard replied in kind.

'Sorry I'm late,' said the man, who seemed to be in his early sixties. 'Got a bloody puncture at the bottom of the hill,' he said, indicating the front tyre of his bike.

Richard found his morbid spell broken. He smiled in sympathy. The man was breathing hard. He walked past Richard straight up to the wall of the building, where he set about securing his bike with a chain to an iron loop. Richard looked a little bemused. Who could possibly steal it?

Mr Wentworth, isn't it?' the man enquired.

'Yes,' replied Richard.

'Don't worry, son,' said the man. 'Nothing supernatural. We get a list from the office every day.'

'I don't suppose you get many appointments?'

The man moved towards the padlocked entrance to the building. 'Oh, you'd be surprised. Sometimes we – that is the other groundsmen and me – get kept so busy with visitors that we don't have much time for the essential work.'

Richard just looked at him. He wasn't sure if he was having his leg pulled or not. The man's expression gave nothing away. He supposed it was possible that a cemetery was potentially a busy place, with any number of people wishing to locate plots in which relations and friends were buried, but it wasn't something he'd thought about.

Anyway, the iron gate had now been opened, and the man had stepped forward to negotiate the wooden door. He fumbled a ring of assorted keys. Richard was amused to see that the key-ring had a blue plastic BMW logo attached to it. The incongruity was refreshing.

A moment later, they both stepped into the cool musty atmosphere of the building's interior. When his eyes adjusted, Richard's vision was met by sturdy shelves full of leather-bound volumes along two of the walls. A desk with stacks of paperwork and a telephone sat in one corner. A pair of lawnmowers and various other items of garden equipment cluttered another corner.

The man asked him to sign a visitors' book, which was kept mainly for chance visitors, before Richard was left to browse freely while he got on with his work.

3

Finding her name was incredibly straightforward. The entries were made year by year, and then each year listed alphabetically by surname. To find the plot, simply note the code following the name and check against the cemetery plan. Simple.

He found the volume for October-December 1978. Emily Reynolds's name appeared on page 585. His eyes had locked on it almost as the page fell, and in spite of the other Reynolds listed there:

REYNOLDS Emily S. 83 4E.121. int.2/1.1978
REYNOLDS George M. 58 3D.234. int.3/4.1978
REYNOLDS Emily L. 22 4F.342. int.6/11.1978
REYNOLDS Anthony I. 4 4F.369. int.23/12.1978

4F 342. Block 4F, plot 342. Emily Lesley Reynolds.

Seeing her name recorded here, in this Book of Death, made his heart skip. He found himself shaking his head gently, as if in disbelief. This simple handwritten record, more than anything else to date, confirmed her status. He looked up momentarily. He was thankful that the old man had left him with the ledgers.

In all of his encounters and experiences, he had been increasingly aware of her life force. She was *alive*. It was in a state that few could understand, but it was true. Here, though, his certainty wavered. Faced with the brutal fact of her death, with her ruined body incarcerated beneath sagging earth, it was suddenly difficult to maintain the clarity of that vision of her.

Well, he thought, whatever the case, whether her spirit lived on as he believed, or whether he was sick and imagining it all, as some claimed or suspected – even Sally, it seemed – he had come here to meditate on his predicament, to employ her grave as a focus for his thoughts.

4

He squatted down in front of her grave. Carefully, he brushed away the dried husks of twigs and leafy mulch that had accumulated below the headstone. In their place he lay a small bouquet of bright flowers, daffodils and tulips.

He didn't believe in using flowers for such ends ordinarily. It seemed too close a metaphor for the nature of life itself: no sooner do we grow and blossom do we begin to wither and die. It seemed more fitting to plant a bulb or a tree instead, which might symbolise the continuance or cyclic renewal of life. But the gesture seemed right here.

He stood up, taking a step back. The headstone was plain white marble, which had lost some of its polished lustre to decades of the elements.

Emily Lesley Reynolds

Aged 22

2 September 1956
27 October 1978 .

In memory of our beloved daughter
Sleep, love, sleep in peace

The photograph in the paper had been taken no more than a few months later. Winter temperatures had precluded the sods of grass knitting together seamlessly to bind the earth, and the stone appeared clean and sharp, yet to be attacked by cycles of weather. Below the stone were vases and bunches of freshly cut flowers.

The sight before him contrasted with the mental picture he had brought here.

He felt the emotions well up, and swallowed heavily. A tear formed in the corner of his eye, perched there momentarily before careening down his cheek and plummeting into the grass at his feet.

He looked around, suddenly self-conscious at the show of emotion. Some way off, he could make out an old woman crouched over a fresh plot, placing flowers. His eyes showed her to him as a blur; the image wavered and flowed through his tears.

It was so useless. He stared ahead, his thoughts capturing Emily's appearance from his encounters and dreams.

The moment overwhelmed him. All the pent-up pain and frustration he had suffered rushed to the surface. The humiliation by friends, the disbelief and lack of understanding by Sally – it all came out, to combine with the intense feeling of sympathy and helplessness he felt for Emily. No-one, not even her fiancé, offered understanding.

'Emily ... ' He was surprised to hear himself speaking aloud. His voice creaked through his sobs. 'Emily, what do you want of me? What more can I possibly do? I contacted John yesterday. He er ... he doesn't want to know ... '

He had mentioned the ring to John Hudson, related its inscription. For a long time it had been the sole thrust of her attempts at communication. And yet, apparently, it had found no recognition with Hudson. Perhaps the information, gained through his trance-like meetings with Emily on the hill and in his dreams, meant nothing after all.

He fell quiet. His breathing slowly returned to normal. He took out a tissue and wiped his eyes. After a few minutes, his composure returned.

A few days ago, it had all seemed so clear, so simple. Hudson would be receptive to the message and the pair of them would be off to Blaxton Hill. Emily would be reunited with him, and find peace. He would be released from his obligation and could finally begin to repair his own life.

Well, all that had been shattered. He didn't know if this was just a setback, or if it was finally over.

Pumfrys had told him to give him a call after he had phoned Hudson, to let him know how it went, but he really didn't feel like talking to anyone about it at the moment. Pumfrys's dossier had given the name of the cemetery. He had decided to come here instead.

He looked at the grave for a moment longer, then turned and made his way back to the path.

5

That night, Richard got drunk again, steadily, deliberately. At the moment it seemed his only refuge from a barrage of thoughts and reflections. Without the alcohol, his mind tended to play over and over on a loop.

While he was here, there was Sally. The house carried her in all its aspects, in the décor, the arrangement of furnishings, and in a hundred little details. Her favourite scent still permeated the air, particularly in the bedroom.

Where was this all leading, other than into personal disaster? He couldn't think straight anymore. A myriad of images whirled around in his head: Hudson, a mental picture of him screaming in slow motion into a telephone receiver; Pumfrys; the newspaper articles, his friends sitting around a beer-soaked pub table in shocked embarrassment; the picture of Emily, coming to life, speaking to him, her grey newspaper-print lips moving, but making no sound. The picture changed shape, flowing into a broader shot of the hill itself. The cars, welded together, surrounded by rescue vehicles and people. Then it began to rotate, to tumble, gaining momentum...

He opened his eyes. The ceiling was spinning above him. He sat up quickly, reeling. Swinging his legs around to find the floor, he tried to get up too quickly, and found himself staggering sideways, catching hold of the arm of the sofa. He made for the stairs, mounting them as fast as possible, just making the bathroom in time.

Immediately, the acid curdling in his stomach subsided, and he felt his head clearing. He flushed the loo, and turned to the sink to wash out his mouth and splashed his face with water. Then he made his way back downstairs and went into the kitchen to make a cup of coffee. The kitchen clock showed 02:15.

Sitting back on the sofa, his thoughts returned inevitably to the last couple of days. Voices and images replayed vividly in his mind, but now they were stable and ordered.

The early hours of the morning before dawn – the so-called wolf hour – the time when, statistically, most people die; the time when the body's diurnal cycle reaches its lowest ebb; the time when the mind seems most tired and vulnerable, stripped of its rational processes and defences; when the trap door of the dark unconscious is thrown back.

The cloying stillness of the hour, disturbed only by the sound of his own breathing and the steady clack-clack of the kitchen clock (why is it that clocks seem to find their voices in the early hours?), allowed Richard to quietly come to terms with the situation.

It was finally over. He made a mental apology to her.

Sorry Emily.

But his tired, still somewhat inebriated mind had come to a sturdy realisation, a conclusion. He had done all that was possible, and at great expense. And no matter the strength of his personal conviction of Emily Reynolds's reality and her plight, he could do nothing about it.

What alternative was there? He could continue to make sorry trips up to the hill and, assuming that Emily continued to appear, make endless futile attempts to help her off the hill.

But, what could he say to her? And how could he further punish her, and himself, by watching her slowly lose her fight for identity?

No, that was to be avoided. It would be too much, for both of them.

He only hoped he would be able to avoid thinking of her, alone and afraid in that terrible darkness in the years to come.

Finally, he drifted off to sleep.

6

A dream formed in the fog of his mind. In it, he saw himself asleep in his car on Blaxton Hill. Emily was with him. She was trying to awake him, shaking him, but although he shifted in his sleep, he did not stir.

He saw her slip a ring from her finger and, uncurling the fingers of his left hand, place it in his palm. She looked particularly sad, her eyes moist, a pained expression creasing her brow.

She leaned forward to whisper in his ear. He watched with that strange detachment of self, as she replaced his hand in his lap, squeezing the fingers gently together to secure his hold on the ring.

The words she had spoken, whatever they were, caused his sleeping self to shift again, uncomfortably. Finally, his eyes blinked open to see her fading away. He reached out for her, but she was already gone.

His attention fell to his hand. Something had fallen into the passenger seat, but in the darkness he could not make it out. It was not on the seat where he felt around trying to locate it.

The ring. Gone again.

7

04:20. He snapped awake. His body was soaked with sweat. Birds chirruped outside in the stirring light of dawn. Dreaming again. Just another dream. Feeling sorry, and torn and exhausted, he rolled onto his back, and beads of tears welled in the corners of his eyes.

8

5:45 p.m.

Richard's phone buzzed in his pocket. He hadn't long been in after a foray to the supermarket. It was on its fourth ring when he answered it.

'Hello?'

'Richard Wentworth?' asked the voice. He recognised it immediately.

'Yes, speaking,' he replied. 'Mr Hudson?'

'Yes.'

Richard felt awkward. Why was he ringing here? How did he get the number? Of course, Pemberton. But what was this about?

'I'm ringing to apologise for the other evening,' said Hudson. 'I'm afraid I lost my composure, and manners. I reacted without thinking.'

Richard was embarrassed, but intrigued. Hudson's demeanour was so different to before.

'Er, no. I'm sorry for the way it came across,' he replied. 'But I wouldn't have bothered you without good reason.'

'The things you said… about the ring, and the pigeon.'

Richard cringed. It had meant nothing to the man before, and it seemed ill-considered and pathetic.

'How did you really find out about them?'

Hudson's tone was cautious, but not accusatory.

'You mean it means something to you after all?' asked Richard.

'It might.'

'She ... Emily told me. As I tried to explain. I know it sounds unbelievable, but – '

'How –' began Hudson before changing tact. 'No, we'll come to later. Please tell me what er ... she said.'

Richard's information had come to him mainly in dreams. The hill encounters were always too brief. All he knew was that the mention of these two things, in particular, should be meaningful. Detail behind them was, embarrassingly, absent.

'I believe the ring was her wedding ring. You put it on her finger before she was buried. She knows it's one of the few things that would convince you – it's inscription and all that.'

Hudson tightened his grip on the receiver.

Richard took a deep breath. 'As for the pigeon,' he said, 'I'm not sure what it means, but I got the impression that it was something you wouldn't forget.'

There was silence for a moment, then Hudson spoke, his voice hollow. 'Wh...' He cleared his throat. 'Why, if she spoke to you, didn't she just tell you what it meant?'

It was a question Richard had asked himself, and he *had* tried to find out more from her.

'I don't know,' he answered truthfully. 'But I do know that she asked for you. It's really important.'

Hudson didn't follow up with the questions Richard expected – about why she had asked for him, and so on. Instead he came out with something that seemed nonsensical, to begin with.

'Are you married, Richard?'

'No. Not yet. I'm engaged.'

Well, he thought, Sally hasn't actually told me I'm not.

'In that case, I think you should bring your young lady over tomorrow night, and we'll talk.'

Richard couldn't believe what he'd just heard. He was speechless. Apparently, his appeal at Emily's graveside yesterday hadn't been wasted after all. Incredibly, it was coming together again.

'So you believe me?'

'I think we should talk about it,' said Hudson. 'Is tomorrow night too soon?'

'No, no. That's fine. We can't afford to waste time.'

'Good, then if you have pen and paper, I'll give you the address.'

'Yes, sure. Only my fiancée won't be able to make it. Is it Okay if I bring a friend along instead? It's someone who might be able to help me explain what's been going on. In fact, I believe you've spoken to him before.'

Hudson was suddenly skeptical at the mention of Pumfrys's name, but Richard was able to convince him that he wasn't including him from any desire to publicise. With due reservations, he agreed.

Richard took down the address, and noted the agreed time: Seven-thirty tomorrow.

'Okay, see you then. Thank you,' said Richard before hanging up.

Richard sat back and closed his eyes.

We're back in business, Emily. I hope to God we're successful.

He picked up his phone again and called Pumfrys's number.

TWENTY-ONE

The following evening, by arrangement, Richard drove over to the *Courier* offices to pick up Pumfrys. Hudson lived in that direction, in the village of Eastleigh, eight miles on the other side of Fordham, so it seemed logical to leave one of the cars and go together.

He pulled around the flower-bed D that fronted the building, and parked in the taxi-rank layby. He left the engine running.

7:05 p.m.

He should be out by now, he thought. He was late himself. The traffic in town had been slowed by an accident.

He waited for another five minutes, then got out and trotted up the flight of steps up to the reception, which was still brightly lit. The main desk was unoccupied, but off to the right, in a booth, sat a security man. Perhaps he could check if Pumfrys was in. He was halfway through the door when he heard footsteps shuffling up the steps behind him.

'Richard.'

He whirled around to see Pumfrys.

'I was just coming to find you,' said Richard.

'I've been looking for you,' said Pumfrys.

Richard shrugged. 'Yeah. Sorry. Traffic.'

'Never mind. Shall we go?' said Pumfrys.

They made their way back down and over to Richard's car.

'Do you think he'll go along with it?' asked Richard, as he unlocked his door.

'I really don't know,' said Pumfrys.

He broke off while Richard got in and leaned over to unlock the passenger door.

Chapter Twenty-One

Pumfrys pulled the door open. 'It all depends…'

Again, he cut himself off. His was looking down, inside the car.

Richard followed his gaze. 'What's up?'

Without answering, Pumfrys reached down the side of the seat and retrieved a small object, which he held up for Richard to see. 'Yours?' he asked, doubtfully.

Richard's eyes opened wide in surprise. He swallowed. 'Let me see,' he said quietly.

Pumfrys offered the ring to him on the palm of his hand. Richard hesitated for a moment, then took hold of it. He held it up to examine it.

His expression changed from awe to suspicion. It was impossible. He found himself looking at Pumfrys. Had he planted it? What for? More to the point, where did he get it?

But from the look that Pumfrys gave him, he could tell he was thinking the same thing of him.

Richard looked at it closely. It *was* the ring, familiar in design and weight. He held it between thumb and forefinger, turning it to check its inner surface. The word *Together* was etched there. He felt a tingling sensation up his spine.

He didn't understand how it could be, but there was no denying it. It was real. It wasn't about to evaporate like it had in his meetings with Emily or in his dreams.

He looked at Pumfrys.

'An apport,' Pumfrys said with wavering voice. His face had paled noticeably.

'A what?'

'A physical manifestation, a solid object that appears out of nowhere. Implied by the term is the assumption that it has passed through physical barriers.'

Richard was thoughtful for a moment. Then he said, 'It'll make our case stronger. This –'

'No. I wouldn't mention it unless we have to,' replied Pumfrys.

'Why not? Emily obviously means me to have it.'

Pumfrys shook his head. 'Richard, don't you see? We still don't know how Hudson will react. The strength of your case is not that ring, but the impressions and details behind it, which is what you have already told him. 'If you just come out and produce the ring, apart from the immediate suspicion it will cause – where you got it, and so forth – it would devalue your whole case.'

Richard fell silent. He could see what Pumfrys meant. How could descriptions of the ring and its inscription (it wouldn't be difficult to guess the other half of the message) mean anything if Hudson believed he had it in his possession all the time? It would make the whole idea of contact with Emily unbelievable and preposterous. And his motives and sanity would be in question. Hudson certainly wouldn't be predisposed to hear him out. He might even call in the police if he thought he might have disturbed Emily's grave.

'Okay,' he said. 'But if he still seems doubtful after what we have to say, then I'll have to take that chance. After all, it's what's driven Emily in her efforts at contact all along, isn't it?'

2

They parked around the corner from Hudson's house, a modest semi-detached with a neat, spacious front garden.

Richard had quickly slipped on a jacket and tie, much as he hated to, before they made their way up the path to the door. Pumfrys seemed to own nothing *but* formal wear. In Richard's right trouser pocket, wrapped in a tissue, was the ring. Pumfrys carried his research dossier, in case Hudson proved to be unfamiliar with the case.

John Hudson met them at the door and, after exchanging pleasantries, invited them through the hall and into a through-lounge.

Hudson offered to take their jackets, while making the introductions.

'My wife, Emily,' he said. She stood around five feet five. Grey-haired and slightly overweight (she had once described herself as 'pleasantly plump'), she still looked young for her age. Her eyes were the kind that smiled at you. Richard smiled back easily, hoping that neither of them had noticed his surprised reaction at her name.

'How do you do,' she said, nodding first at Richard, then Pumfrys.

'Emily, Richard Wentworth,' said Hudson, indicating with his palm up. 'And this is Mr Peter Pumfrys.' He had earlier explained to her that he was the journalist who had written the article the previous year. And that he was coming with Richard as a friend, not to make notes. She hadn't been quite so trusting. Nevertheless, she had no reason to be rude now.

Pumfrys returned her greeting. 'Pleasure,' he said.

3

The lounge area was spacious and comfortable-looking. Two soft, oatmeal-coloured two-seat sofas made an L-plan on the right, while two single armchairs faced them, so that the ensemble formed a broken square. In its centre, on a stylish mosaic-patterned mat, stood a low coffee-table with mock-tile covering. On it were two large oval plates, arranged with a variety of sandwiches and snack items. Glasses with rolled serviettes in them occupied the middle of the table.

For us? thought Richard.

As Richard and Pumfrys were invited to sit down, they

couldn't help but notice the projector positioned between the sofa-chairs. Facing it, collapsed down for the moment, was a screen. Both eyed the set-up with interest, but neither said anything.

Mrs Hudson offered them a drink, reeling off a list of options. Pumfrys asked for a light martini, while Richard, driving and, for once, genuinely not interested in anything stronger, opted for tea. She returned shortly with a tray, and set their drinks before them. She passed a glass of white wine to her husband before sitting with hers.

John Hudson placed his wine glass on a coaster, before directing his attention to Pumfrys: 'I saw your article in the paper last year. I don't recall reading much, though, about your actual – what, sighting?' he said to Richard.

'No, I wasn't actually interviewed,' Richard said, glancing at Pumfrys.

'I'm afraid that was my fault. It was a bit hurried. Last minute thing,' said Pumfrys.

'I see,' said Hudson. It was plain that he and his wife felt awkward. 'So…' he said.

Richard cut in. 'First of all, I'd like to thank you for inviting us over tonight. It's much better than talking over the phone. And hopefully I can convince you that I'm not a nut, despite how it probably sounded the other night.'

'Well,' said Hudson, 'to tell you the truth, you wouldn't be here but for what you told me over the phone, you know.'

'I realise that,' replied Richard.

'You can guess from my reaction the other evening how I feel about these reports of a ghost being connected with Emily Reynolds. Now, I'm sure most of it is rubbish, and sometimes it can be very hurtful.' He looked at Pumfrys, who lowered his sight.

'But,' he said, 'I can't deny that you got to me,' he said to

Richard, 'because no-one alive, apart from myself and my wife knew anything about Emily's ring. I put it on her finger myself and it was buried with her.'

Richard stole a glance at Pumfrys, who remained straight-faced.

'And the thing about the pigeon.' He shook his head, turning to his wife. 'I didn't tell even you about that.'

She frowned. 'Pigeon?'

'Hm-mm. Rather than try to explain, I think the best thing would be to show you.'

Hudson put down his drink. Levering himself out of his seat, he made his way around behind her towards the projector screen. Pulling the screen upright, he hooked it onto a clip at the end of its pole.

'Three weeks before Emily died, we spent a day at Chessington Zoo. I took my ciné camera along, and what I'm about to show you are the last pictures taken of her.'

His voice had lowered, sounding a little strained.

'I hope it's alright. I checked the film earlier, but it hasn't seen the light of day for forty-odd years. I only watched it once, about two months after...'

There followed a brief pause. 'If we're ready, we'll start rolling.' He turned to his wife. 'Can you lower the lights please, love?'

Emily Hudson got up and walked over to the dimmer switch on the wall. She dimmed the lights to their lowest and returned to her seat.

Her involvement in this was her own choice. Her husband had offered to drive her to their daughter's place for the evening, but she had elected to stay, out of curiosity as much as to watch out for him.

The subject was naturally something close to her husband's heart, and she was not sure if he could be entirely objective about it. And she was suspicious of Richard's and Pumfrys's yet unstated motivation. She didn't want to see John getting hurt again.

From what she had already learned, the whole thing seemed to be just too incredible. Though, she conceded, the information regarding the ring was spot on. And, of course, she was aware of the reports that had appeared in the papers over the years.

This projector viewing was the first such occasion in years. Most of their ciné film had long-since been transferred onto digital formats. But not this. Tonight, the old way was the only way.

4

A primitive countdown sequence flickered on the screen. The clacker-clacker of the noisy projector was distracting at first but was quickly ignored as the first proper frames came on. Hudson adjusted the focus.

Richard shifted forward in his seat, forcing Pumfrys to lean a little to get a complete view around him. He could understand Richard's fascination.

The shot was a wide-angle of an open area of parkland. The colour was faded, and the image pitted and streaked here and there, but the film was steady.

Richard sensed movement through the expanding beam of light and the dust motes suspended in it. He noticed Hudson taking the chair nearest the screen, and turned his attention back to it, waiting for Emily Reynolds's image to appear there.

'As I said, this was about three weeks before the wedding,' he said, narrating the film which was without sound.

'But as you can see, the weather was great for the time of year, around the first week of October, or late September, anyway.'

The view changed to closer crops of the cages and pens within the zoo complex, cutting from one to the next with perhaps a little too much haste.

'We went there,' he continued, 'with Emily's friends and the boyfriend of one of them. One was called Julie. I can't recall her surname.'

'Cabot. Julie Cabot?' offered Richard.

Hudson looked at Richard. 'Yes. That's it.'

'I don't recall the name of the other girl.'

'Olivia.'

Hudson nodded. 'Yes, that sounds right. Anyway, we had some tickets and I...'

The first shot of people appeared on the screen. It was too brief to be able to study it before it changed to a close-up of a young woman. Emily.

Richard felt his heart almost stop. Goosebumps broke out on his skin. Pumfrys had also reacted. Richard dared not take his eyes off the screen, but he felt Pumfrys's weight shift on the sofa.

If he had looked around, he would have seen Emily Hudson looking on, elbow on knee, one hand massaging her chin. Hudson himself seemed unable to look at the film for very long. He kept turning from it to watch his guests, particularly Richard, who was captivated.

The girl on the screen, her light hair blowing gently in the breeze so that the drop-curls on one side kept covering one side of her face, was talking into the camera. She looked from side to side, smiling all the time, occasionally brushing the hair out of her eyes and mouth.

The picture bobbed up and down, as if nodding, as she looked back in their direction. The camera zoomed in for a close-up of her face.

She held her hand up, then there was a cut to a wider shot again of the entire group sitting together eating a packed lunch. Hudson had said nothing during the close-ups of Emily, not even an introduction.

'When did she change her hair?' inquired Richard without looking away, and without thinking.

'Hm?' said Hudson.

Richard looked around. 'Her hairstyle… it's different.'

Hudson was nonplussed. He looked back at the screen. Had she changed it after that day? He couldn't remember, and he didn't know if Richard was trying it on or not. He had to let it pass.

There followed another sequence of shots showing animal pens and intercut views of the group walking away from the camera, or travelling between cages. One showed a view of Hudson himself, looking much different with his slimmer build and full head of hair. The figure on the screen launched into an exaggerated grin, and waved his hand frantically like an over-the-top circus clown. Forty years in the future, Hudson cringed at the sight and laughed with his wife and their guests. Clearly, he had forgotten the incident, which had appeared here without warning.

Further along, there was a close-up of Emily and Julie, sitting with her boyfriend on a bench. It was the first time Richard had seen an image of Julie.

It was difficult not to see a mangled car wreck through this peaceful late summer scene. He wished desperately that he could reach through space and time, through the screen, to warn them.

As a sequence of fairground views came to an end, Hudson said: 'This is it.'

The others turned to him, but this time, he was the one who maintained eye-lock on the screen. They followed his gaze.

The screen went dark and then Emily's image appeared. She was laughing, really laughing. The camera panned quickly to the left to show Julie and her boyfriend, and Olivia, all laughing too. Olivia pointed towards the camera.

The view swept back to show Emily. Her laughter had been replaced with a grin, through which she was trying to speak. She pointed above the frame, reaching beyond the camera's focus and beckoning as if she wanted to take the camera. She shrank slightly in the frame as the camera backed away to avoid her grasp. But then the shot changed. It showed Hudson again. Obviously, he had handed the camera to Emily, and she was now filming.

He was saying something to her as Julie came into the shot, holding a handkerchief. Julie was waiting on him as he continued to talk to Emily, then he lowered his head towards Julie as if directed. The camera moved shakily in for a close-up.

The top of his head was plastered with the khaki-and-white of guano. The hanky, having waited for the camera to get a good view, proceeded to wipe and pull at the matted strands of dark hair.

The film cut back to show Julie helping John to remove the bird poo, and then to a gathering of pigeons. They waddled and strutted about on the ground, chasing pieces of bread thrown to them from off-camera, their heads bobbing forward and back like sand-dancers.

Shortly, the subject of the film changed to unrelated shots of a garden, a street, shots of the Haltham of 1978; the photographer using up the last of his film.

Richard turned away from the screen to face Hudson. A three-quarter angle on a familiar car, an early 1970s Consul, flashed on the screen before the film ran out, the reel flapping on the projector.

Hudson said nothing as he got up and went over to the wall to turn the lights up. He turned back to see Pumfrys turn the projector off. The reel came to a halt, leaving the room in momentary silence.

They all felt diminished, somewhat overwhelmed by the film. Hudson, in particular, seemed to have been deeply affected. He appeared to have shrunk in his clothes.

Much of the film had been new to him. He hadn't realised what the years could really do. He felt some guilt at having forgotten what Emily Reynolds had really looked like; some of her mannerisms. Over the years, his mind had formed a hazy mental picture that had preserved her essential personality, but had become neglectful of her true appearance. He had found it more painful than he had expected to view the film. But, it also served a purpose in making her real to him again.

At last, he spoke: 'Well, now you can see why I agreed to see you, Richard.'

'It's incredible!' remarked Mrs Hudson.

'I'm surprised myself,' said Richard calmly, although inside he was glowing.

'You said Emily needs help. Asked for me?'

'Yes.'

'But why? How can I possibly make a difference? I mean, if she really is there, why would she wait forty years before making contact?'

His wife answered, an unexpected ally: 'I suppose, John, that it could be said that she's been trying to do that almost from the beginning?'

'Okay. I'll admit that some of them have been intriguing, but I still feel ambivalent about the whole thing. Not to mention confused. I still can't ... Why now?'

'I can't answer that,' said Richard, 'but ... '

'I think I can,' said Pumfrys. 'Possibly because before now

she may have lacked the means of achieving proper contact? The catalyst in this case is this young man.'

'Are you suggesting that Richard is a medium?'

'No,' said Richard. 'Not at all.'

Pumfrys spoke again, directing his attention to Richard. 'I realise you're not fond of the term, but it is essentially what you are.' Richard looked uncomfortable with the thought, but chose not to argue.

'Let's just call it a psychic ability,' Pumfrys said. 'The well-known medium and healer, Matthew Manning, when he was a young man, described meetings and communications with a spirit who inhabited his home in the eighteenth century. In many ways, the case resembled Richard's experiences. In fact, it surpassed it in a few respects, so this type of experience is hardly unique. Manning saw apparitions; there were physical effects.'

Richard looked up sharply.

'And he maintained communication with the ghost through automatic writing. Anyway, the point is – I came across this really by accident; it seemed very apt – he likened his ability to a key which enabled this character to free himself of the bonds that had trapped him in the house since the 1730s.'

Emily and her husband exchanged glances. Where was all this leading?

Pumfrys continued. 'I think Richard is the key to contact with Emily Reynolds. We can't begin to understand why, but somehow she has become trapped at the scene of her death. It doesn't always follow, but the classic theory of apparitions seems to apply here: that a state of high emotional charge – in this case, the pre-wedding excitement, and the trauma of the crash itself – may have prevented her finding rest. She has unfinished business.'

Hudson's thoughts were in conflict. That was plain to see.

'You still haven't explained where I come into it,' he said.

Richard took Pumfrys's lead. 'I think I explained briefly over the phone that she needs to get away from the hill? Well, I can't tell you how many times I've tried, and failed, to accomplish that. But I know it's the answer; but I'm not strong enough by myself.'

'But I'm no medium!' said Hudson.

Richard shrugged. 'Maybe. But it does seem that Emily needs your involvement.'

'Your relationship may provide its own special energy,' added Pumfrys.

'Wait a minute,' said Hudson, raising a hand. This was getting out of hand, in spite of all he'd heard tonight. 'You're starting to lose me. Let's try to clarify things a bit. It's your belief,' he said, looking from Richard to Pumfrys, 'that I can help Emily Reynolds by providing an energy boost to enable her to get off the hill? How am I supposed to do this?'

'Simply your presence may suffice,' suggested Pumfrys.

Emily Hudson was beginning to look decidedly uncomfortable. 'What... by actually going to Blaxton Hill?' she asked doubtfully.

Her husband said nothing, but his expression reflected his own concern at the suggestion.

Pumfrys decided to try to slow things down. He and Richard were acting unfairly, hitting the man with too much too soon. No wonder he was starting to look lost.

'Richard, I think it'll be helpful if you described your experiences from the beginning, to provide some perspective?'

Richard nodded in agreement.

'Um...before you begin, why don't I make some tea?' suggested Emily Hudson, rising from her seat.

They all appeared to welcome the distraction. While she was away, they talked casually about each others' backgrounds and interests. Hudson responded freely to Richard's tentative questioning about Emily Reynolds – how they had met, how he coped with her death. Pumfrys sat back and listened for the most part.

When Emily returned with the tray, Richard began, taking his time.

Over the next twenty minutes, he told them everything, his dreams, his insights and feelings, and the hill meetings. There was no sense in hiding anything. Some of it was new to Pumfrys.

He described Emily to Hudson as fully as he could. He tried to impart a sense of her personality and her feelings of isolation and despair. He described how she appeared and how he had learned to 'tune in' to her presence, the frustrations at her all-too brief stays, the way she seemed lacking in awareness and vitality to begin with, only gathering by drawing energy from him. How she had finally completed her message to him, asking for John Hudson, and to get the ring to him. How he sensed that she was fading, of how time was running out.

When he finished, Hudson was the first to speak again.

'What is it that you propose we should do – go up there and, what, hold a séance?'

Pumfrys winced. 'I think you should think of it as a soul rescue.'

'Soul rescue?' asked Emily.

'Some people believe it is possible to combine mediumistic talent with prayers and guidance to aid trapped or stranded souls to find the light, so to speak.'

'How can you tell if you've been successful?' she asked.

'Well, the ghost isn't seen or heard from anymore,' replied Pumfrys.

'Look,' said Hudson. 'I don't mean to sound defeatist or anything. If Emily's really there, I want to help her, but I've got to ask a question.'

His attention was squarely on Richard again.

'I believe you've impressed us both with what you've told us tonight,' he said, looking to his wife, who nodded in agreement. 'It would seem that you have a ... a gift. So couldn't all of this come out of this medium-is-tic ability?'

He placed special inflection on the final words. His eyes showed a vulnerability, the unsettled look of a man taken beyond the threshold of reality into a wider world which he was being asked to take seriously, as a matter of life, or suffocating death. A man grasping at straws.

'Because,' he continued, 'there isn't any concrete proof, is there? Not really.'

'What would constitute proof to you, Mr Hudson?' Pumfrys asked.

Richard shot him a wary glance.

'I don't know,' he said. 'All I know is that it all seems impossible. I'm sorry, but I don't think I can go along with it. Emily Reynolds *died* four decades ago.' He stared at the floor.

'John ... ' His wife grew more concerned.

Richard shifted in his seat. He looked at Pumfrys, who seemed to have found interest in a hangnail on his thumb. Without looking up, Pumfrys asked, 'Do you know what an apport is, John?'

Oh, oh, thought Richard. He took a deep breath.

'No. But I have a feeling you're going to tell me,' he answered somewhat wearily.

'Apports are objects that appear from nowhere in some hauntings, although they are particularly associated with poltergeist cases. They can be familiar items that seem to have been teleported. I realise this sounds like fantasy as well. They are objects that appear to move from room to room, or they can be foreign objects which have no known source.

'Some mediums claim that apports are gifts from spirits that are given in appreciation of services rendered – payments, I suppose, for providing a means of communication.'

'Ah, so what is your point, Mr Pumfrys? asked Emily.

'Richard?' said Pumfrys.

Three pairs of eyes were on Richard as he stood. He looked at all of them in turn as he thrust a hand into his trouser pocket and retrieved something wrapped in peach-coloured tissue.

'I want you to know ... I swear ... that I didn't get this the way you might think.' He unwrapped the tissue and picked out the ring.

Hudson grabbed at the arms of the chair, eyes wide. His jaw clenched visibly. He stared horrified at it, and then over it at Richard.

'What is it?' asked Emily, getting up to take a closer look. She slipped on a pair of glasses, and gasped.

'Her ring,' he replied with incredulity.

'Are you sure? asked Emily.

'Let me have it,' he said to Richard.

Richard held it out. Hudson showed the briefest trace of hesitation before taking it from him. Like Richard before him, he turned it over and over, positioning it so that its inner surface was fully illuminated.

'Well, John?'

He looked at his wife, nodding slowly. 'It *is* her ring. It even has the scratch on it where I squeezed the two together the day after she died... I was going to throw them into the river,' he croaked.

'It turned up this evening, in my car, on the way over here. Peter found it,' Richard said quietly. 'Honestly.'

But Hudson didn't need any more convincing.

5

In spite of all she had seen and heard, Emily Hudson had remained reticent, cautioning her husband about going on with this.

But here they were, at Blaxton Hill. Pumfrys had driven them, and now they sat a little way up from the crossroads by The Bull.

'What do we do now?' asked Hudson, looking around anxiously from his position in the rear of the car. 'Just sit here?'

'More or less,' answered Richard. 'We could drive around, but it's probably better to sit tight. Just concentrate.'

Hudson caught Pumfrys's eyes in the rearview mirror. He formed an expression that Pumfrys interpreted as 'what am I doing here?'

Pumfrys glanced at Richard. He could just tell through the dark that he had closed his eyes.

'Do you really think this will work, Richard, with three of us here?'

Richard answered without opening his eyes. 'We can only try. It never happens right away. Give it time.'

Lights behind them announced the approach of another vehicle. Milky shadows glided across them as it picked up speed, dissolving back into darkness as it whined past them, a young woman peering over her shoulder from the passenger seat at them.

'Doesn't that sort of thing have a negative effect on Emily's appearances?' asked Hudson, leaning forward to talk to Richard. 'What about when the pub turns out?'

The question caused Richard to turn to face him. He sat back again.

'I can't recall ever seeing a car or anyone when I'm talking to her. It seems unreal, like time is suspended or something, or it's operating in a different frame.'

Hudson looked over his shoulder, and around again. The lights from the pub looked inviting, comforting, compared to the darkness around them. He had passed this way only a few times since the dual carriageway was built. It looked just the same.

Eleven-fifteen. Just about the right time, he noted. Looking out into the dark, it was easy to overcome the feelings of foolishness he felt even as they were driving over. Even so, he was still having problems trying to assimilate the idea that his erstwhile fiancée could actually be haunting this spot.

They sat there in silence for a while. Hudson was becoming increasingly ruffled, an impatience born of tiredness. Even Pumfrys shifted and sighed, he noted. The night's events had been emotionally debilitating, to say the least. Now, the initial adrenaline rush had subsided and it was proving to be exhaustingly anticlimactic and tedious.

He kept his feelings to himself for the moment. He had to keep reminding himself that this was for real. He had held her ring. He decided to break the silence to ask a Richard a further question.

'Have you ever asked yourself why Emily would choose you as her contact?'

'Many times,' Richard replied. 'Though whether she chose me is open to question. I think she... er gravitated to me, if you like. I was probably just susceptible.'

'Any previous experiences like this?'

Richard almost laughed. 'Er, no.'

'Are you sure?' asked Pumfrys with real interest.

'Nothing I ever thought meant anything,' he sighed.

'Like what?' asked Hudson.

Richard seemed reluctant to pursue this, not least because of the distraction the conversation was causing.

'Oh, I don't know,' he said, 'but when I was a kid I used to wake up in the morning sometimes and think that things in the room had been moved around.'

He paused for a moment.

'One night, returning to bed after going downstairs to get a drink, I passed the open living room door, and I thought I saw what looked like an old man sitting in the chair nearest the fire. It disappeared when I blinked.'

'And you don't think that's significant?' asked Pumfrys.

Richard tilted his head. 'Can't prove anything by it. My mum didn't believe me. She thought it was just attention-seeking. Y'see, my dad had only left us the month before. He didn't even stick around to see my brother born.'

'Classic situation,' said Pumfrys.

6

They waited on the hill for another ten minutes, then agreed to leave, Richard with some reluctance.

Richard dropped Pumfrys off at the *Courier* offices on the way to Eastleigh. No-one said very much on the journey.

It was plain that expectations had been higher than Richard knew to be realistic. He knew that patience would be necessary on Hudson's part for them to be successful, but how could you convince someone to stay with this sort of thing for an indefinite period?

Perhaps Pumfrys had been right when he said he didn't think it would work. At least he felt that his own presence had had a dampening effect. He – Richard – and John Hudson, had belonged there. He had not, and he felt partially responsible for tonight's failure.

'I'm sorry,' Richard said to Hudson as they drove on to Eastleigh. He didn't know what else to say. Hudson rocked his head in denial of the apology. Before he got out of the car, Pumfrys had urged Hudson to try again. Richard took this up.

'Try again tomorrow?' he asked hopefully, glancing away from the road for an instant.

Hudson sighed, stretching his feet into the well in front of the passenger seat. 'I don't know right now. It's been a long evening, a lot to absorb. Do you really think it will make any difference?'

'As Peter suggested, I'm already involved, and you were specially invited. He wasn't. Perhaps it will work with just the two of us there.'

'Maybe,' replied Hudson noncommittally.

'We owe Emily that – to try, at least?' He looked again in Hudson's direction.

After a moment of silent reflection, Hudson relented. 'I suppose so.'

'Thank you,' said Richard, relieved. 'I do understand how it must still seem to you, but I've a feeling it will work next time.'

He hoped his optimism would prove to be well founded.

'Besides,' he added. 'We didn't have the rings – I think that might have had something to do with it. Perhaps you could wear yours?'

As soon as Richard said it, he regretted it. Hudson flinched, his eyes narrowing at the suggestion. He didn't answer. He had never put the ring on, and it didn't seem right now. Instead, he asked, 'What time tomorrow?'

'Eight?'

'Okay.'

'How about if I drive over to your house again, and leave my car there while we go instead in yours?'

'How come?' asked Hudson.

'It'll mean I can sit in the back, relax properly and concentrate. And, if Emily appears, I can try to stop her slipping away. Whenever I've tried to drive off the hill, my attention isn't always on her, of course, so I never actually see her vanish.'

'Okay, I understand. That's fine,' said Hudson.

Richard left Hudson at the end of his driveway, declining the offer to step in for a cup of warming tea, which he felt was offered more out of courtesy rather than any real desire to prolong discussion.

Hudson had offered him Emily's ring, but he had declined that as well. It was meant to be taken to Hudson. There it would stay for the moment.

7

Emily Hudson had waited up for her husband. She made him a drink and listened to his brief report on the night's non-event before taking herself off to bed.

He followed a short while later, after placing the reunited rings into his security box, where he gazed at them thoughtfully before closing the lid.

TWENTY-TWO

Richard lay in until early afternoon. He had had a very restful, dreamless sleep, and he felt fully refreshed. And strangely confident.

Tonight would be different. He could feel it. All the ingredients were right now: Hudson's presence, the ring. Yes, it *would* happen.

On the spur of the moment, he decided to call Sally. Amazingly, he found his heart beating fast as the phone rang at the other end.

'Hello, Wyler National, Claims. Can I –'

'Sally. It's me.'

'Oh, hello,' she said coolly.

'Hi,' he said gently. 'How are you keeping?'

'I'm okay. Er, I can't really talk now. What do you want?'

'I'm just calling to tell you it's almost over.'

2

Hudson was waiting in his car when Richard arrived. Richard raised a hand to indicate that he had seen him as he pulled in to park. He locked his car and trotted back to climb in beside Hudson.

'Evening, John' he said cheerfully. 'How'd you sleep last night?'

'Fine,' answered Hudson as he checked mirrors and pulled away.

'Me too,' replied Richard. 'Do you have the rings?'

'Hmm-mm.'

Within minutes they joined the motorway for the nine-mile journey to junction eleven, a mile-and-a-half north of Blaxton Hill. By now the traffic had died down in this direction and it took only ten minutes before the turn-off countdown markers came into view. The slip road brought them to a junction with the Haltham-Eldonbridge Road, where Hudson turned right, so that they passed under the motorway heading south. A mile further on, they came onto a roundabout interchange at the top of Blaxton Hill. Hudson took the first exit, for Frickley. A hundred yards further along, on the right, was the turn-off for the old Haltham-Eldonbridge road.

In 1978, Hudson explained, the road curved northwestwards from here and then straightened out before entering the outskirts of Haltham. That section of road had been obliterated with the dual-carriageway upgrade in 1982 that made an entirely new Haltham to Eldonbridge road.

The preserved section of the old road retained some of its old menace. The gradient on the dual carriageway over to their right had been reduced, but this old section provided sufficient fall off along its length to command respect, particularly in poor weather when visibility and traction were reduced. Hudson reduced speed accordingly.

The pub came into view at the crossroads. The beat of rock music could be heard even over the noise of the engine. Lights from the small courtyard helped illuminate the traffic and road signs: straight over for Eldonbridge, left for Frickley, right to Broadford and Nedworth.

Giving way to the Valence Lane traffic, particularly that emerging from behind The Bull off the steep descent from Frickley, Hudson edged out and then brought the car into a tight U-turn around the crossroads island so that it faced up the hill. Richard knew that he was acutely aware that this very spot was the scene of Emily's death. He didn't hesitate to pull the car away and up the slope again so that they parked at the same not-too-distant-not-too-close spot as the previous night.

The handbrake secured their position with a *cllunnch*. Hudson extinguished the car's headlamps and then cut the engine, leaving the sidelights on for safety's sake.

'Right,' huffed Richard, unfastening his seat belt, 'I'll get in the back.' He pushed the door open and lurched out into the night. The air was mild, its movement light. The breeze carried with it the sound of traffic from the dual carriageway down away to their left through the hedgerows.

Richard looked up and down the road. He had been up here so often by now, he had almost forgotten the terror of his first encounter. His sense of fear had become depressed over the ensuing months. It would be as well to remember that and try to appreciate how Hudson might feel if his own feelings of optimism tonight proved well founded.

He opened the rear door of the car and swung himself into the seat, pulling the door closed behind him before shuffling over to the right behind the driver's seat. Hudson didn't ask him why he chose to sit there. In fact, Richard did it without thinking, as if unconsciously reserving the seat nearest the pavement for Emily. The thought must have occurred to Hudson too, since he seemed to shudder slightly before speaking.

'So, we just sit here again?' he said without breaking his gaze from the dark lane ahead.

'Yes. But this time,' replied Richard, 'no talking please. Just leave me to concentrate.'

Hudson stifled a yawn. 'Whatever you say.'

Richard closed his eyes and tried to shut out the outside world, John Hudson included. He tried to focus on a mental picture of Emily, calling her, drawing her near. As he gradually slipped into the desired state, his muscles relaxed and his breathing became slower, deeper.

3

Given opportunity to anticipate these events, John Hudson might have come to dread the hill waits as probably the most fraught, frightening and traumatic phase. But he had discovered last night, and was rediscovering very quickly now that, like any other stakeout, it was a tedious business. Boredom and weariness resided in the dark.

Sitting on the hill was not frightening. It looked eerie, and it held awful significance for him, but the ambience he had expected was swamped by his self-consciousness, by that same sense of foolishness that he had felt twenty-four hours previously.

Paradoxically, when he was away from here, at home, the potentials were more vividly realised and he found that if he were not careful, it could get to him. Like late last night. But, of course, at home he wasn't waiting for a stranger or a policeman to tap on his side-window and ask him what he was up to.

He hadn't slept much the night before, despite what he had told Richard. His mind had simply been too active. An hour after retiring, he had slipped out of his bed, careful not to wake his wife, and snuck downstairs. He had poured himself a drink and sat quietly poring over an old photo album which contained pictures of Emily Reynolds and himself, and items of wedding paraphernalia – printed invitations and receipts for what should have been a day of great happiness.

As the alcohol had taken effect, accelerated by his tiredness, he had found himself fighting back a sense of loss and despair that had been denied but not forgotten all these years.

No wonder that tonight he found it a little less difficult to accept being here. In the inside pocket of his jacket were the two rings. He hadn't been able to resist re-opening his deposit box again last night before going back to bed. Emily's ring had been there. It was real.

But, first thing this morning – well, soon after it opened, at nine – he had gone to the cemetery. He had visited often in the weeks and months after Emily Reynolds's death, but less frequently over time, especially after meeting the other Emily, who was to become his wife. Aside from one occasion, his father's funeral, he hadn't been there in all these years, and he felt some embarrassment at not having being able to locate the plot right away. But soon enough, he stood at the foot of the grave.

It was clear that someone had been there recently. It was cleared of debris and a wilting bunch of flowers had been laid at the foot of the stone – almost certainly left by Richard Wentworth.

As he stared at Emily's headstone, the intervening years collapsed under their weight and he was back there again, four decades ago, heartbroken and lost.

But the plot itself appeared undisturbed, and any remaining doubts had evaporated right there. As he said to his wife when he got back, he had to check, had to be sure – else he, and Richard Wentworth would not be here tonight.

He reached into the pocket and, locating the ring that would have been his wedding band, removed it and slipped it quickly onto his finger, not allowing himself time to think about it. He curled his fingers into a fist so that he could feel the ring's cold silky skin against his own.

He glanced around and saw that Richard appeared to have fallen asleep. He had slumped in his seat, and his chest rose and fell sedately. He turned back, resigned to just waiting. With Richard out of sight and silent behind him, he felt suddenly alone, and a little uneasy.

Up the lane, the cats' eyes glinting insipidly in the light cast by the sidelights. The darkened lane outside the dim cone of light consisted of shifting patterns of black and grey. It was easy, with tired eyes and mind, to imagine all sorts of things in that grainy gloom. The wind flicking at leaves on the trees and shrubs suggested forms and movement, waxing and waning. Illusions.

An occasional fleeting shaft of light in his rearview mirror provided some distraction from his mental musings as cars passed through the crossroads or left the pub car park.

The silence somehow made it worse. He reached for the radio, turning down the volume control before switching it on so as not to disturb Richard. The sound of radio chatter, though barely audible, provided some company. After a while, he found his eyelids growing heavier and soon, he closed his eyes and found himself drifting into that woolly state between wakefulness and sleep. He opened an eye just once before nodding off, at the sound of the first drops of light rain pattering on the windscreen.

4

The ache in his neck and upper back woke him. At least that's what he thought at first. Slowly, he lifted his head and reached to massage the nape of his neck. He took a deep breath, coming fully awake.

Squinting through slightly blurred vision, he read the dashboard clock: 22:38. Its green colon pulsed in the darkness. He had been asleep for over two hours. His wristwatch, positioned to take advantage of the spilled light from The Bull confirmed the time.

Outside, the rain was fine but steady. It cloaked the

darkness in a shimmering grey curtain.

He looked around at Richard. He was still out of it. He had slumped in his seat, his chin resting on his chest.

Hudson felt an urgent need to wake him. *Now*. No delay.

Something was happening. He could *feel* it – a numbing coldness that spread down his spinal cord like ice water. The muscles of his middle back tensed in response to signals sent out by a part of the brain he wasn't in control of.

'Richard?' he murmured.

The feeling was growing.

'*Richard,*' he pleaded through clenched teeth.

Richard moved slightly. He could hear that. Hudson sat rigid, unable to move, not even to look round. The gathering sensation, like a cloud of electricity that was overloading his circuits, activating his nerve-endings, spread through his body. He could feel the skin of his groin crawling and tightening, his veins surging with the sudden forceful pumping of his heart.

His eyes flashed to the rearview mirror. He had sensed a change in the quality of light. Yes, it emanated from behind. No, it wasn't another car's headlights, but a smoky blue light that was coalescing next to Richard.

The temperature in the car was also dropping rapidly, falling below that of the outside air so that the misted windows began to clear.

'*Richard!*' he yelped. He fought the compulsion to get out and run.

Then, a clear, distinctly feminine voice called to him from somewhere near. *John?'*

His panic became frenzied.

'RICHARD!'

'Mmm?' came a sleepy reply.

'QUICK!' he screeched, his voice high; his eyes wide in the rearview mirror.

The car rocked gently as Richard straightened in his seat. The bluish haze filled the car, but was stronger in the region of the vacant rear seat. A filament of wavering light joined Richard to it, appearing like an umbilical drawn out of his solar plexus. Another tone, steadily warmer, was developing rapidly into a human outline back there.

Richard bolted upright. 'Emily!' he exclaimed, before he was even properly orientated. He stared at the form rapidly manifesting beside him. Emily's head and shoulders had formed first, but the rest of her was gaining focus and substance, but differentially, as if she were a three-dimensional photograph developing in accelerated time.

It was colder than he had ever experienced. He felt light-headed and a little scared at the force and unexpectedness of her appearance. He turned his attention quickly to Hudson, who sounded like he was close to hyperventilating. He could see his eyes reflected in the mirror. They were screwed tightly shut.

'John, I'm here,' called the voice again, sounding firmer and more natural. Richard glanced back to Emily, now fully formed.

'Hello, Richard,' she said, smiling gently. 'Thank you.'

Before he could return the greeting, she had switched her attention and her concern to Hudson. This Emily was so immediately vital and lucid that he had been thrown off guard. He was used to seeing her in a frightened, confused state, only gradually gaining awareness and sense.

In the front, Hudson was shaking. 'No, no!' he rasped.

His right hand fumbled for the door release. He found it and pushed it open with his elbow.

A hand fell on his shoulder. Hudson yelped, his body tensing under the contact.

'John, stop. It's alright. It's me,' said Richard. 'Relax.' He could feel the cold perspiration through Hudson's shirt.

'Let me out,' whimpered Hudson.

'Close the door!' insisted Richard.

Then, more sympathetically, 'John, please. It's Emily.'

'Yes, John. It is me,' said Emily. 'Really. I'm so glad you came. Please turn around.'

He really didn't want to. But, after a moment, Hudson swallowed and turned slowly, avoiding the mirror. In spite of his attempts to ready himself for this, he recoiled in shock. The familiar form of his long deceased fiancée sat there. The blue haze around her had faded.

Her expression was soft, her eyes smiling and comforting. She looked as she might have on their wedding day, radiant and beautiful. He wondered how he could have ever forgotten what she had really looked like. He found his fear begin to ebb away, giving way to wonder and curiosity. He found the strength to look in her eyes.

'It's like it's been forever,' she said. 'I can't tell you how relieved – and pleased – I am to see you. I'm so sorry for what happened. I wanted to marry you more than anything.'

His tongue felt thick in his mouth, dry of saliva. Tears were welling in the corners of his eyes, his nostrils growing moist.

'I... I ... ' he stammered, 'I know, Emily. I know. And me, you.' He found his gaze dropping from hers. They were too deep.

This was surreal. He heard his own voice as if from somewhere nearby.

'And this is all due to this young man,' he said, finding an excuse to look away for a moment to Richard. He was overwhelmed.

'Young man? Listen to you, John. You sound like you're getting old.'

Hudson managed a smile. 'I *am* getting old,' he said, making eye contact again. 'Look', and he put a hand up to his fleshy face and balding scalp.

His fears were dissolving in familiarity and a remembered love.

'You have changed, but you are looking well,' said Emily.

He nodded. 'Thanks,' he said. 'You look just the same. It's incredible.'

He fell quiet for a moment. He shifted his body to a more comfortable position for looking behind.

'I have to confess to not believing any of this.'

'I understand,' she said.

'I... we both have Richard to thank.'

'Yes,' she said quietly. She looked at Richard as she spoke. 'Richard has been a good and reliable friend. He heard and believed in me, and offered his help when I desperately needed it.'

Richard felt a lump in his throat, his eyes moistening.

'You're welcome,' was all he could think of to say.

Hudson looked at Emily's left hand. There was no ring there.

'It was the only way I could get you to come,' she explained. 'You always were stubborn, but never too narrow-minded,' she said.

Richard hadn't said very much. Aside from feelings of being an outsider, a gooseberry to a unique meeting, he was starting to feel very tired. A queasiness curdled in the pit of his stomach, like his viscera were being slowly extracted. He wondered if Hudson felt the same cramps in his gut. After all, he was the catalyst in Emily's transformation, the source of additional power she required to fully realise herself.

'How did you manage it?' asked Richard.

'I gave it to you,' she said, sounding surprised that he should have forgotten.

Richard frowned. She didn't seem to have any understanding of how she manifested, of how her presence affected him, drew from him. He decided not to pursue it. Instead, he brought a hand up to his forehead, finding beaded droplets there.

'Are you alright?' asked Hudson.

I don't know,' he said. His cheeks puffed as he exhaled through pursed lips. 'But I do think we shouldn't waste any more time here.'

He faced Emily. 'We've got to get you away from here, haven't we?'

'Yes,' she said. 'It's about time. Only I feel so safe and strong with you both here, it's hard not to put off the moment.'

Richard understood her feelings. There had been so many failed attempts to get her off the hill. If they were to fail this time, there would be no hope.

Her next words echoed his thoughts: 'If I stay here, I fear I'll be lost forever.'

She shuddered, something Hudson later considered to be an ironic reaction.

'Promise me you won't let me slip away again?'

Richard found he couldn't lie to her. 'We'll do all we can.'

'Where are we going?' asked Hudson.

'It doesn't matter, as long as we get away from this spot.'

'Take me ... home, John,' Emily said, savouring the word.

Hudson nodded. There was a certain rightness about that. 'Okay, okay, we're on our way.' He reached for the ignition key, starting the engine without delay.

'But *slowly*,' Richard urged. 'Why don't we ... er, just take it easy?'

The engine sputtered. Hudson turned the ignition again.

He winced.

Two hours with side-lights on must have drained the battery. And maybe, Emily's appearance may have something to do with it as well.

'Problem?' asked Richard.

Hudson didn't reply. He tried again, feathering the gas pedal. The engine sputtered again, then coughed, and finally turned over. Hudson closed his eyes momentarily in relief. He revved the engine to keep it from stalling.

"Okay,' he said. He depressed the clutch pedal and engaged first gear. From what Richard had told him, Emily could vanish at any time after a certain distance from this place. They would have to be careful.

A flash thought occurred to him. They knew she might vanish at any moment. Perhaps that would be an end for her.

But what if she didn't – not at all? What then?

He pushed the thoughts from his mind. Neither bore thinking about.

Headlights sheared through the darkness ahead, clearing a path for them as the car pulled out and began a measured acceleration up the lane. None of them spoke as Hudson proceeded through second gear, checking his mirror to catch Emily's reflection, ready to brake quickly if she showed signs of ... well, any sign of discomfort.

His limbs still felt heavy with the unmetabolised adrenaline in his bloodstream, his perspiration-soaked shirt and trousers clammy and sticking to his skin. He noticed for the first time how quiet it was all around them – no sight or sound of other traffic, the pub behind them receding and strangely distant, like it wasn't quite real. The radio was no longer playing. Instead, there was a sizzling static coming from the speakers. Hudson reached down and switched it off.

The car gained speed.

Richard was intent on keeping his eyes on Emily, ready to

shout if there was any problem. In the past, he had only been able to guess at the rapidity of her disappearance. He hadn't actually witnessed it, and he didn't know if there would be sufficient time to act to make any difference. He looked away only long enough to make snap assessments on their progress, looking out for the stretch of road where he thought Emily would be in greatest danger.

During one of these glances, Hudson's left hand came into view on the steering wheel. Richard couldn't help but notice that he had put on his ring.

He checked on Emily again. 'Okay?' he asked.

She nodded but her eyes betrayed her, exposing her uncertainty. Her hands were pressed together in her lap. Even in the poor light he could see that her ring was missing.

He was aware from the familiarity of the hedgerows they passed that they were approaching the critical phase of the journey. It began somewhere before the hill's gradient began to level off, and where the road bore to the left before continuing onward.

Almost immediately, as if on cue, Richard noticed that Emily began to shiver and then tremble. It was as if they had crossed an invisible threshold, like stepping out of doors into winter air and the sudden cold forces goose-bumps to break out on the skin.

They were already well within the danger zone. Emily's face showed alarm, her colour fading momentarily. He reached over to take her hand to offer reassurance. A high-pitched whine, like a generator, immediately coursed through his temple. He shook the feeling off, seeing stars for a moment. Through this, he could feel the unusual texture of Emily's hand in his. It was like putty, cool and somehow malleable like her flesh was losing cohesion. He felt it might easily extrude through his fingers if he formed a fist.

'No,' she wheezed, snatching her hand back and doubling over as if from a blow to the midsection. *'Help me!'*

'John!' Richard exclaimed sharply.

Immediately, Hudson braked – not the sharp application of an emergency stop, but a well controlled deceleration that caused the rear wheels of the car to slew only a fraction.

'We're losing her!' said Richard, his voice fraught.

And, at first, he thought they were. But, as the car stopped, she uncurled herself from her forward hunch, bringing her shoulders back. She regarded him with greying eyes, an expression that echoed the fear and hopelessness he had seen in her before.

'What happened?' asked Hudson anxiously.

'I'm sure she started to slip away,' replied Richard. 'Don't ask me why she's still here,' he said, noting just how far along the road they had travelled. It was a lot further than ever before. And she was still here. There was still hope.

'Hang on, Emily,' urged Hudson.

'I feel like I'm floating,' she said. 'But I'm alright.' She looked at them both. 'For a moment, you two, the car, everything, began to fade away.'

'We're not going to lose you,' Richard assured her. 'Not after all this. I...'

He broke off. He closed his eyes for a moment, his head swaying like he was in a swoon before he regained his train of thought.

He addressed Hudson. 'John, we're gonna have to swap places. You're going to have to take over back here.'

'Why?' asked Hudson. His voice showed some alarm again. He accepted that this was the Emily he had known and loved, but he also knew she was dead. His primal fears dictated his reaction, a case of nerve-endings over rationale. He really didn't want to be any closer.

Richard answered him by trying to explain his reasoning to Emily: 'I don't know how, but it seems you absorb power from whoever is physically close to you, particularly those with some... psychic ability. I know it's not intentional on your part, but sitting here with you has exhausted me. I don't think I'm strong enough to give you what you need to get you off the hill.'

It was an honest assessment. He wouldn't allow personal feelings to get in the way, much as he felt he had earned the right to see it out and take the major credit for Emily's rescue. But, it was Emily that mattered.

John Hudson, though not psychic in the same sense, had that special affinity with her that provided its own power. It was his turn, his love, and his rightful place now to be the one to pull her free of her snare.

He turned to Hudson: 'C'mon, quickly. I'll drive.'

Without further discussion, they hurriedly swapped places, pausing only to note just how dark and silent it had become outside. Nothing seemed to exist outside their little oasis of light.

Wasting no more time, Richard raised the clutch pedal a little too hastily. The car lurched forward and he had to fight to reduce their acceleration in case it had an adverse affect on Emily.

'Sorry, sorry,' he said.

Sitting that little bit further away from her, Richard began to recover quickly, so that driving wasn't as difficult as he anticipated.

It was strange how only now he could really gauge Emily's new vigour and the demands on his mental and biological energy she had made for her appearances. He hadn't noticed the gradual depletion in his self until the pressure behind his eyes had been joined by the cramps in his abdomen. Now, he could appreciate the difference. It was apparent that prolonged exposure might be very taxing, if not dangerous, since Emily's demands would progressively outstrip weakening supplies of whatever form of energy she drew from them.

The realisation set in that they couldn't afford to be overly cautious. If they didn't get Emily away fairly quickly, they would be too weak to save her anyway. He stepped on the gas pedal.

The gradient of the road ahead seemed to be levelling out. Nearly at the top, and they were still accelerating.

'How are feeling, Emily?' he called out.

'Nervous; a little shaky, but alright now. I don't feel so weak,' she called back over the noise of the engine.

'Good, good. John ... ' He waited for Hudson to lean closer, placing his head nearer the seat-back.

'Give Emily her ring.' Richard glanced around briefly.

'Huh?'

'I've a feeling it'll help if she has her ring back – don't ask me why. Just do it, okay?' he added.

Hudson reached into his jacket pocket. He transferred the ring from his right hand to his left before offering it to Emily.

She seemed somewhat hurt that he had chosen to stay near the offside door, reluctant to sit any closer.

She took it from him, unavoidably touching the tips of his fingers. Something passed between them at the contact. Hudson felt his fingers numb slightly, and the small muscles of his hand and lower forearm twitched as if subjected to a mild electric shock.

Though the touch was brief, he could tell that her flesh was different. It was cool, and felt almost artificial, though he couldn't explain exactly how. The coolness of her skin, he surmised was either 'normal' for her current state, or an impression of unnatural coldness gained by Emily's absorption of his own body heat, drawn out through his finger tips.

Whatever the nature of the energy she drew from him, he had felt the drain intensify on contact. The chill that rolled down his spine from his scalp was something more familiar and better understood. Nevertheless, he forced himself to keep his hand there until she took hold of the ring and replaced it on the finger where it belonged.

Emily acknowledged the action, and him, with a passive smile, a mixed expression of regret and understanding of his feelings that caused him to again drop his gaze, embarrassed at his still evident unease.

For the first time, he had a full view of her, and couldn't fail to notice that she was wearing the same clothes she wore the night she died, a light-coloured blouse and dark skirt. Only these, like her body now, were undamaged and whole. She had actually been buried in a dress suit.

Slowly, he adjusted to Emily's presence again. Earlier it had been to the shock of her appearance. Now, to the close proximity to her. He tried to avoid any thought of her death – that she was a spirit, a ghost, a phantom, a wraith – call it what you will – and think of her as Emily. Just Emily, the young woman whom he had loved very much.

'I'm still finding this very hard to believe,' he said to her. 'Not to mention difficult.'

'I understand, John,' she answered.

He smiled at her, and they fell quiet, turning their attention back to the road.

5

Richard saw and felt the change in gradient as the car achieved the brow of the hill. The car slowed as he eased off the accelerator to look around.

It was a strange moment, anticlimactic in its own way. He knew, and Emily knew, that they had escaped the hill's influence. Only Hudson remained unsure. He looked from Richard to Emily, whose expression told him it was over. Her eyes were glassy with relief.

'Is that it?' asked Hudson.

Could it have been so simple?

Richard sighed. 'I think we've done it!'

Emily's reflection in the mirror confirmed her untroubled presence as he brought the car up to the junction with the Frickley road.

At this moment, he realised his fears about Emily's effect on them were unfounded. The danger was over. There was no longer a kind of supernatural tug-o'-war between themselves and the hill.

They had won. Unbelievably, and at last.

Emily no longer seemed to be drawing the same amount of energy from either of them. Richard felt relieved of the residues of his headache. He guessed that Hudson felt the same relief too.

He also realised that, strictly, Emily didn't even have to reach home to be safe. If she vanished now, it wouldn't matter, although it would mean being robbed of the opportunity to say goodbye. He hoped they would be permitted to complete their journey. It seemed appropriate and just that Emily complete her fateful last journey home, begun so long ago.

Emily's mixed expression, of joy tinged with sorrow, suggested she also realised it could end at any moment now. From here on, they were on borrowed time.

Hudson waited for Richard to take the Haltham turn-off – one o'clock on the roundabout at the end of the Frickley Road – before offering Richard directions.

'It's okay,' he answered, 'I know how to get there,' referring to Emily's former home.

'Of course you do,' replied Hudson.

'Just make the most of the time we have,' Richard said.

As they drove through the outskirts of Haltham, Emily and Hudson talked easily about their former lives. They were worlds apart now, but they could each rightfully regard their common past as belonging to a former life.

Richard listened without comment or interruption. Though it was turning out differently to his expectations, hearing two people, long separated and reunited as no couple had ever been, talking fondly and lovingly, made it all worthwhile.

John Hudson had made an incredible adjustment in a short space of time. His voice, as he spoke to Emily, showed that he was deeply moved by the experience.

Emily knew he had married. Richard had told her that. She urged him to enjoy his life, not to dwell on the past. This included an unspoken acknowledgement of the passing of Emily's parents and the deaths of her friends in the same accident.

6

Finally, here it was. Harefield Road.

Emily shifted uneasily in her seat. It couldn't be easy on her. It might be mission accomplished as far as he and John Hudson were concerned, but for her, it meant uncertainty, and some fear.

The three of them were quiet as Richard completed the turn and rolled the car slowly between the lines of closely parked cars.

The moment was near at hand.

Richard had made dummy runs of this very journey on several occasions. He coasted slowly towards the spot in the road that corresponded with number thirty-four, as if to put off the parting.

Then it began to dawn on him that something strange was happening here. The road was completely still, no-one out, no cars moving.

Later, Hudson would also indicate he had begun to notice the change as they approached the road, but it was only at this point that either could confirm to their satisfaction what they were now seeing. All of the cars were old models – vintage cars from the late 1960s or early 1970s. He had seen a few driving around, maintained by a few dedicated enthusiasts, but none had ever looked as fresh and new as those he saw here.

On their left, a Ford Anglia. Also a Zephyr. Further along stood a Vauxhall Viva. Opposite, a Hillman Hunter, a Mark 3 Ford Cortina and an Austin Allegro, all looking new under the streetlights.

Hudson looked at them closely as they passed slowly by. No, he wasn't mistaken. None were more recent than the mid-1970s; some much older. A few of them would be worth a small fortune in such condition.

The houses gave no real confirmation of his suspicions. They looked largely as they should. Except for the absence of satellite dishes and the minutiae of modern times – new styles of aerials and so forth – they passed as comfortably for the 2020s as for 1978.

Richard stopped the car outside Emily's home, where a generous parking space had been conveniently left, as if they were expected. And from the view of the house, there remained no doubt that some kind of temporal shift had taken place.

Hudson looked in wonder at his own car – his first car, a Ford Escort Mark 1, parked on the driveway, its green paintwork looking black under the street lighting. It was like seeing a beloved pet dog alive again. But this was impossible. The car had been sold, and probably re-sold over and over until finally finishing its days in a scrap yard somewhere.

But he had learned already tonight that 'impossible' was a word no longer at ease in his vocabulary. He stared at the registration plate, at the number that he had completely forgotten in the intervening years. Restored here, he knew it was right. It gave him a strange sense of a home-coming of his own, an evocative reminder of his own youth, of days when things had been simpler and the future held bright promise.

Seeing things as they had been, completely restored, made him doubt his own senses in a way he hadn't at Emily's appearance. She was an out-of-place item in a modern world, caught in a whirlpool of time, while the world of which she was no longer a part marched on without her. Here, if anything, it was he and Richard who were out of time. The tables had been turned.

Either that, or he was hallucinating. But he had already started to disregard that possibility. It was clear from Richard's turned face that he was as puzzled and disturbed by their surroundings.

He looked around and back past Emily at the house, from which light spilled from incompletely closed curtains in the living room. He locked eyes with her briefly when she turned to face him. Words escaped him for the moment.

The effect outside was much more vivid and powerful than any illusion. It wasn't fleeting. He was sure that if he got out and walked over to his old car, he would be able to touch its shell, smell its interior. On the face of it, it seemed as real as Emily had proved to be.

'What's happening, Emily?' he asked.

She didn't answer immediately, something Richard also noticed. His heart sank a little. She continued to stare at the house, as if in contemplation of a fitful journey. She seemed to have become a little distant, not quite as alert and vibrant as she had been only a few moments before. But then he recognised that this was part of what was supposed to happen, a partial detachment from them that would ease the separation, allowing her to let go, to move on, her natural time reclaiming her to end things rightfully. There was no sadness in this. It seemed they had truly brought Emily home.

When she finally turned back, she had returned. Her expression spoke of insight and understanding. Her eyes were calm and serious, her pupils dilated. They held a peace she had long been denied.

'I'll always love you, John,' she said. 'I only wish you could stay ... '

Her expression indicated she accepted this as her proper time, where she belonged. Tears began to form on her cheek.

Fighting back his own emotions, Hudson lifted his hand towards her face and, with forefinger, gently brushed the tears away.

'I'm sure we'll be together again someday,' he said.

Hot salty tears erupted from the corners of his own eyes and streamed down his cheeks. They looked into each other's eyes a moment longer before reaching for each other, holding in a tight embrace so that they wept on each other's shoulder.

Richard turned away, feeling awkward and a little overwhelmed. Without thinking, he hopped out of the car, and was immediately struck with the realisation that he had impulsively risked pricking the surreal bubble in which they had existed since Blaxton Hill.

But the strange surroundings remained, although the illusion, or whatever it was, was not perfect. He could sense rather than see flashes of the modern road bleeding into this scenario here and there, like the two co-existed somehow, one grafted carefully over the other.

He opened the door beside Emily, and waited there while she and John made their final farewells.

She pulled away and stepped out of the car, straightening before Richard. Her eyes and cheeks were still wet. She stood on tip-toes to kiss him fondly on the cheek, the fresh fragrance of her hair and skin lingering after her.

'Without you, none of this would have been possible. Don't think I'm not grateful. You saved my life. Thank you, Richard.'

Her eyes remained fixed on his for a moment longer, then she turned, stepping back on the pavement to address both of them, Hudson now standing beside Richard.

'I love you both,' she said, swallowing, fresh tears spilling from her eyes.

'I know now where I'm going. Please don't worry about me. All I can say is that one day, I know we'll all be together again. We'll all have come home.'

She stood facing them for a moment longer. Then, smiling gently, she said goodbye, and turned away from them to make her way up the garden path.

Hudson and Richard watched in awed silence as she reached for the doorbell. No sound came from it, but presently a light came on in the hallway and, a moment later, the door opened. A middle-aged woman welcomed her daughter home.

With one final glance over her shoulder, she stepped into the hall, her silhouette absorbed by a growing brilliance, a dazzling, breathtaking radiance that sparkled as it expanded, and then rapidly dissipated.

Richard Wentworth and John Hudson stood there, overwhelmed, the intensity of the light having painted green and red patterns on their retinas. As their eyes readjusted, the house changed before them, darkening; Hudson's car melting away to be replaced by an unkempt front garden. A child's rusty tricycle lay on its side on the path.

Simultaneously around them, the familiar sights and sounds of an early spring evening of the twenty-first century came flooding back. It took them a few moments to readjust.

Was it really over? Already it seemed as if it had never happened. All of it.

Hudson turned to Richard and, patting him lightly on the back. 'Come on, son. Let's go home.'

Hudson walked to the driver's side, and climbed in behind the wheel. His car, after all.

Richard went around to the passenger side and pulled the door open. He hesitated. Something had caught his attention.

'Wait a minute.' He stepped away, letting the door swing to. He pulled open the back door and leaned in to where Emily had sat. He backed out, closed the door and opened the front passenger door.

'What's up?' asked Hudson.

Richard sat down and pulled the door closed. Then he said, 'This', and held up the ring – Emily's wedding ring.

This time, Hudson's reaction was different. He broke into a grin.

'Here ... ' offered Richard.

'No. You keep it, as a memento. Emily was right. It was all due to you. I'm sure it was meant for you, anyway – a lasting reminder of her thanks and appreciation. And of mine.' He smiled.

Richard nodded. He placed it carefully in his pocket.

7

It was late. 12:05 a.m. Hudson pulled up outside his house. The living room light was still on. He knew his wife would be waiting up for him. At least he could settle her mind by telling her it was over. Not that she'd believe any of the night's events. Not really. It was way beyond all they had heard together from Richard and Peter Pumfrys the night before.

He couldn't even recall accurately right now just how he had felt setting out on this mission this evening, only that his expectations hadn't been high.

But what he had witnessed had changed him forever. What it meant was beyond accurate description. There was no-one with whom he would be able to discuss it in the years to come but this young man, Richard Wentworth.

'Sure you won't come in for a cup of coffee or something? There's a lot to discuss. Emily won't mind.'

'No, I'd better not. I promised Sally I wouldn't be too late.'

'You could phone her. Tell her you'll be a bit later than expected?'

'No. Thanks, but a late call would alarm her, I think. Best if I just get going.'

'In that case, Richard, thanks again.' Hudson offered his hand. Richard reached out and they shook there in the street.

'We'll get together again soon to discuss tonight?'

'That'll be good,' said Richard. 'I'm sure Peter will be keen to hear about it too. And he's sure to have plenty to say about it as well,' he added as he backed away towards his own car.

Hudson grinned and raised his hand in farewell. 'Drive carefully,' he said, then turned to stroll up his driveway.

8

Richard sat behind the wheel of the car. He sighed heavily, at last left alone with his own thoughts. As he waited for the engine to warm up, he realised he was free now to get on with his own life. And there was a lot of re-building to do there. There would be plenty of time to reflect on this amazing experience later. Time to give his own life priority. Sally was waiting at home for him. He smiled inwardly at the thought as he selected first gear and pulled out.

Down the road out of Eastleigh, he came to the roundabout that gave him options for Eldonbridge and the motorway; eastbound for Haltham, southbound for the coast. On impulse, he took the motorway exit towards Haltham. And Blaxton Hill.

With the motorway quicker than the A-road through town, he decided it would be fitting to go home via the hill. It wouldn't take him any longer than the other route at this hour, and it seemed he owed it to himself as a way of rounding off his involvement, of closure.

Before he sighted the junction sign on the motorway, it had started to rain again.

TWENTY-THREE

She had been asleep on the settee. She couldn't remember when she had dozed off. Sally squinted at the clock over the mantelpiece, and did a double-take. It couldn't be. Two-fifteen.

But it was. She swung her legs around to meet the carpet. Where was he?

She sat anxiously, her heart sinking at the thought of being let down again. Perhaps she should have listened to her parents and not rushed over.

She might have been angry but for her worry. Richard really had sounded so fresh and back to normal. She couldn't bring herself to believe he was doing this intentionally.

He had phoned her this afternoon, telling her again that he was sure it would all be over after tonight. She hadn't quite understood what he meant by that, but he had sounded so positive, so like his old self. Tomorrow, he had said, he wanted her to take a day off so they could spend it together; patch things up. He had apologised for all the torment of the past few months, finally able, it seemed, to take upon himself full responsibility for the disruption in their lives.

He promised to tell her all about it when he got home. He was meeting John Hudson at eight. The name was familiar from somewhere. She knew he had something to do with Richard's ghost – but, hopefully, not too late, he would be home. And home meant *their* home, not her parents' place. Would she come back, wait up for him?

Could Richard finally have pulled himself together? It sounded promising. He had sounded so different, so much like his old self that, at first, he had sounded alien to her. After some consideration she had agreed to give it another try. She would be there.

The house hadn't been as bad as she had expected. The last time it had taken her over an hour to straighten the place, but she had been pleasantly surprised to see that Richard had kept the place clean and tidy. There was no washing up in the sink, and the fridge and freezer were adequately stocked. An encouraging sign.

She had prepared a meal for him, leaving it covered in the microwave. Stupidly, she hadn't asked him when he would be back, assuming from the way he had talked that it wouldn't be very long.

She had become concerned as ten o'clock passed. Then eleven, and finally, midnight. Sometime after that she must have drifted off, trying to deny her growing unease, or disappointment – she couldn't then decide which.

A ring at the doorbell startled her out of her musings.

At last! Then: Why hadn't he used his key?

Before she could get to the door, it rang again, an ominously loud and prolonged burst. Dread descended on her. It was all wrong.

She depressed the handle and gingerly opened the door, its base scuffing over the bristle door mat.

The light from the hallway washed over two uniformed officers, one a WPC. Sally immediately went cold. Her eyes widened, her mouth snapping open in fearful reflex.

'Miss Sally Nelson? asked the policeman.

All she could do was nod. A choked question spilled from her lips: 'Wh-what is it?' She had started to tremble noticeably.

'May we come in, Miss?' asked the PC.

Sally looked at the WPC, whose own expression spoke in reply.

Unreality washed over her. A cold explosion of adrenaline shot through her, its chilling flush curdling in her stomach, the sensation spreading to her legs, making them weak.

She started to shake her head vigorously. 'No ... no,' she said. 'You must be mistaken.'

'Can we come in, Miss?' repeated the PC quietly. He removed his cap.

Sally let the door swing free. She was already in a state of shock even before they stepped into the room. The WPC supported her as she led them into the living room on woolly legs; her breathing shallow; thought banished from her mind, lest she make this real by acknowledging it. The two officers were probably in their mid-twenties. Too young for this type of work, observed one part of her mind.

The female officer guided Sally to sit down.

Their part already served by their presence, the PC nevertheless continued with the formalities. He sat opposite Sally.

'I'm afraid I have some bad news.'

Sally stared stonily at him from a place behind her eyes, to which she had already retreated as if to distance herself from this play. The shell of her body felt cold and heavy around her.

'I'm afraid Mr Wentworth was killed this evening in a motor accident.'

After a pause, he added, 'There was nobody else involved.'

Sally dropped her gaze to stare at her fidgeting feet, her mind reeling.

'There must be some mistake?' she pleaded. She had seen this very scene enacted on television often enough. The reactions of the aggrieved to the news always seemed trite, clichéd, as if the police *would* come without being absolutely sure.

She looked up.

The words that followed were also part of the script, but this wasn't fiction.

'I'm sorry, but no,' said the WPC, reading from her notes. 'Richard David Wentworth, twenty-four.'

There followed a strained silence in which Sally just looked into space. Just five minutes ago she was in an entirely different existence, one of hopefulness. Things were supposed to get better, not spiral out of control like this. That's what was supposed to happen, wasn't it?

'What... what happened?' she asked.

The policeman answered her, pausing briefly to note his partner making for the kitchen. The inevitable cup of tea or mug of strong coffee.

'It's not absolutely clear at the moment,' he said quietly. 'But it looks like he lost control of his car. Wet road surface. It was probably instantaneous.'

'Where?' she asked.

'Blaxton Hill, around 12:40 this morning.'

Sally smarted at the name. *Blaxton Hill?*

She shook her head in disbelief. In different circumstances she might have appreciated the irony, but now it all seemed too much.

'Where is his ... where is he now?' she asked.

'I believe he was taken to Eldonbridge General.'

A quiet calm befell Sally.

The reaction was a common one. Full realisation and grief would probably hit her in the privacy following their departure. On that subject, he noted the time. He and his partner would have to leave soon.

'Is there anyone who can come to stay with you, or you can go to?'

She was slow to think properly and to answer. 'Er, yes. I'll call my parents.'

At the same time, the WPC reappeared, brandishing the tray – the one, she noticed as it was set down, the smiling Mickey Mouse pictured on it, beneath three mugs of coffee. The contents of one was much darker than the others. No points for guessing who that was for.

'We'll stay with you until they arrive, or we can take you to them, if you wish?' she said.

'No, it's okay,' Sally replied. 'It'll only take my dad a little while to get here.'

Her expression suddenly changed. 'Oh! Richard's mother? Who's going to tell her?!' Her eyes began to fill up for the first time.

The WPC laid a hand on her shoulder, handing her a steaming mug.

'Don't worry about that for now,' she said. 'Drink your coffee, and then phone your parents. Wait until they're here, okay?'

Sally looked troubled, but acquiesced. She took a sip of her drink, wincing at its bitter-sweet taste.

2

The officers stayed with Sally until her parents arrived half an hour later. She met them at the door. At the sight of them, Sally burst into tears. Her mother rushed to her, and the two of them held each other and they cried together.

Sally's father walked over.

When she looked up, she saw him standing near. She broke from her mother and threw her arms around him.

He looked into her reddened eyes. 'I'm sorry, love,' he said. 'Really sorry.'

Sally squeezed her eyes shut in acknowledgement.

The PC took Sally's father aside before leaving to ask him

to make arrangements for a formal identification of Richard's body.

Sally watched them leave. They walked across the drive past her father's car, which stood, lights on and engine idling. Sally looked over to her father with quizzical expression.

'Come on, love,' said her father. 'It's not going to be any easier, but it's got to be done.'

Of course, they couldn't phone Richard's mother with such news.

Sally disappeared inside to fetch her coat, along with a few things. She locked up and the three of them made their way to the car. She paused to take a wistful glance over a shoulder at the house, now standing in darkness. All the darker after tonight. It was to have been the dream home for her and Richard, and now she doubted whether she would spend another night there.

TWENTY-FOUR

If it were not depressing enough, the weather took a turn for the worse on the day of Richard's funeral. Dark, rain-sodden clouds threatened to inundate the gathering as they stood around the open grave.

The wind was strong and biting this morning, forcing its way through the trees before spreading out unimpeded across the open expanses of the cemetery. It tugged and clawed irreverently at the mourners' clothing and the collection of wreaths and flowers.

The gathering was small, but everyone was there. Richard would have been pleased at that.

Sally and her parents stood at the head of the crowd, before the vicar. Richard's mother, and his young brother, John, stood opposite.

Sally's head lay against her mother's shoulder. Dark semi-circles marked her eyes, tears streaming quietly down her face. She looked ten years older.

Her mother was also crying. Her father remained stoic, though Richard would surely have been satisfied to see that even his eyes were moist.

Sally wore a navy-blue outfit.

Don't ever wear black, Sal. It doesn't suit you.

His words echoed in her mind, the unexpected vividness of his voice bringing new force to her grief. He had said those words when they had attended the funeral of Sally's great aunt only a few months ago. Such a long time ago.

Peter Pumfrys was there. Richard's death had been featured in the paper, together with a small photograph of him. He had

had no part in the article; hadn't known about it until it was pointed out to him before going to press. At least he had been able to prevent his editor from making too much out of the connection between Richard and the hill that had finally claimed his life. Thank goodness, he thought, he had no knowledge of the events that had transpired, and Pumfrys's own part in it.

He stood deliberately apart from Sally and Richard's mother. He had rediscovered new blame for himself in this, and would not let others suffer unnecessarily again on account of him.

Richard's mother had no-one else to lean on. She had no siblings herself, and her husband's and her own parents were dead. She looked drawn, old and frail beyond her years. She had seen a mother's worst nightmare realised. The death of an offspring defied the natural order of things. Parents were not supposed to outlive their children.

All she had left was Richard's younger brother. She pulled John closer, holding onto him tightly. He had been brought along to pay his last respects to his elder brother. He stood quietly, too overwhelmed to react with the open grief displayed by his mother. The implications of what had happened would not sink in for a while; could not be readily absorbed by a boy who had just turned thirteen, a boy who had grown up without a father, and had now lost his only brother. There was no telling how it would affect him. Richard had been more than a brother to him, virtually a surrogate father figure.

Richard's and Sally's friends made up a single line along one side of the grave. Terry looked gaunt, more serious than he ever had. He held hands tightly with Alice, the pain of this moment written across his brow. He stared into the excavation, his troubled thoughts fixed elsewhere ... anywhere but here and what they were here for.

Alice thoughtlessly nipped at the thumb-nail of her free hand as she listened to the vicar's sermon. The others were similarly disposed, standing quietly, emotions simmering, occasionally brimming over. Jennifer Lyle and Tom Peters, Gary Tucker. Even Craig Mountford.

At the end stood an older couple. None of them knew who they were at first; had eyed them a little warily, until Sally had explained. John Hudson had introduced himself to her on their arrival, expressing his condolences.

They had been here for something less than fifteen minutes, although it seemed a lot longer. Richard's casket had already been lowered to its final resting place. No-one wanted to prolong the agony any longer than necessary.

The vicar was reading through his prepared dedication, but the passage he read from the Bible, though meaningful, was not being heard ...

> *For the Lord will not*
> *cast off for ever,*
> *but, though he cause grief, he will*
> *have compassion*
> *according to the abundance of his*
> *steadfast love;*
> *for he does not willingly afflict*
> *or grieve the sons of men.*

A discreet distance away, the caretaker busied about the grounds, raking the grass of windblown leaves and twigs and pieces of litter.

He glanced in the direction of the congregation. He had witnessed the same scene countless times, had played an active part himself on too many occasions. Not in a good while, though, had he felt this degree of sympathy for a stranger's interment.

The sight of children's funerals always affected him deeply, as did those where there were no mourners to see off the departed.

This funeral evoked a similar feeling, for he had learned that the deceased was the young man who had visited here only weeks before. A somewhat troubled lad, he recalled.

He leaned on his rake for a moment, taking time to survey the grounds.

He never enquired why people visited the cemetery. That was an intrusion of a very personal kind. He tried to help as well as he could and leave them be. But, in this case, he found himself wondering why the man had come here that day. Whosoever's grave he had visited wasn't a stone's throw away from where he now lay, he felt sure. Unbeknown to him, two of those present at the graveside could have shown him whose it was.

The faint, wavering recital of the twenty-third Psalm carried to him on the wind. The words were indistinct, but the tempo and pitch made it recognisable. That meant the vicar would be rounding things up very soon. The reverend's voice led them, clear and strong. He was a good one, that Phillips. At least the lad was getting a competent send off. He shook his head gently, lamentably, before returning to his work.

Presently, the crowd began to break up, to drift in his general direction. Reverend Phillips was packing away his vestments and Bible to don a long coat. A few drops of rain had begun to fall.

A few of the people walked slowly alongside a young lady who was being supported and consoled by a man, her father. A hand cupped her elbow, supporting and guiding her away from the grave site. She slouched from the burden of her grief, fully awakened now that it was time for them to leave.

Only now, with Richard's body left behind, did the awful realisation of his loss finally sink in for Sally. Her walk was unsteady and laboured, as if lead weights were attached to her ankles. And doubtless, it felt that way. Terrible, low sobs escaped from her.

Nearby, Terry Andrews helped Richard's mother along. John made his own path, away from her, where she couldn't see the tears rolling down his cheeks. He fought against his own grief, ashamed of it, yet unable to control it. She wanted to go to him, but Terry held her back, advising her to let him deal with it in his own way.

Ahead of them all, the first to pass the caretaker on the main cemetery path, walked Pumfrys and John Hudson, talking quietly. Neither made mention of the irony of Richard's burial not only in the same cemetery, but so close to the body of Emily Reynolds. After the triumph of a little over a week ago, the complete downturn in events was almost too much to bear, much less discuss.

2

Richard's mother had insisted on holding a makeshift gathering for Richard at her own home, from where the funeral had proceeded. She hadn't wanted to burden Sally with the further pain of organising such a thing. Besides, it was her own way of seeing off her eldest son, although from the look of her, she was barely holding herself together. They all made their way back there for a brief drink.

Discrete groups formed in the living room. Richard's and Sally's friends sat together, talking quietly. Hudson, his wife, and Peter Pumfrys stood apart. Sally stood with her parents and Richard's mother. John, Richard's brother, had gone upstairs to his bedroom.

Sally wandered over to Hudson's group. She had calmed down on the way back from the cemetery, all her tears cried out for the moment.

'How are you feeling, dear?' asked Emily Hudson.

'I'll be alright,' said Sally, summoning a smile from somewhere far away.

She faced John Hudson, then glanced at Pumfrys. 'Thanks for coming today,' she said. 'I'm sure Richard would have appreciated it.'

She fell quiet for a moment, a quizzical expression forming as she struggled to find her next words. With them, she addressed John Hudson.

'Mr Hudson, do you believe in God?'

It took Hudson by surprise. 'Er, yes. I think I do,' he answered honestly.

Another question: 'Do you really think Richard was in contact with your fiancée?' she asked, neglectful of the presence of Hudson's wife and her feelings, for which she could be forgiven at this moment.

'I think he pretty well managed to convince us of that. But it's not a case of just believing what he said,' he answered. 'I saw her myself. Richard was right. He saved her.'

He struggled to explain his rationale. 'Er ... not as we understand it, of course. Her body died many years ago. I'm referring to the real Emily Reynolds, her spirit.

'I know how you're feeling,' he said, glancing at his wife, before continuing. 'After Emily died, I thought my world had ended. Really. But I've seen that it isn't really the end. You must try to have faith in that. I know that doesn't help much at the moment, but I believe in my heart that he's fine.'

Sally nodded slowly. 'It'd be nice to be able to believe that,' she said with a hint of cynicism.

'The police gave me something that was with Richard's

personal effects.' She held out Emily Reynold's ring. 'I think this belongs to you?'

Hudson locked eyes with Sally. He could see her thoughts were in turmoil at the moment. She really didn't know what to believe. He took it without comment, dropping it into his inside jacket pocket, where his own ring still lay. He looked at her a moment longer, then Sally excused herself, moving over to her (and Richard's) group of friends.

3

Pumfrys left first; Hudson and his wife next.

The weather had deteriorated. Rain threatened again. It had been a dismal week in that respect, the low pressure making the whole thing more nightmarish.

On their way home, Hudson stopped his car beside the river. Emily Hudson remained in the car. She didn't question what he was doing. He walked over to the river bank and took out the two rings. He held them in the palm of his hand while he regarded them for a moment. Then he closed his fingers around them, and cast them as far as he could across the swirling grey water. They seemed to hover in space together for an instant before plunging out of sight forever. He got back into the car and drove on without comment.

Sally left with her parents at four o'clock, having stayed for a couple of hours with Richard's mother after the others left, helping her to tidy up, allowing time to make sure she'd be alright.

By now, the clouds had finally burst, drenching them before they got to her father's car. The street lighting had tripped in early because of the overcast, punctuating the gloom along the street. Sally's mother sat with her in the back.

As they drove through Haltham, southbound for

Eldonbridge, Sally started to weep again. Her heart felt as dark as the night. Richard was gone, his body left in the cold, saturated soil. It was like a nightmare that wouldn't leave her.

She snuggled up to her mother like a child, surrendering herself to the comforting warmth of her arms and the warm air blown out by the heaters. She allowed oblivion to claim her for a while.

Seemingly ages later, she was awakened by the brightness of headlamps arcing across the ceiling of the car. She sat upright, wiping her eyes. Her mother gave her a comforting squeeze.

'You alright, love?'

Sally nodded. 'Where are we?' she asked, pulling herself upright to look out of the window.

'Nearly home now,' answered her father.

It took her a few moments to gain her bearings. Her heart skipped when she saw they were heading down Blaxton Hill. The light was coming from the busy traffic heading up the hill on the opposing carriageway. She hadn't been asleep for as long as she imagined. She was hurt that her father should bring her this way, but it was the most direct route home.

They followed the sweeping curve that brought them in sight of the Valence Lane crossroads and The Bull, off to their left beyond hedgerow-lined fields.

She didn't know – didn't want to know – exactly where Richard had his accident, but she knew it was over there somewhere.

She turned her gaze away, looking past her father's shoulder at the road ahead. They were travelling through the slipstream of another car, its tyres kicking up a red haze of spray from the wet road surface.

Something ahead caught her attention, on the kerbside, picked out briefly by the lead car's headlights. After that, it all happened so quickly.

It looked like a figure. She stiffened. Her father had seen it too, for the car lurched slightly as he gripped the steering wheel.

'What's the matter?' her mother asked, alarmed.

Sally ignored her. She continued to stare through the windscreen. In the seconds it took to close the distance, Sally's eyes widened in horror.

On the roadside stood a sullen figure, a lone hitch-hiker, thumb cocked in customary fashion before the passing vehicles.

As they sped past, Sally's head tracked quickly to keep it in sight. Through their own rearward spray, she saw the figure had turned to watch them pass, a terrible expression of sadness written across its gaunt visage.

No. It can't be. It can't ...

'No! NOOooooooo!'

Sally broke down uncontrollably as she watched Richard's shade recede, to be swallowed by the gloom that closed in around him.

Notes &
Acknowledgements

No book is ever the singular creation of its author. Knowingly or otherwise, a number of individuals make contributions along the way, either to the story itself (through reference or inspiration), or by serving an invaluable function on its completion.

Included in the latter group are this book's beta readers. I extend my thanks to the following for devoting their time to read, proof, and provide general feedback on the story: Claire Armstrong, Beckie Carwardine, Emma Green, Steve Morgan, Sarah Parmenter, Pamela Tudor, Kerry Webb.

Thanks go out also to my wife and children for their forbearance during the writing process, when I am partly 'away' in the world of the imagination.

The story itself, of course, is inspired by the urban legend, the *Phantom Hitchhiker* (or *Vanishing Hitchhiker* (USA)) and several documented cases of 'real' encounters with hitch-hiking spirits.

In tune with my belief that mixing fact with fiction makes for stronger fiction, several books and their authors from the real world find mention: John G. Fuller's *The Ghost of Flight 401* (Corgi, 1979); Shirley Jackson's supernatural novel, *The Haunting of Hill House* (Viking, 1959); and Matthew Manning (medium, healer and author of *The Strangers* (W.H. Allen, 1978), amongst others).

The Wetherby book doesn't exist, but its inspiration is Michael Goss's excellent *The Evidence for Phantom Hitch-Hikers* (Aquarian Press, 1984).